I0547090

The Pastors

A mystery novel

Mary Ellen Jackson

E&MJ

This is a work of fiction. Names, characters, places, events, and organizations are entirely the products of the author's imagination or are used fictitiously. Any similarity to real persons, living or dead, is coincidental and not intended by the author.

Copyright 2022 Mary Ellen Jackson

All rights reserved.

No part of this book may be reproduced, or stored in a retrieval system, or transmitted in any form or by any means, electronic, mechanical, photocopying, recording, or otherwise, without express written permission of the publisher.

Printed in the United States of America

To Louis Van Woods, WWII veteran.
Thank you for your service, Dad. I love you!

But if the watchman see the sword come, and blow not the trumpet, and the people be not warned; if the sword come, and take any person from among them, he is taken away in his iniquity; but his blood will I require at the watchman's hand (Eze, 33:6; KJV)

The Pastors

Chapter 1

Monaco Valentine was in bra and panties staring at herself in her bedroom mirror. Her large, slightly droopy eyes that Ernest once described as 'bedroom,' focused on the filmy white dress she held against her body. Dissatisfied with the dress she tossed it onto the bed. Living in New York City had given her an eye for the fashionable world of colors, patterns, and fabrics. She loved designing her own outfits as much as buying them in high fashion houses and on dressmaker's row.

Walking to her closet she gazed at the multitude of white suits and dresses lining the clothes rack. Most were out of season.

Monaco grabbed items off hangers tossing them onto a chair for donations. The pile grew larger as she sorted through the racks a second time. At last, satisfied she had purged her closet, she gathered the mass of discarded items shoving them into two large shopping bags. She stashed the sacks in a corner of her bedroom to drop off at another time.

Returning to the closet and full-length mirror, she scanned her wardrobe of newly hung dresses, settling on a white knit button front coat dress. She smiled at her reflection in the door mirror. It was the first time she had smiled anticipating an outing.

Her best friend since childhood, Lisa Marie Gonzalez, decided it was time for Monaco to come out of her self-imposed isolation. Monaco had lost her parents in a car accident, and her only sibling, from a stray bullet.

Lisa persuaded her to attend Hot Springs Cathedral Church where both had grown up, and where they had spent happy years, among family and friends.

As they crossed the threshold into the sanctuary, Lisa guided them to a row of seats in the back. Much had changed during the years Monaco had been away. She noticed the long wooden benches replaced with dark blue padded chairs. Under her feet the carpeted floor replaced by hardwood flooring. The stained-glass insets placed high on the walls remained, and she approved of the skylights. The choir stand was new and featured hanging microphones.

As they settled in their chairs, Monaco read the bulletin in her hands. She looked at the listing of names of members asking for prayers of comfort.

"The church outline has not changed one bit," she whispered to Lisa.

"That's because folks like structure," Lisa whispered back.

"Where's the pastor? His name is not in the bulletin."

"Oh, I didn't tell you? About six years ago, Pastor Clayton's health declined. He decided he needed to retire."

"Oh wow! Does the church have a pastor?"

"Of course! The clergy nominated Paul Mouton from among their ranks, and presented him to the congregation. The church approved, and he has been our senior pastor."

"Why isn't his name in the bulletin?"

"He won't be up there for another month. He took a three-month leave of absence to finish his divinity doctorate."

Two older church ladies sat beside Lisa. She moved closer to Monaco. The white-haired ladies, with their large, embellished hats and stuffed handbags, looked over at Monaco in her mini-dress, and both gave her disapproving glances. Lisa tried not to smirk while Monaco ignored them. Music played as a row of clergy stepped on to the pulpit. Lisa stiffened beside her and peered more closely at the pulpit. Their childhood friends were now pastors in the church they had all grown-up in. Monaco watched as the men clad in black suits, strolled across the platform, followed by a distinguished-looking older man.

"Lisa," she whispered. "I remember when Nick was ordained, but when were Ernest and Steven ordained?"

"It's been about five or six years now," replied Lisa. "I believe Steven was first, and later, Ernest arrived."

Monaco whispered again. "Who is the man next to Ernest?"

2

"David Sanchez."

"What a handsome man!"

"We all love David. He's intense but he knows his stuff."

"Who is the man seated next to David?" Monaco asked, intrigued by the tall, elegant-looking older man.

He had a pleasant face with white close-cropped hair, and white neatly trimmed facial beard against smooth brown skin.

"That is Reverend Dr. Charles Robertson. He stepped in after the deaths of the three elder pastors."

"Oh no! I was wondering where they were."

"Yes girl! Reverend Johnson fell down the stairs at home, Reverend Wallace drowned in his bathtub, and Reverend Harris walked into a speeding car. You know folks afterward said they should have all retired long ago."

Monaco laughed out loud. The older women at the end of the pew glanced in their direction.

"That's people for you. Did the interim pastor approve these new men?"

"Pastor Robertson said he would stay on until the senior pastor earned his degree, and the church approved."

"Who's the attractive older lady in the front pews? The one sitting with Deaconess Whitfield?"

"That's the pastor's mother, Jayne Mouton. Seated next to her is her daughter, Raquel."

"Lord! The daughter is a younger version of her mother. Drop dead gorgeous."

"Tell me about it. Some women receive more blessings than others," said Lisa with a chagrined expression.

Monaco held back a giggle. She noticed a woman with long red curly hair seated next to Raquel.

"Is that Jasmine Carter?"

"Yes, that's Ernest's little sister, all grown up. She graduated from college with an English degree and was working part-time for an insurance company. She was looking for a job where she could use her degree, and Pastor Mouton hired her as his full-time administrative assistant."

"How does she like working for the pastor?"

"She loves it. She's one of the young women in ministry training. I'll tell you more about that later."

The music ended and a minister strolled to the lectern.

"Good morning, church. Do we have any visitors in the house this morning?"

The congregation looked around. Lisa nudged her in the ribs. The two older women on their row stared hard. Monaco reluctantly stood up. An usher rushed to her side handing her a microphone. She cleared her throat. "Giving all praise and honor to God who's first in my life. I thank you for your hospitality. I'm looking forward to hearing today's message. My name is Monaco Valentine and I live in Hot Springs County. My former church was in New York City under Reverend Dr. Van Abernathy."

The minister looked at her and smiled. "Thank you, Sister Valentine. We thank God for you this morning. Please enjoy the service, and we pray and hope to see you again. Church, let's give Sister Valentine a warm welcome."

The congregation clapped. The ushers gave her a welcome folder, and several members came over and shook her hand. Far to the front she locked eyes with her cousin Claudia Ginyard. Both turned their heads at the same time.

"I did not know Claudia had returned to town," she whispered to Lisa.

Lisa smirked. "Pooh on her! She's on every ministry that has to do with finances in the church."

"She is an accountant," returned Monaco watching how alert Claudia was in looking up at the pulpit. "Who is she interested in up there?"

"Oh, you caught that too, uh? I believe it's Steven. I heard they might be dating. It's hard to tell with Steven. You know how private he is, but for now, she's chasing him."

"Time will tell," mused Monaco.

She looked on the podium at Steven with his close-cropped hair and long sideburns. He had been wearing dark oversized sunglasses since high school. People had grown so accustomed to seeing him in them that they failed to notice he rarely took them off.

The service ended. The women prepared to leave the pew. As they walked toward the aisle, Monaco asked Lisa a question.

"How long have you and Nick been seeing each other?"

4

Lisa blushed. "Not long. Just under a year now. It's been slow-going because of our work schedules."

"You look happy Lisa."

"I am. I believe with all my heart he's the one."

As they gathered their belongings, Monaco felt a tap on her shoulder, and turned around. She was face-to-face with the terrible trio. It was the youthful nickname for the young men who had been like older brothers for her and Lisa.

Nick Rodgers was the first to grab her around the waist bringing her in for a bear hug. She had a momentary crush on him as a budding teen. The tax attorney with the light tan skin that complemented his cobalt blue eyes, and sandy brown hair, lifted her in the air.

"Monaco! Glad you made it to church."

"Hi Nick," Monaco laughed. "I'm glad to see you answered the call to preach."

"And he happens to be excellent as a lawyer and a pastor," chimed in Lisa.

Nick smiled at her. "That is truly a humbling statement seeing as your legal gifts are awe-inspiring in their own right."

"Are there any violins in the house? I feel the urge to play a love rhapsody," Ernest said.

"Okay, okay. It's my turn," said Steven Barnes in his deep baritone voice. The psychologist kissed her cheek as he hugged her. "You look great Monaco and I like the fact you've stopped cutting your hair in those crazy styles you sported when we were growing up."

"I like my hair long and straight now. I'm sorry I didn't make it to your celebration party when you received your doctorate, Steven."

"That was many years ago," he responded, smiling hard. "You bring it up like it was yesterday. Besides, you were in the middle of the glow with the publishing success of your first book."

He moved to the side and Ernest Carter, smiling mischievously, came forward. He nursed a mad crush on her going back to their kindergarten days, but had never asked her out. Ernest had matinée idol looks. His pale turquoise, almond-shaped eyes were the focal point of his light reddish complexion and deep auburn hair color. He was Nick's first cousin, and a forensic pathologist.

"Hey darling," he said now as he hugged her. "You're looking beautiful, as always."

"Ernest, you say that every time you see me," she smiled. "How is Nancy?"

"Who?" Ernest looked confused. Monaco shook her head, and everyone laughed.

Lisa sighing stated, "Monaco, Nancy was about two months ago, and I recall she may have been his date for that one weekend when he brought her to my birthday party."

"I don't know why we ask their names anymore," said Nick, quietly.

"Are you staying this time?" Steven asked Monaco.

"I am trying my best to keep her here," interjected Lisa.

Nick kissed his girlfriend's cheek. "Keep trying sweetie."

"Yeah, we miss the old gang," said Ernest in his falsetto voice.

"Honestly, from day to day is a struggle," replied Monaco.

"It takes time Monaco," said Steven. "Don't rush the grief process. Returning home in the aftermath of pain is difficult. Just know we're all here for you. We're family, and always will be."

"Thanks, Steven, I believe that. Being home among my friends has helped me heal emotionally. But seeing you all on the pulpit has been mind-blowing. If our parents could see us all now."

"Yeah, we were a handful for our folks," reminisced Ernest. "Forever in trouble."

"Speak for yourself," said Steven. "You and Nick were a handful."

"Those were the days," murmured Nick, smiling slightly. Everyone laughed.

"Let's get something to eat," suggested Ernest watching a few single ladies as they passed by. He smiled and one gave a little wave. Ernest smiled, waved back, and put on black sunglasses.

"Hold on Ernest," said Nick. "We have a meeting with the pastor."

Lisa turned to Nick. "I'm taking Monaco to lunch today."

"Okay, call me once you arrive home," replied Nick.

"Let's do a group dinner later in the week with everybody," suggested Monaco.

"Sounds great," said Steven, inserting notes in his phone. He looked up, spotted a familiar figure he waved over to them.

Steven said, "Monaco, let me introduce you to Pastor David Sanchez, a friend of ours."

Monaco looked at the handsome pastor in black. He was built like Ernest with a swimmer's build. He had thick, glossy black ,wavy hair, dark intense eyes, and a trimmed goatee. Up close, he gave matinee-idol Ernest a run for his money in the looks department.

David took her hand to his lips. "How incredibly beautiful you are! It is a pleasure to meet you, Monaco."

"Alright, alright," said Ernest. "None of that Latin lover talk in the church."

Everyone laughed, including David, who put his hand to his chest, and winked at Monaco, smiling.

"I'm just trying to love everyone as the Good Book instructs."

"Let's get a move on," said Nick, smiling and shaking his head.

"It was a pleasure meeting you," said David, kissing the back of her hand again. He kissed Lisa on the cheek and followed the pastors heading toward the side doors at the front of the church.

Monaco and Lisa left the sanctuary through the front entrance.

"Hey, let's have lunch at Barb's Bistro," suggested Lisa.

"Sounds great," replied Monaco. "Oh no! I forgot my Bible. I'll be right back."

Monaco turned back to enter the church in search of her Bible.

Chapter 2

Monaco was standing in the pew she had sat in peering down at the empty seats when a light touch on her shoulder caused her to glance around to the figure behind her. She looked up into dark almost black, almond shaped eyes, medium nose, and full lips. He was as tall as Steven and as broad with a rugged look underneath the shirt, knotted tie and double-breasted vest. The voice was low and smooth. He was standing in a relaxed posture but Monaco was aware of the muscled physique beneath the tailored clothes. Something about him appealed to her womanly senses. She was still in the pew as he was blocking her exit.

"Excuse me, but are you looking for this?" He held her Bible out to her.

"Yes, thank you."

"I studied under Pastor Abernathy as a minister."

"Oh? What brought you here all the way from New York City?"

"Pastor Abernathy himself, and you?"

"My parents died and left me a house. I'm a writer and needed a quiet place."

"Ah, a writer. What do you write, your genre?"

"I write children's books. I'm working on my sixth children's novel."

He smiled broadly. "If you're not busy, would you care to join me for lunch?"

"Thank you, but no. My best friend and I have plans."

"Perhaps another time?" he asked, still smiling.

He stepped to the side to allow her to pass. She walked past him and turned around to see he was watching her.

"For the future, I don't accept dates of any kind from men I don't know whether I meet them in church or not."

Throwing her hair back she walked away consciously aware he was still watching her.

How convenient the turn of events! The Sleeper had watched the pastor sit in the back of the pews slyly studying Monaco. It appeared to the Sleeper the pastor's serious attraction to the beautiful vagabond could help him in several ways. If this budding romance flourished, it might speed things along. He would do everything in his power to help in that situation. The sooner Monaco Valentine left that house, the better.

A short time later, seated in the bistro, Monaco told Lisa all about her conversation in the pew with the stranger.

"I tell you the men at that church never change," said Lisa, tossing her dark red curly hair about her shoulders.

Monaco sat up straighter. "Some things about life never change, girlfriend."

"I wish I would have been there. We have about four new brothers who have joined. I'm sure some are more than likely decent, industrious men looking for good women, but you wait for an introduction. I sure would have reported it to our new pastor. He doesn't play with that kind of stuff."

Monaco smiled. "It's okay, Lisa. It's not that deep. He went there and I stopped him." Changing the subject, she asked, "Pastor Clayton believed in patriarchy. Do you think we will have women pastors in the future?"

Lisa cocked her head to the side, and lightly frowned as she thought about her friend's question.

"I want to say yes and no. I don't see them being pastors, but I do believe we will have women reverends. I mean, look who he has as clergy backing him?"

"I saw that. Are they all known as pastors?"

"Yes, Pastor Mouton made that clear at his first meeting with the congregation. He said he can't do the work all by himself. He also spoke about the church needing women clergy in leadership roles."

"How did the church handle that conversation?"

Lisa laughed. "Not well. The old guard opposed it, a few approved, and all the younger people were in favor."

"What's the issue with having women clergy? I've always thought it was highly inappropriate to have men at women's-only events."

"That practice has stopped with Pastor Mouton."

"Good! But I'm surprised they voted an unmarried person in as senior pastor though. I mean, Steven, Nick, and Ernest are not married either," persisted Monaco. "I remember when the church had an issue with single men during Pastor Clayton's tenure. What happened to that argument?"

Lisa smiled. "Well, it takes time Monaco. It takes time but change does happen. The guys replaced the aging clergy that were on board. It's a new day."

"What does that mean?"

"It means these younger men are better educated, matching the educated congregation approving them. Don't forget Nick and the guys are adult men not young boys. They will all marry soon enough. Nick told me that the married men on staff they interviewed did not want the position. And, unlike in times past, the church was not in favor of hiring out-of-town pastors. Steven, Nick, and Ernest are homegrown. David came along with Pastor Mouton who Pastor Robertson taught in seminary."

"So the new pastor is a local guy?"

"Yes. He grew up in the rural part of Hot Springs. He went away to school, and his career took him further. Like you."

"Seems I was ahead of my time. So, what's going on with you and Nick."

"Nick and I have been talking about marriage. But finding your ideal spouse takes time. Nick and I have much in common, but we're taking things slow."

Monaco looked at her best friend. Lisa was an attorney for a firm that managed tax fraud cases. She had dark red hair, black eyes, and a feisty temperament. Monaco was secretly happy Lisa and Nick were a couple, and pleased they had given each other a chance.

The women's food arrived. They were eating when a shadow fell across the table. Monaco looked up into the face of her childhood nemesis, her cousin, Claudia. The brown eyes framed by blondish-beige layered curls looked down at Monaco with thinly veiled contempt.

"I thought that was you this morning," she said between orange hued lips. "Someone told me you were back in town. Condolences on your family loss."

"Thank you, Claudia," said Monaco. "They were your family as well."

"I guessed you would be returning," said Claudia, ignoring the reference to their blood kinship. "Are you staying in the house, or living somewhere else?"

Lisa cut in. "Drop it, Claudia, and go about your business."

"It's okay Lisa," Monaco said. Claudia was fishing for information and not too subtle about it. "I'm remodeling the family home to my tastes. Mom and Dad had the same furniture as when I was growing up."

Claudia nodded her head in an understanding way. "Are you staying in Hot Springs?"

"For now. I miss being home after being away for so long."

"Are you joining the church again?"

"I don't know."

"Well, if you do, and I think you will, there's a spot on the women's ministry for a pianist. Deaconess Whitfield has gotten older, and can't always make the different events. I'm sure they would welcome you."

"That's sweet of you, Claudia, but I have a lot on my plate right now. If I joined the church, it would be only as a member."

"Just consider it. Women's Day is around the corner."

"As I just mentioned, I have a lot on my plate. Besides, I'm certain you are still a capable pianist."

Claudia forced a smile. "That I am. But I spend so much time as the finance director, I really have little time for anything else."

"Well, it's good to know your putting your CPA credentials to effective use doing the Lord's work," Lisa stated between clenched teeth. Claudia glanced under eye at Lisa.

"Well, it was nice chatting with you both. Enjoy your lunch ladies. I have a date with Pastor Barnes."

Giving them a wave, she walked across the dining room, and disappeared into the private section.

"It's always been hard for me to understand why she dislikes you so much," said Lisa.

"I stopped caring a long time ago. Hopefully, Pastor Steven can rebuke that hateful spirit in her."

Lisa giggled, and Monaco smiled.

A week later Monaco was munching an apple, and looking through a rough draft of the second chapter in her book, when she received an impromptu visit from her godparents. Deacon Ed, and Deaconess Mary Joseph dropped off a coconut cake which had always been Monaco's best-loved dessert as a child. Ed, using his quad cane, insisted on bringing the cake to the kitchen. Monaco watched Mary, who was gently napping, in the couple's car. Monaco studied the older woman, who in sleep, was still a stunning beauty. Monaco stood on the sidewalk watching Ed's old, but reliable, Crown Victoria sedan amble up the street.

Returning inside she walked straight to the kitchen where she cut a slice of coconut cake, and waited for the coffee to brew. As she poured herself a cup of coffee, she received a text message on her phone.

Him: Hello there. Are you free for dinner tonight? I know a quaint (!) little place on High Street, Paul.

Her: Who is this?

Him: The man you met in church. I apologize for not introducing myself. I forgot you're a new member. Have you joined yet?

Her: Whether I join or not is none of your concern.

Him: Back to my original question. Are you free for dinner tonight?

Her: NO!

Chapter 3

For several weeks Monaco remodeled her childhood home. She hired painters to paint the outside to a pristine white with black trim on shutters and a red front door. She hired contractors to upgrade the kitchen and dining rooms creating an open floor plan. She favored the idea of being accessible to her guests as she cooked. The enlarged kitchen and dinette areas allowed for more space in the living area where her baby grand piano sat. Monaco carved out a corner alcove to use as her writing space in the dining room. Her house was decorated with distinct types of wall hangings intermixed with family photographs, statues, and knickknacks. When the furniture arrived, she placed pieces as if she were creating works of art in each room.

One day Monaco and Lisa went shopping. They stopped at a consignment shop and bumped into Jasmine looking at a lamp in the furniture section.

"Hi Jasmine," Lisa greeted the redhead who had her back to them.

"Oh, hi Lisa, Monaco," Jasmine stammered softly.

"That's a pretty lamp," Monaco said. "Are you buying it for your bedroom?"

Jasmine smiled shyly. "I wanted something for my office at church. The pastor said I could decorate the office as I see fit."

"That's wonderful," Lisa said looking past her to a piece of wall art. She pointed it out to Jasmine. "Look at that blue, yellow, and green abstract painting. Do you like it?"

Jasmine turned to look at what Lisa was indicating on the wall behind her. "Hmm...actually, yes."

"Look ladies," Monaco found a dresser with eight drawers in a flaking wood pattern. "What do you think?" she asked.

Lisa surveyed the dresser. "Are you painting or varnishing it?"

"I would paint it if I were you," Jasmine suggested. She held the blue lamp and picture Lisa had pointed out.

Monaco took another look at the dresser. "To be honest, that's what I think I will do, ladies. Paint it."

Lisa and Jasmine nodded their approval. Monaco made arrangements to have the dresser delivered as the frame would not fit in her red, four-door Jeep Wrangler. The next afternoon she was in the middle of painting the consignment shop dresser when her phone buzzed.

Him: Hello there. It's Paul. How are you doing?
Her: How did you get my number?
Him: I'm just trying to be hospitable.
Her: I have no need of a welcoming party.
Him: I see. Would you be my guest at a luncheon?
Her: Get it through your head. I don't want to eat with you.
Him: Okay, we'll start slower.
Her: Get off my phone!

It was Monaco's fourth week attending Sunday services at Hot Springs Cathedral Church. She was reading the church bulletin when Lisa sat down beside her.

"Good morning," said Monaco.

"Good morning. Are you joining today?" asked Lisa, surveying her conservative teal lace dress.

"Oh, my goodness! Will you stop? What's the rush?"

"What are you waiting for? You could walk out the church today, and get hit by a car and meet your maker."

Monaco laughed. "Great reason to join a church, Lisa."

Lisa folded her arms. "You know what I mean."

"Will you be quiet if I tell you I intend to join once I finish my new member classes?"

"Do you want me to walk up with you?"

"I think I can manage. I grew up in this church too, remember?"

"Okay. Take your time." She said it so contritely Monaco had to smile. Monaco lounged on the living room couch flipping through television channels. Her phone rang.

Him: Hi, it's Paul. I was just thinking about you. How are you doing?

Her: Why do you keep calling me?

Him: I like you. I want to get to know you.

Her: Please leave me alone.

Him: I'm really a good guy.

Her: Then be good with someone else. Leave me alone!

This was the Sunday Monaco would formally become a member of Hot Springs Cathedral Church, and she was excited and nervous. Her phone buzzed. She ignored it as she zipped up a royal blue dress with balloon sleeves. She slipped the thin belt around her waist. She made sure the outfit was below her knees. She was happily surveying herself when her phone buzzed again.

Him: Hi, it's Paul. I want to apologize if I came off too forward.

Her: You don't need to apologize. Stop calling me.

Him: I'd like to get to know you better.

Her: Do I have to report you to the pastor for you to leave me alone?

Him: No, that won't be necessary.

Her: Thank you!

Lisa suggested they move nearer to the front of the church today and Monaco agreed. The service concluded with a deacon reading out the names of people who had completed new members classes. Monaco was joined by a family of four, a tall man with bright green eyes, and another man in carefully coiffed braids gathered in a ponytail. The pastors stepped forward to welcome the newest members to the church. Ernest caught her eye and winked. The pastor entered the sanctuary from a side door.

Senior Pastor Paul Jerome Mouton was tall, handsome, and rugged looking in his clerical robe with the three black chevron bars on the sleeves. He stood in the center aisle as the congregation clapped their approval of the new members joining the church. Each member of the clergy and deacon boards shook a new member's hand. The pastor himselfstepped forward and shook each new member's hand. When he came to   her, he smiled as he clasped her hand in his, and winked an eye.

Chapter 4

Seated in Barb's Bistro Monaco could not wait another minute to relate her pew experience to Lisa.

"Girlfriend, I have something to tell you."

"Okay," Lisa was looking at the menu.

"The pastor is the man I've been telling you about who keeps asking me out."

She watched as Lisa slowly laid her menu on the table, took a sip of water, and stared at her.

"You're kidding, right?"

"No, I'm not kidding. You wanted to introduce me to him, remember?"

"Holy cow! You're been asked out on dates with one of the most eligible men in the church?"

"That is true."

"So, what now?"

"I don't know. He keeps texting me though."

"Why aren't you answering your texts?"

"I don't know what to say to him."

"That's ridiculous. I'm sure he knew you did not know who he was."

"So how would it look now if I said yes to his dinner proposals?"

"Say yes only if you want to say yes, dummy."

"Just because he's the pastor does not mean his motives are pure, Lisa."

"He's not married," said Lisa offhandedly as she toyed with a piece of roll.

"More so," exclaimed Monaco. "He should have introduced himself properly when we first met."

"Look, I get your point. However, to my knowledge, he's not a womanizer. He's been working on his doctorate, and teaching at the university. Besides that, he's a fitness junkie. I see him all the time jogging in the park."

Monaco side-eyed her friend. "How do you see him jogging in the park? Last time I checked you were so attached to your car your backside carries the logo."

Lisa grinned. "Ha, ha, ha! Nick and I have been jogging together to stay in shape."

"Runners in love, eh? Didn't you tell me that's how you two got reconnected? Jogging in the park?"

"You know I dated lots of men. I think poor Nick could never find a wedge to get in."

"I just don't think you looked at him that way. I mean just think about how protective all three of them were. Plus, we knew their girlfriends...it was just as if we were siblings instead of friends."

"Good point." Lisa agreed and looked up smiling.

Monaco smiled too and looked up into the dark eyes of Pastor Paul Mouton. The Pastor was wearing a three-piece black pinstripe suit with a black print tie and white pocket square. He looked very elegant.

"Hello ladies. Forgive my intrusion, I just wanted to say hello."

Lisa jumped out of her seat. "No problem, Pastor. I was just leaving. I have a date with Nick. Call you tomorrow Monaco."

Before Monaco could speak, Lisa was weaving through the tables to the exit. Monaco stared after the hastily departing form of her best friend. There was an awkward silence. The pastor cleared his throat. He pointed to the seat made vacant by Lisa's vanishing act.

"May I?"

"Of course, where are my manners?"

"Had you two ordered?" He smiled at the startled expression on her face. "I saw you when you came in." He pointed to a sleek black car, a Mercedes-Benz parked curbside.

"Were you waiting for someone, Pastor?"

"No, I was on the phone."

"Oh." She was at a loss for words.

He smiled again. "I usually eat alone. This is one of my favorite spots."

"Usually?"

"Unless my mother or sister are in town. Otherwise, I eat alone."

"Pastor, we have a large congregation. You can find no companion to dine with?"

He stared at her. "You're correct, I'm the senior pastor. But the Good Book warns pastors about messing with God's flock. I don't chase women in the church."

She returned his stare. "Well Pastor, you're certainly chasing me."

He laughed. "Good point. Let me formally introduce myself. I'm Dr. Paul Mouton. And please call me Paul. You're the first woman I've become attracted to since coming to town."

"Spare me, please."

"Ah, but its true Sister Valentine. Ask anyone."

"Didn't you tell me you spent time in New York City? There are hundreds, I mean, millions of attractive women in New York. No one caught your fancy?"

"There were two or three but nothing substantial."

"Substantial? What does that mean?"

"I mean it was nothing more than physical attraction, or to fill the void of loneliness."

"I see. Well, I don't date for physical attraction, nor do I use people to fill any voids. My life is pretty fulfilling on its own."

He smiled and she looked away. He was still smiling as he responded. "You asked me a question. I'm being honest with you because I like you. In fact, I'm strongly attracted to you. It's only natural your attractiveness would play a factor in my interest."

"Well, let me be brutally honest with you, Pastor. I don't do one-night stands, weekend layovers, friends with benefits, or any other type of sexual entanglements. That's why I'm still single, regardless of my attractiveness."

He was staring intently at her. "Good to know."

He was making her nervous. She looked at the menu and decided to change the subject.

"When did you receive your doctoral degree, Pastor?"

"Two weeks ago. The ceremony is coming up. Will you come as my guest? You can bring Sister Lisa if you choose. I welcome the company, and I'm certain Nick would not object."

"Don't you have family?"

"My family is my widowed mother and younger sister."

She softened her approach. He was handsome when she looked directly at him. There was a clean-cut, ruggedness about him. He glanced at her as she was studying his face, and she looked down quickly. The waiter appeared and took their orders. As they waited for their food, they exchanged life stories.

"Tell me about your life here in Hot Springs," he said, sipping his wine.

"Normal, small-town life with family, friends, and good times. I grew up with a tight-knit group of friends. Three of them are your pastors. When I graduated from high school I went away to college and never returned. That is, until the death of my parents and sister. My friends are my family. I have no one else."

He stared at her the entire time she was speaking. She appreciated the attention, but the direct gaze was unnerving her. She took a sip of her wine, and her slight hand tremble caused her more anxiety.

"Okay, Pastor, it's your turn."

"Yes, it is. But I'd really like it if you'd call me Paul. I have one or two questions if you don't mind. What is a normal, small-town life? What does that look like to an outsider like me?"

"What I mean by small-town life is a place of about twenty thousand, give or take a few hundred, with every third person related by blood or marriage. To introduce new blood into the marriage pool outsiders are warmly welcomed." She gave him a huge grin after the last sentence.

He nursed a smile. "I see why you're a writer. You're amusing in a low-key way. One last question, why didn't you want to return home?"

She leaned back and sighed. "I just wanted to see what was on the other side of the railroad tracks. I wanted to live somewhere no one knew my name or could place my face. I wanted to live without judgments, or having to please everyone else, but myself. Living under the lens of a town like Hot Springs can be stifling in many ways."

"What did you do after college?"

"I worked full-time for media publications where I started as an intern. Then a few years ago I decided to try my hand at my first love; authoring stories for children and youth. No one was more surprised than me when it blew up the way it did. I bought a town home with my hard-earned cash in Harlem. I was living the American Dream on my own terms."

"Until your parents death," he finished.

She nodded. "Okay. That's enough about me. What's your story?"

"My story begins with my late father. He was a pastor his entire life. He knew when he was a young boy, he wanted to follow his father into the ministry. I had the same epiphany when I was in middle school. I knew I wanted a life as a preacher."

"Three generations. It's good you knew early what you wanted to be," she said.

They smiled at each other. She turned her head first. He had a way of looking at her that made her uncomfortable.

"Are you staying in Hot Springs? I mean, are you settling in, or will you be leaving again? Returning to New York?" he asked.

"To be honest with you, I haven't figured that part out yet," she said. "I originally moved back here with the intent to sell the house and never return. But after a while, I realized the house brought back as many pleasant memories as sad ones. I also live next door to my best friend, and she's alone as well since her mother passed a few months ago."

"So, you bring each other friendship and sense of family? At least, for now."

"For now?" Monaco frowned with the question. "What does that mean?"

"Surely you don't think she's going to be alone forever. She and Nick are compatible on many levels. I don't see them dating long-term. He's not that kind of man."

"Well...yes...but..." Monaco stammered. She had not consciously considered Lisa's single status would ever change. Paul, watching her face and the conflicting emotions playing across it, changed the subject.

"What, if anything, are you doing with your house now?"

"Huh? Oh, I saw the house needed to be brought up to date and hired a remodeling company to do renovations. My furniture arrived from New York, so I was able to get rid of the old and replace it with the new. My last

21

step was to join the church after being hounded and nagged by Lisa to no end."

He laughed. "She's looking out for your soul. Don't be too hard on her."

"Yeah, right," Monaco said, smiling despite herself.

"How's the writing since settling in Hot Springs?"

"My writing has been doing well. It's easy to write here. Fewer distractions. It's a magical place."

"I agree with you. Hot Springs is a magical place."

"What brought you here and do you intend to stay?" she asked him.

"Your former pastor extended an invitation to me to join his ministry if I were ever considering settling down. I discovered one of my mentors, Rev. Robertson was the interim pastor, and here I am. In a few months I plan to tell the Board whether I'm staying on or leaving."

"I see. Which way are you leaning at present?"

"Not subtle at all. I like that about you. If I stay it will be because I am envisioning a life here. I don't intend to play the field forever."

They sat in their respective seats looking at each other awhile. He smiled and she looked away. He drove her home.

"Thank you for having dinner with me."

"Don't thank me. Thank Lisa for her speedy retreat. Makes me think it was planned."

He laughed. "You'll never know."

She smiled and looked out the side window. He pulled up in the paved driveway and turned off the engine. He stared at the large, white two-story Colonial home edged with boxwood shrubbery, and framed by enormous oak trees.

"You grew up in this house?"

"Yes, it has four bedrooms and three baths. Are you looking for some prime real estate?"

He laughed. "It looks like a great family home."

"Lisa lives next door in the red brick."

"And I take it, that's your red Jeep Wrangler?" Paul stepped out of his car to inspect her parked vehicle.

He walked around it inspecting the tires. Monaco stood quietly by watching him. She had seen Steven, Nick, and Ernest show the same concern when the truck arrived.

"Yes. She arrived last week. I didn't need to drive her much in New York. But it's another story in Hot Springs."

He walked her to her door and shook her proffered hand with a slight smile. She stood on her porch and watched his car lights vanish from view.

Chapter 5

The Sleeper easily entered the one-story, small church making his way to the Trustees Office. This church in Wood Haven Township was on the town's social registry as an historic landmark. He stood in the middle of the small room, and looked around. In this office was where it all began for him. This room was the major point at which he discovered his talent for numbers. The Sleeper recalled a long history with a team that made them more than, and forever, friends. Yes, the Sleeper would miss them, but the honest to goodness truth was that they had become threats to the assignment at hand. They needed elimination for him to move forward. That was the only way the mission could be salvaged. They all had to die. The Sleeper could not have anyone searching the past right now. Looking around the tiny room, the Sleeper shook in disgust at the disheveled mess in the office. The church had been closed for a good number of years. The room smelled like mildew and mold. He looked at the thick layer of dust on everything, and noticed the thick cobwebs crisscrossing in the corners behind the desk. He poured kerosene over everything in the tiny office, and outside on the walls. He struck a match, and in a moment, fire was spreading rapidly. The Sleeper changed clothing, and joined the rest of the crowd on the sidewalk watching the fire engine trucks as they hurriedly tried to contain the raging flames. Police arrived, and the uniformed officers, pushed the crowd away from the growing blaze. Dark puffs of smoke circled the fire. When the Sleeper saw the approaching news vans, he casually walked to a vehicle parked three blocks away, and made a hasty retreat in the opposite direction.

Chapter 6

The next morning Paul called and asked if she would attend a book reading later that day with him. She spent fifteen minutes selecting an outfit. She chose a powder blue smock mini dress, and threw her hair on top of her head in a messy bun. He smiled when he saw her.

The Holly Oak Bookstore combined a two-level building with indoor/outdoor dining on the top floor. They attended a reading by the religious author of a philosophy book on ethics and Monaco noticed Paul taking notes. They were not the only members of Hot Springs Cathedral Church in attendance as she saw Steven and Ernest seated a few chairs behind them. Ernest smiled but Steven ignored them as he was taking notes.

The reading over, Steven joined Paul at the author's table with their purchased books. Ernest came over to talk to her.

"Hi Monaco, I didn't know you knew about this event."

"Actually, I knew nothing of this book signing."

"Sign up at the library in our town. That way you receive invites to all book signings and other unique events all the libraries in this area hold."

"Thanks, Ernest. I did about two weeks ago. I'm not fully in the library system yet, I guess."

"How's the house renovations coming along?"

"It's almost complete."

"Excellent. I'll stop by and inspect it. I'm out. Tell Steve I left."

"Oh, you didn't come together?"

"Nah, we usually meet up at places. We both live busy lives and have other places to visit, people to see." He giggled and she smiled.

She watched him walk out to a yellow Corvette Stingray coupe, his eyes on his phone. The car speed off toward the highway.

"Hello lady," said Steven, his deep bass voice modulated to a low pitch.

"Hi Steven. Ernest left. He said he had an appointment."

"The man always has appointments. He's a doctor. Do they sleep?"

Monaco laughed. "Ernest works to meet women."

Steven grinned. "I doubt that. He loves being a scientist, and he doesn't have problems attracting women."

"That's true."

"Let's talk about you. I'm glad to see your active though. Lisa told me about your self-hibernation routines."

"I'm over it now."

Steven looked over at Paul who was gathering his laptop and new book purchase. "Glad our pastor is able to fit you into his busy schedule."

Paul grinned. "I do my best to tend to the needs of the flock."

Steven's chuckle was a deep grumble. "I see. Catch you folks later. I've a date with a certain blonde beauty, and I dare not keep her waiting."

"See you later, Steve," called Paul.

Monaco watched Steven stroll to a black two-door Porsche parked strategically toward the street. She noticed three women who nearly collided into each other watching him as he strolled by.

She mused aloud. "How can Steven see out of his car's black windows wearing black sunglasses?"

"You'll have to ask him," stated Paul. "Are you hungry?"

She nodded and he took her upstairs. Paul ordered tomato soup and grilled cheese sandwiches for them. They took their trays to the seating area. The server brought them a pot of coffee.

"What are your thoughts on the book reading?" he asked.

"The topic is engrossing to you, as it should be. But it was a waste of my time," she replied, sipping her coffee, and looking at him over the rim of the cup.

"That's what I like about you. Straight and to-the-point." He gazed thoughtfully at her. "Are you in a relationship?"

"No." She steadied her eyes on her food.

"I'd like to seriously date you," he said.

"What does that mean, Pastor?" she asked.

He was silent for a time. She looked up. He smiled.

"What would you consider serious?"

"I don't know, Pastor. It's your statement."

"Let me put it in a question format. Will you seriously date me?"

"Same question, what are you asking specifically?"

"Fair enough. I don't want to see other people, and I want you to call me Paul."

He had stopped eating. Their eyes met.

"Okay."

He resumed eating. "The end of this month is a four-day weekend. I'd like us to take a trip together."

"I don't do that. I never have, and I'm not going to start now."

"How about if I reserve separate rooms for us?"

"Why is a trip necessary? What's the purpose?"

"I want to spend time with you away from the church."

She looked at her water glass for a minute. In a controlled voice that was barely above a whisper she spoke her mind.

"Spending time away from the church would be dating. Dating is not the means to an end by itself. Dating is when you attend events and indulge in activities without being on church premises. Dating evolves into courtship which is where intimacy occurs because by now you are both certain of the outcome."

Monaco kept her head down because she was feeling herself becoming angry, and she was fighting a powerful impulse to walk out on him. They finished their meal in silence. As they walked toward his car, she resigned herself to the fact that she would never see him again except on the pulpit. Oh, well! He would not be the first would-be suitor or the last.

"Would you care to walk around City Park? The trees and plants are blooming now that winter has passed," he said.

She looked up at him. "Sure, okay."

They did not talk on the drive to City Park. They strolled on the walking paths, and Paul spoke to her about the difficulties he faced growing up as the son of a church pastor. He told her humorous tales of growing pains and lessons learned. He shared with her his love and admiration for his late father and his respect and love for his mother. He told her about his romantic interests and the breakups. Throughout Monaco never interrupted, and at no time appeared bored, giving him her full, undivided attention. He brought her home as the sun was falling. At her door, they shook hands. He did not smile this time.

Monaco settled on a blue two-piece belted skirt suit to attend Paul's commencement. Paul wore a plain black suit with a white shirt and black tie. He asked her to hold his jacket as his robe would be too hot if he wore it. They met his mother on the university lawn, and Paul introduced her to Monaco.

Jayne Mouton at sixty-six years old was a stunning woman. Her complexion, a light beige coloring with a subtle buttery undertone was offset by wavy, waist-length black hair, and dark brown eyes. Tall and elegant she was the picture of poise and sophistication. Paul guided the women to their seats before leaving for the commencement line up.

Raquel, attending with David, sat next to her mother. Claudia, sat on Jayne's other side, with Steven beside her. Monaco saw the top of Lisa's dark red curly hair in the crowd and the deep blue of Nick's smiling eyes. She beckoned them to their row. Monaco, seated next to Lisa, was scanning the program for Paul's name, when someone sat beside her.

Monaco looked up and smiled. "Glad you could make it Ernest."

"I wouldn't miss this for the world."

Ernest took off his dark shades to briefly look around. The bright sunshine illuminated his turquoise eyes calling attention to their brightness against his light cinnamon skin color, and defined bone structure. Several women bumped each other in their haste to present him with a program. The squabble took less than a minute for the victor to emerge.

The well-endowed blonde purposely stepped on the downed loser's hand after elbowing her rival onto the opposite aisle. Slightly out of breath, she presented Ernest with a bent program, and he rewarded her with a dazzling smile. She stumbled up the aisle fanning herself with the rest of the damaged programs as her comrades managed to straggle by gazing at him with forlorn appeal.

Monaco struggled to keep from laughing, and put a handkerchief to her eyes. Ernest giggled beside her.

"You rascal," she said under her breath.

"It's not my fault I'm pretty," he returned.

Nick and Lisa, having seen the women's antics, were quietly laughing. Nick leaned across Lisa, and still laughing, said, "Ernest, put your glasses back on."

Two-and one-half hours later Paul was standing among them receiving hugs from his family and friends. The group celebrated with dinner at Le Château Restaurant.

On the way home Paul spoke about his future in Hot Springs. Monaco listened but said nothing.

"Could you envision a future in Hot Springs?"

"Depends on what the future holds."

"Understandable. I like this town and the people in it. I like the slower pace of living when it comes to raising a family."

"How large a family do you want?" she asked gazing out the window.

"Well, at first one child and about two years later add a second one. Unless the Lord saw fit to make us parents of twins, triplets, quadruplets, etc."

Her head snapped around. She stared at him. She was speechless for a minute. His eyes were on the road. "Twins and triplets?"

He gave a little smile. "You have to keep your options open with God."

"Hmm," was all she said causing Paul to laugh aloud.

The next morning Paul called Monaco and made a date for the movies that evening. They saw a romantic comedy starring several blockbuster film stars. After the movie they stopped at Barb's Bistro for hamburgers and French Fries. They discussed the film's overlapping themes and argued their points of view with good humor. Paul took pleasure in how enthusiastic she became when arguing her viewpoint. Monaco admired his intelligence with conveying his opinion. He kept the conversation going as he watched the dimples that danced around her lips. She was glad for the stimulating verbal exchange as it gave her reason to feast her eyes on his handsome face. At her front door, he shook her proffered hand. This time he walked away with a thoughtful expression on his face.

The Sleeper had had a long and trying day. Parked between two other dark vehicles, he watched the large white house in the next block. He saw when Monaco and the Pastor arrived from their date. Observing the pastor's expression with the staid handshake Monaco gave him struck the Sleeper as wryly amusing. Judging by the pastor's face and body language he would have appreciated more than an old-fashioned farewell. The Sleeper smiled. Monaco Valentine had always been a prim and chaste person. It was encouraging to find she had remained in touch with her morals in the chaos and confusion of the modern world around her. The Sleeper admired that about her.

Chapter 7

The four-day weekend dawned, but neither of them mentioned it. Instead, they enjoyed a day in City Park, and made their way to an outdoor festival.. Monaco chose to wear a long multi-floral navy sundress. Paul wore a white knit pullover that clung to his muscled abdomen. His loose-fitting sweatpants were a departure from the dress pants and tailored denims he usually wore. He found a semi-secluded spot under a leafy tree and spread their blanket. Few people were in the area. He had brought along a large picnic basket loaded with different cheeses, fruits, tiny rolls, and two bottles of wine, one red and the other white.

They stayed there for two hours talking. The afternoon sun was waning, and a gentle breeze brought the scent of lavender to their nostrils. David and Raquel waved at them on their way to David's car. He was carrying a blanket and picnic basket.

"Today is a perfect day for a picnic in the park," said Monaco, watching David and Raquel.

"Yes, spring has turned into summer. I'm here for it."

"Wow, that's some car David drives."

Monaco stared at the elegant-looking, silver metallic luxury car parked across from them in the parking lot. She watched David open the car door for Raquel before walking around to the driver's side. They were a good-looking couple. Monaco looked at Paul who was looking at her.

"How long has he had it? It looks brand new," she asked.

"He bought it a few months ago."

"What make is it?"

"I believe it's a Rolls-Royce Shadow."

"Those cars cost a pretty penny."

"David is a Wall Street stockbroker. I'm sure he can afford it."

"Seeing him and Ernest together always makes me smile."

"Yeah? Why?"

"Ernest is the lazy one. David seems so intense, so focused."

"Lazy Ernest? No. Ernest is one of the leading authorities on forensic pathology. He knows his craft, loves traveling and meeting people. He handles cases all over the world. That's one of the reasons for his success. In that way he's just as driven and focused as David."

"Wow! The terrible trio grown up."

"Nick is the one to watch out for. He's always the quietest one in the room, but he's one of the sharpest. I tell him all the time he missed his gift of being a great detective."

"Nick was always that way. He and Steven were the quietest among us. But Nick was mischievous and Steven played by the rules."

"That pretty much sums up their personalities now."

"How did you come to be collaborating with my friends, and why no women pastors?"

"To answer the first question. I met your friends when we attended a men's conference a few years ago, and we clicked. Steven has become my best friend followed by Nick and Ernest. David, I've known a long time."

"You didn't answer my question about women pastors."

"I'm coming to it. The prior leadership did not endorse women leaders. That was the old mindset. We know in today's culture, you need women as well as men leaders. To that end, we have hired seminary-trained women clergy who will oversee some of the neglected women's ministries."

He looked at her closely. "Does that bother you?"

"No. I was curious. I have no plans or desires to become clergy."

The gentle wafting of the wind brought with it the fragrance of the wildflowers close by. She looked over at him lying on his back with his hands behind his head gazing at the sky. She was sitting across from him with the picnic basket planted firmly between them.

"What are you thinking about?" she asked.

"How much I like you and how well we get along together."

"I like you too."

"I have enjoyed your company immensely these past few months."

She smiled. "Likewise. Your easy to talk to, and we seem to have much in common."

"I want to ask you a serious question."

"Hmm...," She was listening to the music. "Is that the Doves?"

"Yes. The song your enthralled by is entitled, *I'm All Yours*. It's from their greatest hits collection.*"

He sat up and pushed the picnic basket from between them. He pulled her down on the blanket under him and kissed her lips, neck and collar bone. He allowed his lips to wander down to her cleavage. She stiffened and pushed him away. He raised his head and looked at her.

"Kiss me back," he said.

"Let me up," she said sternly. "I told you..."

He smiled. "I'll let you up when you return my kiss."

"Paul..." she said as he kissed her again. He let her up, and put the picnic away as she watched him. He rose to his feet, helped her to hers, and they walked down to the car in the parking lot. She scrutinized the area. She had seen the bridge adjacent to the grassy lot from where they had sat earlier.

Monaco made her way to the bridge. Looking down over the wooden railing she saw a little stream with water flowing languidly on jagged rocks and stones. She watched the water a moment. Paul came and stood beside her. As she turned to look up at him, she smiled, and he lowered his head to hers and kissed her full on the mouth. This time their arms wrapped around each other.

Paul walked into his town home and a sharp pang of loneliness hit him. He looked around his living room. A large brown leather sectional was the focal piece of the room besides the wall television and floor lamp. His open kitchen held a table and two chairs. He walked upstairs to his bedroom and looked at the king-size bed, dresser, and nightstand. Everything in a black or brown color. His spare bedroom was where he had his home office. A wall of books. One large desk and armchair. That was it. There was a patio off his main bedroom that wrapped around to the living room. There was no furniture out there because he never used it. In the five years he had lived here he had come home alone. When he wanted or needed female companionship, he traveled to them.

He asked Monaco to come home with him once, and she firmly put him in his place. Far from being discouraged he found himself more infatuated with her. He believed he had found the woman he wanted to spend the rest of his life with. He had never experienced these feelings he had for her in any previous relationships, and it was both intriguing and exasperating. He believed she was hesitant to open her heart to him because of a prior hurt, and he did not want to risk making her uncomfortable.

One evening they drove through the countryside. The quietness within the dark interior of the car added a dreamy ambiance against the colorful scenery flashing outside the windows. She asked him how he could stand driving with so much silence. He was quiet for so long she grew uncomfortable.

Turning to her, he said, "I have you now. You fill the silence whenever I think of you."

Leaving the kitchen, Paul paced about the living room before going downstairs to his home gym where he stayed for an hour. He took a shower, and called Steven. They had a lengthy conversation about sports, religion, travel, politics, guns, women, fishing, and Monaco. Paul rambled on for some time about her without specifically narrowing or naming any topic associated with her. From his end Steven listened with his therapist ear as he watched NASCAR. At last Paul hung up and Steven smiled to himself. He suspected Paul was falling in love with Monaco.

The day had been a productive one for Monaco. She had finished editing a chapter in her new book and found extensive research on the subject matter she previously assumed she would have to postpone for another day. She took a shower, threw on a loose white tank and khaki shorts, and made a Caesar salad. She heard the front door, and Lisa had entered the kitchen. She set a large shopping bag on the counter.

"Hey doll face," said Lisa. "I had a tough time settling on the fish until I saw the bass. No contest."

Monaco smiled. "I set up the coffee table. That British mystery series I like comes on in about thirty minutes."

"You mean the one you've been watching with your new boyfriend?"

"He's not my boyfriend. I mean..."

"He's not seeing anyone else. Are you?" Lisa snapped her fingers in her face startling her. "Are you okay?"

"I'm fine, Lisa. Come on, let's eat."

"Don't try to change the subject. Paul is not seeing anyone else. You do know that, right?"

"Yes, he told me he wanted to see me exclusively."

Monaco brought the salad bowls and ice water pitcher to the table. Lisa had picked up an order of garlic-roasted sea bass from their favorite deli. Monaco turned on the television. Lisa turned it off.

"What's going on with you? Do you like him or not?"

Monaco sighed. "I'm crazy about him."

"That's all I needed to hear!" Lisa smiled. "I feel the same way about Nick."

Lisa reached for the salad bowl. Monaco smiled. She listened as Lisa described her blooming relationship with Nick. In her mind, Monaco believed Paul wanted more of a commitment from her than what she had been giving, but she was not certain if she trusted him enough with her heart or her body.

One afternoon after church services, Paul took Monaco for a drive through the countryside. She soon was aware they were on a different route than they usually traveled. All Monaco saw were acres of wooded areas as they sped along a two-lane highway. Soon they parted from the wide road to one lane which interconnected with bypasses to other roads. Paul turned onto a solitary road leading to a circular driveway with a flowing fountain.

Monaco looked up at the mansion built on the Georgian Colonial style. It was a large, two-story brick structure designed with overlapping gables, wide windows, and a double door entryway under an arched column. Taking her by the hand, Paul pointed out the natural waterway built around the home. A private garden looked on the water where a small boat sat anchored by a dock obscured by wild flowers, buttonbush shrubs, and wild berry bushes.

"What a beautiful home. Is it really built over this stream?"

"Yes, it was quite daring, but dad insisted this was the spot."

"Who designed this house?"

"My father working with my great-grandfather."

"I thought he was a church pastor?"

"That was my grandfather. My great-grandfather was an architect."

"Wow! So you grew up in this house?"

"Yes."

"Who lives here now?"

"My father passed about ten years ago. My mother and younger sister live here now. I live in a town house in the city."

"We're visiting your boyhood home?"

"Yes, as well as, formally meeting my mother, Dr. Jayne Mouton."

"I met your mother during your commencement, remember?"

Paul smiled. "Watch the heel of your shoe along here."

He guided her around to the front door. Monaco panicked. "What? Why didn't you tell me? I shouldn't have pulled my hair up. I should have worn something else."

Monaco wore a black A-line dress with lace three-quarter sleeves and a full skirt in velvet. Paul smiled as he pulled her along.

"That's why I didn't tell you because we wouldn't have ever made it here. Relax. Mother won't bite, she may snarl but never bite."

Paul smiled at the panic stricken look on her face, and rang the doorbell. When the front door opened, Monaco's fears vanished. Jayne opened the door with a smile, bringing Monaco into the home with an embrace. She seated them in a living room decorated in French Provincial-style. Monaco loved the bone china platter trimmed in gold braiding which held an assortment of French pastries, tarts and cakes with a similar platter holding a coffee urn.

Jayne artfully steered conversation away from herself. She asked Monaco questions about her parents, her education, and her career. For her part, Monaco was direct, and to the point. She did not fear Paul's mother, and responded honestly to her questions.

They were finishing tea when a younger version of Jayne entered the room; Paul's sister, Raquel. She had hazel almond-shaped eyes, and full lips enhanced by the halo of thick, wavy black hair cascading about her shoulders, and down her back. Raquel was a healthy woman with solid curves she emphasized in snug fitting attire.

Staring at Monaco, she walked over to her mother and hugged her. She kissed her brother on the cheek.

"Hello brother dear," said Raquel. "Who's this exquisite creature?"

"Raquel, this young lady is a friend of your brother's. Her name is Monaco Valentine," said Jayne.

Raquel sat next to Monaco and extended her hand. "Hello, my name is Raquel Mouton. Pleased to meet you, Ms. Monaco Valentine."

"Likewise, Ms. Mouton," said Monaco, shaking her hand.

"How long have you been seeing my brother?"

"I would think you would ask him. I believe though it's been several months."

Raquel snorted. "You believe? You mean you don't know how long you've been dating?"

"I'm horrible with numbers."

Raquel looked at her brother with a mocked smile on her face. "She's not much into you dear brother if she can't remember how long you've been dating."

"Slow down, Raquel," said Paul.

He was smiling at Monaco pretending to be inspecting her shoe heel.

"I'm glad you brought your friend over Paul. Please don't be a stranger Ms. Valentine," said Jayne.

"Thank you for a lovely evening, Ms. Mouton. I enjoyed myself. But next time the conversation will focus on you."

A huge smile spread across Jayne's face. She looked at her son and hugged him before turning to hug Monaco.

"I meant what I said. Do come back."

Monaco smiled. "That will be up to Paul."

Raquel smiled and waved from her chair. "Bye-bye Paul, and Ms. Valentine."

In the car Paul looked at Monaco. "My mother likes you."

"I like her."

"Don't mind Raquel. She's jealous."

"She didn't bother me."

"Somehow I didn't think she did."

Chapter 8

On stealth feet the Sleeper put in the pass code and made his way to the Trustees Office. He looked down at something on the floor. A piece of note paper had fallen. There was an address on it. Whose? He read it and smiled. Ah, this would come in handy someday. He moved to the safe, opened it, and took out the ledger and checkbook. After writing the check he forged Claudia Ginyard's signature and put everything back in the safe. He booted up the computer and sighed. The system was outdated, and it surprised him that it turned on. He did not blame the pastors for using their own laptops. It was a sin and a shame the way some churches stayed so far behind the times with technology. The computer at last booted up. The Sleeper deftly balanced the spreadsheet and tallied it with the ledger. He shook his head. Such mundane, outdated bookkeeping systems. An idiot could help themselves to free cash if the need arose. He was about to exit through the side door when he spotted a flashlight. Who was that? The figure with the flashlight is a woman. What is she doing? Why can't people mind their business? Move the dog away from the bushes and turn off the flashlight! Not much time, and he needed to be somewhere else and soon. Wait a minute, that's not a dog. She was pulling a child's toy wagon with bags of garden soil. Did she intend to plant flowers along the church driveway at this time of night? Wait, that looked like Sister Agnes Wright. He vaguely remembered her and assumed she was in a nursing home. He scanned the neighboring houses across the wide street. Moving with stealth form he kept one eye on Agnes bent body and another on the street.

Not a soul was out. Putting a hand over her mouth and another around her throat he snuffed out what little breath she had before dragging her across the yard to the back of the church.

The teenagers wanted a quiet spot unseen from the highway. Brad and Sondra had been flirting in school for a few weeks when he asked her to the movies. He was happy she accepted. Sondra was glad he overcame his shyness. Brad drove his mother's Ford Exhibition sport utility vehicle onto the back parking lot without being aware they were on church grounds. Their fear of anyone noticing the car or them was of little concern as they were from a neighboring township.

Brad looked around. "No one can see us from the street here."

He smiled at her. Sondra was looking over the dashboard. She noticed something in the bushes when Brad turned the car's headlights off.

"What's that over there? Under that brush?" She pointed, and he squinted in the darkness to see where she was pointing.

"I don't see..."

Brad, inquisitive by nature, wanted a closer look. He decided to get out of the vehicle, and followed by Sondra, they walked to the bushes. As Brad pushed back discarded tree branches and debris, Sondra screamed when she saw the lifeless body, and ran back to the vehicle. Brad took out his phone and snapped pictures before calling the police. As they waited for the police to arrive, the teen uploaded the pictures to his social media account. By the time the police were on the scene, Brad's pictures had amassed twenty-two thousand votes in under twenty minutes.

Detectives Matt Osborne and Joe Grant worked out of Oakland Heights Police Station. Osborne was fifty-years old, married, and had been a police officer for thirty years. His partner, Grant, was twenty-seven years old, single, and had aced the detective exam on the first try. He was entering his ninth year in law enforcement. The partners, in their fifth year working together, pulled up to the church parking lot, and immediately noticed the absence of spectators.

"No one interested in murder?" asked Osborne sarcastically; his pale blue eyes surveyed the street.

"This is Oakland Heights," responded his partner, looking around. "More than likely they're watching us behind their drapes."

"You mean from their camera monitors. Look at all the cameras on these homes. You think anyone was filming over here?"

Grant laughed. "If they were they've erased them. Don't want their names in the media. This is a well-to-do retirement community. They're not looking to get involved with the outside world."

"Humph, we should be so lucky," responded Osborne. He spied a patrol officer coming toward them. "Hey Parker, whatcha got?"

"Good evening, Detectives. Not much so far. Two teenagers discovered the body."

"I won't ask what the little angels were doing on a back lot this time of night." said Osborne wearily as Grant grinned."Go on, Parker," continued the sergeant.

"That's it, Detectives."

Grant looked at the cop. "That's it?"

"The medical examiner had the body moved to the morgue."

Osborne's irritation was apparent. "Are you kidding me? Why would Feinstein move the body before we get a chance to look at it? What's up his craw tonight?"

The officer looked surprised. "Oh, it wasn't Dr. Fienstein. The new medical examiner is a woman, but I didn't catch her name. Oh, here it is, Dr. Karen Newbold. She's the new chief."

"Chief, uh? Good for her. Call on her tomorrow, Joe."

"Right. Did you get the victim's identity, Parker?"

"The name of the woman is Agnes Wright, and she wandered from the Oakland Heights Nursing Home about a mile from here."

"That's just great," said Osborne. "Anything else, Parker?"

"No, that's it. The teenagers are over there if you want to speak to them."

Osborne looked over at them. Both had their heads down, their eyes on their phone screens. He let out a breath.

"Get their names, addresses and names of their parents. Make sure they both get home safe. Thanks, Parker."

"No problem. You guys be safe."

40

Osborne turned back to his partner. "Joe, when you talk to the new medical examiner. Let her know not to move the body until we've seen it in all its blood and glory."

The black detective grunted. They returned to their cruiser.

The detectives parked alongside the hedges in front of the Oakland Heights Nursing Home. They showed their badges to two security personnel before reaching the registration desk. A slender, wiry redhead with a spiked haircut and periwinkle blue eyes was at the desk. She was not in the best mood.

"I don't care who you say you are. You aren't going anyplace in this building unless Dr. Keener approves. If you want to play tough guy, go right ahead, and I'll call the actual police."

Grant stepped in front of Osborne. "Look nurse. We don't have time to flirt with you. One of your patients escaped her cage, and ended up dead a block or more from here."

The nurse stared up at him a moment. She sat down and put her face in her hands. Another nurse walked up. She looked down at her colleague. She was taller with black hair and gray-blue eyes.

"Dorothy, what's the matter?"

Dorothy said, "Kristie, that patient we were looking for? The police found her. She's dead."

Kristie turned her gray-blue eyes on them. "Oh, no! I'm the supervisor for this shift. Kristie Reynolds. May I see your badges, please?"

They showed her their badges and waited.

"Thank you," said Kristie. "What can I help you with, Detectives?"

"Was Agnes Wright a patient here?" asked Osborne.

"We use the word client," she said. "Hold on. Let me retrieve her file."

She walked behind the registration desk to an area where a desktop sat. They could hear typing on the keyboard. A few minutes later Kristie returned to the counter.

"Detectives, is this the woman you saw tonight?" Kristie showed them a photograph of a smiling Agnes Wright in a blue dress with colorful balloons behind her.

"Yes. May we keep this?"

"Yes, that's your copy. Is there anything else I can do for you?"

"Simple bio."

"Widowed. Initial entry into dementia. Predeceased by her husband and one son."

"How old was she?"

"She turned eighty-eight last week."

"How long has she been here?"

"Going on eight years."

"What did she do before she retired?"

"She was an accountant. When she retired, she volunteered her services in a tax clinic and in her church."

"Did she ever have visitors?"

"Only when the church ladies showed up. She played piano when she remembered."

"Thank you for your time."

"Oh, wait, Detectives," called Kristie after them. She was looking in a heavier manila folder in her hands. "I remember something that was never put in her file. She belonged to Hot Springs Cathedral Church in Oakland Heights."

Grant wrote it down in his notes. The detectives left the hospital.

Chapter 9

Steven's two-story condominium sat on the back end of a multi-apartment building complex. The home boasted high ceilings, twelve-foot picture windows, and a swimming pool. The first floor was an open floor plan centered by a large white leather sectional which served to anchor the living room from the dining room. On the second floor, Steven designed the master bedroom with a walk-in closet that led to the bathroom. The guest bedroom had its own bathroom. The third floor was on the roof and housed exercise equipment. The garage held a redesigned 911 turbo Porsche vehicle. The newest additions to Steven's garage were hid behind a wall panel.

Steven and Claudia had been seriously dating for six months. They had grown comfortable in each other's spaces. When Claudia stayed overnight her iced pink BMW sat next to his Porsche in the garage.

Steven invited Paul and Monaco to his home for Sunday dinner. One hour before their friends arrival, Claudia let herself into Steven's home with a shopping bag laden with food items. Using the house key she called out to him. He was in the kitchen tending to the garlic-basted chicken and new potatoes in the oven.

"You found everything?" he asked, intent on basting the chicken.

"Yes, I was in the market last night. I didn't want to shop in this outfit today," replied Claudia.

He glanced at her. The slinky black dress was appealing. He understood her point and smiled. She returned his smile.

"I bought some flowers for the dining room table and your coffee table."

"Thank you," he replied moving from the oven to the refrigerator.

He took out a bowl of tomatoes and hunk of mozzarella cheese. She handed him a jar of black and green olives. Claudia watched Steven for a minute as he expertly sliced the tomatoes. He had learned how to cook from his parents, and she silently thanked them every day because her culinary skills were non-existent. She moved to the sink to put water in the empty flower vases stashed under the sink. Steven kissed her cheek in passing, and she smiled.

Across town Paul picked Monaco up a few minutes ahead of the time he had text he would. She was sitting on the sofa and saw him when he drove up. She wore a pink multi floral lace mini dress with ruffles on the long sleeve cuffs and around the hem. The back tied at the neck and opened to the waist. She pulled her hair in a loose ponytail and when she walked in front of him, Paul had to put his mind to other thoughts. Between her delectable back and the long, shapely legs he had a challenging time maintaining his decorum throughout the evening.

When Paul brought her home, he parked in the driveway and walked her to her door. As she unlocked her front door he reached out and turned her around by her shoulders.

"I'd like to take you out for a fancy evening tomorrow night."

"How fancy are we talking? All our dates have been fancy."

"Black tie fancy."

"Oh!"

"See you at nine o'clock sharp." He smiled as he walked away. She watched his car until the taillights faded.

The next afternoon Monaco called Lisa for help. She showed Lisa the two dresses in black; Lisa rejected both.

"For goodness' sake Monaco, you're going on a fancy formal date. Wear something in a fabulous shade that's a little bit daring!"

"How about this?" She pulled out a long gold-colored gown.

Lisa was now raking through the back of her closet. She looked at the gown Monaco showed her.

"No, that simply won't do for a formal evening."

"I don't know if I trust your fashion advice," said Monaco, sighing. "I wore that floral dress with the back out you like. Paul didn't say one word how he felt about the dress. He usually says something, but he was mute the entire evening."

Lisa, preoccupied with her search, murmured, "Uh huh."

"I'm serious, Lisa. I think I pushed the envelope too far. He is a pastor, after all!"

Lisa laughed. "Honey, he's a man first! And, he's a man that's into you. Why not highlight what he's missing?"

"Stop it, Lisa. I'm not trying out for the role of the scarlet woman."

"Girl, please!" Lisa's eye caught something. She pulled out her find. "Oh, this will have him proposing!"

Monaco shook her head. "Oh no, I can't wear that. I don't know why I let you talk me into buying it."

"Because it's your style, the color looks gorgeous on you, and your legs look great."

"I guess it will be alright..."

"Wearing this dress will only highlight your assets!"

Two hours later, Monaco examined herself critically in her bedroom mirror. The light aqua-colored sleeveless gown was a snug-waist wrap style that opened slightly above the knee. The neckline hung into a low cross neck drape. Paul smiled when he saw her.

They drove to Le Château Restaurant where a private booth with lit candles and calla lilies as centerpieces awaited them. They danced to deejay-inspired romantic ballads including the tune by the Doves which had caught Monaco's attention in the park. But it was the following Doves tune, '*I love you most of all*' that Paul sung to her as he wrapped her in his arms. As they were eating dessert, Paul had one of Monaco's favorite show tunes dedicated to her. The older patrons in the restaurant sang to it, and Paul laughed to near hysteria when Monaco, cheerfully and musically off-key, loudly joined in.

The drive home was quiet. Paul played a series of love ballads. He parked in the driveway and walked her to her front door.

"May I come in?"

"Yes."

"May I have a glass of water?"

She looked at him. She returned with the glass of water. He sat on the sofa, took the glass from her, and placed it on the table. She frowned as there was no coaster on the table.

"Come sit here with me."

"Paul..."

"Sit down Monaco."

"It's late Paul and I have to work on..."

He pulled her down next to him on the sofa. "Look, I'm crazy about you. How do you feel about me?"

She smiled nervously. "The same."

"What is it about me that's keeping you from loving me? What's the matter between us? Aren't you attracted to me?"

"That's not it."

"You didn't answer me."

"Yes. I'm attracted to you."

"Okay, what is it? I'm listening."

Monaco sighed. "I guess I've been overly-cautious because of former betrayals and disappointments. I'm too old to play the virgin queen, but I'm not streetwalker sullied either."

"I understand about betrayals," he replied, staring intently at her.

"Do you? I dated Brian for three years. I was certain he was the one for me. Our families had grown close, we had no hidden lovers jumping out of the woodwork issues. Everything was perfect."

Monaco stopped speaking, holding herself tight as if to hold in the pain. She gave him a tight-lipped smile.

"About a week before the wedding, Brian decided we should hold a party at his place. It was a wild night. Long story short, the next morning I woke up in bed with another woman...and Brian was beside me with our future best man."

Monaco lowered her head so as not to look at Paul. When Paul reached for her, she pulled away, and stood up shakily.

"You don't understand. I had no one to ask advice from. I was too ashamed to ask the guys for their advice, and I darn sure did not want to give my sister another reason to despise me. The funny thing is, Paul, I was happy being alone. I had a great job, great benefits, and loved my life.

46

But my family kept pressuring me to meet someone and marry. My upbringing in the church contributed to me feeling guilty for enjoying my single life so much."

"Sweetheart, you've been punishing yourself for behavior that was not your fault. That guy was a jerk."

"It doesn't matter if he was a jerk or not. I've failed at finding love numerous times. I'm as impure a sinner as they come, and not fit to be a pastor's wife."

"So what you've been doing? Avoiding men? You don't believe your pure in God's eyes? Let me tell you, baby, you're human. God forgives our mistakes, whether they are one or one hundred. That's the eternal grace and mercy He gives us. We repent, and he forgives us."

Paul walked over to her and took her in his arms, and for a few minutes, as he held her tightly, he could feel the tension in her body slowly release.

Monaco buried her face in his chest. "I'm sorry I didn't tell you when we were exchanging life stories, but it was embarrassing. Desperately seeking love and affection, after Brian I doubted my sexuality. I wondered if I were attracted to women."

"Are you?" Paul quietly asked.

"No. I'm attracted to men. I'm attracted to you."

"Look at me, please," Paul put his hands on her shoulders. "Look at me. I want you. I've wanted you since the first time I saw you in church. I've watched you in church and outside of it. But if you were the village idiot, I would still want you. We are kindred spirits, you and I. And, I've waited a long time for a woman whose intellect, humor, personality, and charm kept me stimulated beyond her sexual attractiveness. I wanted you for mine the moment I laid eyes on you."

"But you didn't know the damaged woman I was."

"Your not any more damaged than the rest of us. You've put up a fence of resistance against being hurt again. Given the betrayals you suffered, that's understandable. But baby, it's time to move forward. Mistakes don't define you. Now, to change the subject."

He reached inside his coat pocket and produced a silver sequined jeweler's box. She looked at him with a surprise look on her face. Bending to one knee he opened the box and a sparkly diamond solitaire ring nestled on silvery fabric gleamed.

"Will you marry me, Monaco Valentine?"

She was speechless and happy. She nodded her head, smiling through fresh tears. He slid the ring on her finger and kissed her softly.

"When do you want to set the date for?" he asked.

She gave him a half smile. "I don't know. Do we have to set a date this minute?"

"No, tomorrow's fine. My only request is that we make it sooner rather than later. Now that I've found you, I don't want to be without you."

"I have never planned a wedding before. I will need to ask my godmother if she will help me."

"My mother will help if you need her."

"Oh no, thank you. I have my best friend Lisa, and my godparents."

"Who are your godparents, if I may ask?"

"Deacon Ed, and Deaconess Mary Joseph."

"The Josephs?" Paul laughed. "I didn't know that."

"I hate to throw you out, but I've some planning to do."

"Okay. Don't forget to let me know as soon as possible our wedding date. Anything you need me to do besides plan the honeymoon?"

"I will let you know."

He wrapped her in his arms and kissed her deeply.

Chapter 10

Monaco watched Paul's car until his taillights disappeared from view. She immediately called Lisa who answered on the second ring. The excitement Monaco was feeling came out in rushed sentences.

"Lisa, are you busy? Paul proposed, and I said yes, and now I must plan a wedding because we don't want to wait a long time to get married. Can you help me?"

"Honey, breathe. Congratulations!"

"Thank you."

"Did you call your godmother yet?"

"No, I called you first."

Lisa laughed. "You want me to come over?"

"Yes."

"Okay, I'll leave a text for Nick. Let me pack a bag. I have a feeling I'm going to be spending the night."

"Okay. I'm calling Mary next."

"You do that." Lisa hung up. Monaco dialed Deaconess Mary Joseph.

"Hello?"

"Hi Mary, it's Monaco. I'm sorry to be calling you so late."

"Hello sweetie. Oh, that's fine. I'm waiting for Ed to tuck me in. I've been a little sick since I last saw you."

"Steven told me. How do you feel now?"

"Slowly regaining my strength. Ed has been a remarkable husband. My concern is whether I will be able to get into some of my clothing. His style of doing laundry is not to my taste but at least he tries. When are you coming to see me? Your family. You know you never need an invitation."

"Mary, I have something to tell you. I'm getting married! Pastor Mouton asked me to marry him, and I said yes."

"Congratulations! What a wonderful surprise!"

"Yes, we've been seeing each other for a little bit now. He proposed tonight. We want to marry soon."

"Soon? How soon?"

"As soon as possible. That's where you come in. I need your help. I don't know where to begin."

"Okay. Grab a pen and paper. First, you need to set a date. I'm sure your ceremony will be in our church, so you'll need to contact Jasmine to determine if the church is available ..." she stopped. "Can you come over here tomorrow morning, and we can begin working on your wedding together?"

"Are you well enough to receive visitors?"

"Are you kidding my dear? With news like this I'm cured of the melancholy that attached itself to me feeling worthless lying around this house." She laughed gaily and Monaco laughed too.

"Lisa is coming over to spend the night and help as well. Do you mind if she comes with me?"

"Lisa will bring the Latin flavor we love about her. She has a gift with floral arrangements. I'm glad you returned home, sweetie. We all missed you." After a pause, Mary said, "I'll see you both tomorrow morning."

Monaco took a shower and threw on her pajamas. She heard the front door open and close. Lisa had let herself in with her house key. They flung their arms around each other.

"Let me see the ring! It's beautiful, girl. That dress took him over the edge," said Lisa, gazing at her hand.

They both giggled. "It was such a magical night. The way he was behaving I thought we might have the honeymoon ahead of the wedding."

"Tell that to someone who doesn't know you. When's the date?"

"Mary wants us to come to her house tomorrow morning."

"Okay," said Lisa. "You know I will do the floral arrangements for my best friend."

"That's what Mary said. Oh, Lisa, I am so happy."

"Wow! To think a few months ago you didn't want to go out with him at all!"

"I know, right?"

"Okay, girl. Let's go to sleep. We've got work to do tomorrow."

Monaco laid awake in the dark of the bedroom. She could not believe she was engaged to Paul. She sighed happily. She was relieved he had not condemned her or seen her as less worthy of committed love. She had hid the agony, disappointment, and humiliation of those affairs from even her best friend. The final betrayal by Brian left her emotionally demoralized, and she determined to never give her heart or body away again. With that decision meant she cut herself off from falling in love because she no longer trusted herself or the men who pursued her. Monaco looked at her ring in the semi-darkness of the room. The light drifting in from the moon's glow illuminated the sparkle of the diamond. She heard Lisa snoring softly beside her and smiled. Slowly, and without trying, she fell into a gentle sleep.

The next morning Monaco woke to the smell of coffee brewing, and knew Lisa was downstairs in the kitchen making breakfast. The day had dawned bright with sunlight beaming through the drawn curtains. Monaco decided on a simple outfit of navy striped top and navy slim pants. She gazed happily at her engagement ring with thoughts of Paul and the previous evening.

When Monaco walked into the kitchen, Lisa in a long bib apron, beamed happily as she set two cups of coffee on the kitchen counter. Next to the coffees were plates of toasted corn tortillas holding refried beans, avocado, cheese, and sunny side up eggs topped with salsa.

"Oh, my goodness!" exclaimed Monaco, her eyes on the food before her. She sat in the highchair, pulling a napkin across her lap. "I haven't eaten your Mexican breakfasts since forever."

"Well, after all that excitement last night, I figured we might forget to eat today. I believe a good breakfast will ensure we're fortified for the day."

Grinning they both attacked their breakfast plates. As they ate, they pulled up online wedding catalogs.

An hour later the women were on the road to Ed and Mary Joseph's sprawling home. When Ed opened the front door, he smiled broadly at his goddaughter. Kissing her cheek, he swallowed her up in a bear hug.

"Congratulations," he said. He pushed her away, and peered in her face closely, smiling the entire time. "Let me get a look at you. What a little sight you are. You look exactly like your mother."

"Now Ed, you let them in, and close my front door. Bugs are flying in here."

The voice came from behind Ed, and in the darkened room, Monaco found it difficult to locate her godmother. Once the lights were on, the room expanded. Monaco saw her godmother seated on the sofa in the living room. She walked over to her, and the women hugged. Monaco stepped back so Lisa and Mary could embrace. Ed came out the kitchen carrying a tray loaded with refreshments and placed it on the living room coffee table.

"Hi Deaconess Mary," Lisa said.

"Hello Lisa," said Mary. "How's that gorgeous blue-eyed boyfriend of yours?"

Lisa blushed. "Nick is fine."

"When are you two marrying? With that pretty color hair of yours, and his gorgeous eyes and skin tone, I would expect your children will be stunning visions of you two."

"We've been talking about marriage, but our workloads are heavy right now."

"Oh posh! He's a managing partner, isn't he?"

"Yes but..."

"Yes, but what?"

"You should have been a lawyer," smiled Lisa.

"Come sit over here next to me on my left Lisa. Come over here on my right-side Monaco."

Monaco slightly upset, viewed Mary's physical appearance on the sofa with a light blanket across her lap, and her eyes fell on the folding walker. Mary was in her mid-seventies, and had practically raised her alongside her own mother. She had been a vibrant, energetic woman in her youth with gardening and horseback riding her two chief loves. She had been a tennis instructor, and played the game fiercely with the young people in the church.

Mary took the teacup from Ed before looking at Monaco sitting stiffly at her side.

"I know you're upset about my health, child. It's been a long time since you've been home. Please don't be upset about this. The doctors are doing what they can, and I do my part. I never knew this was a degenerative disorder or that it ran in my family."

"What do you have?" Monaco asked, her voice almost a whisper.

"The long form is multiple sclerosis. You've probably heard of it as MS."

Ed passed a teacup to Monaco. "It's a disease that affects the central nervous system. Think of it as the immune system eating the protective covering of the nerves."

Lisa's eyes swelled with tears. "Is there a cure?"

"Not yet, but they're working on it," replied Ed.

"All is not lost," said Mary in a cheerful voice. "The symptom I'm experiencing right now is difficulty walking sometimes, and problems with my coordination when I do walk."

"And you tire easily now, sweetie," added Ed, handing Lisa a teacup.

"Yes, it's why I can no longer ride Starbuck, my horse. We sold him to a family looking for a gentle horse for their son. Occasionally, they invite us over to their farm to watch their son ride. They are a sweet family."

Ed stood up. "Well ladies, I'm going to take my leave. Congratulations, sweet girl. We'll do whatever you need." He turned and walked towards the kitchen. "I'm going into the garden if you need me, Mary."

His wife watched him walk through the kitchen and out the back door before turning to the two young women seated on either side of her.

"Ed worries too much about me, but I'm doing fine. I do my weekly aerobic exercises five days a week, and that keeps me going. He lets the medical staff scare him too much." She laughed gaily. "Now, let's plan for this fantastic wedding of yours."

An hour later Ed came in and hovered about in the kitchen. After a few minutes he walked into the room.

"Girls, I know you're in a state of happy excitement with the wedding planning, and I imagine my sweet wife is too. But she tires easily now."

Monaco and Lisa moved swiftly to pack their belongings. Mary, folded her arms loosely across her chest.

"Oh Ed, now you've scared them. Come here Lisa, and give me a hug, darling girl."

Lisa hugged Mary, and immediately the tears fell. Mary hugged her as she did when Lisa was a teenager, and crying over some mishap or other. Ed shook his head with a wistful smile on his face.

"Now that's enough of that, you two," he said.

Lisa wiped her eyes, and kissed Mary's cheek. Monaco hugged Mary around the neck holding back tears. Ed kissed Monaco's forehead and Lisa's cheek. He gently picked up his wife, placing her in a wheelchair Monaco had not noticed was behind the sofa. Ed wheeled his wife out of the room. Mary had passed out with a gentle smile on her face. The women let themselves out the house quietly, their eyes rimmed with tears.

In the bridal shop Lisa, in her bridesmaid gown, whirled about in front of the full-length mirror. Raquel and Claudia were agonizing over the flow of the lower portions of their gowns. Mary in her wheelchair was having a grand time directing the parade of women and the gowns they tried on. The saleslady stood to the side as Mary worked. It was well-known throughout their community that Mary was a fine seamstress.

"I love the style of these gowns on you girls, but I don't like that color on you, Lisa. Try a darker shade."

"Claudia let's tighten this area in the waist, and add a thicker padding in the chest."

"Raquel, we need to emphasize your beautiful waist to hip ratio. Your gown needs tightening right here."

Jasmine exited the dressing room and Mary smiled. Her gown needed no alterations. Raquel playfully pinched her, and Jasmine grinned. Lisa returned in a darker version of the bridesmaid gown, and Claudia and Raquel applauded.

"That shade is gorgeous with your hair color Lisa," crooned Claudia.

"Thank you, Claudia," said Lisa. "I like that color on you and Raquel as well."

"Okay, now that I've got you girls together, where's the star of the show?" asked Mary. "I want to see the wedding gown she selected."

The saleslady rushed to retrieve Monaco. The gown Monaco tried on had a deep sweetheart neckline, and clung to her body down to the fishtail hemline. The front sported a low neck line with the back view lower.

Claudia gushed. "Wow, you look great."

Raquel whistled softly. "Wow! That gown showcases your curves to perfection. I love the back view."

Lisa clasped her hands together. "The ideal dress."

Jasmine murmured. "I want a dress like that for my wedding."

The saleslady preened. "How stunning you look, dear."

The ladies all turned to look at Deaconess Mary who was sitting quietly with her hands folded. She smiled sweetly.

"Are you all finished? The dress is beautiful, and she is gorgeous. If she were anyplace else, marrying anyone else, it might be the ideal gown. But she is marrying the senior pastor in our church. Young man though he is, he is conservative in his speech, manners, and personal grooming. You're about to become a senior pastor's wife, future mother of his children, and first lady of Hot Springs Tabernacle Church."

"Yes, but..." Monaco stopped as Mary had lifted up her hand.

"You're in a unique position and one, not a few women envy you for. As first lady, you are going to lead the women's groups, and be an example of beauty, grace, modesty, and humility for all women, regardless of age, socioeconomic status, or education. Walking down the aisle half naked in God's house is disrespectful to yourself, your future husband, and the church. But this is your wedding, Monaco, what do you think?"

Monaco swallowed. She whispered, "I have another gown to show you."

She fled the room, and Mary had the bridesmaids give their gowns to the seamstress with instructions on alterations. Jasmine's gown needed no alterations, and was wrapped for her to take home. The bridesmaids changed back into their street clothes and waited. Monaco returned and the ladies were silent. Mary inspected Monaco in the next gown. She had Monaco turn to give her front, back, and side views. She made her walk back and forth in the room. She had the headpiece brought out and pinned to the back of Monaco's hair and the saleslady placed the bride on the dais.

"Okay ladies, what do you see?" asked Mary.

Raquel said, "I like this one much better. It looks more elegant for her."

Claudia whispered, "I agree with Raquel. Her figure is as impressive in this gown as the previous one, and I like the long sleeves."

"No one should be upset over this choice. She looks gorgeous," said Jasmine.

"This dress is classier and fits her style as well. It ties in with the bridesmaids gowns," observed Lisa.

The saleslady offered her remarks. "Make sure her hair is worn up like this. She will be stunning in this gown. Do you wish to see the headpiece?"

Mary gave the saleslady the headpiece Monaco had selected earlier. The bridal party was silent. Everyone looked at a beaming Mary.

"You are stunning in that gown. Slight alterations right here by the bust line but otherwise, we have a winner," exclaimed Mary.

The bridesmaids clapped with approval, and turned their attentions to the colorful racks of party dresses. Mary sat in the back dressing room with Monaco, and approved the purchase of a second dress. Mary understood it was typical these days for the wedding couple to be hosted by their close friends after the traditional reception. She smiled to herself as Monaco tried on the gown for her. It was sleek; it was sexy, and it was Monaco. She doubted if the wedding couple would be present for the after-party once the groom saw her in this gown.

Chapter 11

The Sleeper was in the Trustees Office manipulating the account ledgers, and had gotten everything set up the way he wanted when he became aware of someone else in the room with him. He turned around. Damn! Minister John Bergson was in the file cabinet by the side wall. Why can't people mind their own business? The minister bent down looking in the lower cabinets, unaware of the coming danger, raised up in time to see a heavy object come crashing down upon his skull. The Sleeper surveyed the still body of the minister who had a reputation for being fastidious and eccentric. The Sleeper thought of positioning the minister as someone who might have had a heart attack, but the severity of the wound threw the idea out the window. Instead, he wrapped the body in an old blanket he found in the stockroom, and transported the corpse to his vehicle. He returned to the Trustees Office and the bookkeeping ledgers, and double-checking his work, replaced the files in their safe space in the cabinet. He looked up the minister's address and drove to his home. Dragging the man's body from his vehicle, the Sleeper pushed it violently against the siding of the house. He watched as the dead man's body slumped across the vegetation, and laid in an unflattering heap on the boxwood shrubbery lining beside t h e h o m e . With distaste souring his senses, the Sleeper shoved the prone body onto the flower bed.

It was late and the exhausted young woman had been on her feet all day as a cashier for a local grocer. Because they needed the extra money, Ann had asked to work overtime. She would be glad when her husband Mike's internship was over, and she could return to regular hours. Usually, he arrived home ahead of her and walked their dog. But tonight, it was her turn. The woman and the dog were returning home, and as they rounded the corner, the dog pulled the leash hard. Ann stumbled on the broken edge of sidewalk that jutted from the ground. Releasing the leash to break her fall, the dog sensing the situation, ran into the overgrown grass. Oh, for Pete's Sake! She was about to yell for the dog when she noticed the strange lump he was sniffing. The dog backed up with a funny cry. She walked over, picked up the dog's leash and tried to make out what the odd shape was in the dark. Ann crept closer peering as hard as she could in the dense shrubbery. She made out the figure of a man lying in a heap in the middle of the flower bed. His vacant eyes were wide open as was his mouth with one side of his face covered in something dark. Her scream, when it broke free from her throat, was long and high-pitched.

Grant, with Osborne in the passenger seat, pulled up behind a thick convoy of black and white police cars. They surveyed the scene. The wide, tree-lined block jammed with ambulances, fire trucks, and unmarked vehicles. The medical examiner's large white van parked prominently in the middle of the street helped to shield the neighbors view of the body. The community slowly came outside as word spread there was police presence in the middle of their quiet suburban neighborhood. The police questioned residents who had gathered on their front lawns.

A black Camaro cruised to a stop alongside a police car. A tall, broad-shouldered man with dark, deep-set eyes, a straight nose, and a thin mustache set in a chocolate brown face surveyed the scene as he stepped out of his vehicle. He walked over to the area where the dead body laid. Immediately, uniformed police officers gathered around him. He stood nodding his head in response to what they said to him.

Osborne and Grant walked to their police cruiser, their attention riveted on the newcomer. His name was Lieutenant Jim Hawkins and he worked the Major Crimes Task Force Division in Chicago. His appearance in Hot Springs guaranteed this was no, run-of-the-mill criminal case. The detective had been in their town several years earlier to solve a string of armed robberies.

Hawkins spotted the detectives across the street, and headed toward them. "Gentlemen, how are you?" he asked, by way of greeting.

"About the same as last time we saw you," grunted Osborne.

Hawkins smiled. "What do we have so far?"

"John Bergson, seventy-nine years old and a widower. A neighbor, Ann Jaworski, walking her dog found him in those bushes over there. Medical examiner says it's been four to six hours since his death," said Grant.

"Cause of death or did he die of old age among the bushes?"

"No, ageism did not shorten his life. Bashed in the head with a blunt object."

Hawkins looked at the house. The forensics team in white hazmat suits were swarming in and around the home and premises.

"Is that the victim's home?"

"Yes, but we don't think he was killed in there," said Osborne, dryly.

"The front and back doors are locked and all the windows. It wasn't robbery because his wallet was on him, and his house and car keys were in his pocket."

"He was killed somewhere else, and brought home?"

"Yeah, you saw the body. There's no blood splatter on the bushes, grass, side of house..."

"Wasn't there another older person found recently in this area?" asked Hawkins.

Osborne, leaning on a patrol car, wearily watching vehicles entering and exiting the street, closed his eyes to the scene. He waved his arm down the street.

"You're thinking about that widow whose body was found behind the church a few blocks from here."

"What was the cause of death for the widow?" asked Hawkins.

"She was smothered."

"We're still piecing together how she got to the property," said Grant. "All indications suggest she walked the five miles pulling a child's wagon loaded with dirt and flowers she dug up along her journey."

Hawkins stared at Grant who returned the stare. Hawkins looked around Grant to the woman talking to the police officer. She was now holding her dog close to her chest.

"What was the name of the church?" asked Hawkins.

"Hot Springs Cathedral Church."

"Send me the witness interview statement in the morning." Hawkins looked tired. "Contact that church and see if they know this man, or that woman who died on their property."

"Okay," said Grant, his fingers moving over his keyboard.

"Where are you staying?" asked Osborne. "You know I'd put you up. We have a guest room we hardly use."

"Thanks, Matt. But I love my privacy," said Hawkins, smiling. "Besides, Maggie's going to have dinner guests every other night with a single woman showing up who just happens to drop by."

The detectives laughed. Osborne said, "I don't know what to tell you. It's why I can't get Joe over except for our annual summer barbecues."

Grant smirked as he headed for the police cruiser. Osborne, still grinning at the image of his wife and her antics, got behind the wheel.

Smiling, Hawkins drove away from the scene musing of the chaos that murder brought to a community.

The Hot Springs Police Administration Building was housed in a sprawling structure across the street from City Hall. On the ninth floor, in a spacious office with a scenic view of the city, Hawkins was typing his monthly notes. A light knock on the door claimed his attention.

"Come in," he shouted.

Two plainclothes detectives walked in and closed the door. He beckoned them to the two chairs positioned in front of his desk, and finished typing. A minute later, he walked over to the two men, and shook their hands.

"We have a new assignment, of sorts. Instead of being passive observers, you will now enter the community. Here is what you need to hone in on."

He handed both men folders. Walking to a side wall, he darkened the room, and pulled up photo images on the white board.

A week later a police officer led Paul and Nick led to an interview room at the Oakland Heights Police Station for questioning. Detectives Osborne and Grant walked into the room. Both pastors remained seated. Osborne surveyed them. The senior pastor, with the piercing, almond-shaped eyes, stared directly at him in an openly curious way. He was broad-shouldered, and physically fit. The other pastor had deep blue eyes and an aura of calm about himself. He too, eyed the detectives, with genuine curiosity.

Osborne cleared his throat. "My name is Sgt. Osborne, and this is my partner, Detective Grant. We're investigating the possible homicide of John Bergson, a minister at your church."

"Good to meet you gentlemen. I'm Dr. Paul Mouton, senior pastor of Hot Springs Cathedral Church, and this is Mr. Nick Rodgers, legal counsel for the church."

"Dr. Mouton, how long have you been at Hot Springs Cathedral Church?"

"This will be my fifth year."

"Where were you previously to arriving in Hot Springs?"

"New York City. I was an associate pastor under Rev. Van Abernathy."

"What brought you to Hot Springs?"

"I enrolled in Hot Springs University for my doctorate. When I joined the church, Pastor Clayton installed me to the clergy board."

"You've identified the deceased as John Bergson?"

"Yes."

"Dr. Mouton, did you know John Bergson personally?"

"I knew him as one of the ministers in the church, but we didn't have a personal relationship away from the church, if that's what you mean.."

"As the senior pastor you supervise the clergy on staff. Am I correct?"

"I oversee the entire church administration, Detective."

"How long was he a member of Hot Springs Cathedral Church?"

Paul consulted his tablet. "Minister Bergson and his family moved to the area over sixty years ago. His wife died ten years ago."

"Is there anything else you can tell us about the deceased?"

"Such as?" asked Paul.

"What were his church assignments?"

"Minister Bergson was a chaplain in a nursing home."

Osborne leaned forward. "Okay, one last question, where were you when the minister was killed?"

"Dr. Mouton would have no idea when the minister was killed, Detective," said Nick.

Grant cast a furtive glance at Nick. "We believe he was killed a few days to a week when he was found."

Osborne turned to Paul. "The minister was a member of your clergy board, but you didn't miss his presence in the church?"

"He often gave communion and baptisms at the nursing home where he was a chaplain. Most of our clergy staff have Sunday assignments on any given Sunday."

"Aren't you marrying soon, Dr. Mouton?"

"Yes, I am," replied Paul, a smile softening the intensity of his gaze.

"The church must be excited about your upcoming marriage."

"Is there a question?" asked Nick, quietly observing the detective.

"No one missed the minister's presence at the church?"

"How do you mean, Detective?"

The detectives stared at Paul. "Dr. Mouton, wouldn't he be, oh I don't know, kind of expected to be seen in church services?"

Paul smiled. "The role of chaplain is similar to being a church pastor or priest. He was on staff at the nursing home."

"Didn't you announce your engagement in church recently?"

"Yes."

"Was the deceased on hand to offer congratulations?"

"I honestly don't recall. It was a Sunday service, and the announcement came at the end."

"Had you prepped your staff that you would be announcing your engagement to the church?"

"Yes, Detective."

"Do you recall if the victim was at the prepped meeting?"

Nick interrupted. "Dr. Mouton has confirmed the deceased spent his time as a nursing home chaplain."

"Wouldn't it be required for church leadership to attend meetings called by their senior pastor?"

"Our meetings are virtual for those who cannot attend."

"Do you have any idea why anyone would want to harm the deceased?"

"No," replied Paul. "Why is his death being treated as a homicide?"

"If you don't mind, we'll ask the questions. The deceased death is being treated as a homicide, because of the way he died," Osborne stated.

Grant spoke next. "Repeat question, do you know why anyone would want to harm the deceased?"

Paul sighed. "No. The minister was a generous man with his time, money, and influence, and well-respected by the community. The church is managing the grief and dismal circumstances of the minister's death."

Nick spoke next. "If there are no more questions for Pastor Mouton, we'll be leaving now."

"Excuse me, Counsel, but when we've finished with our questions, you and your client can leave," said Osborne, brusquely.

"Let's move backwards, say about two months prior," said Grant. He was looking through a folder. "Does the name Agnes Wright sound familiar, Pastor?"

"No."

"Agnes Wright is the name of the victim found in the back parking lot of the church you pastor."

"Is there a question for the Pastor?"

"How was she connected with your church, Pastor Mouton?"

"I don't know, Detective," said Paul, looking Osborne straight in the eye. "The name is not familiar to me."

Grant pulled out several sheets of paper. "She was a member of Hot Springs Cathedral Church for over thirty years before succumbing to Alzheimer's disease."

"We'll ask you again, Pastor," said Osborne. "Did you know the victim, Agnes Wright?"

Nick intervened. "I believe that's enough for today. Dr. Mouton has already addressed your question. If what you're stating is true, any information on her would be in our church records."

Nick and Paul stood up. Osborne and Grant stood and shook hands with both men. The detectives watched the pastors walk down the hall to the staircase. They walked next door. Hawkins turned from the two-way window.

"Well, Detectives?"

"I didn't get any vibe from either one. You, Joe?"

Grant shook his head. "No."

"They are huge dudes. I saw that when they stood up," said Osborne, subconsciously pulling in his stomach.

Hawkins murmured more to himself. "Just mild-mannered pastors."

Grant snorted. "Well, I don't know about the mild-mannered part."

Hawkins looked sharply at him. "Meaning what, Detective?"

"The pastor with the blue eyes is a practicing tax attorney," said Grant.

"And the deceased was a retired tax attorney," added Osborne.

"Well, the church is a business," said Hawkins. "They collect tithes and offerings and pay bills gentlemen. It makes sense they would have accountants on staff as trustees."

Grant said, "just throwing you food for bait, Hawkins."

Hawkins smiled. "Thanks, Joe. What was the victim's occupation who was found on church premises? The one from the nursing home?"

Grant looked through his notes. "Accountant."

"From what I heard," said Hawkins, "this last victim was a minister and chaplain and had assignments that took him outside the church. The female victim had been in the nursing home for several years."

"You think someone targeted these older people?" asked Osborne.

Hawkins nodded. "Have there been similar crimes in other townships?"

"We'll need to check," said Grant, writing in his notes.

"You do that," said Hawkins, walking away.

Chapter 12

In the shadows of Hot Springs Cathedral Church, the Sleeper moved insidiously along the walkway placing each foot carefully on the pavement as to not disturb the flower beds. He unhooked the central alarm system, and moved stealthily back to the front of the building, and round to the side. He carefully lifted the loosened window and climbed into the room. Making his way down the hall to the Trustees Office, he unlocked the door and entered. He booted up the computer system, and located the ledger and checkbook in the safe. He easily forged Sister Ginyard 's signature as she wrote in a large, florid script with a slight curve to it. He worked diligently, and fast. Leaving the Trustees Office, the Sleeper took the concealed stairs to the church basement. Entering the maintenance room, he dragged the body of Robert Lewis to the side door, retrieving a piece of cinder block, and jammed the door open with it. Dragging the body, he transplanted him among the dank flower beds, making sure it was visible if anyone was walking close to the vegetation, but not seen from the street. Returning inside the building he removed the cinder block, and closed the door. He reset the alarm. The Sleeper changed clothing to light-colored ones and placed the black clothes in a brown shopping bag. He walked the three blocks to his vehicle and drove home.

Seated in Paul's office, Jasmine was in tears. Paul had called Monaco. He told her where to drive and park as the police were scattered about on the property. He saw her car when she arrived and hurried to the door to open it. He almost smiled. She had forgotten to change, but he did not care. She wore a bright yellow and white floral wrap mini dress with tied spaghetti straps on the shoulders, and a ruffled hemline. The heeled sandals added more curves to the curvy silhouette. She glanced up at him with concern.

"Where is she?"

"In my office. You want me to wait out here?"

"For now? Yes."

She disappeared into his office. Paul walked to the front of the church. He looked at all the assorted colors of vehicles in the parking lot. He walked down and around the hall, and was confronted by Steven and Nick.

"Why are you out here?" asked Nick.

"I sent for Monaco to be with Jasmine. I couldn't get Jasmine to stop crying."

"Where's Ernest?" asked Nick to Steven.

Steven, leaning against the wall, was looking at the commotion on the church lawn. "He's out of town. We'll take care of her."

Nick said to Paul. "I saw the detectives outside. I'll handle them. Get ready to go over to the precinct. The sooner we get rid of them, the better."

"I'll take care of the information to the media," said Steven.

Paul said, "Jasmine found him. They'll want to question her, too."

"I got this." Nick left them.

Monaco came into the hall followed by a visibly shaken Jasmine.

"I'm bringing her home with me since Ernest is out of town. Can her car stay on the lot?"

Steven said, "I'll take care of her car. Come here, Jasmine."

Jasmine walked to Steven and collapsed in his arms in tears. Paul watched as Steven whispered to her. Jasmine nodded her head a few times and stopped crying. She smiled at Paul.

Paul found his voice. "Jasmine take the day off. If you're not feeling better tomorrow, don't come in. Okay?"

"Thank you, Pastor." She turned and left with Monaco. Paul noticed she already had her purse on her arm.

He looked at Steven. "What did you say to her?"

"Huh? Oh, nothing much. Listen, I'm going to write that item to send to the media. I'll send you a draft, approve it, and send it back to me."

"Where are you going now?"

"I have a couple of classes this afternoon. I'll call you tonight."

Nick had returned and was standing behind them. "We must meet them at the station in an hour. Did you talk to Jasmine?"

"Yes. She found him," said Paul. "Steven is writing a piece for the news media and..."

He stopped speaking when Nick handed him a tablet.

"Why'd he send it to you first?" asked Paul. He thought about the question and shook his head. "Never mind, Nick."

He read it quickly, approved, and returned to Steven. He had to keep it together. He was about to marry the love of his life. Whoever was killing these people would be dealt with. But for now, he had to focus on this one beautiful major moment in his life. He looked at Nick whose dark blue eyes were solemnly surveying him.

Hawkins nearly jumped out the police cruiser before it stopped rolling. He raced toward the church stooping underneath the yellow and black caution tape. Osborne and Grant were examining the body and straightened up.

"Good morning," said Osborne. "As you can see we have another old person found among the bushes. He was placed along there," he said, pointing along the landscape edge.

"What's his name?" asked Hawkins.

"His name's Robert Lewis, and he's eight-six years old."

"Who found him?"

"Young lady by the name of Jasmine Carter. She's the pastor's private secretary."

"She identified him?"

"Yes. She said he's a church deacon."

"Where is she?"

"She's in the building," said Osborne.

"Who's in the building now?" asked Hawkins.

"Dr. Mouton arrived a few minutes ago followed by two other men. Mouton's fiancée arrived, and the secretary left with her."

Hawkins listened without interrupting. He turned his back to them a moment, and they heard him sigh, before turning around again.

"Who's in the building now? Remember, I don't like repeating myself."

Osborne said, "I believe the three men are in there. No one else."

Grant, cleared his throat. "Two men are in there. One left."

"Who's the man in with Mouton now, and who left?"

"The pastor with the blue eyes is in there."

"The lawyer," said Osborne. "That figures."

"Who's the man who left?" Hawkins fairly shouted over Osborne's comment.

"I don't know. I've never seen him before," said Grant.

"Did you ask the secretary where she was going since you allowed her to leave the scene of a crime?"

Both detectives remained silent. They could see and hear Hawkins anger. He glared at them.

"Detectives, let me refresh your memories about police investigations. No one enters or leaves a crime scene before you question them. I know this is a church, and they're pastors, but don't become superstitious on me. Alright, I'm going to view the body again. Preferably, alone. Locate the secretary. Find who the anonymous man was. Question everyone at your station house. I'll observe."

Grant was visibly upset which was unlike him. Hawkins gave Grant his full attention.

"This job getting to you, Joe?"

"Lieutenant, this man wasn't killed here, and I doubt if he died here. His medic alert bracelet gives a home address in Exeter Heights."

"Yes, I noticed the head gash, too," murmured Hawkins.

"He was killed somewhere else and brought here. Why?" asked Osborne, looking up at the church structure.

"If he wasn't killed here, do you have his address in Exeter Heights?"

"Uh...no," said Osborne. "She was leaving as we arrived. We didn't know... the pastor told us her name and that she was the one who found the body. I assumed he told her to go home."

"Find out if the deceased was a member in this church. Send me see the secretary's statement," said Hawkins.

"Here comes the medical examiner now."

Hawkins walked around them keeping his back to the advancing medical examiner. The detectives stepped in front of the doctor. She was in a white hazmat suit with her goggles around her neck. The hood was fitted to her head with her face out.

She smiled. "Good morning. Can I help you, Detectives?"

"I'm Sgt. Osborne and this is my partner, Detective Grant. We mostly work homicide cases. We wanted to introduce ourselves as you're new."

"Thank you. I'm Dr. Newbold. Glad to meet you," she said. "I'll be able to give you a positive identification on the victim soon."

Grant held up his hand. "The victim is an elderly man found by the church secretary this morning. If you could give us an approximate time of his death, we can wait on the autopsy report."

"Not a problem, Detectives."

They moved to allow her to pass, and followed her. Osborne saw Hawkins car as it sped past them.

Paul and Nick seated in the interview room of the Oakland Heights Police Station awaited the detectives who had summoned them. Detectives Osborne and Grant entered the room. Osborne stood in the corner, across from his partner's chair, watching the pastors. Grant sat across the table and opened his notebook. The pastors quietly assessed both detectives. Osborne tried not to squirm, and decided to sit down a seat away from his partner at an angle to watch the men.

He noticed their clothing this time. Expensive, well-styled suits. Silk, tailored shirts with French cuffs. Not much jewelry but those wide black wristwatches. The blue-eyed pastor wore what looked like a light blue beaded bracelet, but it was under his jacket sleeve. They both looked physically fit.

"Good afternoon, gentlemen," Grant began. "We won't take up too much of your time. This is a murder investigation and the body was found on the church property by one of your staff."

Grant looked up from his tablet. Both men were giving him their direct attention. He felt uneasy for reasons he could not fathom. He deepened his voice to ask the first question.

"Your secretary found the victim's body this morning. Is that right, Pastor?"

"What time did you arrive at the church?"

"I was there at eight."

"You didn't see the deceased lying in the bushes?"

"My parking spot is on the opposite side of my secretary's."

"Who was the man whose body she found?"

69

"Robert Lewis."

"What is or was Mr. Lewis' role at Hot Springs Cathedral Church?"

"He was a deacon and a trustee."

"Active status?"

"In what, Detective?"

"In the church, Pastor? Was he active as a deacon and a trustee?"

"He no longer worked in the trustee office. His deacon status was emeritus."

"Are you aware that the victim's body was on the premises for fifteen hours, Pastor?"

"No."

"Was the deacon in Sunday service?"

"I wouldn't know."

"What can you tell me about the deceased."

"Deacon Lewis was loved by the church and community. He was retired and held double duty in the church as an ordained deacon and had volunteered in the trustee office. He worked tirelessly as a civil servant, was a war veteran who saw combat in Germany before being honorably discharged. He outlived his devoted wife, Camille, and their two sons, Robert, and Michael. He had no other living relatives."

"You stated Mr. Lewis was retired. Do you know his profession before retirement?"

"I believe he was a federal employee."

"Would you know why Mr. Lewis was on church premises over a weekend?"

"No."

"Don't you find it strange, Pastor, that these trustees keep turning up dead on the church property?"

"Misleading question calls for assumption on the part of Pastor Mouton," said Nick.

"Who else was in the building with you earlier today?"

"Pastor Barnes and my fiancée."

"Is Pastor Barnes and your fiancée in the station house?"

"No."

Nick said, "Pastor Barnes arrived when I did. Neither of us knew of the events that transpired. We were picking up assignment notes, messages, and the like."

"Where is this Pastor Barnes now?"

"He's out of town for several days. Do you want him to come in when he returns?"

"That won't be necessary," said Osborne.

"Why was your fiancée there? Was she picking up notes and messages as well, Pastor?" asked Grant. His voice held an edge of sarcasm.

Paul smiled. "I made the call for my secretary. She was near hysteria, and I couldn't get her to stop crying."

There was silence. Paul closed his tablet.

"Did your fiancée know the victim?"

"No."

Nick spoke. "Are you charging Pastor Mouton with a crime, Detective? If not, we are leaving."

Nick waited a minute. He and Paul walked out the room, down the hall and out of the building.

Hawkins stood in the hall at windows adjacent to the parking lot. He watched the pastors leave the parking area. He was admiring the blue-eyed pastor's bright blue and yellow striped sports car. Grant walked to the window.

"What make of car is that?" asked Hawkins.

"That's a Dodge Viper," said Grant. "They've been known to clock at well over two hundred miles per hour."

Osborne watched the sports car head toward the highway. He gave a low whistle. "Whose driving that beauty?"

"Pastor Rodgers," said Hawkins, as he walked back down the hall, "the lawyer."

An hour later Nick accompanied Jasmine to the Oakland Heights Police Station for her interview with the detectives. Jasmine wore a dark green dress with a white collar making her large green eyes pop. The thick red, curly hair and light dusting of freckles across her nose, gave her an angelic look. Grant took one look at her, and immediately became tongue-tied.

"Good afternoon. I'm Detective Grant. May I have your name?"

"Jasmine Carter."

"You work for the ... I mean, your boss is Pastor Mouton. Correct?"

"I work for Hot Springs Cathedral Church. My immediate supervisor is the pastor. I'm the church secretary."

"How long have you been in that role?"

"Four years full-time and about five years part-time."

"Are you married?"

Nick, in a clear voice, said, "her marital status is not relevant."

A momentary pause. "What are your work hours?"

"I work Mondays through Fridays from nine in the morning to five o'clock in the evening."

"What about the weekends?"

"What about them?"

"Do you work on the weekends?"

"I told you my work hours, Detective."

"I know but..."

Nick cleared his throat. "My client has answered your questions regarding her work hours."

"Okay. Tell me what happened yesterday morning."

"I drove to work and arrived at eight-thirty in the morning. I parked in my slot in the back and was walking to the door when I saw a body on the ground."

"How do you know the exact time you arrived?"

"I always look at the clock on my dashboard because sometimes I get there a few minutes later. It's a little game I play with myself."

"Okay. You mentioned you have a 'slot in the back.' What does that mean?"

"My parking spot."

"Is it a designated spot? Your name or initials?"

Jasmine sighed. "It's says 'church secretary.'"

"How many parking slots are there?"

"I don't know."

Nick interrupted again. "Detective, are you charging Ms. Carter with a crime?"

"Did you recognize the deceased immediately?"

"Yes."

"Is he related to you?"

"No. I grew up in this town and in this church. Deacon Lewis was in school with my grandparents."

Tears fell from Jasmine's eyes. She put her face in her hands. Nick stared at Grant, stood, and taking Jasmine by the hand, they left the station.

Hawkins was standing at the end of the hall looking through the windows at the parking lot below. He turned to the detectives.

"Did you check for similar crimes in other townships?"

"We found nothing other than a fire in an old church in Wood Haven Township," replied Osborne.

"How long ago?"

"About two months before the victim from the nursing home."

"How old was that church?"

"Historic to the town. The entire church wasn't destroyed," said Grant, reading from his notes. "There was only one area affected by the fire."

"What area was that?"

"According to the arson report, the fire began in the trustee office, and died there."

"Any computers or software saved?"

Grant smirked. "Uh, no. The church is on the town's social register. At the time of closure they were still using paper and pen."

"How long has the church been closed?"

"About fifteen years now."

"What does the fire report read?"

Osborne looked surprised as Grant pulled up his notes. "Fire inspector labeled fire as suspicious and deemed it arson. A full investigation is underway as only the one room burned down. Fire inspector states there is evidence to suggest fire was contained to that room."

"Meaning someone knew what they were doing," said Osborne.

"How far is Wood Haven from Hot Springs?"

"About sixty miles or up highway 102. That's a straight shot."

"Okay, thanks, guys," said Hawkins. The detectives parted.

Chapter 13

A week before the wedding Monaco hosted a bridal luncheon for her attendants at her house. She chose a white sequin wrap mini dress with long sleeves. The luncheon was nice, and Monaco was glad she had taken such pain to make it memorable.

Raquel gushed over the robe she received in her bridal bag. "These are gorgeous, Monaco."

Jasmine tried on her robe. "Where are we meeting before the wedding?"

"Right here," said Monaco. "I have four bedrooms in this house. I think we will be fine."

Lisa was checking off her list. "Ladies, pack your gowns and your overnight duffel bags you received, and be ready to come here from the rehearsal dinner."

The doorbell rang. Ed had come to retrieve his wife. Claudia and Raquel had taken her out of her wheelchair on her instructions, and placed her on the sofa as she wanted to sit near Monaco.

Jayne and Mary hugged. "You get yourself home now, honey. I'll see you at the wedding," said Jayne.

Mary said, "I'm fine. Everybody makes such a fuss. Ed has come too early."

Ed smiled. "Behave yourself, Mrs. Joseph."

The ladies laughed and all of them whirled around the old, crippled deacon as he carried his wife in his arms out to his car. Raquel and Jasmine folded up her wheelchair, Claudia wrapped cake and appetizers for Ed in a goody bag, Lisa tucked Mary's blanket about her legs as she nodded off. Monaco, on the porch observing the scene before her, was touched by the effortless way in which the old deacon took such tender care with his wife. She prayed that she and Paul were like this couple in their older years.

It was two days before the wedding. Monaco was restless. She threw on a loose tank and light blue denim shorts. She looked at her wedding dress hanging upside down on her closet door. The doorbell rang. She ran downstairs. It was Ed carrying a white gift bag which he handed to Monaco.

"Hi Ed, come in," said Monaco.

"Hi, darling. I don't want to bother you. Mary asked me to bring you this. It's your something blue."

"Thank you, Ed. Would you like some coffee?"

"Oh, no, thank you, sweetheart. I've got to return home to Mary. I left her sleeping on the couch. She could wake up. Sometimes she tries to walk about without her walker or cane, and every time she does, she ends up falling and hurting herself."

"Ed, I'm sorry to hear that," said Monaco.

"Don't you worry your beautiful head about us. It's such an honor to be a part of your life. I wish you nothing but happiness from here on."

They hugged, and Ed kissed her forehead before leaving. She watched him limp to his tan Crown Victoria car. He was leaning hard. He waved and slowly drove down the street. Monaco looked inside the bag. It was her *something blue,* a satin laced garter belt.

An hour later the doorbell rang again. Steven, Ernest, David, and Nick walked in. She looked at them and grinned.

"Is this a new wedding tradition I don't know about?"

Steven chuckled. "Paul sent us over here to get whatever stuff you want in his place."

Monaco frowned. "Like what?"

Ernest looked around. "Furniture, pots and pans, books. Whatever it is you want from here to there."

"Why didn't he come?"

Nick smiled. "I don't think you'd want to chance him hurting himself lifting something would you?"

She sighed. "No, I guess not."

David looked around. "Just tell us what you want us to bring. We each have our cars."

"How big is his place? I've never been there," she said.

The men digested that bit of information in silence. She looked at them. She noticed Ernest had turned a deep shade of red and avoided looking at her, Steven moved to the kitchen, and was in the pantry, and David was busy with his phone.

"What's good to eat?" Steven asked. He opened the refrigerator and found some cake.

Nick put both hands in his pants pocket and cleared his throat. "Don't worry about furniture. He has a lot of that. What about clothes? Pack some bags and we'll take those over."

"Ok, guys help yourself to whatever is in the kitchen. Lisa and I are shopping tomorrow for our sleepover the night before the wedding."

"We should come back," said Steven, placing some leftover foods in the microwave.

The men stayed downstairs in the kitchen talking low while she went upstairs to pack. She looked about not sure what to pack. She decided to call Paul.

"Hey lady, are you okay?"

"Yes Paul. The guys are here. They wanted to bring stuff over. I told them I have never been to your place. I didn't know what to have them bring over. Nick suggested clothing."

There was silence on the other end.

"Paul?"

"I'm here. Listen, some of your clothes for now. We'll figure out the rest later."

"Okay. Are you alright?"

"I'm fine."

She hung up and packed two suitcases of clothes, one suitcase of shoes, and a suitcase with underwear and pajamas. She looked at her Hope Chest and put her favorite quilts, blankets and the new towels and wash cloths she had bought. She packed a duffel bag of her favorite jewelry and gave Steven her laptop and charger.

"Okay guys. I have four suitcases and my Hope Chest."

Ernest giggled. "Four?"

The men packed the items in David's car. David removed his white straw Panama hat before hugging her. Ernest kissed her cheek staring at her with glimmering eyes until Steven pushed him across the door sill.

"Good night, baby girl. We love you," said Steven, kissing her forehead.

"I love you guys too," she said.

Nick kissed her cheek. "Stay sweet, gorgeous."

Monaco was restless and sleep was eluding her. Tomorrow evening was their wedding rehearsal with the dinner to follow. Her chest was heavy as if she were having an anxiety attack. Her phone rang. It was Paul suggesting they have dinner. She jumped at a chance to get out of the house not paying attention to the time. Because she had been in white the last several days she decided on a form fitting, sleeveless dark blue dress with a low-cut front neckline, and a mid-thigh slit. She looked in the mirror. Oh no, the dress was too body skimming. She opted for a strapless bra and thong panty set. Looking in the mirror again she smiled. Much better. She tied multicolored sandals on and was ready when Paul knocked on the door. Their drive to the restaurant was in silence. Once seated they kept staring at each other.

"The guys delivered your stuff."

"I never saw your place."

"You should see it."

Without saying a word, they left the restaurant without eating. On the drive to his place, he played the Doves, *'I'm all yours,'* and they listened to it in silence. Paul opened the front door and they entered. Monaco conscious of Paul behind her walked through the living areas as if she had never seen a sofa or a wall-mounted television. She ambled into the open kitchen, and over to the sink. It was pitch black outside, but she peered out the window into the darkness. She stood there a few minutes. She left the kitchen, and sat on a high stool to unlace her sandals. Paul took off his jacket. Out of the corner of her eye she saw him, and her heart pounded in her ears. She knew she had to get a grip on her nerves.

She walked up the stairs slowly, each step labor-intensive. She was acutely aware of him behind her. The fact that he was so silent was making her extremely nervous. At the top step there was one door open, and she walked toward it. Her breathing became shallow. There was a slight glow like candles flickering softly in the room. She crept a little nearer seeing rose petals on the bed trailing to the floor.

Paul moved closer to her, unzipped her dress, and it slid in a puddle at her feet. He turned her to face him and kissed her, wrapping his arms around her. Something inside her mind exploded. She draped her arms around his neck and became engulfed in his strength and his tenderness, and all reasoning flew out the window.

The next morning Paul helped Monaco unpack, sort, and hang her wardrobe in his closets. They laughed about the need for a bigger house for closet space. Her shoe collection fascinated him. The dresses that shrunk or folded into nothingness amazed him. For her part, she mused about his extensive wardrobe of suits and dress clothes. He had drawers of black outfits. They spent the morning cleaning the house, and arranging her belongings to complement his. They were finished by early afternoon.

At the church Charles organized and instructed the placement of the wedding party. Ed would give Monaco away. Mary had promised she would be quiet to conserve her strength. Ed set up his tablet on video-audio and was taping the wedding rehearsal in case she nodded out during their time in the church.

Three hours later, Hawkins sat in his vehicle in a spacious parking lot hidden between two other dark vehicles. His gaze stay directed across the street at the upscale restaurant, Le Château. He watched the Valentine-Mouton wedding party as they exited from the rehearsal dinner. He closed the folder of pictures he had been studying for a few days. He knew them all by sight now. He watched the senior pastor and the gorgeous woman beside him. Her parents and sister's deaths was one of the reasons he was in Hot Springs.

Directly behind them was the eminent psychologist in the sunglasses with the voluptuous blonde at his side. Hawkins had not been able to find a single photograph of this man without dark eye shades. Behind them was the attorney with the deep blue eyes and his redhead Latina girlfriend, also an attorney. Something caught his attention behind them. A slight scuffle between two women with the winner gaining an opportunity to walk alongside the pastor with the blue-green eyes. Hawkins smiled at the way she gazed adoringly up at the man's face. Hawkins was sure the pastor was aware of the commotion behind him the way he was smiling.

Following them was the Puerto Rican multi-millionaire who was currently dating the pastor's younger sister. He spotted his detective, Rick Emory, with the pretty redhead who was the light-eyed pastor's younger sister. He would have to speak with Emory. The detective was smitten with the young woman, and it showed in his face and body language.

The old man wheeling out his invalid wife were the godparents to the future bride. The old man walked with a deep limp, but he was careful with the wheelchair holding his wife. Hawkins picked up the folder again and looked at their photos. She was a knockout in her prime, and not too far from being considered a legendary beauty now.

Behind them was the distinguished pastor from New York escorting the pastor's mother. As he watched the valets retrieve their cars, Hawkins mused how this group of clergy were always together.

Chapter 14

Monaco and Paul's wedding day arrived with Hot Springs Cathedral Church's parking lot crowded with vehicles. The older parishioners recalled in times past when pastors married in their home churches. They counted this wedding in Hot Springs Cathedral Church as a sign that this pastor led by divine favor.

Pulling up to the front of the church in a white limousine sat Monaco with her bridesmaids. Jasmine, Claudia, and Raquel were wearing purple satin gowns with sequined spaghetti straps and crossover necklines. Lisa as maid of honor wore a purple cold-shoulder chiffon gown fitted at the waist and tied in a long sash on the shoulder. A deacon opened the car door, another deacon began helping the women onto the sidewalk.

The ladies circled Monaco. Lisa inspected the back of the gown ensuring each hook and eye closure securely fastened and the bowed sash in place. All four ladies gasped with delight. Monaco's dress boasted a rich overlay of beaded lace embroidery in floral motifs with long sheer lace sleeves. The slight cowl neck in front gave way to a low-cut back fashioned with the sash bow and floating effortlessly in a train. She had chosen to wear her hair in an intricate bun at the nape of her neck with her ivory tulle veil secured on top of the bun with a pearl-encrusted headpiece. She stepped into lace covered satin pumps and placed her engagement ring on her right hand. A cascading arrangement of orchids, peonies, and lisianthus made up Monaco's bouquet.

"If I didn't say it before, welcome to the family," said Raquel.

"Thank you, Raquel, that means a lot."

"You look beautiful," said Claudia.

"Thank you, Claudia."

"I'm sincere, cousin. Simply gorgeous."

Monaco teared up. Lisa shouted in a loud voice. "Okay, stop! We can't have the bride's makeup smeared."

The organist began the wedding march. The bridesmaids grabbed their nosegays of orchids and lisianthus and walked down the aisle with the groomsmen. Lisa walked behind the bridal party. In a black tuxedo with a purple tie, Ed greeted Monaco in the hallway, and walked her down the aisle of the church.

Hawkins attended both the ceremony and the reception afterward. What he noticed about the church was its size. It was a typical megachurch size with an amphitheater sanctuary and a pulpit built to accommodate events. The pastor's family filled the groom's side of the congregation, the clergy, deacons, deaconesses, and ministry leaders filled the bride's side. That gesture touched Hawkins. It showed they had adopted the soon-to-be pastor's wife as one of their own. Hawkins watched the newly-married couple throughout the afternoon. He spotted detectives Stewart and Grant among the crowd as he was leaving.

Hours later the wedding party drove to David's home for a private post-reception affair. David lived in a converted six-bedroom Spanish-style mansion. The first floor boasted a grand ballroom which held the reception for Paul and Monaco. It opened to an enclosed rose garden where David cultivated white roses. In the center of the garden was a white gazebo framed with ivy and white roses and a heart-shaped love seat. An hour later, David and Raquel took Monaco, with Paul by her side, on a tour of the air strip where his helicopter sat and promised her a passenger ride. He bypassed the spacious garage that housed his limited-edition jet warplane. Nor did he show her the bedroom he had recently redesigned for his Raquel with whom he had fallen in love.

Directly after the tour, Steven and Claudia drove Paul and Monaco to their hotel where they spent the night.

Four days later, on honeymoon in Jamaica, Monaco and Paul, received the video footage of their wedding day from her godparents. Ed supplied the videography and Mary narrated. Monaco could not stop the flow of tears that fell from her eyes. Paul was happy to comfort his new wife.

Three weeks later, stretching luxuriously, Monaco grimaced at the bright sunlight falling into her eyes. She laid back on the bed pillows and gazed at her engagement ring and wedding band. She could hardly believe it. She was the wife of a pastor. She slipped out of bed and threw on a robe walking about the room. She thought Paul's town home was nice, but she missed the spaciousness of her house. She needed to return to her writing. She texted Paul she would be at her house for the morning. When Paul left the church he drove to Monaco's home. They decided to spend the night in her house.

Wait a minute! The Sleeper slowed down as he drove past the large white Colonial on the corner and saw the lights on downstairs. Why were they in the house this time of night? He looked at the house next door where Lisa lived. The night light on the porch was on but no other lights or signs of life
was evident in the large house. He scanned the other house on the opposite side and noted dimmed lights on the second floor in the back of the house. Oh! The downstairs lights were turned out. He waited watching the front door. A light came on in the bedroom upstairs. Drat! Why were they in this house? She was married now. She should be at his place not here. He tolerated her being in the house when she was single but not now. He clenched his jaw and drove on. She was getting on his nerves!

Monaco acquired the vacant office next to Paul's. One morning Monaco was hanging a mosaic print on the wall when Claudia visited. She leaned in the doorway with crossed arms, and a sarcastic smirk on her face.

"I know you're excited about being called First Lady, but please remember this is a church. What picture is that you're hanging?"

"It's an abstract. I like color, remember?"

"I see," said Claudia. "What did I warn you about regarding your clothes? No matter what the pastor says, these church women will judge you, my dear."

Monaco looked down at the deep pink smock mini dress and smiled. She crossed the room and put up another picture. When she looked around, her cousin had left. The next day, Monaco wore a royal blue and white geometric print knit dress that came to her knees when she attended her first meeting with the women's committee. The ladies' expressed joy when she asked questions and took notes.

A week later, Monaco invited to a deaconess meeting, carefully chose a deep yellow knit dress that stopped below her knees. At the meeting Mary sat beside her to explain any protocol with which she was not familiar. Monaco received a budget for an upcoming holiday program to approve. After going over each line item, and with Mary's approval, Monaco approved the budget. Claudia slipped in uninvited and sat in the back row.

"Sister Monaco, why don't you play the piano for the Women's Choir this Sunday as a lead in for the holiday program?"

Deaconess Mary smiled. "Thank you, Sister Claudia, for the suggestion. Please refrain from making remarks here. You are not a deaconess."

One of the older deaconesses made a motion on Claudia's suggestion. Monaco smiled warmly and stood up.

"Thank you for the vote of confidence, but I would prefer one of the other deaconesses to play. I am still transitioning to wife status and all that entails. I would not be able to make the rehearsals and that wouldn't be fair to you all. There will be a time and space for me but not now."

Deaconess Mary spoke up. "Sister Claudia was out of turn. Deaconess Slater will play for the program as she always does. Deaconess Slater's backup is Deaconess Thomas. Let's not forget First Lady Mouton is a newlywed and her schedule is new. It needs the pastor's approval."

The rest of the deaconesses nodded their heads in agreement, and the meeting continued smoothly. Claudia's eyes were like slits in her face as she looked at Monaco.

Monaco and Lisa were speaking to several women in the hallway when Claudia approached. She raised her voice to a roar.

"Sister Monaco! You can't approve the budget for the deaconess project."

"Sister Claudia, with all respect, yes I can."

"That approval has to come through me first," said Claudia with a scowl. "Matter of fact do not interfere in any church business. You don't know this church to think that you can make decisions."

Monaco smiled. "I know the financial procedures, and the buck does not stop with you."

"I've been here longer and know more than you about church business. Oh, and that dress needs to be longer and looser. Please don't let me have to talk to you about these matters again." She turned on her heel and walked away.

Monaco shook her head and walked on with Lisa to her church office. But, standing with other senior deaconesses at the end of the hall, Mary became highly upset.

She spoke to Paul about the scorn and public disrespect. After speaking to Monaco, Paul held a private meeting with Claudia.

"Have a seat, Sister Claudia. I want to be perfectly clear with what I am about to say to you."

"Excuse me, Pastor, but you didn't pray," interrupted Claudia.

"Let's get something straight here, Sister Claudia. I do not need your approval to oversee church administration. That is Pastor Steven Barnes' role, and he does an excellent job in that area. Further, I don't care how long your family's been in this town or this church, and I don't care about your kinship connections to my wife. What I care about is my wife, and you will not disrespect her, or pave the way for others to do so. She is my wife, and she reports directly to me as to her role and positions. It's not your place as finance director to chastise her about church budgets which you're aware receive approval from the trustees and the pastors. And, since it's on my mind, I happen to like how my wife dresses and trusts her judgment on wardrobe choice. If I hear of your nonsense again, you will sit down from all ministries in this church. Do I make myself clear?"

Without waiting for her assent, Paul walked to his office door, and opened it. He returned to his desk and took an incoming call. Claudia quietly left.

Much later, Paul held a private meeting with Steven in his office. Steven, unbuttoning his black suit jacket, and taking off his dark glasses, gave Paul his attention.

"Steven, I understand Claudia's your lady and that's why we're here. I can't have her disrespecting Monaco in front of the women in the church."

"I wondered when you were going to say something to her."

Paul stared at Steven. "You knew about Claudia's behavior?"

"Who didn't? Claudia is assertive and always has been. Monaco ignores her and for that matter no intervention needed. But with Monaco's new role as your wife, this public disrespect needed to stop."

"Hmm. I'm learning a great deal about all of you."

"Did you think I was going to give you a tough time because I'm seeing her?"

When Paul nodded, Steven laughed. "Oversee your role, Paul. If it were me, I would have gotten with her a long time ago."

"I was trying to be patient, and I didn't want to cross horns with you."

"I surmised that. But in the process, Claudia's sour behavior toward Monaco increased. The one time there was a truce was doing all the wedding excitement."

"That's why I didn't know when something had changed. She was an immense help during the wedding planning phase."

Steven laughed. "I believe she imagined Monaco would be a stay-home wife making appearances on Sunday mornings. It had to be a shock there was a First Lady in the house, and she had to take a back seat."

They both laughed. Paul shook his head. "I value Claudia, don't misunderstand me. She was the lifeguard I needed when I came to this position."

"Oh, I agree. She's well-versed with church politics. But trying to deflect status from Monaco was not wise on her part."

"But man, she's your lady though. Why didn't you talk to her?"

"She's my lady, not my wife."

Paul nodded his head. "I see. All's good with you and me?"

"Indubitably," said Steven. He replaced his dark sunglasses, and got up to leave. They shook hands.

In a minute, his black Porsche soundlessly pulled off the lot. If Paul had not been watching him, he would not have known the vehicle had left the premises.

Chapter 15

Sitting in Paul's office, waiting for him to finish with his pastors meeting, Monaco decided to head to the church fellowship hall for a snack. She smoothed down the ruffled skirt of the blue sprig sundress she wore before venturing out into the hall. She walked into a tall stranger in black. Looking up she gazed into a handsome man's face. As she looked up, she realized he was as tall as Paul.

"Pardon me, Sister," he said in a deep bass voice with the tinge of a Southern accent.

"Oh, I'm sorry. May I ask your name?"

"Ma'am, my name is Jim Hawkins."

"Well, Brother Hawkins, I don't believe I've met you. My name is Sister Mouton, I'm Pastor Mouton's wife."

"How do you do, ma'am, I'm lost. I was looking for an exit."

"It's easy to get lost until you learn the formula. This hall goes around the building except for back here. These are the main church offices. The door you're standing in front of is my husband's office. You came down and around too far."

"Seems like it. Sort of a maze, isn't it?"

Monaco smiled. "Most members are not aware of the circumference of the church unless your staff. Let me walk you out."

"Thank you. I appreciate that."

"Have you joined our church yet, Brother Hawkins?"

"No ma'am, but I might. I don't know yet how long I will be in town."

"I see. Are you visiting our town or is this a job placement?"

"Are you naturally nosy or is that part of being a good church wife?"

Despite herself, Monaco giggled. "I'm sorry, Brother Hawkins. I swear my momma didn't raise me this way."

Hawkins laughed. "You're okay, I was teasing you. I am here on business. It's not a secret. Thank you for directing me safely to the exit doors. Have a good night, First Lady."

"Thank you, Brother Hawkins, same to you."

She watched him stroll to a glossy black car and speed off, turning his lights on as he neared the street. She stood looking through the glass doors at the blackness in the parking lot. A few cars remained in the clergy parking section.

"Hey Monaco, you looking for Paul?" a falsetto voice behind her.

"Hi Ernest, no."

"Are you okay?"

"I walked a man out who was in the back hallway. He was lost."

"Did he have a car parked back here?"

"Yes."

Ernest pale turquoise eyes glinted in the darkness. There was no smile on his face and his red skin tone had deepened in coloring. Steven, David, and Paul walked up.

"What's going on? Why are you out here?" asked David.

"Hold on," said Steven. "Is everyone out the building?"

"I turned the alarm system on. They'd better be," replied David.

Ernest said, "Monaco was telling me someone was in the back hallway where the main offices are, but he parked back here."

"Can you describe what he looked like?" asked Steven.

"I can do better than that. I can tell you, his name. It's Jim Hawkins. He's new in town and hasn't joined the church yet."

David twirled his fedora hat. "How'd you find out his name?"

"I asked him. It might be the wrong one, but that's what he gave me."

Ernest looked at David. "I have a feeling it's the right one. Women are amazing creatures."

Paul laughed. "Shut up, man. What was he doing when you saw him?"

"Nothing. I opened the door to come out, and he was standing there."

Steven was looking out the door. "What kind of car was he driving?"

"It's jet black. Looks like your car, Steven."

They heard footsteps and turned around. Paul was coming down the side hall in a hurry.

Paul said, "I checked the cameras. His car was in between my car and your car Steve. His is a Camaro. I couldn't see the license plate numbers though."

Steven looked at Monaco. "Looked like my car, huh? Remind me never to ask you to describe a vehicle."

The men laughed. Monaco smiled. "Whatever."

"Listen, let's be vigilant about these doors. We have new members and not everyone is honest. I don't believe Brother Hawkins was up to any mischief, but let's err on the side of caution." said Paul.

"Agreed," said Steven. "I have a deacon meeting scheduled for next week. We have younger deacons I want to incorporate onto the church roster. It's time we gave them their Watchman duties."

"Is that it?" asked David. "I have an early day tomorrow."

"Yes, that's it," said Paul. "Have a good night, Dave."

David squeezed Monaco's hand as he passed through the door.

"Okay people. I'm out of town until next week. Don't let anything exciting happen until I return," said Ernest, smiling.

"We'll save all the excitement for you," said Steven. "Which conference are you attending?"

"The one in Santa Monica, you?"

"Boston."

"Okay, catch you when I get back." Ernest waved, exiting the hall.

"What's the name of this conference Steven?" asked Paul.

"*The Abnormal Deviant Among Us*," replied Steven. "Monaco, which way was the man facing when you found him, and whose office did you come out of?"

Paul looked at Monaco who frowned trying to remember. "I came out of Paul's office and ran right into him. He was standing still though."

"Whose office was he standing near to?" persisted Steven.

"The front office door but his back was to the door."

"Okay. I must run. I need to sleep. My plane leaves early tomorrow. Stay safe people. Good night."

Steven looked at his wristband as he entered his vehicle. Paul had sent him a message: *Who is Jim Hawkins?*

"Why was Steven so specific about where Brother Hawkins was standing?" asked Monaco.

Paul smiled. "That's the therapist in him. I'm sure he is analyzing why the man was standing there."

Paul set the pass code on the doors as Steven zipped past them honking once. He placed his arm around his wife's shoulders.

"Come on beautiful, let's go home."

"Paul?"

"Yes?"

"Did I do something wrong?"

"No, why do you ask?"

"Seems the guys were upset."

"It's about safety, not just for you, but us all. We can't have people in the church after hours unsupervised."

"Do you think he was up to wrongdoing?"

"I don't know, but I've learned to err on the side of caution."

"You said that earlier"

"It bears repeating and hearing again. Look, I just found you. I don't want to lose you. I love you, Monaco."

"I love you too, Paul."

Hot Springs Cathedral Church's men's fellowship was growing. Paul welcomed two men to the monthly group. The first was Clay Stewart, an accountant working at a city firm. Stewart was of Jamaican heritage, wore conservative dark suits and had a pleasant but quiet disposition. He was medium-height, slim build, with a trimmed full face beard. Stewart wore his long hair in braided styles.

The tall, tan skinned, Rick Emory, worked for the postal service as a letter carrier. He wore his straight black hair cropped close to his head with long sideburns. His hooded grass green eyes were his most striking facial feature inherited from his Barbadian mother.

After the group ended, David took the men to the conference room to complete their membership cards.

David hit the intercom button. "Sister Jasmine, would you bring me back the files I gave you earlier?."

When Jasmine entered the room with the file, her eyes locked with Emory's, and they both smiled. Emory watched the pretty redhead until she walked to the door. Their eyes locked again as she closed the door.

David paired the men together for the next several weeks. Steven passed Emory and Stewart as they were leaving the conference room. He continued to Paul's office. He pulled up the camera monitors watching the young men in their cars. Emory drove a matte black Audi sports car, and Stewart drove a black, two-door Jeep Wrangler. David walked in with a frown on his face.

"What's the matter, Steve? They've been coming for a few weeks now. Deacon Joseph told me they finished their new members classes. The taller one is Jasmine's friend. Both men joined our group tonight."

"Jasmine's friend may be a detective. I'm thinking the other guy may be one as well."

"You think they're plants?"

"That's a possibility. Let me see the files."

"Which one?"

"Both, especially the one Jasmine is becoming infatuated with," murmured Steven. He scanned the files. "Emory works as a letter carrier for the post office."

"Yes, something wrong with that?" asked David.

"What about his veteran status?"

"His veteran status?"

"I think he served in the military."

"Why wouldn't he put that down?" asked Paul who had walked in, and was seated behind his desk.

"That style Audi drives no less than one hundred fifty miles per hour," mused Steven, studying the stilled photo David had snapped.

Paul, walked over to the screen, and stood with folded arms, looking at the monitor.

"That's an expensive car for a letter carrier. He's new along with the other man Stewart, and Hawkins. Are they all working homicide?"

"That's what I'm wondering." replied Steven. "I'll search military backgrounds on all three, as well as police data banks."

"Let's meet up later this week. I need to prepare for my talk with the Hawkins character who was wandering around here last week."

Steven closed the panel and the pastors departed the office.

When Sunday service concluded Paul asked one of the deacons to locate Jim Hawkins for a private meeting in his office. Paul was hastily writing an outline for a sermon when a deacon knocked on his door.

"Brother Hawkins is here, Pastor."

"Thank you, Deacon Howard. Send him in," he said.

Paul turned to his wife, seated on the sofa, reading a magazine. "Could you wait for me in Jasmine's office? I have a meeting with someone."

"Yes, certainly." She collected her purse as the door opened, and Hawkins entered.

"Hello Sister Mouton. It's good to see you again."

"Hello Brother Hawkins, same here. I saw you in service today. Did you receive the message?"

Hawkins smiled. "Thank you, Sister Mouton. I did enjoy today's message of hope and redemption. I took lots of notes."

"That's the best way to learn, Brother Hawkins. You have a good day!"

"Thank you, Sister Mouton. Same to you."

Hawkins held the door for Monaco to pass through before closing it gently behind her. Something about his mannerisms with Monaco annoyed Paul, but when Hawkins looked at him, he merely beckoned to a chair near his desk. They shook hands.

"Good afternoon, Pastor Mouton."

"Please sit down, Brother Hawkins. Let me be brief. The church is not a playground nor is it a tour museum. On the night that you were wandering about the building fellowship had been over for the better part of five hours. And, you were parked in the back side section that is clearly marked for clergy."

Hawkins stared at Paul whose dark eyes gave him unwavering eye contact. Hawkins reached into the breast pocket of his jacket, producing a silver badge and card.

"My name is Lieutenant James Hawkins. My specialty is major crimes. The simple truth Pastor is that I did become discombobulated in that spacing with the way the halls loop into each other. Your wife graciously lead

91

me to the correct way out. As to the parking situation, I had parked where I was earlier, and none of your ushers, standing at the doors, informed me otherwise. I suppose with all the heavy traffic I wasn't paying attention to any posted signs in the parking lot."

Paul was writing as Hawkins spoke. "Your I.D. has a Chicago logo. Are you working with the police department in Hot Springs, or on vacation?"

"I'm not on vacation, Pastor. I'm investigating a string of suspicious deaths in churches in this area."

"Suspicious deaths?"

"Yes." Hawkins smiled.

"People die, Lieutenant."

"That is a normal assumption, Pastor. As with the victims found on this property, these deaths are suspicious for reasons I can't divulge."

"I see."

"I understand you want to safeguard your congregation, and that is my concern as well. We are on the same team."

There was silence as Paul wrote on a pad, turning it over when he finished. He looked at Hawkins.

"Just so we are clear here, Lieutenant. Do not intrude on the privacy of this congregation that will cause problems, or I will be alerting your superiors. If you need any further information, I would appreciate it if you would give me the courtesy of speaking to me directly."

"I understand, and that won't be a problem. I'd like to keep my anonymous identity. Even regarding your staff."

"Not a problem," said Paul.

"Thank you, Pastor." The men shook hands.

Chapter 16

Lisa was on the highway headed home. Exhausted with a blinding headache, she glanced sideways at her tote bag, which housed her tablet. She was taking a night class at Hot Springs University in taxation laws and had downloaded every document the instructor suggested. She had one more class to attend in her professional development classes. She was near her home when her phone rang, and her car phone picked it up.

"Hello beautiful, home yet?"

"Three blocks away handsome. How was your day?"

"Better now that I'm speaking to you."

"Oh Nick, you are too charming for words."

"I was wondering if you'd consider a serious proposition?"

"Whoa, a serious proposition? You have me intrigued, Counselor."

"I would like to take you to dinner at the remodeled Riviera Restaurant. Does that sound feasible to you?"

"Quite feasible, Counselor."

She drove off the highway ramp to a street stop sign. She looked over her shoulder, and drove down the street.

"Let's pick a weekend that's good for both of us, and I'll make reservations. Wear that black sequin dress you have hanging in the closet. I've never seen you in it."

"Hmm...that sounds like a plan. I don't know if I want to wear that dress. I think I'll make a shopping date with Monaco."

"Whatever you wear you will look gorgeous, baby."

"I think... Oh... Oh!"

"Lisa?" All Nick heard was breathing. "Lisa, what's the matter?"
"Nick! I... I..."
Nick heard a crash, and the line blacked out. Nick signaled Steven and put in a call to the police department as he turned his car around.

Paul pulled up to the site of the crash. Vehicles of every size and description were in the street and partially on the sidewalk. The number of spectators were increasing with time. Paul scanned the crowd and spied the solitary lone figure in black he was looking for. Steven, in dark sunglasses, was standing beneath a scraggly-looking tree surveying the scene. The expertly tailored worsted suit in black wool obscured the well-toned, muscled physique.

"Did you arrive here before the police?" asked Paul.

"Yes."

"Where is the other vehicle?"

"See the skid marks on the ground here?" Steven pointed to faint markings barely seen in the vanishing evening light.

"Yeah, looks like the person intentionally sped up to block her view."

"Agreed."

"Disgruntled client?" Paul offered. "She's a lawyer who specializes in tax fraud cases."

"This is no hit-and-run though. Look at the size of the tire treads."

"Large vehicle..."

"I took enough pics to send you and Ernest."

"Okay," said Paul. He noticed Steven heading toward his black Porsche. "Where are you going now?"

"To see Lisa before going home. I'm cooking for a hazel-eyed beauty who needs consoling after being reprimanded by her pastor a few evenings ago."

Paul laughed. "Any excuse will do."

Steven grinned as he strolled to his car which had caught the admiration of several police officers as they circled the vehicle. They were busy talking about the car and discussing its engine. They barely noticed the car parts strewed about the accident site. The officers slowly became aware of the man in black wearing dark shades who grew larger the closer he came toward them. They wordlessly watched him as he folded inside the car, and silently drove down the street. Paul passed them going in a different direction. Steven played the recording he received from Nick as he drove.

At hospital. She suffered a slight concussion and sprained ribs. Her car totaled. Someone intentionally ran her off the road. Hospital releasing her in a couple of days.

Steven stopped at the nurses' station and asked for Lisa's room. The nurse heard the deep baritone voice, surveyed the chiseled somber face behind the dark eye shades, eyed the powerful built body in the expensive suit, and sensed he was law enforcement. She personally directed him to Lisa's room. She was consciously aware as they walked down the hall how the silent stranger's size dwarfed other men in the hallway.

Lisa was sitting up in bed with her head bandaged, and smiled when she saw Steven. The tears fell as he walked toward her. He held her until she managed to pull herself together. He pulled up a chair by her bed rail.

"Tell me everything you remember," he said. He turned on the audio recorder on his wristband.

"It was a large vehicle like a bus or something. All I saw were these large wheels like on a tractor trailer. It's a one-way street and I saw something parked there. That's when I decided to back out."

"What do you mean something parked?"

"I don't know what kind of vehicle it was. All I know is that it was huge. He turned his high beams on as I got closer blinding me. Steven, I didn't know he was coming at me until I turned around in my seat and saw him. I jumped out the car just in time."

Lisa put her face in her hands and began crying again. Steven looked around. Nick stood in the doorway.

"You got everything you need, Steve?"

"Yes, thanks."

Nick walked to the bed, and Lisa folded herself into his arms. Steven looked back once, saw the couple embrace, and his jaw clenched before closing the door. He passed the nurses' station with such speed all they felt was the wind. He took the fire exit down to the street below.

David saw Nick seated in the visitor's lounge, and walked over to him. The men hugged.

"How is she doing?"

"The doctor says she has a concussion, sprained ribs, but no broken bones. Her car is totaled, Dave."

"Did you get a chance to talk to her?"

"Yes. She told Steve everything. She said the other car was coming at her. She was blinded by the lights. I saw her truck. It was nearly wrapped around the pole..."

Nick stopped talking and walked away from David keeping his back turned. He stood looking at a nondescript hospital wall poster. David watched him. He texted Paul.

Hospital with Nick. Staying with him.

Paul sat in the driveway a moment praying before venturing into the town house to see his wife. Monaco was setting the table for dinner. The blue and white mini dress accentuated by sparkling blue ankle bracelets, she turned and smiled at him. He walked toward her.

Monaco cried but was not hysterical. He called the hospital and left word for Nick to call her. No sooner he hung up, Nick called and he and Monaco spoke for several minutes before she spoke to Lisa. Paul listened to happy chatter for fifteen minutes before gently reminding his wife that Lisa needed rest. A few minutes later, Monaco received a call from Steven. She was quiet and reflective when she hung up the receiver. A few moments later, Ernest called, and she giggled nonstop. When she hung up from Ernest he noticed she was calmer. Lying together on the couch, watching television, Paul mused this group of five friends were closer than he imagined.

Chapter 17

Nick lived in a four-bedroom home he had bought years earlier as a tax shelter. Although the house had a two-car garage Nick had widened the driveway and installed fencing around the outer perimeter of the house. Lisa's new purple Cadillac Escalade truck was parked inside the garage along with the new black Dodge Viper Nick owned.

Monaco pointed to Nick's bright blue Dodge Viper parked on the side of the driveway. "There's his blue angel."

Paul smiled. "He must be showing it off. Usually he keeps it garaged unless he's driving it."

"Everyone's here," said Monaco eyeing the cars parked on Nick's widened driveway.

With an exaggerated sigh, Paul said, "I hate being late for parties"

Monaco giggled, "You need to stop. No one told you to come into the shower with me."

Paul grinned as he angled the Mercedes-Benz sedan on the other side of the driveway facing the street. Lisa opened the front door in a yellow floral sundress, and the ladies squealed and hugged. Paul escaped to the backyard. Nick was grilling steaks, Steven was eating, David was drinking, and Ernest was lying in the hammock with a hat over his face. Paul glanced at David.

"Gentlemen, it's good to see you," Paul said.

"It's good to be seen," replied Steven.

"You drinking now, Dave?" asked Paul watching David open another bottle. David, Steven, and Nick laughed.

"That's non-alcoholic beer and there's non-alcoholic wine there for the ladies. You can thank Lisa for helping out on the beverages."

Ernest waved from the hammock. "Thank you, Lisa."

"The ladies are among us," announced David picking up a glass of frothy beverage for Raquel who had come out onto the patio.

"I think the man is smitten," remarked Steven.

"I think you're correct, Dr. Barnes," said Paul. "I never did ask you about the conference. How was it?"

"Quite interesting. I bought a few pamphlets back with me, if you want to look at them."

Paul shook his head smiling. "Thanks."

Steven smiled. Claudia walked over to them.

"Hello Pastors, nice day for a party."

"Would you like something to drink Claudia?" asked Steven.

"Yes, thank you, Steven." They moved away with Claudia hooking her arm through Steven's as he lowered his head to hear what she was saying in his ear.

Nick put on some music and couples were dancing on the patio to love ballads. Ernest sat watching his sister and Rick. It was evident to him that the young couple were attracted to one another. Neither one was concerned they were in a mixed group of people who were observing them. They paid attention to each other. After one slow song ended and another was put on, Ernest decided to deejay. He abruptly changed the music to uptempo beats. Rebounding, David and Claudia, lead everybody in line dancing steps. Lisa danced with Ernest and Nick finished grilling.

"Okay good people. The grill master is finished."

"Long as we had to wait, it better be good." said Steven to laughter.

"Boy, what a spread!" said Ernest.

"What's the occasion? You got promoted, started your own business, what?" asked David.

Nick grinned. "Dig in. Surprises await after dinner."

"Dessert is an assortment of goodies so save some room," said Lisa.

Ernest watched his sister and Emory throughout the evening, but kept his distance.

The Sleeper driving by Nick's home noticed the pastors' cars parked in the driveway. He had been watching them before and after church services. They were unaware of being studied and evaluated. The blue-eyed pastor he observed more closely than the others. A likeable gentleman but his quietness was disarming, and he saw more than he let on at times. But again, he was a lawyer by training and profession. He watched them climb into their specially designed cars. None of them were aware their covers were blown. Small town boys returning to the community and church that helped raise them. Regardless they were sent to interfere in something that was none of their business. The Sleeper looked at his watch. He needed to get home. Tomorrow was another day.

The evening was winding down. Nick had lowered the music and switched on the overhead lights in the yard. Fanciful streamers, fairy lights, and white glowing lanterns strung across the patio created a sweet, melodic end to the day. The women had gathered in the house with Lisa all except for Jasmine who was playing a game of chess with Emory. Moving a good distance from the house, with chairs angled where they could view the women and Jasmine, the men spoke in private.

"How was your meeting with Hawkins?" asked Steven.

"I believe we had a good discussion," said Paul. "He's a police lieutenant investigating a string of deaths in churches in this area."

David mused. "Must be something more than regular small-town homicides. Since when do police lieutenants climb down off their lofty perches to get their hands dirty? This is the same guy who was wandering about the church halls several hours after closing services."

Ernest stretched out on a hammock, said, "I think we need to examine the other churches. We've only focused on this church and our people,"

Nick looked at him. "I did investigate other area mishaps. Hawkins lied. Other than the arson at the church in Wood Haven Township, there have been no incidences at local churches."

"What exactly did he say he wanted in our church?"

"He said he's received orders from his superiors to investigate a string of church deaths, including ours," said Paul. "He said the deaths were suspicious for numerous reasons."

"Those reasons being?"

"That part he left out," said Paul.

"Hawkins has been snooping around this church for quite some time now."

"Paul, I remember seeing him during your wedding ceremony. He stayed for the reception."

"He's been more faithful than some long-term members. He's at every church gathering, event, Bible study, and Sunday service," remarked Steven. "I've been watching him watching us."

"Now that his cover's blown, I wonder what he'll do next."

"You want to inform the good brothers here of your findings, Nick?"

"Lt. James Aaron Hawkins is a third-generation lawman out of Buford, South Carolina. He attended college on a football scholarship, and earned a degree in criminology," said Nick, reading from his tablet. "He's known as a hound dog when it comes to solving crime."

"Hound dog, uh?" replied Ernest. "I like that description."

"I don't," said Paul. "All it means is he's persistent, and can slow us down. For instance, he said none of our staff stopped him from parking in our private spaces."

"He's trying to say our security is poor."

"I get he's saying don't blame him for being on the premises five hours later. Although I do wonder where he was, and what he was doing by the time Monaco met him in the hallway."

"Relax. He doesn't know who we are, and he's made a name on the local police level in Chicago as a homicide detective. In fact, he's never lost a case he's investigated in his fifteen years there," said Steven.

"I don't think he's working alone."

"The two men who joined the church recently work in Major Crimes in Chicago, too. The one with the braids is Detective Clay Stewart. American born with Jamaican ancestry. Youngest of six children of Marcus, a retired college dean, and Louisa, a retired neurologist," said Nick.

"What's Stewart's occupation?"

"He's a forensics accountant," replied Nick.

"That's why he wanted to volunteer in the finance department. Okay. I know how to keep him busy."

"What about the other guy who's infatuated with Paul's secretary?"

"You mean the tall, talented, tan Adonis courting baby girl Jasmine?"

"Yes. They seem infatuated with each other."

"The infatuation seems mutual if you ask me."

"Oh, they're both smitten with each other. No doubt about it!"

"Doesn't Jasmine know how to play chess? I thought I heard her tell him she wanted to learn."

"Oh, that's why they're playing chess? She's learning?"

The lowkey laughter was met by silence from the figure lying in the hammock. It was known by Nick and Steven that Ernest tended to become quiet right before he pounced. Steven was positioned where he could detain Ernest should his temper get the better of him.

"If you mean the guy with the bright green eyes, that's Detective Rick Emory, a computer forensic scientist, out of that Chicago department. He did a stint as an Army Ranger."

"Oh! A Ranger like Steve and Nick. He might be okay."

Steven looked at Nick. "I saw him at the gun range the week you couldn't make it."

"Since Paul and I are Navy SEAL," said Ernest, his humor returning. "Seems you're still the lone Marine, Dave"

"Only because I'm special," murmured David, smiling.

"What's Emory's history?"

"He's a second generation cop. His dad is Wilson Emory."

"What? The guy who put the word undercover in the dictionary?"

"The one and only. He retired in the middle of his career only to resurface as an undercover drug lord."

"Wiley Wilson Emory! Man! I'm old! I trained under him at Quantico!"

"Hawkins reminds me of someone as well."

"He's the son of James Abner Hawkins, the Black police chief out of Tulsa, Oklahoma."

"They come from great law enforcement legacies."

"All that talent and skill in Hot Springs, though? Why? To solve a couple of elderly homicides?"

Paul cut in. "What about the Oakland Heights detectives, Osborne and Grant? What do we know about them?"

Nick returned to his tablet. "Osborne is a thirty-year veteran, married with two adult children and four grandchildren. Nearing retirement soon. Dedicated public servant. Has a degree in criminal justice. Grant, his partner, has a degree in criminology and a high I.Q. He's trained at Quantico, and is a Black Belt in the Martial Arts. Passed the detective exam on first attempt."

"Sounds like two more great cops."

"Interesting set-up though. Three out-of-town homicide cops brought in to solve the deaths of the same people we're investigating."

"This is Hot Springs police sending for back-up. Hawkins and crew are from Chicago, right? This is small town thinking."

"I agree. Hot Springs is a small-town with non-existent crime stats. The last time Hawkins was in Hot Springs was several years ago solving that-string of armed robberies."

"Yeah, I think Hawkins is pursuing the untimely demise of this town's older adults."

Paul stood up. "I would believe that premise if he were investigating other churches. This church has lost clergy and trustees, and all under suspicious circumstances."

"I paid a visit to Hawkins hideout," said Steven.

Steven passed around a folder with photos and diagrams. "This first pic is police headquarters where Hawkins has an office on the ninth floor. But, for the last several weeks, he's been in the Oakland Heights station house. His loaner office is on the second floor in the back wing. The apartment building where he's living currently. The back is a diagram of the layout. His gun of choice is a Beretta M9."

"Really, now?" said David. "I think I'm in love."

The roughness in Steven's voice matched the stiffness in his form. His deep base voice resonated through the night air as he spoke.

"Hawkins is no fool. He has the architect's layout of this church. When Ernest and I searched his apartment we found the printout. What he doesn't have are the renovations we've made to the building. We need to tighten up the deacon ministry. We need to install extra lighting, and a sound system for the back since our women use that entrance and exit."

"Who interviewed you at the police station, Paul?"

"Osborne and Grant," replied Nick. "I was there. Why do you ask Steven?"

"Those guys are out of the Oakland Heights area. Small town cops who handle soft soap crime like missing bicycle chains."

"Soft soap," Ernest giggled. "Where do you get this stuff?"

"Ernest, we need the medical examiner's notes on Wright, Bergson, and Lewis. Do you think you can retrieve them legally?"

"I have some free time this week. I'll pay a visit to the medical examiner's office tomorrow," said Ernest.

Nick looked at him. "The new chief medical examiner's name is Dr. Karen Newbold. She replaced Feinstein as of a few months ago."

Ernest smiled. "Thanks for the heads-up."

"Gentlemen let's all stay on our toes," said Steven. "More than usual."

"We should have Monaco on the team. She seems to know how to grill people," said Nick, quietly.

Paul laughed. "Leave my wife alone, Nick."

"How's Lisa doing, Nick?" asked Ernest. "In all the hoopla I haven't forgotten her."

"She's doing well, thanks for asking. She suggested this barbecue."

"We're staying in Monaco's house until she is much better health wise. She's in that big house by herself, and Monaco was worried about her."

"I'll be taking care of that soon, Paul. Thanks for looking out!"

"Is Monaco better?" asked Ernest.

"She's fine. Once she spoke to Lisa, she calmed down," said Paul.

"Good," said Ernest, looking at his phone.

"Gentlemen, one more event awaits. Follow me." Nick walked toward the house. As they gathered in the large kitchen, Lisa and Monaco, brought out a rolling cart packed with pastries centered around a two-layered, chocolate glazed cake.

Lisa said, "Ladies and gentlemen, may I present Nick Rodgers the newest partner of Smith, Jacobs, Parks, and Rodgers."

Ernest was the first to hug his cousin. "Aw man, I'm so proud of you!"

"Great job, boss!" said David.

Steven hugged him in a bear hug. "You deserve it man!"

Paul said, "Wow! Congratulations Nick!"

Nick laughed as the women rushed him, giving him hugs and kisses, and each holding on to him. The party ended an hour later. Ernest allowed Rick to bring Jasmine home in his car and he followed them. He parked in the garage. As the couple walked up to the front door, the outside floodlights snapped on, illuminating them. Emory shook Jasmine's hand.

Ernest opened the door, and Jasmine fairly floated by him, with a smile on her face. Emory was smiling as he drove away.

Ernest visited Hot Springs Medical Center early the next morning. He was directed to the seating area in the hospital lobby where he sat for thirty minutes watching the passing crowds. The receptionists, a middle-aged man of Hispanic descent, and a young African American woman in braids kept glancing his way. They were curious about the tall man with the red skin attired in black with black eye shades who sat still as if he were a robot.

Ernest watched a young mother adjusting her child's stroller. From where he sat he diagnosed the baby was cranky because he needed to walk. He observed the mother needed a prescription of vitamins and some sunshine.

A trim figure in a white lab coat caught his attention at the receptionist desk. Ernest looked at the smart, low-heeled pumps up the shapely calves pass the shapeless white lab coat to the thick wavy brown hair. She turned around and he smiled appreciatively. She was an extremely attractive woman, and he had no doubt she was aware of it. He stood to his feet as she walked toward him. Wow!

He took off his shades and extended his hand. She shook his hand as they both smiled at each other. The attraction was immediate and mutual.

"Good morning, I'm Dr. Karen Newbold, Chief Medical Examiner. I'm told you were waiting to see me?"

"Dr. Ernest Carter. I'm inquiring into the recent deaths of several members of Hot Springs Cathedral Church."

"Please follow me to my office, Dr. Carter."

They took the elevator in companionable silence. Ernest's heart was beating out of his chest. He loved the excitement of sexual tension, but this was something else. But what?

She ushered him into her office and sat behind her desk indicating the guest chair. Ernest sat down. It was obvious she did not know who he was. He put his shades in his pocket. She was beautiful to look at, and he enjoyed looking at her. The midnight dark eyes, straight nose with a slight hump in the middle, and the full lips balanced a slightly heart-shaped face. He sat looking at the smooth skin that was a golden tan in coloring. She

10

was wearing a black dress under the white coat. The colors were extremely complementary.

"Dr. Carter, I'm sure your well aware we have confidentiality policies to uphold. I am curious why you would waste my time with such a request."

Ernest handed her his badge and identification card. She looked at both, and at him before returning them. Her brows came forward in an arch indicating she was irritated. He waited. She was worth him taking his time.

"Agent Carter, why are you impersonating a medical doctor?"

"Dr. Newbold, there's no pretense involved."

"Your credentials state FBI. Last time I checked that is not a medical facility."

"But I do have medical training."

"What is your medical specialty?"

"Forensic pathology."

A slow smile spread across her face. "I see. Follow me."

"Where are we going?"

"To the morgue. I want to see what you know about forensics. That will determine what information you receive without a court order."

Ernest opened the door for her. They smiled at each other as she walked past him. He looked down at the shapely calves. My! My! My!

Chapter 18

The two-story picturesque cottage Samuel Bennett had shared with Sarah, his beloved late wife, sat in the middle of a family-friendly block of comparable homes. Samuel and Sarah had not had children of their own, but had been loving caretakers of several orphaned children. His beloved Sarah had died a few years ago, and Samuel remained in their first home, cherishing her presence in each room. Tonight, after a light dinner of clam chowder and oyster biscuits, he read a murder mystery by an up-and-coming young author. A few moments later, he sat dozing lightly in his brown leather armchair. The figure of the Sleeper crept nearer. Samuel stirred in his sleep and woke up with a smile on his face. He had been dreaming of his sweet Sarah when they were young. He felt a presence near him and looked up. He smiled initially before sensing something was wrong. The first blow he felt. The second blow he did not.

Paul was deep into research of a scripture passage when he heard what sounded like something heavy falling in the front office. He opened the door. He was certain he was the only one in the building. He waited to hear the sound again. Nothing. He returned to his desk, and noticed the blinking light on the desk phone. Oh, oh!

"Paul? Are you still at the church?"

"Hi sweetie, I'm sorry. I started researching and time left me."

"Oh? Time left you, huh? It's okay when you do it, but not me?"

"I'm sorry. No, it's not okay when I do it."

"Why didn't you answer your phone?"

"I had it on vibrate."

"Vibrate? I could be getting killed over here, and you wouldn't know about it, because you can't hear your phone?"

"I know you're angry, but that sentence makes no sense."

She hung up on him. He sighed. He looked at his watch. No wonder she was angry. It was past midnight. He shut down his system, turned out the lights, and reset the alarm for the building. He had exactly two minutes to exit before it locked. He heard the click as it closed.

Hours later Paul and Monaco were sleeping peacefully when Paul's house phone rang incessantly. Osborne was on the line. There was a problem at the church, and Paul's presence was requested. He shot a message to Nick.

Something's going on at church. Osborne wants me there.

Monaco insisted on accompanying Paul to the church. She threw on a blue denim jumpsuit and pulled her hair into a ponytail. When they arrived, the area around the church was lit up like a gigantic Christmas display. Police car strobe lights and other emergency vehicles encircled the church property. To the far right of the church Paul saw the news trucks. He sighed. Monaco saw a familiar face talking to a policeman and two other men.

"Look, there's Brother Hawkins," she pointed, and waved. Hawkins returned the wave.

"Stay here," said Paul. He was about to cross to Hawkins when Nick and Lisa drove up.

The women clutched each other, looking at the scene around them. Nick walked with Paul over to Hawkins who was now coming toward them. They met halfway. Paul recognized the other two men as Detectives Osborne and Grant.

"What's going on, Detectives?" asked Paul.

"A body was found in the grass over there about an hour ago," Osborne pointed.

Paul looked confused. "What? On church grounds?"

Nick raised his voice slightly to be heard over the noise of the ambulances, fire trucks, and other emergency vehicles. "What is meant by found? Is there a missing person report?"

107

There was silence for a second. Hawkins took over. "The police received an anonymous tip that someone planted a body on church property earlier tonight."

"Why call us? The church is closed. Who is he?" asked Paul.

"We don't have an identity yet on the deceased. His pants pockets were stripped bare," replied Osborne.

"It could have been a robbery or made to look like one. The fact that this is the third body found on this property won't bode well publicity wise for the church," said Grant.

"Was the man killed here or did he die of natural causes?" asked Nick.

"We won't know that until we get the coroner's report," said Osborne. "Might I ask where you gentlemen were tonight?"

Paul responded curtly. "You called me at home."

A police officer handed Hawkins a folder. He scanned it briefly before passing it to Osborne and Grant.

"Gentlemen, the person has been identified as Samuel Bennett. Does his name ring a bell?" asked Osborne.

Paul frowned. "He's a member."

"Before you were called at home, where were you, Pastor Mouton?" asked Grant.

"I was here working late."

"How late, Pastor? When did you leave?"

"Unless you're charging Pastor Mouton, this conversation is over," said Nick. "Come on, Paul."

Hawkins spoke. "Gentlemen, the police are going to need to know more about the deceased."

Nick turned to Paul. "I'll manage this, Pastor. Take the ladies home. I'll talk to you later."

"Counselor," said Hawkins. "This is a murder investigation. The police need to talk to your client."

"We can be in your office tomorrow morning. In the meantime, I can get you whatever information on the deceased you need now," said Nick.

Hawkins nodded at Osborne. Paul watched Nick and Osborne enter the church with Grant following them. He became aware Hawkins was watching him.

Much later, Nick sent out text messages to Steven, Ernest, Paul, and David.

Tonight the body of another trustee was found on church property. Samuel Bennett. Managed the legalities with the police. Lisa is doing well. Still suffering with nightmares, and tonight didn't help.

I'll be with Paul in the morning at the police station.

The next morning Paul and Nick appeared at the Oakland Heights Police Station. They were put in an interview room where they waited for an hour. Paul typed on his tablet and Nick, seated beside him, read court briefs. In the room next door, Hawkins with Osborne, and Grant, sat viewing the pastors through the two-way mirror.

Grant grew impatient. "What are they doing?"

"Mouton is typing a sermon, and the lawyer appears to be reading court documents," stated Hawkins.

"Well, they darn sure don't seem like they care about time," said Osborne.

Hawkins smiled. "The lawyer just made partner, and he's dating a lawyer who works for a multi-million-dollar firm. I'm sure he's using his time wisely."

"They need to be worried about all these victims turning up on church property," blurted out Grant.

Hawkins looked at the young detective. "What did you find out about the recently deceased?"

Osborne answered. "I pulled up his resume off their website. He retired as a certified public accountant."

Hawkins smiled. "Start there. I'm staying here."

When the detectives walked in the interview room, neither pastor was in a hurry to end their activities. Grant cleared his throat twice. The pastor closed his tablet and folded it into its case. The lawyer gathered his documents into a folder, and stashed them into his briefcase. They gave the detectives their full attention. Grant's irritation showed on his face, Osborne surveyed them with slight amusement.

Osborne said, "I'm sorry to be keeping you from other matters in your lives. Our job is to find the murderer who's killing your congregants. Pastor Mouton, what can you tell me about the deceased?"

"What is it you want to know, Detective?"

"Name, age, married, role in church, Pastor. Standard questions about a person."

Nick responded. "The information I gave you last night has not changed during the past few hours. His name was Samuel Bennett. He was eighty-eight-years old, and a widower. He and his late wife had no children. He was a former trustee in the church."

"You said former. Was he sat down for some reason?"

"Most of our trustees serve for a period before stepping aside. They are retired, after all," responded Paul. He was reading from his notes.

"How long ago was he a trustee?"

"Fifteen years ago."

"How long was his term of service?"

"He served five terms."

"What does that mean, Pastor?"

"In our church the trustees serve five year terms. In total he served a period of twenty-five years."

"That's interesting," muttered Grant. "Did the other deceased members who were trustees serve with him?"

Paul looked at his screen. "Seems the years overlapped. He was the president of the trustee board for the last fifteen or more years."

"Pastor, can you shed light on why the former trustee was murdered on church property?" asked Grant.

Nick stood up. "Are you charging Pastor Mouton with a crime?"

"Not at this time. But don't leave town," said Osborne.

The pastors walked out. Hawkins was at the end of the hall standing by the window. The pastors had arrived in separate cars. For the first time Hawkins noticed the type of car the senior pastor was driving. He beckoned Grant over.

"What's the make and model of that black Benz?"

"You kidding me?" said Grant, looking at Hawkins incredulously. "Not only is it the most expensive of the Benz, but it's the fastest clocking at a cool two hundred twenty miles per hour..."

Osborne whistled softly. "What do these guys do for day jobs? They drive the most expensive and fastest cars known to man, and they're only church preachers."

"Have you seen their women?" intercepted Grant. "These guys aren't human, man."

Osborne laughed. Hawkins stood perfectly still. He thought of the giant in dark shades who drove the Porsche. He recalled the bright blue Viper of the attorney, and the yellow speedy Corvette the turquoise eyed pastor drove. He knew the Puerto Rican pastor was a multi-millionaire business-man, so driving a Rolls-Royce was in keeping with his wealth.

He turned to Osborne and Grant. "You two need to find out what these five pastors' day jobs are, and pull their financial records. Do it sooner rather than later, detectives! I want to see every scrap of information you dig up!"

As they turned to leave, he called them back. "Don't give the media any more details on these crimes or any others. From here on out, skeletal information only!"

It was late evening and the pastors had decided to meet in City Park. They gathered on a bridge overlooking a scenic landscape.

"What did the medical examiner tell you?" asked Paul, trying not to remember the times he courted Monaco in this section of the park.

"Such a lovely woman," purred Ernest.

"Never mind all that, man, what did you find out?" said David, grinning despite himself.

Ernest turned on his wristband to the notes section. "Victim one is Agnes Wright. She was smothered. She was suffering from advanced stage dementia and had wandered from the nursing home. The police believe she was killed on church property."

"Police found a child's toy wagon loaded with dirt and dug up wild-flowers pushed in the undergrowth not far from where she was found," said Paul.

"The reason the police can't make their belief stick is because of the flowers and dirt Agnes dug up on her journey towards the church," added Nick.

"Victim two is Agent John Bergson. The autopsy showed he was hit so hard his cranium cracked in four places. Our killer is right-handed by the angle of the blows. Forensics showed he was killed somewhere else, and dumped at his home."

"What about Deacon Lewis?" asked Paul.

"Our third victim was hit with a blunt object. Forensics showed he was killed on church property."

"Wasn't it Lewis whose body was found in the closet?"

"Yes."

"Where exactly was he killed on church property?" asked David.

"Forensics found trace evidence of blood splatter in the closet where his body was found. It matched with samples taken from the corpse," said Ernest.

David said, "I'm surprised Hawkins hasn't brought in forensics to sweep the church offices."

"He would need a search warrant, and in order to obtain a search warrant, he must have probable cause," stated Nick. "The bodies were found outside the church, not in it."

"But didn't forensics determine Lewis was killed inside the church."

"No, they found trace evidence of blood splatter in the closet where his body was stashed," Ernest corrected. "Deacon Lewis was always cutting himself as a do-it-yourself handyman. His blood droplets was everywhere in the church building, not just the trustees' office."

"Hmph," said David.

"Last, our fourth and final victim is Sam Bennett. He's just arrived in the morgue. The medical examiner will give me the forensics as soon as its completed."

"Great work, Ernest," said Paul.

"Something's not right here," said David. "Why hurt all these older people?"

"The question is, why was Bergson here that time of night?" asked Steven. "He lives on the other side of town. How did he get here?"

"Yeah! How did he get here? At eighty-six-years old I doubt he was out jogging at three o'clock in the morning."

"Suppose Bergson wasn't here? Suppose he was planted here to throw us off the track?"

"Too much forensics point to the church grounds as his burial plot.

Paul said with despondency. "This stinks to high heaven."

"Gentlemen, I think we need to reevaluate our positions here," stated Steven.

"What do you mean by that, Steve?" asked Paul.

"Since we're here and this is our last official assignment, I think we can solve the murders of these older church folks and tie up the domestic terrorism piece without infringing on one over the other," came the reply.

Ernest sighed. "Make your sentence make sense, Steve."

Nick smiled. "What he's saying Ernest is we might be able to help our church with these murders without jeopardizing the mission."

"I'm all for that," said David. "Deacon Lewis was the trustee who showed me the ropes in the finance department when I took it over. He did it without an ego. I think he was happy a younger man was taking on the task."

"We need to update the deacons as soon as possible. See if they've finalized their security plans."

"In light of all this, I created safety plans and checklists myself," said Paul. "It's time I put my dormant skills to use."

"Dormant skills? Never my friend. Well, gentlemen, looks like we all will need our skill sets intact if this church is to survive these murders."

"Steve, did you send the news item for Brother Bennett?"

"No. We didn't receive any requests for comments."

"Hawkins!"

"Exactly! We'll leave it alone unless directly contacted by the news agencies," said Paul.

"What's the commonality to all these people being murdered?"

"They're older members of the church."

"They're former trustees."

"David, are you still auditing the church finances?"

"Thanks for the reminder, Steven. Look Paul, could you please get Sister Ginyard out of my hair. My team has been complaining because she is disrupting my staff and delaying the work."

"Okay, tell me what you need. She is the church finance director. I can't very well stop her from doing what she is supposed to do."

"Well, that's part of the delay. The lovely Sister Claudia."

Steven interceded. "I might be able to get Sister Ginyard out of your way for a few days but give me precise dates."

David said, "I will send you dates and times tomorrow, Steven."

"Cool beans," Steven replied.

Paul looked at his watch. "Gentlemen, let's call it a night."

Steven put his face in his hands. "Gentlemen, there's a black cruiser parked across the lake. Sitting inside is a lone person with binoculars fastened on us."

David was scanning the coordinates on his wristband. "I believe it's the cop, Hawkins."

"Want to play merry-go-round with him?" asked Ernest, giggling.

"He's a police officer, Ernest. Leave the brother alone," said Nick, laughing.

David laughed. "I must be tired because I'm game."

"You are tired," agreed Steven. "I have a date with a delectable honey. I'll leave you to your games."

Paul stretched his back and arms looking over his shoulder in the direction of their watcher.

"Okay, everyone. I'm tired, too. Talk to you later. Be careful, Ernest, I don't think Hawkins is into games."

The group disbanded, and Hawkins lost sight of them.

Chapter 19

Paul was fixing his pocket square on his beige jacket and looking at his reflection in the hall mirror when he saw the black Lincoln Town Car pull up in front of the house.

"Sweetheart, they're here."

Monaco in a silver embellished dress with sequined long sleeves and wrapped low cut neck, smiled one more time at her reflection, before joining her husband in opening the front door. Charles Robertson, had expressed an interest in meeting Paul's widowed mother, Jayne, outside the formality of the church setting. Monaco suggested to Paul entertaining them in her house as it was bigger than his townhouse, and he agreed. Charles had picked up Jayne at her home.

The dinner went well, and Paul was a happy man. The evening had been pleasant with conversation and company. Monaco was pleased the Cornish hens had turned out as delicious as her godmother Mary said they would. Monaco was about to bring in the dessert tray when the oddest feeling came over her. Paul walked into the kitchen followed by Charles.

"Listen, sweetie, could you continue without me for a minute? I need to visit a member, this may be their last night on earth."

"Oh! yes," said Monaco.

"Are you sure you don't want me to go with you?" asked Charles.

Paul smiled. "Positive. You stay and entertain the ladies. Tell them all those stories about my first year in your seminary class."

Charles laughed as Paul rushed from the room.

David and Raquel were playing a game of strip poker. David had taught her how to play the card game. She was still wearing clothes, but he was down to his boxers. They were both having a great time, although he suspected she was cheating. David looked at his wristband.

"My darling, I must leave you for a few moments. An emergency has come up. Will you be here when I return?"

"Yes, but I'm going to bed. It's late. I'll see you in the morning."

"Okay, sweetheart. I'm setting the house alarm."

They kissed. He calmly walked until he was out of her field of vision. He ran to his room, threw on a pullover and slacks, taking the back stairs to the kitchen. He grabbed his keys, set the house alarm, and raced to his vehicle taking the back routes.

They unpacked their groceries. Steven was showing Claudia how to wash off her fresh fruits and vegetables. He was teaching her how to cook simple dishes. She had a few mishaps like soggy spaghetti, burnt eggs, and cement mashed potatoes, but she met her trials with humor, and had gotten better.

"Do you want to try that shrimp with Alfredo sauce tonight?" he asked her.

"If you make it," she said, giving him the evil eye.

He smiled. "No worries, my love. How does caramelize pork chops, baked potato with chives, and steamed string beans sound?"

"Mmm. ... delicious! Where do you want me to put this bottle of spices?"

"Right here." As he pointed, he looked at his wristband. "Baby, I'll be back! Lock up!"

Claudia immediately walked behind him, turning on the house alarm. She did not know how he knew, but the last time she had neglected to turn it on, she heard an hour's lecture on the importance of safety.

Ernest met with Karen in her office. This time the doctor's lab coat was on a coat hanger, and she greeted him in a yellow tweed suit with a pink blouse underneath. The suit was just snug enough for him to imagine the curves beneath. She beckoned to a chair and sat behind her desk. This morning Ernest kept his dark eye shades on which unnerved her. She began by clearing her throat.

"I received Sam Bennett's autopsy report this morning. The victim was beaten to death. There was enough force to sever his head from his shoulders. It was a gruesome sight. This killing was brutal and personal."

"He was an old man, Karen."

"I am aware, Ernest. He was eighty-eight-years old, physically fit, and clear of vision and hearing. He died in his armchair where he suffered the atrocities of violence."

"Calm down, Karen. To live that long in near-perfect health, and have your life involuntarily snuffed out is difficult to grasp."

Karen looked at her folded hands, and under eye at Ernest. "What's going on at your church, Ernest?"

"I wish I had an intelligent response for you, but I don't know."

"Here's a copy of the forensics. I put it on this USB drive as you suggested."

"Thank you. Might I ask you if you're seeing anyone?"

"No, I'm not seeing anyone."

"Would you mind seeing me?"

"Be specific with me as you are in your work."

Ernest smiled slightly. "I was wondering when you would look me up."

"I felt foolish as I read your resume. But what I found interesting is that it was pieced together by someone else. How come you haven't compiled a resume of your achievements?"

"I have for my records."

"Interesting."

"Back to my question, can we date?"

"I heard you the first time. I rarely have time, but when my schedule permits, I'd like to see you."

Ernest smiled. "You have a full schedule, Dr. Newbold?"

"Doesn't every doctor?"

He stood up. "You're not ready for me. Have a nice day."

"Just what is that supposed to mean?"

It means you're still involved with a surgeon who's in residence in Milwaukee. You're also involved with a podiatrist with a private practice in town, and you intend to go on a hiking expedition with your gang of girlfriends the end of the month."

She sat with her mouth open. "You investigated me?"

"Have a nice day, Doctor."

"Wait a minute. Just like that? You give up?" She had followed him out to the hall. He turned around.

"I didn't give up. I stopped pursuit. No longer interested."

He looked down at his watchband, and walked briskly down the hall. Karen stood in the doorway watching him until he stepped on the elevator. Ernest never looked back.

Chapter 20

Nick arrived home from a long day of legal wrangling. He parked his car in the garage, and took the black box out of his coat pocket. Inside was the sparkling engagement ring he intended to give Lisa this weekend. He had made plans for their weekend at a popular resort, and there is where he was asking her to marry him. The mere image of the fiery redhead brought a smile to his face. As he exited his vehicle, he remembered the next day was trash pick-up day. Loosening his tie, he grabbed the full trash can placed beside the garage wall, and rolled it to the curb. Nick would always remember afterward that he sensed rather than saw a presence near him. He turned at an angle in time to see an upraised arm. His reflexes kicked in, and he ducked sideways. He rolled to his feet with a left jab to the stranger's rib cage and a right uppercut to his chin. He gained leverage before the Sleeper kicked upward and over, sending Nick flying overhead. The Sleeper twisted swiftly and grabbed Nick by his jacket swinging him into the garage wall. Nick shoved away from the wall to leap kick the giant. He underestimated the giant's agility and strength. The Sleeper struck him violently by the side of his head. Nick nearly lost consciousness, before managing to hit his wristband alert. He groggily saw the giant coming at him and moved sideways. The blow struck the side of his damaged head. A large truck approached with high beams on and sped up. A man's shout. Darn! A woman opened her front door, and saw the large, dark figure standing over the man lying motionless in a pool of blood. Her scream was loud enough to wake the living and the dead. The dark figure vanished.

Steven silently walked around the front perimeter of Nick's home. He surveyed Nick's vehicles inspecting them top to bottom. He moved further inside the garage noting immediately that no one had been in there. He moved to Nick's study securing the panel that concealed his weaponry and identification. He locked the garage from inside and reset the house alarm. Moving stealthily, he did the same to the inner alarm on the second floor backroom and exited the home as soundlessly as he entered.

Outside, Paul collected what evidence he could from the driveway and took photographs of the area circling around to the back. He located a random footprint on the grass. As he gathered forensic clues, he caught a glimpse of something stuck on a fence rail. Upon closer inspection, it was a tiny thread. Paul took it and put it with his samples.

In the meantime, Ernest was kneeling by his fallen friend, examining closely the head wound. He stopped the flow of blood, took his pulse, and laid his face sideways. He would not choke on his own body fluids that way. David, beside him, removed Nick's wallet, his ankle weapons, phone, and wristband. The men stood together, and prayed over their friend. The four men left the area in separate cars.

In less than two hours the area was flooded with vehicles of various shapes and sizes. Police were dispatched over the grounds. There was a heavy cake of blood where the victim laid on the sidewalk. Hawkins followed the trail from the driveway seeing the dark splotches on the garage door and a long smear of blood. He saw blood on the grass by the side of the garage wall. The pastor had put up a fight. The detective stood still and prayed. Was there a connection between the old trustees and this young pastor? The medical examiner walked over to him. She was in a blue hazmat suit.

"How's he doing, Doctor?"

Karen wiped her brow with her arm. "He's still breathing. They're transporting him to the hospital now."

"What's his prognosis? He's lost a great deal of blood."

"Someone stopped the flow of blood and nicely bandaged his wounds."

"What?"

"Whoever it was has had medical training. The victim sustained head trauma, but the way the head and neck were bandaged showed a level of expertise only a trained medical professional would have."

"Was anyone with him when you arrived, Doctor?"

"No." Karen gave him a steady look. "I'll let you know something as soon as possible."

"Thanks. I'll contact his pastor," said Hawkins, walking away. He left a message with the church answering service.

Detectives Osborne and Grant drove up. Osborne looked around.

"What's happened here?"

"One of the pastor's was attacked tonight," recounted Hawkins.

"Which one?"

"The attorney."

Grant was looking at the ground. "Is he alive?"

"Barely it seems," returned Hawkins.

"He's also a pastor at Hot Springs Cathedral Church, isn't he?" asked Grant.

"Yes, why, Detective?" asked Hawkins.

"Why? You don't think all this is coincidental, do you?"

"No, not really."

Osborne sighed, writing on his notepad. "This is where the lawyer lives? It's crazy he's got to get hurt before we know his exact address."

A police officer came over. "Detectives, the guy over there drove up as the assault occurred. And a lady over there in the house across the street, the one with the wreath on the door, spotted some men in black scouting the premises before the police showed up."

All three men stared at the police officer before Osborne said, "thanks, Smith."

It was Grant who spoke into the silence that followed. "Some men in black were here before the police arrived..."

"But they didn't touch the body?" finished his partner.

"They must have, or at least one of them did," said Hawkins. "The medical examiner said someone with extensive medical training dressed the victim's wounds."

"It could have been a neighbor."

"Why would he leave? He'd want to talk to the police about how he saved his neighbor's life," argued Grant.

"You two talk to the man. I want to talk to the lady," said Hawkins.

Emory and Stewart drove up. Hawkins beckoned to them. The door opened before they could knock. Hawkins and the detectives showed her their badges which she barely looked at. She was attractive, well-kept, and fighting to remain calm.

"Ma'am, what is your name?" asked Hawkins.

"Margaret Jones," she said.

"Do you live here alone?"

"No. I live here with my husband. We have two kids in college."

"Is your husband here now?"

"No, he's out of town on a business trip. I expect him home tomorrow."

"May we have your husband's name?"

"My husband is Ted Jones of Finch, Jones, and Porter."

"How long have you been neighbors with the victim?"

"We've lived here twenty years. Nick is a sweetheart and so, good-looking! He and his girlfriend are a striking looking couple."

"Was she at the house tonight?"

"Oh, heavens, no! She might have gotten attacked as well."

"Could you tell us what you saw?"

"Men in black clothes. I saw them when they left, but they weren't the ones who attacked Nick."

"How do you know that? Did you see who attacked the victim?"

"Nick was already on the ground, and bleeding when I saw them walk up. One bent over him, the other ones were putting stuff in lunch bags."

"Could you describe these people?"

"They were in black clothing."

"Yes. What about their faces?"

"Their faces?" she repeated. She seemed confused by the question. The detectives waited.

"Were they wearing masks?" asked Emory.

She turned vacant dark eyes to him. "I don't know. I don't remember them. I was so focused on Nick."

"You said these people walked up. Were there cars out?" asked Stewart.

She frowned. "Come to think of it, no. I mean, I didn't see any."

"How did they leave?" asked Emory, he stared at the woman as if he did not believe her statements.

"I don't know," she said with such an element of surprise Hawkins wanted to laugh.

"Could you tell if these people were men or women?" asked Stewart.

"I think two of them were women but it was so dark."

"How many people would you say arrived before the police got here?"

"Oh, my gosh! Maybe five or six..."

"Thank you for speaking to us," said Hawkins. He handed her a card with the police department phone number on it.

Hawkins and the detectives walked back to the street and met up with Osborne and Grant. Grant read from his notes in a monotone voice.

"George Hayward, 37, lives with his wife, Nancy. They have four school-age children. He's a private contractor with Zion-Moss, and she's a trauma nurse at Hot Springs Medical Center. When Hayward drove up he spotted one man standing over the fallen body with a long object in his hand that dripped blood. Unfortunately, because of the darkness and the trees, he didn't get a good look at the man. All he remembers is that the guy was a giant either wearing a black suit or in all black. He thinks the man might have climbed the trees because he didn't see a car or truck anywhere for the guy to drive away in."

"What did the witness do after that?" asked Emory.

"He checked on his family and called the cops. He said when he came back to the window a group of people were with the victim. He said they left when they heard the sirens."

Hawkins looked at Grant with interest. "Did he see where any of the people went? What direction?"

"He said they vanished into the darkness... or climbed the trees."

The detectives looked at each other in silence. All five of them looked up and down the street. Using flashlights, the detectives scanned the outer perimeters of the home noting the nine-foot safety fence and the heavy foliage. The home itself, secured by an advanced alarm system, had not been entered.

After a few minutes of silence, Hawkins suggested Osborne call the senior pastor's home.

"Hello, Pastor Mouton, Sgt. Osborne. I'm sorry to bother you at home, but there's been another situation."

"Good evening, Sergeant. What do you mean by situation?"

"Your lawyer, Rodgers, was attacked tonight. I need to see you at the Oakland Heights police station as soon as possible."

"What do you mean he was attacked? Where?"

"At his home, Pastor."

"Where is he now?"

"Hot Springs Medical Center."

"I need to check on my pastor first, Detective. I'll see you tomorrow morning," Paul hung up. He looked at his wristband message from Steven.

Nick's seriously injured. Hospital with Lisa.

Paul parked in the emergency area of the hospital and clasping his wife's hand walked into the Hot Springs Medical Center. As they made their way down the corridor they saw Lisa, in silent tears, as she sat alone in the waiting room. The two women rushed into each other's arms. Steven and David appeared with cups of coffee to calm the women's nerves. Monaco and Lisa were now speaking in soft tones seated beside each other with Lisa gently sobbing on Monaco's shoulder.

The men walked down to where Ernest was standing guard over Nick's room. They moved away from the door.

"What's the update on Nick?" asked Paul.

"The surgeons may have to operate to relieve the pressure on his skull, but he needs to get through the next twenty-four hours."

"His house was untouched. I reset the alarms, and turned on the surveillance monitor."

"Police want to see me at the police station tomorrow."

"As Nick would say, speak only what you know."

"Take Monaco with you. He won't want to say too much with her present."

"Since when? I've never known a cop to not ask questions, regardless of who you are, or are with," said Paul.

"True, but for whatever reason, Hawkins likes Monaco. He won't want to upset her."

Paul looked at Steven and behind him to Lisa and Monaco huddled together on the couch. David pulled Paul to the side.

"What is it Dave?" Paul was watching Lisa and Monaco.

"Listen Paul, the media is going to have a field day with this once it's made known this is one of our clergy. You might want to address the church. Nick is one of the most popular pastors among us."

Paul said curtly, "I don't deal with popularity contests."

"Get a hold of yourself, Paul. I know you've had a lot coming at you these past few months, but you've got to get a handle on this situation. We don't want our congregation worried about who's next. The past ministry leaders being targeted, has a lot of the older members apprehensive."

Paul look directly in David's face. "I do need to get ahead of this. I'll speak to Steven as soon as I speak to the police."

"What do you need me to do?"

"Take care of the financial matters. All these trustees being murdered is not a random or prejudicial act. This is a deliberate pattern."

"That's my feeling, too. I'm going to reset pass codes and do a smaller forensic audit. Claudia's excellent at this."

"Raquel called me earlier."

"I'm going home now."

Paul breathed through his mouth before walking toward his wife and Lisa.

Chapter 21

The desk sergeant at the Oakland Police Station looked up into the face of the large man in the midnight black suit. Sgt. O'Hanson's eyes fell on the white clerical collar around the man's neck. Beside the man stood an attractive woman who could have been a model or a movie star. He vaguely pondered if his fellow police officers were pranking him.

"May I help you folks?"

"We're looking for Detectives Grant and Osborne?"

"Both of you?"

When they nodded, he had an officer escort them. "This way, folks."

The police officer walked ahead of them down a long corridor. Monaco noticed the police were moving out of their way. What was going on? The officer guided them to an interview room. He brought in another chair.

Monaco looked around. The room had one tiny window near the ceiling and a long mirror covered one wall. On the opposite wall was a clean white board. In the middle of the room was a table with two chairs placed opposite each other. She walked to the mirror and checked her makeup, and smooth down the black double-breasted dress she was wearing. Paul was seated typing on his phone. Detective Osborne walked in the room, smiled at Monaco, and sat behind the desk. Monaco sat beside Paul.

"Good morning, Pastor, and Mrs. Mouton. I apologize for having you come down here this morning. Let me get to the point. We have a problem that is escalating. As you know by now, Nick Rodgers was attacked last night at his home."

Monaco stiffened in her seat. Paul holding her hand remained mute. Grant, walked in and stood by the door.

"I wanted to ask you both if you know of a reason Mr. Rodgers would have been attacked?"

"No," said Paul. Monaco silently shook her head.

"What about anyone who might hold a grudge against Mr. Rodgers?"

Paul spoke. "No, no one in the church."

"His place of employment?"

Grant pulled up notes on his tablet. "He recently became a partner with a law firm. Has he spoken of any disagreements? Someone upset because they didn't make partner?"

"No. Nick's a hard-worker. I don't believe anyone would begrudge him success," said Paul.

"In a perfect world, no," murmured Osborne. He looked directly at Paul confident his partner was observing Monaco. "Pastor, when did you arrive home yesterday?"

"My last class at the university was over by five-thirty in the evening. I was home in about fifteen minutes. My wife and I hosted a dinner for my mother and Pastor Robertson."

"What do you teach at the university?"

"An advanced seminary course in practical religious ethics."

"What's your schedule like?"

"I teach that course once a semester. It's a required course for grad students only. And I mentor doctoral students."

There was momentary silence. Osborne looked at his phone.

"You were home all evening then, Pastor?"

"Yes, I was."

"When did you know of Pastor Rodger's condition?"

"When you called me at home, Detective."

"Would your mother and Pastor Robertson corroborate your story?"

"They should," replied Paul. "We had a grand time together."

"When did they leave your home?"

"Pastor Robertson left our home close to ..." Paul looked at Monaco. "Did you notice the time, sweetheart?"

"It was close to midnight, and he left before she did. We drove Jayne, my mother-in-law, home."

"Had she arrived with Pastor Robertson?"

Paul smiled. "Yes, but my mother is old-school, Detective. She was not about to allow him to drive her home at what she termed an 'indecent' hour."

Both detectives nursed smiles. Grant asked, "Mrs. Mouton, any old girlfriends vengeful enough to do this?"

Monaco smiled with her lips, but her eyes held tears. "Nick is a sweetheart of a man. His two serious relationships before Lisa ended amicably."

Grant looked at her. "How long have you known Pastor Rodgers?"

"We grew up together."

"Could you tell us about the two relationships, if you don't mind." Osborne gently prodded.

"Nothing to tell. The first girlfriend was in middle school and her family moved away. The second girl was a high school crush that ended when she left for college. He always cared for Lisa, but she never believed he was serious about her because of how girls chased him."

"Is Lisa who he's currently dating?" asked Grant. "What's her last name?"

"Yes." Monaco's eyes began to look teary as she looked at the detectives. "Lisa Gonzalez."

"Do you have an address and phone number for Ms. Gonzalez?"

Once Monaco supplied the information, Osborne smiled. "Thank you, Mrs. Mouton."

Turning to Paul, he handed him a business card. "If you should think of something that may be useful, please contact me immediately."

"Thank you, I will."

"We have police stationed at the hospital. I need you both to understand that we are working all we can on this."

"Thank you, Detective. We know you are," said Monaco, in a soft whisper, her voice shaky with emotion.

Grant looked at Monaco who was gazing at him with large, expressive eyes.

"Pastor, could you come outside with us a moment? We need to ask you something. Please excuse us, Mrs. Mouton."

In the hall the detectives moved to the interview room next door. Osborne looked at his phone.

"Pastor, last night we interviewed two separate neighbors who swore there was a gathering of people around the fallen pastor last night. Could you enlighten us as to your theory of who those folks were?"

Paul looked from one detective to another. His face slowly formed a scowl.

"Are you serious? I'm a pastor, not a detective! If you have suspects, you need to be questioning them."

"They had left before we arrived."

Paul stared at them. Osborne said, "We don't know what to think."

"Me neither. Did these people attack Pastor Rodgers?"

"We don't know. We were hoping you could give us some type of theory or reasoning to help us in identifying the pastor's attacker."

"That's not my field of expertise, Detective. Is there anything else? I would like to take my wife home."

"Speaking of your wife," said Grant, "I don't believe you need to involve her in these situations unless she's already on site. She's showing signs of stress. You don't want her to have a nervous breakdown on you."

"I don't know what to do," said Paul. His posture slacked, and his face fell with misery. "She doesn't want to be alone anymore."

"That's understandable," said Grant. "I'm not married. I can't speak to couple issues. But I've been doing this job a long time. I know the signs of secondary trauma and stress."

Osborne remained silent, watching him. Paul nodded. This cop was alerting him to a potential issue in his marriage.

On the drive home Monaco wanted to visit Nick. "We're going the wrong way. Aren't we going to the hospital?"

"No, baby, he's still unconscious."

"What about Lisa?"

"Steven is with Lisa. He and Ernest will take care of Lisa. Let me take care of you."

"But what about Nick? Shouldn't we...?"

"Stop it! Get control of yourself. You're not a medical professional. Do you want to do something? Let's go home and pray for our friends, the police, and the poor soul who's causing all this havoc."

"Lisa is my best friend. I can't abandon her. She loves Nick," said Monaco, her voice cracking with grief. "Why didn't you mention you had left to see a member last night?"

"Because I don't want them harassing our members. We're all going through enough."

"But if the member can corroborate the time..."

At the stop sign, Paul looked at his wife. "Can you call and speak to Lisa on the phone for now? Nick can't have visitors. He needs to heal."

"Yes, I can do that."

Paul smiled. He surreptitiously left a message on his wristband.

Nothing to report. They're trying to figure out who we are!

Nick struggled to open his eyes; the bright light brought pain. He closed them again. He was in a dark, cloudless space breathing heavy mist. Why was it damp and dark in here? He opened his eyes slowly as they felt extremely heavy. He saw a head of red curls. A long slender arm draped across his chest. He studied the pink fingernails. Tiredness overcame him. This time the darkness was in shades of gray, and he could breathe. Nick smelled a scent like gardenias and opened his eyes. A woman in a white dress with long black hair was speaking. Wait! She was reading a book. He tried to speak to her...eyelids heavy. He was running through the dark misty night toward something. He saw two figures in black. One figure was near him seated in a chair, and the other was leaning against the wall. He struggled to hear what they were saying. He was so tired. He needed to rest. It was labor-intensive to open his eyes. He closed his eyes again.

Nick opened his eyes to a bright room. He saw Steven seated in a chair by the wall with his tablet on his lap, and Ernest seated in a chair by his bed completing a crossword puzzle. Steven noticed him move first.

"Well, it's about time you joined the land of the living," he said, softly.

Ernest closed his book. "Hey, Nick."

"I know your head is hurting like hell, but do you remember anything?" asked Steven.

Nick smiled and let out a breath. He looked at the open door. Ernest closed it. Steven turned on his recorder.

"I don't remember anything," said Nick, slowly. Ernest and Steven looked at each other.

"Don't worry about it, Nick. Be well, buddy," said Steven.

Nick had fallen asleep.

Nick, seated in a hospital chair, was looking at the bright sunshine flowing in through the open blinds. He looked down at the deep blue silk robe and matching pajamas set Ernest had brought for him. He clasped the box containing the ring Nick had returned to him. A light tap and Lisa entered the room.

Nick's smile lit up his entire face. "Hi, gorgeous!"

"Well, good morning, handsome," said Lisa. "Why aren't you in bed?"

"I'm feeling much better."

"You're not out of the woods yet, Nick. You've had a traumatic brain injury. Ernest said you have to take it easy."

"Please stop talking."

Nick was feeling dizzy. He stood up. Lisa rushed to him, and putting her arm around his waist, helped him to his bed. Nick laid back on the pillows she propped beneath his head. He grabbed her hand.

"Lisa, baby. You have brought me so much happiness these last few months. When you had that accident, I knew without a shadow of a doubt, I didn't want to be without you for the rest of my life."

"Nick, if you're thinking of breaking up with me, forget it!"

"Shut up, woman!"

"I love you, Nick. I always have."

"I love you too," said Nick. "Although it's not the romantic weekend I had planned, I'm asking you to marry me when I get better."

Tears fell from Lisa's eyes. "I'll marry you whenever and wherever. I love you so much."

He slid the ring on her finger, and they hugged. Lisa crawled onto the bed beside Nick and snuggled in his arms.

Chapter 22

Grant was typing up his interview notes when he looked up and saw Osborne's pale blue eyes staring at him.

"What's the matter with you?"

"What are you doing?"

"Finishing reports I never get to finish. Why?"

Osborne grunted. "Leave that for later. We're going to visit the pastor-lawyer in the hospital. He's conscious now."

"I'm game if we can stop by the church. I like looking into the green eyes of that church secretary."

Osborne grinned. "I know you do but be careful. One of those pastors is her brother. Come on, let's go."

The detectives arrived in time to find a fully awake Nick. The men stood transfixed for a moment. The room was resplendent with floral arrangements. A large bulletin board leaned against the wall filled with chalk-written messages, taped postcards, and photos of people with notes attached. Seated in the chair was a woman with thick, curly dark red hair framed around dark eyes, turned up nose, and full lips. The man seated next to her stood up when they entered.

The first thing Osborne and Grant noticed about the man was his red skin coloring. The bright blue-green eyes fixed on them in a mesmerizing stare. With difficulty, they transferred their attentions to the man in the bed. His head, heavily bandaged and eyes half-closed, the detectives noted the silky black pajamas he wore.

"Mr. Rodgers, we'd like to ask you about your attack."

"Who are you, gentlemen," asked Ernest.

"We're from the Oakland Heights Police Department. I'm Sgt. Osborne, and this is my partner, Detective Grant."

"Who are you people?" asked Grant.

"Hello, Detectives" said Lisa. She held tightly to Nick's hand. "I'm Lisa Gonzalez, Nick's fiancée."

"Pastor Ernest Carter from Hot Springs Cathedral Church," said Ernest.

"Did you receive clearance from his doctor?" asked Lisa.

"No, we didn't," said Osborne.

"But we need to know what happened to Mr. Rodgers," said Grant.

"As his attorney, I cannot allow you to question him when he's in a fragile mental and physical state. It will have to wait," said Lisa.

"With all respect, Ms. Gonzalez, you are not a doctor. Who is his doctor? We'll get clearance from them."

"I'm his personal physician," said Ernest. He had put on dark sunglasses. The dark brown suit he wore intensified his skin color.

"I thought you were a pastor," said Grant, clearly irritated.

"My day job is medicine and my weekend gig is pastoring," said Ernest, smiling.

Osborne looked at Nick. "Do you remember anything from your attack?".

Nick smiled. "I remember I was in the driveway of my home. Someone came at me from the back. That's all I remember."

"You said someone. You didn't see who attacked you?"

"No."

"Was it one person or more than one?"

"I don't know."

"You put up a helluva fight, Pastor," observed Grant.

"Do you have any martial arts training?" asked Osborne.

Nick smiled and closed his eyes. Ernest stepped to the bed and looked at Nick before turning to the detectives.

"He needs to rest now. If there's anything else, I'll call you or you can wait until he's released and/or remembers something of that night."

Grant asked, "Doctor, what medication is he on?"

"Privileged information," said Lisa, sharply.

The nurse appeared and the detectives left. Grant did not forget Nick's silence when he asked about martial arts training. He later relayed the interview to Hawkins, word for word.

A few evenings later, Ernest parked in the visitor's section at Hot Springs Medical Center. Grabbing his medical bag he made his way to Nick's room. The police officer on duty nodded at Ernest. Steven stood and stretched when he knocked and entered the room. Ernest glanced at the bed. Nick was sleeping.

"How's he been the last few nights?"

"The nightmares appear to have eased up. He hasn't been shaking the last six hours."

"That's a relief. A few nights ago when I was here I had to chain him to the bed to keep him from jumping up and hurting himself."

"No worries now. The worst of it seems over. You want anything before I leave?"

"No, Karen is bringing me something later."

"Who?"

"The medical examiner."

Before Steven could reply, Lisa walked in carrying brown shopping bags with a pink floral duffel bag. She was dressed in a khaki jumpsuit and slip-on sneakers.

"Hi, guys!" she said brightly. Ernest gave her his chair.

"He was conscious for a minute, but he's sleeping now," said Steven. "What's in the bags?"

"I brought over snacks, sales catalogs, and pajamas. The nurse said a family member can stay with him. They'll bring the cot soon."

Ernest pulled out a catalog. "Furniture?"

"I'm redoing one of the upstairs bedrooms for my work area. I'm also redecorating the living space. There's too many dark colors in that house."

"Sounds like you're moving in," observed Steven.

"I am!" Lisa laughed gaily. "Nick is going to need someone to take care of him until he's well again. As his fiancée, that'll be me. There are no at-home nurses over age 50 in this hospital."

"You came up with a plan?" asked Steven.

"You know it! I'm his girlfriend. I'll take care of him myself."

"I'm sure he'll appreciate that," murmured Steven.

"Yes, he will," she responded brightly. She turned to her shopping bags. Ernest giggled. Steven looked amused.

Monaco's visit with Nick and Lisa in the hospital produced tearful hysterics Paul had a difficult time soothing. They stopped at the grocer on the way to the town house and ordered a pizza for dinner from Barb's Bistro. Monaco ate two bites of her slice and wanted to lie down. She took a shower and crawled into bed. Paul watched her feeling defeated. The detective's advice about Monaco suffering stress stayed with him on his drive to Steven's home. Steven and Claudia were preparing dinner when Paul visited.

"I'm sorry. I didn't know you two were having dinner. This could have waited until tomorrow."

"No problem, you're here now," said Steven. "Come in. Would you like something to drink?"

"No thanks. I'll only be a minute."

"Hi Paul." Claudia waved from the kitchen. Steven led him to his den and quietly closed the door.

"What's going on Paul?"

"I know you saw Nick earlier. How's his medical condition?"

"I stopped by for a few minutes. Nick's medical progress is slow but hopeful. He still doesn't recall anything from the night of the attack. It's safe to say he has a concussion, but he's healthy he'll survive. Osborne and Grant visited him."

"Were you there? How did it go?"

"No, Ernest was. He said the detectives are intuitive and smart. We need to respectfully stay on our toes."

"Thanks for that update. How's Lisa taking all this?"

"Lisa plans to move in to take care of Nick. He proposed to her once he came out of the coma. Ernest and I moved two large suitcases and a trunk to Nick's home. Lisa and Claudia were talking about bed linens this morning. Jasmine shopped on her lunch break for food items that Monaco's bringing over either today or tomorrow."

Paul's head snapped around. Steven managed to keep a straight face as he updated Paul on the women's activities.

"I'll talk to Nick and Lisa about a wedding date," said Paul slowly.

Steven cleared his throat. "Better yet, marry them at the hospital. That way you won't catch hell from the deacons about a pastor shacking up with a church member."

Paul's head jerked again. "I'll call them as soon as I get home."

Steven waited. "Anything else? You look like something else is on your mind."

"It's Monaco. We have relocated to my house. Steven, I don't know what to do. We visited Nick in the hospital, spoke with Lisa, and as soon as we reached the parking lot, she had a cry fest. She barely eats, and now she's home in bed. I don't know what to do to help her over this depression."

The silence became so acute that Paul found himself staring at Steven. That was when he noticed Steven was wearing his dark eye shades in the house. Steven walked away from him to the window.

"You may or may not have heard the family story from Monaco. She had one older sister. They were not close because the parents favored the older one, and ignored Monaco. That's how Ernest, Nick, Lisa, and I became her family. We're all only children except for Ernest. However, Jasmine was a surprise baby, hence the age difference between them. But the five of us were the siblings the other never had. The community connected us, sealed us, and protected us."

He turned and faced Paul. "When Monaco was working and living in New York I visited every other weekend although she technically and visually 'saw' me when the five of us planned outings. When I couldn't make it Ernest or Nick was there. Our bond is tight. I'm telling you all this because you're her protector now. And yes, Ernest loves her. He always has. She has never felt that way about him, and he knows that as well. But, if anything happened to her on your watch, he would come for you."

Paul smirked. "I don't think he wants to get into a fight with me."

Silence. Steven sighed. "I wouldn't want either of you in a fight. You would kill each other. Don't forget he has skills too as a Navy SEAL. But this is not about you or Ernest, it's about Monaco. You must put her first. I know you love the church, but it will remain standing when you're visiting your wife in the asylum, or the graveyard."

Paul's head involuntarily twitched for the third time.

Steven continued. "David is keeping tight reins on the finances at the church, and Charles is there in the interim we're not able to make it. Ernest is keeping a close watch on Nick's medical condition. I have control of the church administration. Your job is to take care of your wife. We've got your back and always will have it."

"Dave believes we need to be talking to the congregation. Do you think I should call a town hall?"

Steven smirked. "You're a pastor, Paul. Call a church-wide meeting but air it on social media. That way, other towns will know what we're dealing with here."

"Great idea! Thanks, man!"

"I'm the licensed head guy, remember?"

Chapter 23

Monaco found it difficult to keep up with all that was happening. The local news always lagged a day behind the live drama they were all struggling to move ahead of. Nick was doing better. She was helping Lisa with moving into the home she would share with Nick on his release from the hospital. Monaco looked around the living room of the town house. She was finding it cozy living here. What she once considered cramp had turned into quaint and comfortable. She threw on a navy striped pullover and blue denim shorts and sandals. She had not been in her house for several weeks now. She needed to check the mailbox. Fifteen minutes later, Monaco pulled her vehicle into the driveway of her house and parked. She walked through the fallen leaves up the path. She looked over at Lisa's house and saw the large for sale sign on the lawn. The sign gave her cause to pause as the years fell away, and memories of their childhood surfaced. She came back to reality with a jolt. Time to move on. Climbing the stairs to the front door she noticed the porch needed sweeping. It occurred to her as she unlocked the door that the house needed cleaning as well. When Monaco turned on the lights she fell over the crumbled rug, and landed sprawling on the carpet in the spot where the coffee table had once stood. From her position on the floor, she saw the dishevelment of the house with lamps knocked over, cushions tossed about, and chairs upturned. She heard what sounded like running in the rooms overhead. She scrambled to her feet and ran outside to her Jeep. She could barely start the engine; her hands were dead weights as she struggled to turn the key in the ignition.

She backed the vehicle out the driveway with screeching tires. She was on the road trembling when the tears forming in her eyes fell onto her cheeks.

Steven received the alert alarm from Paul as he was leaving the campus for the day. Taking back streets and highways he parked in the back of Monaco's home, and made his way inside of the house. He was too late. Whoever had been in the home had vacated the premises. Looking about he surveyed the damage on the first floor. He eased the front door closed with his foot before taking the stairs to the bedrooms. The rooms were untouched, but he noticed a dusty smudge on the bottom of the balustrade. He collected samples. Returning downstairs, he jumped lightly over the railing, and as he landed saw police had arrived. He exited as he entered.

Monaco, sitting in Paul's lap, had both arms around his neck. She was quietly sobbing.

"Alright, your safe now. Calm down. Breathe, baby," said Paul, soothingly in her ear. The doorbell rang. Paul gently deposited her on the sofa, straightened his shirt and jacket, and opened the door. Steven, and Ernest entered.

"Are you okay, Monaco?" Steven asked. He was not wearing his dark glasses, and looked like he had not slept in days.

Monaco nodded but kept her face in her hands. She had wrapped a blanket around herself as if she were cold. Ernest sat beside her and kissed her cheek. She leaned her head on his shoulder. Paul cast a glance at them but said nothing. Steven walked ahead of Paul to the kitchen.

"What's up?" said Paul, watching Ernest and Monaco.

Steven suppressed a smile. "I checked out the house. I called Hawkins and company. They're over there now."

"What did you assess from the situation?" asked Paul.

"Someone was looking for something. The damage is on the first floor. The typical overturned chair, discarded table, and so forth."

"Maybe they didn't get a chance to go upstairs," offered Paul.

"They were upstairs. What they want is not upstairs. She startled whoever it was," said Steven.

"Does that house have a basement?"

"No, attic. The rooms weren't touched upstairs at that time."

Paul frowned. "What do you mean at that time?"

"I need to throw Hawkins off track for a minute; nothing grand."

"That man is a homicide specialist," Paul said with a hint of laughter in his voice. "He will throw you beneath the jail for obstruction of justice, tampering with evidence, and/or stealing."

"That is a possibility," mused Steven."However, he would have to prove I did something, moved something, or stole something first."

They both laughed. They returned to the living room where Ernest sat close to Monaco with his arm around her blanketed shoulders. Paul cleared his throat, and Ernest looked up. His pale turquoise eyes gleamed beneath half closed lids giving him the look of an angry feline. Paul stared at him hard a minute before walking purposely toward him. Steven intercepted by moving in front of Paul, lifting Ernest up by his arm, and shoving him forcefully toward the front door in one fluid motion.

"Well folks, have a good night. Tomorrow is another day. I expect you will hear from the police soon."

When the door closed behind them, Monaco said, "Paul? What's the matter with you and Steven?"

"You're my wife, not Ernest's. His hands, arms, and lips should not be on you."

"Oh, Paul. We grew up together. He treats me like a sister."

"I have a sister, remember? So does he. How would you feel if Lisa or Claudia hugged me around the neck, and kissed my cheek barely missing my lips?"

Monaco sighed. "They wouldn't do that."

"Oh? Why not? Because it's not appropriate? You wouldn't get angry?"

"I just never thought anything of it. Ernest has always had a crush on me."

"It's time he moved away from boyhood fantasies, and its time you stopped encouraging it. You're my wife not his playboy centerfold."

"Don't speak to me that way."

"Good night, Monaco. I won't argue with you."

"There's no reason to be jealous of Ernest."

"It's not jealousy. It's about respect. Just as I was on your side when Claudia disrespected you. I would think you would be the same way about me. Good night."

"Don't you want anything for dinner?"

Without answering her, Paul went to their bedroom. She sat on the sofa. She had grown up with Ernest, and he had never disrespected her. She sighed. She sat there awhile remembering the years of loneliness; remembering how she wished she had someone to love, and who loved her. She reflected on her childhood home. It was her past. Her present and future was upstairs. She sighed and turned out the lights. She saw Paul under the bed covers. He usually waited for her to come upstairs. She walked into the bathroom and showered. Climbing into bed beside him, she saw he was sleeping in a thermal pullover and sleep pants. He rarely slept in clothing. She laid down beside him, snuggling against him. He turned over and hugged her. He took off the clothing, and laid beside her, wrapping her in his arms. She kissed his cheek, and he kissed her lips. They were soon engaged in the age-old ritual of making up.

The Oakland Heights police pegged Monaco's house break-in as nothing more than vandalism. They suggested the couple do an inventory of the house contents. When Paul got off the phone with Grant, he found Monaco sitting on the patio. The once empty, bleak space now held a colorful swing, a bistro table with two chairs, and a cabana umbrella. As Paul stepped onto the patio, he noticed the addition of two large plants and vaguely wondered if they were real or potted. Monaco, in a navy print wrap dress, was seated on the swing. She smiled at him. Paul sat beside her.

"That was the detective about the break-in. The police believe it's nothing more than simple vandalism."

"Simple to them. I was terrified."

"Where's the homeowner's insurance policy?"

Monaco frowned. "Good question. I don't think I found one in any of the documents I've gathered so far."

"You need to check that out. Unless you want me to do it?"

"I can manage. Thanks, honey."

"Okay. You want to reserve a table at the Riviera for dinner?"

"Can we stay in tonight? There's new movie releases."

"How's about ordering in?"

"Okay. Whatever you want."

"Please eat something. You're worrying me."

"Okay, order some Chinese or Thai. I promise I'll take a bite."

She grinned and he shook his head.

Chapter 24

Osborne drove through a stop sign, and grunted in annoyance with himself. He and his partner had been working on the senior citizens death cases nonstop. He did not blame his wife, Maggie, for being upset. The weather forecasted clear skies for this weekend. But he had volunteered to pull desk duty because he had to finish paperwork for his quarterly review. Driving home, he turned a corner and recognized he was on the block where the injured pastor lived. He looked at the homes he drove past. This was an upscale neighborhood. Far nicer than where he could afford to live. He remembered the pastor was a practicing attorney which would explain how he could live in this posh area. As Osborne drove past Nick's home he casually glanced over, and immediately turned his vehicle around. He had spotted someone climbing over the back fence into the yard. He radioed his coordinates, and parked his vehicle. Inside the yard, the Sleeper spotted the police vehicle. He ran to the other side of the yard, but that was a nine-foot iron railing fence with two-foot-high spikes on the edging. Oops! He scaled the side of the house crouching on the roof ledge. Osborne took his weapon out of his shoulder holster and moved forward quietly and carefully. The detective was perspiring as he carefully opened the gate. He crept in slowly and pulled the gate behind him. The Sleeper watched the detective below him; how he was holding his service revolver. He held the hypodermic needle firmly between his fingers as he watched the advancing cop. When the detective was directly beneath him, the Sleeper eased down onto his back. He wrapped his arm around Osborne's neck in a choke hold, and emptied the needle contents in one fell swoop.

By the time his partner pulled up to the house, Osborne had been dead for thirty minutes.

Hawkins, pulling up in an unmarked cruiser, spotted Grant standing by a patrol car with his arms crossed, and his head down. The handsome detective's face bore a look of profound sorrow.

"Are you okay, Joe?"

"He was already gone when we got here," stated Grant, not looking at Hawkins.

"I'm sorry you lost your partner. He was a good cop."

"He was not only my first partner here but my mentor," said Grant, tonelessly.

"I know, Joe. What happened here?"

"The dispatcher said he called in a possible intruder alert on this house."

"Intruder alert? So, why didn't he wait for backup?"

"That's what I can't figure out. That wasn't like Matt to take risks. He must have seen something that stoked him."

"How did he die?"

"I don't know. There's no visible bruising on the body. The autopsy will tell us."

"Where was his body when you arrived?"

"Right here on the sidewalk; but I don't think that's where he was killed. Looked like he had been placed there."

"Forensics pick up anything that you know of?"

"Haven't asked. Matt had his badge, gun, wallet on him. It wasn't robbery unless Matt spooked the robber."

"Go home, Detective."

"I'm going to the hospital, Lieutenant."

"The hospital?"

"Maggie, his wife, is going there. I need to talk to her."

"Okay, I understand. Take Officer Parker with you."

Hawkins turned and looked at Pastor Rodger's home with the police tape around the perimeters. Was this a simple case of a burglary gone south, or something else?

Paul was on the phone with his mother when Jasmine knocked and entered his office in a rush.

"Excuse me, Pastor. There's a huge argument going on in the Trustees room."

"What? Sorry, Mother, I'll have to call you back."

Paul walked into the hall and could hear the loud shouting. He opened the door to the Trustees Office where David was in a heated verbal battle with Claudia. He was so furious he was speaking rapid-fire Spanish, his anger taking him back to his native culture. Claudia, who spoke fluent Spanish as well as French, was not dissuaded by David's Latin temper, giving as good as she got in English and Spanish.

He stood between them. "What is going on in here? Your heard all over the building."

"He's accusing me of being fraudulent," yelled Claudia.

"I'm not accusing you of anything. I'm telling you you're a liar!" yelled David.

"You can't call me a liar when you have no proof!"

"This is all the proof I need. Liar!"

Paul raised his voice to a small roar. "Shut up! Both of you!"

He looked at Claudia. She was clearly distraught. Few things could knock her off her proverbial ice float. Claudia's spiritual calling involved anything to do with money. As finance director, she was the second signature on church checks behind David. The finance activities kept her on the church grounds throughout the week.

"What's going on?" Paul asked. He saw David was sweating.

"Pastor David is accusing me of cooking the books."

"Cooking the what?"

Claudia looked at David who was quiet for the moment. "What it means Pastor is I'm being accused of manipulating our financial records."

"Hypothetically, why would you do that?"

Claudia flailed her arms. "That's my point."

Paul turned to David. "Okay, Dave, what's going on?"

"I'm no fool, Paul. I didn't accuse Sister Claudia of anything yet. I merely asked her with declining income from tithes and offerings, why is the church looking financially solvent when we should not be. That's when the screaming and yelling started."

Claudia was sitting in a chair, softly sobbing. "Show him the receipts, Pastor David."

The fight seemed to have gone out of David. He handed Paul a stack of papers.

"These are copies of bank statements for the last quarter. Look at the amounts circled in yellow markings."

Paul scanned the documents and gulped. The room shrunk. He sat down at the table. Claudia continued crying. David loosened his tie and sat in the other chair.

"Pastors, I swear I did not write those checks nor approved such figures. I swear on the Bible I did not do this. Someone is setting me up."

Paul looked at David. "What do you suggest Dave?"

"I have a meeting with the bank manager who services our accounts in an hour or so," said David.

"Naturally."

"What I suggest is having Trustee Martin begin to look for the discrepancies. Is that all right with you, Sister Claudia?" She nodded. "Okay, work with him on it. You're the president. Trust no one. Okay?"

She nodded and tears sprung up again. David gave her his handkerchief.

"Let's keep this in this office," said Paul, "and let the trustee know not to share any information with anyone."

David looked at Paul's retreating figure. "Where are you going?"

"To see Nick at the hospital. Lisa brings him home next week. I'm marrying them today. Trying to put out fires before they start. Call me if you need me. Jasmine's coming with me."

When Paul and Jasmine entered Nick's hospital room, the first-person Paul saw was his wife wearing a yellow wrap dress seated in an armchair, and Lisa in a white suit standing by Nick's bed. Nick was looking better. He was proudly showing off his neck brace to the women. Ernest had arrived earlier with the tailored black suit Nick now wore.

"Hello Nick, you look great. How are you feeling?" said Paul as he kissed his wife.

"Like I've been hit with a ton of bricks. Can't move my head too much yet. I must wear this neck brace to keep my neck stiff."

"Your handsome face is intact. That's all I care about," said Lisa.

"Is that all, Lisa?" murmured Ernest in a low voice and giggling.

Lisa blushed a deep red, and Nick laughed out loud. Paul shook his head. Steven and David entered the room. A young nurse came by to read Nick's chart. Ernest handed it to her. They smiled at each other. The falsetto voice was melodious in its pitch.

"Excuse me nurse, when can Mr. Rodgers sign out?"

"His doctor cleared him for next week. When you're ready Mr. Rodgers, we will send a chair for you," she said, gazing at Ernest. "It's hospital rule."

Steven, standing to the side, deepened his voice pitch to a lower than usual scale.

"Pardon me nurse, but where are your vending machines?"

The nurse switched her adoring gaze from Ernest to Steven. Breathing heavily, she managed a reply. "Down the hall."

"Thank you," said Steven, holding the door open for her to pass through.

As he closed it, Monaco and Lisa giggled as quietly as they could. Ernest merely rolled his eyes. Paul laughed and turned his attention to Nick leaning against the hospital bed. Steven stood on Nick's right side to hold him steady, and Ernest stood behind him to catch him should he fall.

Nick and Lisa held hands as Paul recited the wedding oath. Monaco and Jasmine stood to the side of Paul gazing at the couple with misty eyes. The end of the ceremony Paul handed the license to Ernest and Monaco to sign as witnesses, and Steven helped Nick into a chair.

"Ladies if you'll excuse us. We need to talk to Nick alone," said Paul.

Ernest opened the door. "This way, ladies. Don't get lost. The waiting room is at the end of the hall where the snack machines are."

They ignored him. Nick and Paul laughed, and Steven smiled. With the ladies' departure Paul filled the pastors in on the drama with the church accounts.

"I highly doubt Claudia would do something that transparent," said Steven. "I mean, she's well off financially, and she's good with her personal finances. She's helped me with my investment portfolio."

Ernest looked at Steven. "Investment portfolio? Why didn't you come to me?"

"Many reasons. You're pretty, but she's prettier with a much better figure. I can do things with her, I'm not interested in doing with you."

Paul and Nick laughed out loud. Ernest grinned, and waved him off. "Leave me alone, man."

"You took the roller coaster to the top, not me," said Steven. His phone buzzed. "Hey guys, are you good here without me? Claudia's car is in the shop. I'm going to get her."

"All's good, Steve. Tell Claudia not to worry. We'll figure out what's going on."

"Tell her I said hello," said Nick, weakly.

"You got it, and congratulations," said Steven. He and Nick hugged.

"Come on Nick, let's get you back in bed," said Ernest.

Chapter 25

The night nurse checked in on Derrick Hines. He was lying in bed watching a comedy on television. He smiled when he saw the pretty nurse at the door.

"How are you doing tonight, Derrick?" asked Anna, the night nurse.

He waved slightly. "Oh, you know, so-so and more so-so."

They both laughed. "What are you watching?"

"I think it's the Late Show or a corny movie. Take your pick."

"Okay, I will check on you later. You need anything now?"

"No, sweetheart. Thank you. Get off your feet. I'm fine."

The nurse smiled before closing the door. She checked the rooms of her other patients on the floor before retiring to the nurses station. She and Nancy were on duty tonight. It was usually quiet in the Mount Pleasant Nursing Home for Veterans.

"Hey Anna," her partner, Nancy, walked up to the counter. "Are you staying here awhile? I want to take a smoke."

"Oh sure! My group's been inspected. I'll sit here. Enjoy."

Nancy walked down the hall and Anna watched as she sat on the iron bench to the right of the glass double doors. Anna pulled out her phone, located the pinball game she loved playing, and soon was involved in a tournament with hundreds of faceless gamers. The Sleeper waited in the hall closet until both nurses had settled down. The hall lights automatically turning off was his signal to move. He looked down the hall at the front desk. Both nurses now seated at the counter and both on their phones. He crossed to Derrick's door, pushed it inward, and stepped inside. The nurse had returned and shut down the television. He walked to Derrick's bed, and took the extra pillow off the chair. With little effort he smothered him. Checking his watch he crossed back to the hall closet, changed his clothing, and secured his backpack. He set off the fire alarm and waited. In the general melee he calmly, but efficiently, left the premises as one of the male night shift workers.

Hawkins seated in his office in the Police Administration Building greeted Emory, Stewart, and Grant. He beckoned to chairs facing his desk while he looked at his computer screen. A knock on the door and a woman entered. A slow smile spread across the woman's face as Grant walked toward her. They hugged.

Logan Sanders was five foot ten inches of solid woman. A former heavyweight boxer in the Army, she was a firearms specialist. She came in with seven years experience in the police department; all of it working undercover. The blue-eyed blonde earned high marks in hand-to-hand combat.

"Grant, meet your new partner, Detective Logan Sanders. Sanders is coming off vice."

"We graduated the Academy together," said Grant.

"How did your orientation go this morning?" Hawkins asked her.

"Excellent, sir," said Sanders. "Pleased to meet you guys."

Sanders shook Emory and Stewart's hands. Hawkins waited with folded hands on his desk. When they regained their seats, he gave each a folder.

"You four are on special assignment with me until this case is cleared; whether that is next week, next month, or next year."

"Are we still working the older adult murders?"

"The short answer is yes. Nothing has changed but the focus of our investigation. Hot Springs Cathedral Church is our target as all these victims have had or have a connection with it. Study the information in your folders and the pictures provided. We need to find and stop this murderer."

"This is such a heinous, cowardly crime."

"I agree," Hawkins said, looking at his desktop screen. "This is what will happen per direct orders from upstairs. Doesn't matter who gets killed or hurt at Hot Springs Cathedral Church, we are not to report it to the media."

"What?"

"That will be impossible. Calls are radioed out."

"There is a way to receive calls that won't relay across general wire, but I don't know how safe that will be for us when, and if, we need backup."

"Why not just have an operator use a special code only we know? That way every cop in a twenty-mile radius won't be responding."

"Great idea, Stewart."

"Okay," said Hawkins, who had been writing. "I repeat, under no circumstances are interviews given to the media about this case."

"Look me wrap my head around this case. Somebody is killing old people at this church? No other church?"

"No other church."

"Sounds like vendetta killings."

"These people are senior citizens."

"The way they're attacked is hit over the head with a blunt object. A woman could be the murderer. How much strength does it take to wield some heavy object at someone?"

"Or a young person with some kind of vendetta against these older people."

Hawkins interrupted with a cough. "Someone smothered an older man in a nursing home a couple of towns over."

"Did they catch the perpetrator?"

"No."

"I'm going out there to see what happened. Set up the code system, and check the local hospitals."

A knock and a uniformed policewoman handed Hawkins a manila envelope. He opened it, scanned it a minute, and looked at them.

"This is the toxicology report on Sgt. Osborne. Seems he was injected with a fast-acting poison. No pain but instant death."

The silence that followed was deafening.

Nick was released from the hospital in the care of his new wife. Once she had Nick firmly settled in, Lisa set about decorating the house with color and light replacing dark window coverings with light, sheer curtains. There were two doors with specialty locks that used a coding system, and Lisa was curious about them. Nick refused to explain about the locked doors saying it could wait until he was well. Though she was irritated by his response she sensed it was better to allow him his vestige of privacy.

After consultation with Steven, Nick gave her the code for one of the rooms where he kept his technology. In this room he gave her the password to the computer terminal and fax machine. He showed her how to use the phone system as well as the new monitoring system he had installed by Steven after his attack. She was pleased by his trust in her and fascinated by the technology. She forgot about the other room.

Hawkins drove the two hours away to Exeter Township where the Mount Pleasant Nursing Home for Veterans was located. He met with the two regular night shift nurses on duty that evening. Neither had seen nor heard anything out of the ordinary. The nurses were still shaken by the incident. The nursing home facility installed a security monitoring system and hired a security company. The doctor, specialized in geriatric medicine, pronounced the eighty-two-year-old Derrick Hines 'healthy as a horse,' and confirmed asphyxiation as the cause of his death. He showed Hawkins on microfilm the two broken ribs in the victim's chest that had been crushed by his attacker. Hawkins examined the man's room and found nothing out of place. On his way out the room he glanced down and spotted on a low table a black binder Bible and a workbook. He looked inside. Hawkins called Hot Springs Cathedral Church and left a message for Paul.

Chapter 26

Trustee Glenn Martin lived in a renovated mansion a half mile from the church he had attended all his life. With over sixty-years' experience in the world of finance, Glenn listened silently as Claudia explained the problems with the forged checks, church ledgers, and the accounting system. He asked her pertinent questions, and made one request, which she granted. Later, in his office at home, researching the reported discrepancies, something caught his eye among the numbers. He peered closer. There was a telltale sign he had seen once before. It was an involuntary tic in the handwriting, and one person possessed that tic. He walked to his desk and pulled out an old photo album. He turned to a selected page. His finger trailed the page of anecdotes, poems, and well wishes. He peered closer. Ah, yes! The telltale tic. He looked down at the photograph with the signature beneath it with sorrow. He called Claudia's home number. After the third ring, he sighed, and left a message for her to call him. A shadow fell across the page. Glenn looked up too late into the face of his murderer. A look of hurt and disbelief crossed his handsome face before his life was violently snuffed out. His body slumped across his desk and slid to the floor leaving a bloody trail. The Sleeper removed the evidence that had caught the man's attention.

The next morning Paul was in his office when Jasmine knocked and entered.

"Good morning, Sister Jasmine. May I help you with something?"

"Mr. Jones wants to see you right away in the back hall. He says it's urgent."

"Okay, thanks. Here take this USB. I'll be right back."

Paul found Harold Jones of Jones Cleaning Crew in the back hall. Harold was the grandson of the original Harold Jones. He was seventy-five years old and the last of his lineage. The older man stood with his hat scrunched in his hand in his faded gray overalls and loose pullover. He looked to Paul as if he were about to burst into tears.

"Good morning, Brother Jones. How can I help you?"

Harold could not speak, only point with a gnarled finger toward the broom closet. Paul pulled the door wider. Inside was the crumpled, bloodied body of Glenn Martin.

Grant and Sanders examined the body in the closet. The medical examiner had taken him out of the closet. Other than the split skull, neither the medical examiner nor the detectives could find any other wounds on the body. Harold was questioned and released. Paul sent Jasmine home and fended off news reporters as he headed home. The church closed for the day as police, medical technicians, media, and attention seekers laid siege on the embattled church grounds. Later that evening, Paul and his ministry team returned for intercessory prayer on the church grounds. Monaco insisted on coming with him. The women ministers and deaconesses were thrilled to see her and embraced her into their women's prayer circle.

Paul was lounging in the living room absently turning channels on the television remote. Monaco was not feeling well, and Paul had made her lie down. The door bell rang. Charles was standing on his doorstep.

In the living room Charles talked about the relationship between the pastor and the community. He stopped when he saw the look of resignation on Paul's face.

"Look son, you're facing wicked machinations, but you can't grow weary. Your congregation is looking to your leadership and spiritual strength. Not to mention your pastors need to see in the man of God those prophets of old who relied on the sovereign power of God."

"Just seems like a Pandora's box of evil has been unleashed on the church."

"It has,"Charles confirmed. "Now what are you going to do about it?"

"Pray," replied Paul. "Prayer changes things,; provides comfort and healing."

"I don't disagree, but you also have to think about the earthly safety of your congregation."

"What?" repeated Paul.

"This is a large congregation, Paul. Trustees being murdered, pastors injured, and now losing Glenn. You're going to have to devise a plan to keep the church solvent, while protecting your congregation and its leadership."

"The financial aspect I'm not concerned with because that's David's area."

"Oh, of course not! Highly competent man. Listen, Paul, while we are on the subject of planning, I would like to ask your permission to ask your mother to marry me."

Paul stared at him without full comprehension. The elder pastor waited. Paul swallowed and looked out the window.

"Mother's been alone a long time. She raised me and my sister without a stepfather. Are you sure you can manage an independent woman like my mother?"

Charles smirked. "It's not about 'managing' another human being, Paul. She and I are kindred spirits. I don't need to control her, nor does she need to play the bimbo with me. I'm asking your permission out of respect for your role as her eldest son. She may say no. But if she says yes, I want your blessing beforehand without condemnation or hesitance."

Paul smiled. "Mother does deserve happiness. I know she gets lonely which is why she spoiled my sister rotten."

"I have a feeling a certain pastor under your church roof has plans for your sister."

"Yeah, she and David have been seeing each other." Paul stood up. "As for you and Mother, I wish you both the best."

Charles smiled. The men shook hands.

During Sunday services Paul informed the congregation of a church-wide meeting to be held that evening. The news spread fast. By that evening, the parking lot was crowded with vehicles.

A knock-on Paul's private door and Steven entered. "You ready?"

"Yes."

Steven nodded. "Let's go. Showtime."

Paul adjusted the collar of his jacket, and followed Steven to the pulpit. The congregation hushed as Paul walked across the platform. The organist crept down to the pews. There were murmurings among the applause from the congregation. Paul raised his hand for silence.

"I understand the great fear you all have, and I want to assure you that no bad deeds go unpunished on God's children. The culprit will be caught. Our church deacons have implemented safety procedures, and we are going to need your full cooperation until this thing is over. We will be holding prayer vigils every night this week. I ask currently that you group up. Try to move about in groups. Leave no one behind. Watch out for each other. Any questions or concerns, please contact the local police department."

As Paul continued with the meeting Monaco looked around worriedly. Why would anyone want to attack Nick? Her godmother Mary, seated behind her, reached out and touched her shoulder. Monaco laid her head on Mary's hand. Mary's other hand stroked her hair. The older ladies looked solemnly at Monaco. They understood her fears. Thank God for Deaconess Mary, her godmother. At least she had someone to look after her in these dark, troubled days. Seated among the congregation the tender moment between the old deaconess and the young pastor's wife was observed without emotional attachment by the Sleeper.

Mid-week Paul was in his church office writing a eulogy for Glenn Martin when his desk phone buzzed

"What is it, Sister Jasmine?"

"Pastor, Detective Grant is on line four for you."

"Good morning, Pastor Mouton. I need you to come down to the Police Administration Building today."

"Why? I have a job to do, same as you."

"I understand that Pastor, but my job is finding the murderer who is plaguing your church. To that end, I need to see you down here."

"I'm sorry, Detective, you're right. You need me to do that today?"

"Yes Pastor, today. It's urgent at this point."

"Okay, let me phone my wife and I will be there by late this afternoon."

"Thank you, Pastor."

Paul was leaving the police station less than an hour later when he met David in the parking lot.

"You were sent for I gather?" asked Paul.

"Yeah, what is going on? It's like someone wants the church to be destroyed with all this."

"Yes, it's deliberate. Martin's death is ricocheting this insanity."

"How much should I tell them?" asked David, twirling his Panama hat before placing it on his head.

"I talked to Nick before I came here. Let them talk. I did. They don't know about the entangled finances yet. I think that's why they're calling us in. Hoping one of us mentions it as Martin's body was found on church premises."

"Ernest saw the autopsy and police reports, Paul. Glenn was killed in his home, and transported to the church. "

"What's the matter, Dave? I know that look."

"Steven, Ernest, and I checked out the victim's home. He had a study without a laptop or any kind of financial records."

"Someone killed him and stole incriminating evidence."

"It has to do with what we're working on but so far, we can't find the glitch," said David with a sigh. "I'm beginning to think we need to run these trustees backgrounds."

"Personal vendetta for some imagined wrong?"

"Hey! Nothing beats a failure but a try, my friend!"

"I don't know whether that's good news or bad news at this point."

David sighed. "Have you spoke to Sister Claudia yet?"

"Yes. She's pretty upset about Glenn. Go on in. We'll talk later. I'm sure they're watching us."

"Gotcha, call you later."

Hawkins surveyed the pastors from a two-way window in the hallway of the building's second floor. Pastor Mouton's back was to him and the other pastor's face was obscured by the brim of the Panama hat he wore. Hawkins timed their conversation. Ten full minutes.

THE PASTORS

Chapter 27

Clara Whitfield was always inquisitive what her husband kept in the locked box in his bottom right desk drawer. She heard him on the phone earlier. He had left the house ten minutes ago. She waited another five minutes. Over the fifty-nine-year run of their marriage, she had learned that if her husband after a fifteen-minute time span, did not return home for some forgotten item, he was going to keep going to his destination. She found the locked key in one of his coat pockets. The drawer contained one ledger. She opened it and read the names all the way to the bottom. Clara had retired as an elementary schoolteacher. After forty-five years of teaching algebra and geometry to high schoolers, she had become adept at catching mistakes and mathematical quirks. She saw the mistakes immediately and caught the quirk later. But the numbers looked odd. In fact, this was not their household ledger at all. She looked at the front of the ledger and read the stamped imprint. A look of alarm mingled with confusion spread across her delicate face. Oh, no! A shadow fell across the desk, and she looked up into the face of the killer who took her life and the ledger. Her husband walked in the room as her lifeless body was laid under the covers in their bedroom. Raoul had no time to react. For fifty-nine years they had withstood the struggles and triumphs that came with life and marriage. It was fitting that they should see death together as well.

Sanders, with Grant in the passenger seat, stopped their police car alongside a patrol vehicle. They pulled on hazmat suits. They walked up the long driveway to the house surveying the grounds along the way. Beautiful shrubbery and the lawn looked well cared for. The porch was neat and tidy. Inside the home, the downstairs area looked more like a museum with the number of knick-knacks on shelves and table tops. The home was well-lived in. Family photos lined the mantel and a wall-in curio stand. The detectives looked toward the stairs. A police officer was walking towards them.

"Hey guys, the couple's upstairs. Looks like they're asleep until you see the blood on the pillows and bed frame."

"Who are they?" asked Sanders.

"Raoul and Clara Whitfield."

"Ages?"

"She's eighty-two and he's eighty-five years."

"Who found them?" asked Grant.

"Daughter over there." He pointed to a woman sitting in the kitchen with another officer. "Her name's Susan Whitfield Smith."

"Thanks, Mark," said Grant.

Upstairs in the master bedroom they find the couple lying side by side. They appeared to be asleep. Walking closer they saw the heavy blood splatter on the pillows and headboard. They had met their fate in the bed.

The daughter was a younger version of her father but with the thick, shoulder-length auburn hair of her mother. She sat at the kitchen counter with her hands resting in each other and tears lightly forming in her hazel eyes. They heard noise. A young man had entered the home. The woman ran to the man, and they hugged. Grant and Sanders situated them both in the living room.

"I'm Susan Whitfield Smith and this is my husband, Robert."

"Mr. and Mrs. Smith, Detectives Grant and Sanders."

"We understand you found your parents, Mrs. Smith?"

"Yes."

"What time did you arrive?"

"I got here a little past nine-thirty."

"What made you come here?"

"Mom wasn't answering the phone. I had called Dad, and he told me he was at the store. When he said Mom was home, I thought she might have fallen, and hurt herself or something. She always answered her phone. Always."

"Had she fallen or hurt herself previously?"

"No. It's just she's such a tiny little woman, I've always felt protective of her."

"What time was it when you first called your mother?"

"Oh, maybe about six o'clock or so. I was cleaning the kitchen and making sure our boys took baths. They're at the age where water is a repellant. Supervision is a must."

Sanders smiled. "When did you call your mother again?"

Susan sighed. Her husband, holding her hand, was staring off in space. "I guess maybe an hour or so later."

"Where were you, Mr. Smith while your wife was cleaning the kitchen and supervising your sons' baths?" asked Grant.

"Getting an oil change and changing the flat on my wife's car. I was at the mechanic when she called me to say Mom and Pop weren't answering their phones."

"What time was that, Mr. Smith?"

"A little past eight o'clock. I know that because that's when Derek, my mechanic, finished with the tire and began working on the oil pan."

"What did you do when the car was ready?"

"I came home to my wife. Sue was pretty upset by this time."

"What time was it?"

"I don't know exactly. Sue wanted to come over here. I stayed home with the boys."

Sanders turned to Susan "What happened when you got here?"

"What I thought odd was that Dad had returned home yet no one was still answering the house phone or their cell phones."

"How do you know your father had returned home?"

"His car was in the driveway. It's the black Volvo. I called the police and waited, but I couldn't wait for them. I came inside."

At this point, Susan broke down and could not continue though she tried hard. Grant had the medical staff look at her. Sanders spoke quietly with the husband in a corner. As the detectives were leaving the home, Hawkins was pulling up. He waited for them leaning on the hood of his car. He listened to the crime details silently.

"What church do they belong to?" was his only question. The detectives looked at each other.

Wearily, Hawkins said, "could one of you please go ask?"

Sanders, eyeing Grant, returned inside. Grant looked at Hawkins who was in dark track sweats. Sanders returned.

"Their church is Hot Springs Cathedral Church in Oakland Heights. They were church trustees. The wife is eighty-two-years old, and the husband eighty-five-years old."

Hawkins looked around at a news truck that had just arrived. "Keep all this information out of the media."

David walked into his home and sat down by the front door. He looked about the house. David had earned his money the hard way through grit, determination, and sacrifice. He became a millionaire as a teenager playing the stock market. He was now a multi-millionaire, and last time he checked finance periodicals, considered one of the richest men in the world. Not bad for a Puerto Rican kid from the Bronx, New York.

He sighed. He was lonely, incredibly lonely. For all his wealth, he had no one to share it with. He was tired of playing the field. He wanted to come home to someone. He fell in love with Raquel by accident. He was supposed to meet a blind date set up by Ernest when he spied the most beautiful woman he had seen in a long time. Their eyes met and hers flashed with annoyance as she turned her head. From that moment on, he had to have her. It took time. Lots of time but he was patient. For the first time in a long time, he felt alive again.

He had asked Raquel to spend the weekend, but she had refused saying she wanted to be home with her mother. He had not seen her except in church. He longed to see her, to touch her and kiss her. He called her, but she was not home according to Jayne. Where could she be?

He decided to drive to her home. As he pulled up he saw Raquel getting out of her car with an armful of books and her tablet. He rushed to help her.

"Hi David," said Raquel.

"Hello, my love. What are these for?"

"Mystery novels to read this weekend."

"Why not bring your mother over to my home. You know I would make her comfortable there."

Raquel looked at David. "What are you talking about?"

"I was thinking of what you said earlier. You and your mother can spend the weekend at my house from now on. I was thinking you should move in."

"David, we are dating. I am not your wife. Spending every weekend and part of the workweek at your house is becoming too much."

"We love each other. I want to be with you all the time. Don't you want to be with me the same way?"

"Yes, I agree. We do love each other. But we aren't married. I'm not going to pretend to be your wife. I'm your girlfriend!"

"Okay, okay, calm down," said David. "Can we go to dinner? I saw a new restaurant that just opened on the highway near Palmer Drive."

Raquel slammed down the trunk of her car. "No! Go home! Leave me alone." She ran into her house in tears.

David was confused and angry. What just happened?

Chapter 28

Claudia was a conscientious professional. Her expertise in financial and business matters were keys to her successful career. Tonight though sleep eluded her. She paced her bedroom trying to recapture the moment when Trustee Martin had had his eureka. He had phoned her excitedly about his finding, and afterward, she had heard nothing for the rest of the evening. She had been busy in Steven's arms and had not bothered to return his text messages until the following morning. By then, it was too late, the trustee was dead. Spending time with the handsome psychologist and pastor had been rewarding. But now she had to put her well-honed financial skills to use. Claudia slowly walked downstairs to the kitchen. There was a glitch, and she believed, based on the quiet excitement in Glenn's voice when he'd left the message on her answering service, that he had resolved the matter. She opened a bottle of wine, and it hit her. Why not input the data into her home computer? A half-hour later she struck gold. The answer had been in front of her all this time. She needed to call the pastor. She noted the time. Oh! Well, she should wait until morning to speak with him anyway. In the meantime, she would text him her intentions.

Hi Pastor, this is Sister Claudia. Good morning to you and First Lady. I wanted to inform you I believe I have found the identity of the person behind the missing money. I will be in your office around nine in the morning. I hope I'm wrong. See you soon, Sister Claudia.

Claudia lived in a three-bedroom, two-bath chalet-style home she bought when she was twenty-two-years old. The value of the property had continued to double over the years. It was soon to triple with the continued expansion of the area under gentrification. But for all her intellectual savvy, Claudia omitted safety in her portfolio of personal needs. As she walked up the stairs to her bedroom, she met someone standing in the dark on the top landing. As she opened her mouth to scream, the uplifted arm came down with great force causing her to fall over the side of the railings to the floor below. The Sleeper ran down the stairs to finish her off, and heard someone coming inside. He ran back upstairs and left through the window.

The alarm on Steven's wristband informed him an illegal entry was occurring in Claudia's home. With his heart pumping, he sped through backstreets pushing the Porsche past its' celebrated speed. He easily entered her residence cursing silently to himself. He saw Claudia's crumbled body at the foot of the stairs. She had a gash on the side of her forehead and a broken right arm. Steven set her broken arm, and bandaged her head. He picked her up, and carried her outside to his car where he deposited her in the back seat. Wrapping her in blankets he returned inside the house. There was a faint gaseous odor at the top of the stairs. After checking the bedrooms and baths, he found her desktop shut down, and both laptops missing. Claudia's phone was missing, including the extra one. Steven sent David a text to track the laptops and phones. When he heard police sirens, he poured dissolving fluid on the back of the desktop, and exited the residence.

The police forensic team was busy dusting for evidence when Hawkins drove up. Police were putting up barricades and tape. He did not see the medical examiner. He hastily pulled on a hazmat suit, and walked into the home. He automatically knew a single woman lived there by the soft, muted wall colors, the pastel-colored furniture, and vases of flowers everywhere. The downstairs area was immaculate with nothing out of place. Hawkins walked through the dining room to the eat-in kitchen. No signs of a struggle. Where was the body?

Hawkins retraced his steps to the front of the house. In the hall, Hawkins stooped and assessed the blood spot on the floor. Looking up he saw the broken railing. He walked up the stairs slowly. He looked over the railing to the floor below. He walked through the bedrooms and baths.

Nothing was out of place. Hawkins returned downstairs, and followed the trail of police.

Grant and Stewart were in hazmat suits. The room was a nice size and appeared to have been an office. There was no equipment other than a landline phone and a desktop. He smelled something like leaking gas. Where was the body? A police officer appeared.

"Detective, the medic wants to leave as there's no body present."

Grant looked at the officer. "What do you mean there's no body present?"

"We didn't locate a body here. The victim's probably already been taken to the hospital."

Grant walked away, pulling out his phone.

"How did we receive a tip to come to this residence?" asked Hawkins, standing in the doorway.

"Anonymous caller," responded the officer. "So, it's okay for the medics to leave?"

"Yeah." Hawkins wearily waved the officer away.

Grant returned. "The three local hospitals have reported no check-ins"

"Okay, Stewart. I know the look. What is it you've found? Top secret missile contracts?"

"You might wish that after I tell you my findings here. This desktop was not only cleanse bare of data, but dissolving fluid was used to permanently destroy the hard drive."

"Somebody's covering something up."

Emory entered the room. "Another pastor?"

"Not this time. A member of the congregation."

"Kelly told me there's no body?"

They both heard a soft whistle. Grant had walked into the room. He found a photo in a gold edged frame on a low table.

"What a beautiful woman."

The detectives looked over Grant's shoulder at the photo.

Emory smirked. "Who takes a picture with your lady wearing dark glasses?"

"Someone who doesn't want to be easily recognized," said Stewart.

Hawkins, had quietly entered the room, and overheard the conversation. He pondered that statement as he gazed at the photo. Sanders walked in.

Grant looked at her. "Where were you?"

"Doing police work. That man across the street has been on this block about nineteen years. His name is Carl Peterson, age 42. Wife's name is Marge."

"Okay? Did he see or hear something?" asked Emory.

Sanders rolled her eyes. "He said he heard a scream and looked out his bedroom window. He saw what he believes was a shadow man coming out of the side of the house over here. He called the police and when he returned to his window he saw another shadow man coming out of the house carrying the woman."

"Shadow men?" said Stewart, with a hint of laughter in his voice.

"He couldn't describe them because both were dressed in dark colors and moved fast," continued Sanders. "They may have had vehicles but he didn't see or hear any."

"Where did the man go carrying the woman?"

"He said they disappeared behind the trees."

"Oh, Brother!"

"The lady's car is still parked in her garage."

"There's blood on the hall floor so we know she's injured."

"Kidnapping ring?"

"By who? Why?"

"We found a body at the church a few weeks ago. Does this lady attend that church?"

"Who's her next of kin?"

"Hold on a second," Sanders found a purse she opened that was sitting on a chair. She read the driver's license. "Her name is Claudia Ginyard, and next of kin is Steven Barnes, Ph.D."

"Address?"

"None. Just a phone number."

Grant picked up a white Bible. "Hot Springs Cathedral Church bulletins. There's a floral ink pen with the church name on it."

Hawkins took the driver's license and walked away.

Steven guided Ernest to his bedroom where Claudia laid on the bed. Ernest checked her arm for other broken or damaged limbs, and applied a splinter and cast. He lightly cleansed and gave Claudia light stitches for her head wound. He gave her shots for pain and infection. Steven tucked her in, set the monitor on in case she woke up, and left the room with Ernest.

"How's she looking?"

"Here's a couple of painkillers but only give to her if she complains too long, and too loud about pain. Her arm will heal. It was a clean break."

"I got there just in time. He was going to finish her off."

"Damn."

"Right."

"You keeping her here?"

"Yes, for the time being."

"Okay, man, I'm out. Get some sleep. She will sleep for at least twenty-four hours. You have classes tomorrow?"

"No, not this week. Thanks."

"Call me if you need me."

Steven set the alarms. He took a shower. Turned on his surveillance cameras, lowered the lighting, and laid down beside Claudia. In a moment he was sleeping soundly.

David was downstairs in his laboratory checking through the information they had gathered so far at the crime scene involving Nick. He looked at the photographs he had processed and in one set he saw a shoe image. The print was light but if he could magnify the caption, he might be able to examine the sole of the shoe marking in detail. He remembered the random samples he had collected from Paul. The footprint in the grass did not match the other print, but he would compare it more closely with his first print. The tiny thread he put on his microscope with fluid.

David felt the light vibration on his arm and looked at the message.

Claudia attacked. Both laptops and phones missing!

Without blinking, David moved to a keyboard and typed a set of coordinates assigned to Claudia's laptops. His screen showed they self-destructed after three failed attempts to open them. He checked the phones and saw someone was attempting to open them. He destroyed the main frames on both phones and waited. After a few seconds he locked into the coordinates. The phones had disintegrated. He sent a return text message.

Laptops and phones destroyed. No info leaked.

After a glance at his wall clock, he returned to his samples. It was only two in the morning. He would be in bed in two hours. Tomorrow was another day.

Chapter 29

The next morning seated in an interview room in the Oakland Heights Police Station Paul and Nick waited for the detectives' arrival. A police officer brought the pastors coffee and Danish. Paul, for want of something to do, typed out a sermon on his phone. Nick sat in quiet contemplation watching the passing traffic outside the open door. Grant walked into the room and sat across from them. He had Paul's phone and another phone placing both on the table.

"Do you recognize this phone, Pastor Mouton?"

"It looks like mine."

"What distinguishes it from say, this black one here?"

"The one I'm claiming as mine has my initials etched in black on the cover."

"Okay. I'm going to play a recording. I need you to verify its accuracy."

Grant looked at Nick who was staring at him with a placid look. Grant turned on the phone recorder.

Hi Pastor, this is Sister Claudia. Good morning to you and First Lady. I wanted to inform you I believe I have found the identity of the person behind the missing money. I will be in your office around nine in the morning. I hope I'm wrong. See you soon, Sister Claudia.

He looked at Paul. "Do you recognize the voice on the recording, Pastor?"

"Sounds like Sister Claudia Ginyard."

"What missing money is she referring to Pastor?"

"Something she was working on."

"Did Sister Ginyard come to your office the next morning?"

"No."

"Have you heard this phone recording before now, Pastor?"

"Yes."

"What did you do after you heard it?"

"I waited for Sister Ginyard."

"Did she ever show up?"

"No."

"Did you call her?"

"No."

"Why not?"

"Because I assumed she would call me when she was free. She works full time, Detective."

"She made the appointment time?"

"Yes, she did."

"Let's talk about Derrick Hines. Are you aware he's dead?"

"His social worker recently notified the church of his death."

Grant nodded his head. "Was Mr. Hines a trustee, deacon, or both?"

"Trustee," said Paul quietly.

"Had you met him when you came on board, Pastor?" asked Hawkins.

"If I did, I don't remember him."

Grant laid a worn Bible and a workbook with a faded cover on the table, pushing it toward Paul.

"Have you seen the workbook before?"

Paul nodded. "That's the workbooks we use for our Bible studies classes."

"Could you explain how he obtained this workbook?"

"That's an old workbook, Detective. Look inside at the date," replied Paul.

Grant looked inside. The date was twelve years earlier. He looked up at the pastors who were watching him. He called the front desk.

Hawkins entered with two young men and closed the door. Paul and Nick stood up. They were face to face with Stewart and Emory, the young men who had joined the church. Hawkins spoke first.

"Pastors, these young men are detectives with Major Crimes Task Force in Chicago. Meet Clay Stewart and Rick Emory. You know them as the young men who are members in your church and men's ministry."

"Pastors, please be seated," said Grant, who had not stood up. Nick and Paul sat down. A police officer brought in two chairs which Emory and Stewart sat in. The door opened and a chair was handed to Hawkins, who remained standing.

"How do you do, gentlemen?" said Paul. "How can the church help you without compromising her mission?"

"Pastor, we're here to investigate the deaths of Victor, and Cynthia Valentine; your wife's late parents," said Hawkins.

"They were in a car accident," said Paul, staring at them with wide-eyed amazement. "Are you saying it was something else?"

"The Valentines worked for the federal government."

"Okay, but it's my understanding they were retired. But even if they weren't, what does any of this have to do with the church?" asked Paul.

"We don't know yet. But what we do know is that the Valentine's were trustees in that church," said Hawkins.

Emory spoke to Paul. "When my partner and I arrived at the home of Claudia Ginyard, another trustee at the church, I had the distinct impression someone else had been there previous to us."

Paul stared at Emory. "Why were you at Sister Ginyard's home? Has something happened to her beyond all this?"

"We don't know," replied Hawkins. "We have not been able to locate her. We thought you might know where she is."

Paul shook his head. "I have no idea what your talking about."

Nick intervened. "We were unaware Sister Ginyard was missing. Why do you believe she is?"

"We received a phone call that there was a disturbance. When the police arrived the front door was open, there was blood on the floor, and she was nowhere to be found," said Hawkins, watching Paul closely.

Paul shrugged. "I can't help you."

Stewart, usually quiet, spoke up. "We think one of your staff may have been with her before she disappeared."

Nick spoke directly to Hawkins. "Unless you're bringing charges against my client, we're leaving."

172

"We would like to keep the identities of these detectives secret for now."

Emory and Stewart looked at Hawkins who was looking at Paul who had put his face in his hands. When Hawkins remained silent, Nick tapped Paul on the shoulder, and they left. Hawkins did a slow half-smile and turned to the detectives.

"Find out all you can on Dr. Steven Barnes."

"He's a pastor and a psychiatrist. What more is there?" asked Emory.

Hawkins snapped. "First, he's a *psychologist*, professor, and author of best-selling books on criminology and the pseudo-science behind deviancy. Second, he never takes off those dark glasses, and he wears thin hand gloves that don't leave his fingerprints. Last, you always do your research, Detective. The most harmless people turn out to be the deadliest."

Stewart looked at his phone. "Lieutenant, Dr. Barnes is in charge of programs at the church that deal with mental health issues, trauma and crisis. He earned his PhD at Hot Springs University where he teaches an advanced grad course four times a year, and it's mandatory. He was also engaged to Cynda Valentine."

Hawkins cut in. "Thank you, Stewart. Dr. Barnes was seeing the missing woman, and the attorney stopped the line of questioning in that area. They must know or suspect something. We need to know what they know. For all their advanced educations, and dual professions, they are laymen. We are law enforcement."

"Why does the pastor wear those type of gloves? You think his hands are disfigured or something?"

"Maybe that's what's wrong with his eyes, too."

"If that were the case about his eyes, he damn sure wouldn't be driving a Porsche!" said Hawkins, his patience worn thin.

On his way to the Police Administration Building, he put in a call to Hot Springs Cathedral Church where he spoke to Jasmine.

"Good afternoon, Sister Carter, this is Lt. Hawkins at the Police Administration Building. I need to get a message to Pastor Steven Barnes."

"Good afternoon, Lt. Hawkins. What's your message for the Pastor?"

"Tell him I need to speak with him at police headquarters sooner rather than later."

"Okay. Is that all?"

"Yes, and thank you," replied Hawkins.

"You're welcome." She hung up.

Nick was parking his car in the garage when he received the text from Steven that Hawkins had sent for him. Nick looked around the garage. He was a married man coming home to his wife. He liked the feeling, and he loved Lisa. He walked in the back door and smelled the most delicious aroma. He knew she could cook but these days the smells were more than his senses could bear. He found himself working out conscientiously because he was eating more. He smiled at that thought.

Where was she? The house was too quiet. He drew his Glock out of his ankle and deftly scanned the first floor. He checked the alarm system on his wristband. Nothing. He eased up the stairs. He saw her laying on the bed, moving about the room, determined nothing was amiss. She sat up, and he walked over to the bed.

"Oh, hi honey. I'm okay." She smiled happily at him.

"Lie down, Lisa," said Nick sternly. "I'm calling Ernest."

"No, you don't have to do that."

"For the last few weeks, you've been falling asleep any time of the day, and last night I heard you vomiting in the bathroom."

"I'm a woman first, Nick."

"We're lawyers, baby, not doctors."

"I know that. That's why I saw Lydia this morning."

"Lydia? Who's Lydia?"

"You've met her before. Dr. Lydia Khan."

Nick looked confused and scared. "Doctor?"

"Dr. Khan is my obstetrics-gynecologist, or OB-Gyn. I'm pregnant, or we're pregnant."

Nick pulled Lisa to him, burying his face in her neck and shoulder. She wrapped her arms around him. They sat still holding on to each other.

Steven received Jasmine's message, but was busy changing Claudia's bandage on her head. One side of her face was bruised, but the swelling had gone down. He checked the light cast on her arm before carrying her downstairs to the kitchen. She had developed a healthy fear of being alone, and he was only too happy to accommodate her. He alerted Nick regarding Hawkins summons, and they set a time to meet at the police station. He kissed Claudia, and set about preparing dinner for himself, and his fiancée.

Chapter 30

Ernest and Jasmine lived on a tree-lined street directly across from an open field. The five bedroom home had four bathrooms and sat in the middle of a five-home row of residential property. When their widowed mother passed, Ernest brought his younger sibling to his home where she had remained ever since. Ernest loved his younger sister because she reminded him of their mother, not just in physical looks, but also personality. He knew she was falling in love with the young man, and he had sized up Emory. He was certain it was a mutual attraction, but he preferred them to slow it down.

Tonight, Ernest seated in the living room, waited for Emory to bring Jasmine home from a date. He had been tracking Emory's car on his phone. As the young couple walked up to the front door the outside flood-lights snapped on illuminating them. Ernest opened the front door and stood there. Emory shook Jasmine's hand. Jasmine was furious with her older brother for embarrassing her with his obnoxious behavior. She flounced past him into the house to her room. Ernest closed the door unfazed.

Steven entered the Hot Springs Police Administration Building and asked the desk sergeant for Hawkins. The sergeant had another officer walk him to the office where Hawkins was writing on a legal-size notepad. The officer knocked and Steven entered. Hawkins stood and shook hands with Steven. Hawkins had to look up with his head leaning back on his neck. Hawkins knew his hands were large, but Steven's hands seemed to engulf his. As soundlessly as he entered his office, Hawkins suspected his feet were in sneakers.

Hawkins asked, "I'm six feet three inches tall. How tall are you?"

"Apparently, taller," said Steven, and smiled.

"You wear your dark eye shades all the time?"

Steven smiled but the shades remained. "You asked me to come down?"

"Have a seat please, Pastor. This is not formal by any means. Just a conversation."

Steven remained silent. Hawkins noted the expensive black striped suit, white silk shirt, black silk tie, and the onyx shirt cuffs. Hawkins wore his police uniform.

"You know by now Claudia Ginyard was murdered?" stated Hawkins.

A knock on his door and Nick entered. Steven got up and gave Nick his chair and took the seat closest to Hawkins. There was silence for a minute as Hawkins evaluated the two men.

"Thank you for joining us, Mr. Rodgers, I was expecting you," said Hawkins smiling.

"Thank you," said Nick, but his face remained stoic.

"Where were you on the fifteenth of this month, Dr. Barnes?"

"I believe I was in teaching lectures for most of the day."

"What about the evening of the fifteenth?"

"More than likely in my bed resting."

"What is your relationship with Claudia Ginyard?"

"We've been seeing each other."

"For how long?"

"Several months now."

"When was the last time you spoke to Ms. Ginyard?"

"Sunday evening. We had dinner together."

"What happened afterward?"

"I drove her home."

"What time did you drive her home?"

"Between eight-thirty and eight-forty-five. The Château Restaurant closes at eight-thirty every night but Saturday night."

"Once she was home, what did you do?"

"Drove to my home."

"How long were you at Ms. Ginyard's home when you drove her there from your dinner date?"

"A few minutes."

"What is a few minutes?"

Steven smiled. "Five or ten minutes. I didn't stay."

"When did you become aware Ms. Ginyard was missing?"

"I was not aware she was."

"You were unaware the woman you're dating has been missing for over eight days?"

"Has a missing persons report been filed?" asked Nick.

Hawkins ignored him. "Dr. Barnes, do you have any idea who would want to harm Ms. Ginyard?"

"No."

"Did she have enemies in the church? Had anyone threatened her?"

"Not that I know of."

Hawkins leaned forward on his desk. He took a recorder out of the desk drawer. "I want you to listen to something."

Hi Pastor, this is Sister Claudia. Good morning to you and First Lady. I wanted to inform you I believe I have found the identity of the person behind the missing money. I will be in your office around nine in the morning. I hope I'm wrong. See you soon, Sister Claudia.

Hawkins looked at Steven. "Do you recognize the voice on the recording?"

"It sounds like Sister Ginyard."

"What missing money is she referring to, Dr. Barnes?"

"This recording was not sent to me."

"My sources say otherwise. Pastor Mouton's wife and Ms. Ginyard are related. Cousins on their late mother's side."

"Is there a question?" Nick asked.

"Were Ms. Ginyard and Mrs. Mouton close?"

"I don't know."

"You don't know. You five grew up together. You knew they were cousins. Why jerk me around?"

"Lieutenant, do you have a reason to have Dr. Barnes down here? If not, I'm taking him out of here."

Hawkins glared at Steven. "The question remains, Dr. Barnes. What missing money is she referring to?"

"Pastor Barnes handles church administration," said Nick.

"He's dating the finance director. Did she mention missing money to you, Dr. Barnes?"

"No."

"Gentlemen, it would appear your church has financial improprieties that Ms. Ginyard was working on which put her life in danger. Now we can continue to play this dodge and evade game, or you can help me locate her."

"I cannot tell you what I don't know," said Steven.

"If there are no more questions?"

"Dr. Barnes, for an intimate relationship, you don't speak to Ms. Ginyard every day?"

Nick stood up. "My clients have cooperated with your investigation, and will continue to do so, Lt. Hawkins. These men are merely pastors, and someone is working overtime to destroy the church. If you have nothing else, we are leaving."

Hawkins said, "I have one more question."

Nick remained standing. Hawkins eyed the cane Nick was leaning on. He looked at Steven, still seated.

"What happened to your hands, Dr. Barnes?"

"Nothing that I know of."

"Why do you wear those hand coverings? Is it to hide your fingerprints?"

Steven smiled. "Early onset of arthritis. Keeps my hands warm."

Hawkins stared at Steven, which was an arduous task since the black eye shades were opaque and covered most of his face.

"If you have nothing else significant to ask my client, we are leaving now."

Hawkins waved them away and sat back in his chair. He listened to the taped recording of the interview. What was he missing?

In the parking lot, Nick relayed his news of impending fatherhood to Steven. The men embraced.

"Man, that was quick! Weren't you married like two minutes ago?" asked Steven, smiling.

Nick's face was sporting a large grin. "Man, I'm so happy I don't know what to do."

"Take care of yourself ,so you can be around for little Nick or Nicole. Second, Lisa's your wife now, keep her safe. In-between pregnancies, teach her how to defend herself against physical assault."

"I caught the 'in-between pregnancies' snippet," remarked Nick, still grinning.

Steven gave a soft chuckle. "I knew you would. Everything is set up in the house, including the alarms. The guys left you a honeymoon present in the kitchen. Now that she's pregnant though, you'll have to wait a few months. When are you moving in?"

"The weekend. You guys coming over?"

"Saturday evening, okay?"

"Yes. Everyone will be there."

Together, they looked at their buzzing wristbands.

Please relay message to Pastor Ernest that his sister was in a car accident. I'm with her at the hospital. Emory

Chapter 31

What a long and crazy day. Jasmine had been crying off and on for most of the day. She could not believe Claudia might be dead. Why was the murderer doing this to the church? Jasmine texted Steven the message from Paul advising him to be careful. She gathered her belongings, and locked the office door behind her. She fairly ran down the long hall to the exit door. Deacon Hancock, standing watch inside the church on guard duty, waved to her as he reset the alarm. Jasmine sprinted to her vehicle locking herself in. She was driving down the one lane street before she noticed how close a large dark vehicle was behind her. She turned a corner in case he was following her. She looked in her rearview mirror. The large vehicle was following her, and gaining speed! In a moment of panic, Jasmine hit the accelerator and tried to outdistance the vehicle, but it gained steadily on her. She drove onto the highway hoping to lose him in the evening traf- fic. In her panic she entered the wrong ramp, heading back towards the church. She saw the shadow of the large vehicle and in a state of blind panic she took another exit ramp leading to a bridge off the beaten path. Here the larger vehicle easily overtook her smaller car pushing it over the guard rails to the valley below. Jasmine closed her eyes and prayed. The car, thrown onto the rocks, caught fire, and exploded in a haze of rocks, rubble, gray smoke, and heat. Jasmine had not had time to buckle her seat belt. Her body was hurled from the vehicle with such force she lost con- sciousness. She was dimly aware of someone carrying her. She struggled to open her eyes. People were speaking, there was a siren, and someone was holding her hand. Her beeping phone, laying wedged between rocks on the embankment, received a text message.

Jasmine, this is Pastor Paul. Please go home immediately. Do not return to the church until this is over. Be safe and text me once you're home safely.

When Paul and Monaco arrived at Hot Springs Medical Center, they found Ernest in the waiting room. He was unusually quiet. He kept his dark glasses on covering his eyes. Monaco walked over to him, and Paul did not stop her. He had come to understand they had grown up together. There would always be some type of bond, and, as long as his wife was in his corner, he would tolerate some interaction. Monaco sat beside Ernest who turned away from her. Paul stretched out his hand to his wife, and she came to him, and they sat together. Steven walked in, looked at Paul and Monaco, and sat beside Ernest. Paul could not hear what Steven said, but Ernest rose and followed Steven to the elevators.

Monaco was crying. "Oh Paul, this is awful! Why attack Jasmine?"

"What makes you think it was an attack? Could have just been a car accident."

"Paul, I'm scared. Seems a lot is happening to church members. Suppose that driver was trying to seriously hurt Jasmine?"

"I gave her time off with pay until this is over."

"There's Brother Rick who brought her in," said Monaco. "Hello, Brother Rick, how is she?"

"Good afternoon, First Lady. The doctor said she will be fine. She was shaken up a bit. I'm taking her home."

"That won't be necessary," said Ernest, behind him.

Nick said, "Paul, do you mind if Monaco and I go visit with Jasmine?"

"No, not at all," replied Paul. He turned to Monaco. "Go see how she's doing, sweetie."

When Nick and Monaco had walked from view, Paul along with Ernest, and Steven, stood in an arc in front of Emory. They turned on their wristbands.

"Mind telling us what happened?" asked Paul.

"When I arrived, I saw her car demolished on the rocks and her belongings on the shoreline near the water, and debris everywhere. There's a narrow road that leads down the side of that embankment and that's how I drove there. I swam out to parts of the vehicle, which had blown into the water, and didn't see her. I looked around and saw where she had landed on the muddy ridge. After checking for any serious injuries, I put her in my car, and drove up to the highway. The medical ambulance was pulling up as I arrived."

"Did you see the accident occur?" asked Paul.

"Were you following her?" asked Ernest.

"How did you know about the narrow inlay?" asked Steven.

Emory looked up at Paul and Steven who dwarfed him, and traveled to Ernest whose skin shone unusually red under the harsh fluorescent lights in the hospital waiting room. He shivered, but before he could speak, he heard Steven's voice, as from a great distance.

"He's drenched. He needs a change of clothes. Interrogation can wait. Rick..."

Emory collapsed. Ernest picked him up from the floor, and hoisted the detective over his shoulder. Steven sent Nick a text. They left the hospital down the emergency fire exit. Nick brought Monaco back to the waiting room and left to take Jasmine home. Monaco put her face in her hands and began crying again. Paul sat beside his wife and pulled her to him.

"Oh, Paul. What is going on? Who is doing this and why?"

"I don't know, baby. I'm as scared as you are because I don't know."

Hawkins standing outside the door of the waiting room, listened to the couple with a heavy heart. He walked away; the heart-wrenching soft sobbing of Monaco filling his senses.

Emory woke in bed under a thick quilt. He was wearing a hospital gown. His head was pounding, and he had the chills. He tried to get up. He heard a voice and looked up.

"I'm glad you woke up," said Ernest, seated in a stuffed chair across the room, reading a book.

"How long have I been out?"

"Three days. You caught a case of the chills wearing those wet clothes. I appreciate you taking care of my sister."

"Is she okay? Is she better?"

Jasmine came to the door with a tray. "I'm all better thanks to you. You've been sick, Rick. My brother and I have been taking care of you."

She set the tray on the side table. "I've made you vegetable soup. I'll make you some lemon tea later."

She left the room. Emory looked at Ernest who was now leaning by the wall staring at him.

"Where am I?" he asked Ernest.

"Our home. My sister takes care of you during the day. I have a meeting to attend, but I'll be back. Eat the soup and get some rest. Your boss knows you're here, too. You can check in with him. Your phone is there on the night stand."

At the door Ernest looked at him. "There's a bathroom in this room. It's over there. I left you a pair of pajamas for when you're better. No walking around. You're not out of the woods yet."

"Why didn't you leave me at the hospital? I could have seen a doctor."

"I am a doctor. See you later."

Emory laid back on the pillows. He closed his eyes, and drifted off to sleep, smiling at the image of the pretty redhead bringing him a tray.

Hawkins shut down his desktop, put on the answering machine, and slipped on his jacket. He was glad to hear from Emory. Grant tried to get the call traced without success.

A knock at his door and Grant and Sanders entered. Hawkins looked at the two detectives.

"It can wait until tomorrow," said Hawkins.

"You wanted us to gather information on these pastors at Hot Springs Cathedral Church," said Grant.

Hawkins sat down. "Alright, Detectives. Speak your piece."

Sanders sat down as well. She shoved a folder across the desk to Hawkins. Inside was a printout of the pastors church salaries. Hawkins looked up at the detectives.

"Are you telling me only Paul Mouton is drawing a salary?"

"Yes," replied Sanders.

Grant shoved a thicker folder across his desk. "Here's the folder of their real careers, and they all do very well financially, including the pastor."

"Where did you get the resumes?"

184

"The church site. But the write-ups came from the news stations. The salaries of the companies they work for is public record access."

"Something else. They all have post office boxes as their addresses," said Sanders.

"Thanks, Detectives."

Once Grant and Sanders left his office, Hawkins remained seated at his desk scanning the folder's contents.

Hawkins studied the grinning profile picture of tan-skinned, blue-eyed Nick Rodgers. It was the face of a winner. Nick was an unbelievably successful tax fraud attorney. He specialized in international business law. Nick's recent status as partner in a multi-billion-dollar firm had made news headlines for several weeks. His personal biography highlighted an upbringing by scholarly parents as an only child in Hot Springs. Hawkins was impressed with his stint in the Army as a Ranger.

He looked at the next profile. David Sanchez, the only son of a hard-working Puerto Rican barber and housewife, grew up in the Bronx, New York. David was not only a certified public accountant, but a multi-millionaire. His business savvy was the subject of curriculums taught in business schools. He looked at the picture of the businessman. David's handsome face wore the intense scowl that was his trademark image, and which Hawkins believed came from his time as a Marine.

Hawkins transferred his attention to Ernest Carter, considered a subject-matter expert in the field of forensic pathology. He had earned numerous scholarships and awards and held honorary doctorates. Ernest was the oldest son of college professors. He had one younger sister who he gained custody upon his widowed mother's death. Hawkins looked at Ernest's profile. His reddish skin coloring and unique red-brown hair color along with the brilliance of his eyes gave him the appearance of a devil as he stared into the camera lenses. Hawkins searched and found one line stating Ernest had been in the Navy.

Hawkins studied the senior pastor's profile picture. As a theologian, he had amassed an incredible amount of education and experience in theology and religion. Third generation pastor. He had written a theoretical book on religion and ethics. It was in its sixth printing. Recently married to hometown beauty who also coincidentally happened to return home after parents sudden deaths. He almost closed the folder before looking for any military service. The pastor had been in the Navy.

But it was Steven Barnes, clinical psychologist, and college professor, who caught and held Hawkins interest. The big man had drafted several best-selling books on criminal deviancy. Hawkins looked at the book he had on the side of his desk. It was Dr. Barnes latest and included more researched cases than his previous books on the subject. This man intrigued Hawkins. Who was he? Even on the jacket back cover, there was no picture of him. No biography of his life. No mention of military service. Yet, Hawkins was certain he had a military background.

Hawkins closed the folder and look out into the dark night sky. He had no doubt these successful men had amassed their success by their own blood, sweat and tears. Yet, someone was trying to destroy the church they pastored and, by the physical attacks on the clergy staff, wanted them out of that church. His job and focus was now seeing to it that these pastors and their families survive through the horror.

The Riviera Restaurant with its purple, green and gold theme was celebrating a Mardi Gras wedding by one of its patrons. Charles and Jayne had enjoyed dinner and dancing to show tunes and were now heading toward her home. Jayne's intentions were to change into lounge wear and read one of the science fiction novels on her nightstand. She was looking forward to a nice quiet evening alone.

Charles was extremely nervous. He wanted to return home to New York but the thought of never seeing Jayne again made him despondent. The suburban home he had shared with his late wife was large, airy, and now, stifling. Until he met Jayne, the loneliness of living a decade without someone to intimately share his heart, his bed, and his life had passed him by. Jayne had secured the first part, and he was praying he could get her to share the remaining two.

Charles parked in the driveway and walked Jayne to her front door. Turning her key in the lock she turned to him with a smile.

"Would you care for coffee, tea, or some wine?" she asked.

"Yes, coffee sounds good," he said.

She hesitated slightly, but they went into the living room where she deposited him. She headed toward the kitchen, and he took the ring box out of his coat pocket. He had been studying the jewelry she wore. He looked at the solitaire diamond ring before placing it back in its box and walked into the kitchen.

She turned around. "I was coming back. Just starting up the espresso machine. I want espresso instead of straight coffee."

"Whatever you prefer is fine with me."

She glanced at him. "Are you okay? You seemed preoccupied at dinner tonight? Is it the problems with the church Paul's tending?"

"Yes, that and other things."

"I've told him he needs to leave, but he's like his father. Stubborn and caring more about others than himself."

"Well Jayne, I wouldn't say..."

"No Charles, it's true. Paul can't behave in that singular, bachelor mind-set he held when he had no one in his life. He's married now. All those murders are taking a toll on Monaco. She's a nervous wreck. I told him the other day it's not good for her to be constantly surrounded by all this danger to him. He could be next."

Charles was quiet as Jayne spoke. He was feeling desperate about how to propose now that she was riled up about her son's marriage and the danger, he was posing to himself.

"Paul is a grown man, and he's in love. He won't let anything happen to his wife. Trust me on that."

"Men are all the same. Stop trying to sell me. She was alone the night she returned to her house, and found it vandalized. He couldn't have helped her if that maniac had caught her."

Charles believed it was in his interest to remain quiet. She loved her son and daughter-in-law. Charles and his wife had never had children. Paul reminded him of the son he had always envisioned having. He did want Paul to return to New York instead of remaining in this town with its antiquated ways. He envied and was wary of these young pastors surrounding Paul. There was something about them when they were together, he could not put his hands on. Those four were always together, although there were several other reverends and about a dozen ministers and elders. He sighed.

Jayne had walked near him. Staring up at him, she offered him a coffee mug. He smiled and placed it on the counter. Taking her in his arms he kissed her. She returned his kiss and tried to push him away. He held onto her. Her pleasant face turned serious.

"Charles, what are you doing?"

"I would like you to stop talking for a minute."

"What?"

He released her and took the box out of his pocket. "This is for you."

She looked at him before opening the box. "Charles?"

"It's all I've been thinking about all evening. I don't want to return to the life I had before meeting you. I don't want to live my remaining days without you. No matter where you are I want to be with you. Will you marry me, Jayne Mouton?"

She smiled. "It's about time and the answer is yes."

He placed the ring on her finger and wrapped her in his arms.

"It's time I moved out of this home I shared with Paul's father," she said, smiling up at him. "There used to be too many memories, but they've been fading every day."

"I'm selling the home I shared with my late wife as well. We can find our own home together whether here or in New York."

"Let's stay here. We can be near our grandchildren."

"Grandchildren?"

"The future Charles, I always look toward the future."

"I love you, Jayne." He wrapped his arms tighter about her.

She smiled and gently but firmly loosened herself in his grasp. Smiling she said, "It's time for you to go home."

"We're engaged now," he said smiling.

Her smile broadened. "Engaged, but not married. Good night, Charles."

"Good night, Jayne."

Chapter 32

The Sleeper had one more person to visit on his list. He stood in the shadow of the tool shed watching Cora Novalski with her granddaughter, Gloria, as they cleaned the kitchen. He had always had a crush of sorts on Cora. Such a beauty in her day. She still carried herself with refinement and grace. He sighed. She was part of the team, and in time, the slow thinkers would remember her. He had no doubt she was as mentally sharp now as she was back on the team. Cora and granddaughter left the kitchen with the back door wide open. He snuck in and hid behind the dining room drapes just as the teenager returned to the kitchen to close and lock the back door. The Sleeper sat cross-legged on the floor underneath the dining room table. He watched Cora and her granddaughter on the couch in front of the television set. The movie ended, and the granddaughter helped her grandmother tidy up the living room. An hour later, the house was still. The Sleeper peeked in on the granddaughter. She had fallen asleep with her laptop on the quilt beside her. He closed the cover and placed it on her nightstand. He found Cora in bed with her Rosary beads in one hand, and the Bible opened, and resting underneath her arm. She struggled a few seconds before going limp.

Hawkins drove the cruiser up on the sidewalk and parked. The street was lined bumper to bumper with ambulances, news crews, and police cars. In another unmarked car, Hawkins guessed the dark cars were undercover as there were no government tags on them. He walked through the police barricades and up the steps to the house. Just inside the dining room he saw a teenager in tears being hugged by a middle-aged couple. He spotted Grant and Sanders and walked over to them.

"What happened here?" asked Hawkins, keeping an eye on the group in the dining room.

Grant read from his notes. "Teen's name is Gloria Novalski. She spends every weekend with paternal grandmother, Cora Novalski. She got up for a glass of water, noticed backdoor opened, and checked on grandmother. She thinks she saw someone leave the room. She found her grandmother with a pillow over her face."

"Did she describe the someone she thought she saw?" asked Hawkins.

"A shadow man is what she called him," replied Sanders.

"How old is the girl?"

"She's fifteen."

"Who are the people?" asked Hawkins.

"Her parents, Sam and Diane Novalski."

"Isn't he the police commissioner?" asked Hawkins.

"Yes, and the murdered woman was his mother."

"Oh! All right, walk with me."

Emory and Stewart had arrived and stood listening.

"Lieutenant? There's something you should know," said Grant.

Hawkins eyed Grant. "Okay, I give up."

Sanders, looking at the worried expression on Grant's face, looked at Hawkins.

"Sam Novalski is best friends with Paul Mouton. He and his family attend the Hot Springs Cathedral Church where the police commissioner is a church deacon."

Hawkins stared at her a moment, sighed, and turned away. For the first time in his career, he wondered if his legacy was in jeopardy.

In his private office in Hot Springs Cathedral Church, Paul hung up the desk phone, stood up and walked around to the front of his desk. The seated pastors watched him. He crossed his arms, and leaned against the edge of his desk.

"That was Sam Novalski informing me of his mother's murder."

"Where?"

"In her home. Gloria was spending the night. She woke this morning to find her grandmother smothered to death."

"Aw, poor kid. Thank God she's safe."

"Sam said she described the man as a 'shadow' man."

"He's purposely dressing in black clothing."

"Or, she."

"Excuse my pronoun lapse... or, she."

"We don't have a positive identification of the suspect."

"Nick, do you remember anything of your attacker?"

The attorney shook his head slowly. "No matter how much I try I can't remember anything but pulling a trash can and sensing someone was near. After that, nothing but blackness."

David looked at Steven. "Did you try hypnosis with him?"

"His brain has blocked the entire event," said Steven. Ernest remained mute.

"We also have this, gentlemen," said Paul. He turned on a taped recording of Claudia's voice. The men listened in silence.

Paul said softly, "I didn't hear that message until afterward."

Nick, seated on the sofa, responded. "The attack occurred after she sent the text regardless of what time you received it."

"She had figured out the identity of the person stealing from the church." Ernest was seated at the other end of the couch. His jaw tightened.

David spoke with a voice full of anguish. "Her attack is on me. I should have been collaborating with her instead of accusing her. If I had been with her this wouldn't have happened."

Paul told them. "Hawkins is leery about her disappearance."

"Well, what are we telling the congregation? People are scared."

"Lisa is pregnant. She can't be stressed out by all this," said Nick.

"Can't you take her away awhile? Visit family?"

"She has little to no family, believe it or not. She was adopted. Our home is here, and our family is here."

Steven, seated in an armchair, stood up. "We need to shutter the church doors until these murders are solved. However long that takes. Put a series of teaching videos on social media, send the reverends on assignments, and stay out of this church. Whatever bills need to be paid; David can oversee. Sit all the trustees down from handling church finances. Make sure the media and the congregation know that. We might be able to save a deacon or trustee's life. I'll inform the deacons so they can get their membership lists together. If there's nothing else, I'm going home. It's been a long day. I'm tired, hungry, and I've got work to do."

After a minute of silence, Steven collected his briefcase, and walked out. Into the silence Nick spoke.

"I'm in favor of taking the finances away from the trustees. I'm also in favor of David managing the bills. I'm sure Steven's already prepared the ministers' listings. What I'm confused about is the videos he's talking about."

Paul said, "Steven's referring to the sermons, Bible studies, and workshops I've taped, but that was many years ago."

"Could they be of use during a time such as this?"

"They would be programmable for social media today. But I'm beginning to be worried about Steven," said Paul.

"I'm not."

Paul said, "I don't want him destroyed over this, Nick. He was in love with Claudia."

Nick spoke over Paul. "Steve lost Cynda when a bank robber shot her in cold blood because she walked into the bank he was robbing. They were due to get married that weekend. We all know this. Fast-forward he's dating Claudia, and she's been attacked. His first instinct will be to protect her at all costs."

"Steven has never been one to go off on emotional tantrums," said Ernest. "He's given some clear counsel which we need to implement."

"Besides," said Nick, "she's with him."

"I'm going to use his suggestions," said Paul, "and I do believe we should close the church doors temporarily."

Paul walked around to his desk chair, and sat down. He frowned, and looked at the men who were watching him.

"Did I hear you correctly Nick?" Paul asked. "Did you say Claudia's with Steven?"

Ernest giggled before saying, "Steven arrived at Claudia's house ahead of the police. I looked her over. She had a slight gash on her forehead, and a broken arm. Otherwise, she's fine."

"So, all of you knew but me?"

"We needed you not to know because we knew Hawkins was coming for you first," said David.

"You've been under a lot of strain, Paul," said Ernest.

Nick leaned forward. "The rest of the clergy board are in the conference room. We should inform them of our decisions, and as a body, meet with the deacons and trustees."

"I'm on board," said Ernest. David nodded his head. Paul agreed.

The town hall meeting was better than Paul anticipated. The mayor, deputy-mayor, and town council president were courteous, thoughtful, insightful, and respectful of the pastor's situation. Paul answered the questions posed him as truthfully and with as much compassion as he could muster. There were times he stuttered and often the anguish of the situation was telling on his face, but he persevered until the public relations staffer ended the session. The applause was deafening. The mayor and his team were proud. Paul was pleased that countless members of Hot Springs Cathedral Church were in attendance, with a full house of deacons and trustees, cheering him on. Paul seized the moment to inform the church and the public that Hot Springs Cathedral Church would be holding a church-wide prayer vigil by way of social media in lieu of the church's temporary closing. Again, robust applause greeted this final announcement. Hawkins sat in the back and kept his shades on. It was some time before Hawkins realized Pastor Carter was missing. Where was he?

Visiting hours in Hot Springs Medical Center was over. Seated in the hospital cafeteria Ernest, in his dark sunglasses, watched a table of young nurses as they ate their meals, and talked amicably among themselves. He noticed how only two of the eight at the table were not wearing wedding bands. Neither one was his type. He rubbed the empty coffee cup between his palms. His thoughts centered on Karen. He had to pull himself together. He liked her and what he was feeling was no more than physical attraction. What made this one different? Out of the corner of his eye he saw shapely calves in sensible shoes approach. He could hear his heart pounding in his ears. He looked up. Karen sat across from him.

"Hello Ernest. Before you say anything, I want to apologize. I've only been in Hot Springs a few months. The resident surgeon in Milwaukee asked me to marry him right before I left. We had been together a long time. But it's over between us now."

She became quiet as she looked at him. He kept his eye shades on. She leaned forward on the table.

"The podiatrist was a mistake, a one-night stand. He wants to make it more. I don't, and I haven't." She smiled, half-heartedly. "My girls' trip is an annual event. My friends work mostly in the health care profession as I do. None of us ever have what you call free time. You know that. Our annual trips are stress relievers, nothing more. That's the truth. You don't have to investigate me. I'm attracted to you."

She stopped talking. Ernest was sitting still. She looked at him, got up and walked away. She stepped on the elevator. A swift gust of wind ruffled her hair. She looked up. Ernest was in the elevator with her, and he was not wearing his dark eye shades.

Chapter 33

The Sleeper decided David was becoming a nuisance. Following him to Claudia's house, it would have been child's play to loosen the machinery under his vehicle, and allow the brake fluid oil to gush out. None of that slow leaking business. But it would take too long, and dawn would appear too soon wiping out the darkness he needed to accomplish his tasks. David came out and hopped into his vehicle. The Sleeper loved the elegant look of the Rolls-Royce and mused it was going to be a pity to see it destroyed. David glanced in his rearview mirror. There was a large vehicle following him without headlights. David's blood ran cold. He sent out an alarm, set the vehicle tracking system on, clicked off his own lights, and headed toward the highway. This time of night few cars were on the highway, and David wanted to take no chances hitting a pedestrian. David's car was high-powered, having a redesigned engine, and he could clock at two hundred fifty miles per hour smoothly. But when he looked in his rearview mirror, he saw the other vehicle was right on his tail, and had turned on their high beams. The bright lights streamed into his car. David pushed the accelerator until he clocked three hundred forty-five miles per hour, but the machinery behind him remained on his tail. He decided to push to five hundred praying he did not die in a tangle of machinery. He pressed a button near his left knee and a camera from his left taillight began filming the advancing vehicle. The right taillight threw smoke pellets behind him. David saw the lights fading on his pursuer, and slowly stepped off the accelerator, so he could make a turnaround. David was driving back towards Hot Springs when his warning sensors came on as the machine crashed into him from the driver's seat sending his car over the guard rail. David jumped out, rolled, and prayed. He was unable to gauge how high he was. He rolled into a tight knot with his head tucked in and holding his calves tight to his thighs; he hit the water at full velocity. The vehicle pursuing him kept going and exited at the next ramp.

Under the bridge in the pitch-black river where David's car had catapulted, Paul and Ernest, in scuba suits, pulled to the surface the lifeless body of David. Once on dry land, Ernest gave him CPR, and when he heard soft moaning, he hooked up an oxygen mask to his face. Working swiftly, he assessed David's injuries, putting casts on his arms and legs and a brace around his neck and rib cage. Gently, they transferred David's body to a wooden raft securing the body from head to foot with heavy cording.

As stealthily as they arrived, they transported David's body onto the plastic lined trunk of Steven's Land Range Rover parked strategically in the tall grass. Driving steadily through the dark night Steven drove two towns over to the veteran's hospital in Exeter.

Returning to the bridge Ernest located David's car underwater. He dislocated the camera from the left taillight and found the black box underneath the steering panel. He brought the items to the surface and handed them off to Paul who placed the items in Ernest's Corvette. A minute later Ernest returned with the arsenal box. Both men dove underwater to set timed explosives inside and around the car's exterior now wedged firmly on an underwater boulder.

On the ground, Nick scoured the accident scene marking measurements and taking photographs. He cleaned the road removing the markings, and tape. He placed his equipment in his black Viper, and the three men left the scene.

Returning home, Paul's night goggles detected no one in sight of his house. Garaging his car, he crept steadily to the bedroom to check on Monaco. She was still sleeping. He listened to her shallow breathing for a while. He had given her crushed melatonin tablets earlier in her cocoa for her nerves. Now he was glad he had because when he received the SOS from David alerting he was in danger everything in him sprang into action. He changed clothing watching the sleeping form of his wife, took a shower, and returned to the bedroom. He sat on the floor in the dark at the foot of the bed. He looked at his wristband.

He's alive. Broken legs, arms, crushed rib cage, broken collarbone.

In the darkness Paul lowered his head and prayed. He prayed long and with so much emotion he fell asleep. Monaco woke an hour later and was startled that her husband's side of the bed was empty. In the darkness of the bedroom with the moon for light she saw her husband asleep on the floor at the foot of her bed. She woke him, and he pulled her down beside him on the floor. Like lovers everywhere they were soon embraced in a tender knot of kisses and caresses that slowly evolved into lovemaking.

Ernest returned home and checked on Jasmine. She was sleeping soundly. Earlier, she had been distraught having heard about the injured detective. He assured her Emory was unharmed, and when she received a phone call from him, she seemed more at peace. Ernest showered and changed into a pullover and sweatpants. He took the camera box and dislocated it, processing the photographs in his lab. He worked steadily through the night. The evidence he unearthed was tying the pieces of the puzzle together but there was still more to discover. He looked at his wristband.

He's alive. Broken legs, arms, crushed rib cage, broken collarbone.

Ernest set the house alarms and taking his Corvette drove to Steven's condominium where he picked up Claudia, and her luggage, and brought her to his home. He deposited her in his guest suite. She hugged him and he left her.

Nick garaged his car, and stealthily made his way to the bedroom. Lisa was sleeping soundly. He showered, threw on pajamas and robe, and went to his office. He pulled up his second computer where he kept forensic information. The pictures were coming in from Ernest's computer. He looked at his wristband.

He's alive. Broken legs, arms, crushed rib cage, broken collarbone.

Nick turned his attention to the black box. He set the timer for an hour. After which he would shut down everything and join his wife in bed.

In the Mt. Pleasant Nursing Home for Veteran's, Steven seated on the floor in David's room, sent out text messages to the team.

He's alive. Broken legs, arms, crushed rib cage, broken collarbone.

He sent a long message to Claudia with explicit instructions. She sent a return text back. A half hour later, he received a confirmation text from Ernest. Steven checked on David. Tapping on David's forehead in Morse Code he let him know he was near him. He saw tears falling from David's eyes.

"It's okay, Dave. I'm here with you," he said, softly. "We're taking this psycho out. That's a promise!"

An hour after the accident, Hawkins arrived at the crash site. He stood in the middle of the road wearing a deep frown on his face. Symonds, the forensic specialist replacing Stewart, was on site in his white hazmat suit. He and his forensics team stumped as well. The broken railing was the single indication an accident had occurred on the road. There were no skid marks on the ground and other than the damaged guard rail, nothing indicated any activity had occurred here. To them all, the driver purposely took this road as it was off the beaten track. Looking at the eighty-five-foot drop into the river, Hawkins doubted if the driver was still alive. But where was the body? Who had cleaned up this site, and why?

For two days scuba divers from the Coast Guard explored the water looking for a body. An elegant Rolls-Royce was fished out of the river. Forensics confirmed it was clean of paperwork except for the owner's manual and vehicle registration. Hawkins looked at the name on the registration card: David Sanchez.

Chapter 34

Stewart lost Pastor Barnes on one of these connecting streets, but he determinedly kept driving. The young detective's reputation was on the line and his pride bruised, allowing the pastor to slip through his hands like that. He had earned high praise for his tracking skills in the Academy, and he intended on retaining those accolades. He thought about the pastor's solid black Porsche. He had read where the cars clocked at two hundred twenty miles per hour. The pastor's car had no distinguishing marks on it, and even his tinted windows were regulation. Whoever redesigned his motor was an engineering genius because the car was as stealth and silent as its owner. Stewart drove down another street slower this time. There were dark cars parked in the driveways, and on the street. That was when he spotted a lone dark figure going up a side wall and disappearing into an open window. Was that the pastor? He texted his partner Rick, and his boss Hawkins, about a possible burglary in progress. Stewart parked his vehicle around the corner, took off his jacket, put on gloves, and strapped on his bulletproof vest. He made his way to the back of the house. The back door was open. Stewart crept in. He heard and saw nothing moving downstairs. He heard rummaging upstairs. He unsnapped his gun from his holster. He was near the top landing of the steps when the lone dark figure appeared out of nowhere. Stewart instantly assessed he was at a disadvantage and decided to jump over the railing to the floor. The figure calculated the position of the detective's body, and used the instrument he had in his hand to sail it with force at his head. The weapon hit his temple caus-

ing Stewart to lose consciousness. The Sleeper jumped over the railing and retrieved his instrument. Two intentional violent bashes ensured the detective would never rise again. Then the Sleeper noticed the police vest. An undercover cop! Sirens in the distance.

Grant and Sanders came through the front door with guns drawn. They immediately spied Stewart in a pool of his own blood on the floor. Fifteen minutes later they returned to the front hall to find Emory on his knees by his fallen partner. The medical team carted the injured detective out to the waiting ambulance and Grant watched a sullen Emory climb in the back with his partner. Grant was stone-faced, having lost his own partner several months earlier, he empathized with his colleague.

"I can't wait until we catch this maniac!" said Sanders, with venom in her voice..

Hawkins, clearly irritated, walked up to them on the sidewalk. "Why didn't he wait for his partner and backup? None of you should be investigating anything alone. This guy is extremely dangerous. He's killed multiple people, including a police officer, and now has seriously injured another police officer. He has no boundaries and its time we tightened up."

With that said, Grant watched the lieutenant disappear inside the house. He looked around for his partner.

"Logan, whatcha got?"

"Not much to go on, Joe. Blood everywhere as you saw but it's contained on the first-floor hall. Seems like our killer did the most damage right there."

"Do we have the murder weapon?"

"No, must have taken it with him." She looked around Grant. "Here comes Officer Lewis."

"Hi, Detectives. Neighbors along here saw and heard nothing. However, in the house painted red directly behind this one lives a sixty-six-year-old convalescent. His name is Al Davis, and he's lived in the area all his life. He says he saw a huge man crawl into a second floor back window followed by another man. He only saw the first man leave though."

"Could he describe the man he saw?" asked Grant.

Officer Lewis looked at his pad. "He said the guy was dressed in black from head to toe with only his eyes showing. He looked like a bat."

The detectives looked at each other, thanked Lewis, and left the crime scene.

The next afternoon the five pastors met in the café area of the Holly Oak Bookstore for an impromptu lunch meeting. They sat on the third-floor open air balcony with their backs to the wall and placed the billboard where it reflected off the open doorway. They could see whoever entered the balcony, whether server or guest.

"I put in a call...we might have two different cases," said Nick.

"How so?" asked Ernest.

"The clergy deaths we're investigating might be tied into something else," said Nick.

"Fun times at the zoo," muttered Ernest. "Feed me."

"Paul, there's information we need to fill you in on," Steven said, "namely, the identity of the woman you've married."

Paul looked at the three men casually spaced apart. They were all watching him. He could feel his temperature rising. He folded his arms.

"What do you mean by identity?"

"Monaco Valentine is the youngest daughter of Victor and Cynthia Valentine."

"Her late parents were forensic scientists."

"They helped design some of the technology currently in use by the Bureau."

"What were their assignments?" Paul asked.

"At the time of their deaths, they were solidly retired as Bureau agents."

"What were their covers before they retired?"

"Investment banking for Victor, and accountant for Cynthia."

"Could someone have discovered their identities?"

"The Bureau came to that hypothesis when Agent Harris was murdered. Excuse me, when he actively walked into a moving vehicle."

Paul leaned forward. "Wait a minute, what was Monaco's older sister's name?"

"Cynda Valentine. She was Steven's fiancée."

"Cynda was an accountant but she worked for a private corporation."

"Why didn't you guys tell me this was Monaco's family?"

"We didn't know how serious you were."

"You were so smitten you didn't register her surname."

"We thought it best not to remind you."

"One thing you need to know is that we haven't shared any of this information with Monaco."

"Much of it is classified. We only learned about her parents when we took the assignment."

Paul sighed. "The Bureau didn't look at the deaths of Johnson and Wallace until Harris began the inquiry."

"That's right. Don't forget Harris' specialty was bank fraud. His death is what sparked this investigation."

"We should have kept Clayton here. He knew the banking system inside and outside. He would have been an asset for David."

"Clayton was terrified he was next."

"To my understanding Cynda Valentine was not an agent. What's the operating theory on her death?" asked Paul.

"The bank robbery was a planned event. The fact that she entered the bank as it was in progress? An unlikely occurrence."

Paul put his head in his hands. "How do we protect our families, the congregation, and the church?"

"We have to operate as pastors, gentlemen."

"That's our covers; and why we're here"

"There's a sleeper in the church," said Steven, "and for whatever reason, he's been resurrected. He's killed six agents and our mission is to find him and bring him in."

"Or... her. These are elderly people. Our sleeper could be a woman."

"I don't mean to sound sexist, believe me."

"We have a good deal of women in the church who are active in ministries. She could be hiding in plain sight of us."

"Okay. So what about the trustees?"

"What about them?"

"Shouldn't we try to solve their murders?"

"No. We stick to our assignment. Hot Springs finest are on the job!"

"Right. We have Grant and his new partner to watch out for. These local murders are on their turf."

"Not to mention Hawkins' undercover guys, Emory and Stewart."

"Five homicide detectives? Overkill much?"

"Oakland Heights is a well-off, suburban community. As the saying goes, money talks and everything else walks."

The deep bass voice interrupted the conversation flow. "Gentlemen, I think Agent Bergson's murder is why Hawkins is here. Bergson was on assignment in Chicago for several years before being sent here."

"So far, all the change of identity information we've put out on Bergson has surfaced."

"But, in time Hawkins may discover our identities. Right now, we have the jump on him. But we must stay ahead of him or get bogged down in Bureau red tape."

"Hopefully, Hawkins doesn't lose his mind and decide to search the church premises with his forensics team."

"He did, Ernest. When Martin's body was found in the closet, Hawkins sent forensics out later that day."

"They found nothing."

"How is Dave doing?" asked Paul. "I'd like to pull guard duty. Monaco would love spending time with Lisa."

"Paul, right now we need you to focus as a pastor. Pretty soon all hell is going to break loose. With David and Claudia missing, the cops are on high alert."

"That's not all. I heard this morning from my police informant that Stewart was seriously injured. He's in the Intensive Care Unit in a coma."

"How's Claudia doing now, Steve?"

"I proposed to her. We'll be married in a few weeks."

"Aw, man! Congratulations!"

"Joy and pain." Paul shook his head. "What the hell are we doing here?"

"You know the saying. Keep your friends close, and your enemies closer."

Steven stood up. "I'm out guys. Going ring shopping with my lady. Stay safe." The group disbanded.

When the server stepped onto the balcony, it was empty except for the man with the red complexion, and bright blue-green eyes. Ernest looked up and smiled. Mesmerized, she stood holding her pad to her chest, staring down at him as if in a trance. God! He was gorgeous!

"Hi, I thought there were more of you," she smiled shyly.

"They had to leave, but listen, here's a tip for the table, and a little something for you."

She smiled. "Oh, thank you, but I can't..."

He stood up. "Tell you what? When are your days off?"

She stuttered looking up at him. Wow! "My days off are Mondays and Tuesdays. I'm a graduate student at the university."

His smile was disarming, and his direct eye contact hypnotized her. The silky voice added impact. He was a lot bigger than he looked seated.

"Perfect. You keep all that, and one day I will return, and you will dine with me."

"Oh sure! Thank you."

Ernest smiled and donned his dark eye shades before leaving the building. She was too young for his taste. He preferred older, seasoned women. He located his yellow Stingray as a woman with glistening chocolate brown skin wearing a snug deep pink sundress that clung to hourglass curves walked by. Her dark curls blew tantalizingly about her shoulders. The dark, almond-shaped eyes, pert nose, and full lips were hypnotic. They smiled at each other in passing. He watched her in his rearview mirror licking his lips before he put the car in gear, and sped out the parking lot. My! My! My!

Chapter 35

In the Mt. Pleasant Nursing Home for Veterans, David laid semi-comatose with his head, arms, torso, and legs wrapped in heavy bandage. His friends stood silently by his bedside watching him breathing. The nurse on duty, after being beguiled by Ernest and his silky voice, had granted them a time to pray with their fallen friend.

"I'm still developing the film we took out of his car."

"He clocked at nearly five hundred miles per hour."

"Did you find evidence of more than two vehicles?"

"No, only that vehicle's and Dave's."Mt.

"Have you processed the film yet?"

"Photos are fuzzy. Working on clearing them up."

"I feel like we're in a damn science fiction movie!"

"Where was Dave's last stop before he was tagged?"

"Claudia's home."

"Secure Dave's home. We need to pull guard duty until he's out of here."

"Agreed."

"Gentlemen, let's pray."

The men bowed their heads. When the doctor entered the room, he paused and bowed his head as well.

Drifting in and out of consciousness, David could not hear his friends, and was unaware they were in the room. Pain coursed through his body.

Pain in his body threatened to drown his mind. His senses clouded with dark gray shadows growing and dissolving in empty black space. David's thoughts were on Raquel. He had never expressed the depth of his feelings for her; had never told her how much he truly loved her, and needed her in his life. Emotional pain enveloped his heart, his soul. Baby, no, don't leave! Please, don't ever leave me! Shooting pain traveled throughout his body. Images in shades of gray except for his exquisite Raquel who brought color and life to his world of grays. He dreamed of her tan skin, dark hair and eyes, and sultry, mischievous smile. How he loved her! She made him feel so powerful when he was beside her. Darkness approached and with it the image of his soulmate being swept away by some invisible force. No, Raquel, don't leave me!

Hawkins was in no mood to play games. He sent out a summons for each of the remaining pastors to meet with him at the Police Administration Building. Nick called in and scheduled timed interviews on the same day which Hawkins allowed.

The first pastor interviewed was Nick. Hawkins walked in and sat across from him. He looked at Nick's deep blue chalk-stripe suit down to the white French cuffed silk shirt with deep blue pearlized cuff links, and the white tie with subtle deep blue stripes. A thick gold wedding band, and black wristband completed his attire.

Nick folded his hands on top of the table. Unknown to Hawkins or the detectives behind the glass, Nick recorded the session.

"Pastor Rodgers, thank you for being here."

"Of course."

"What's your legal specialty, Pastor?"

"Tax law."

"Pastor, you're also a certified public accountant, aren't you?"

"Yes."

"What is your role in the church besides being a pastor?"

"My expertise in tax law."

"Have you ever volunteered in the trustees office or on the finance teams?"

"No."

"When was the last time you saw Pastor Sanchez?"

"Last Saturday in the church?"

"What was he doing?"

"Playing chess with me."

"How long was this chess game?"

"About ten minutes."

"Where were you with your chess game?"

"The conference room. We were waiting for the pastor's appearance."

"What was the nature of the conference?"

"Our monthly clergy meeting."

"Have you seen or heard from him since?"

"No."

"As a tax attorney with CPA credentials, do you work with Pastor Sanchez?"

"No. I'm not involved with the church financial matters."

"Why is that?"

"Ethical reasons, for one."

"Were you aware Pastor Sanchez was in a road accident?"

"No."

"We found a registration card belonging to David Sanchez in the vehicle we hauled up out of the river."

"Is there a question?"

"What did Pastor Sanchez do as the finance director?"

"I don't know."

Hawkins almost smiled. "Wasn't Ms. Ginyard also on that ministry?"

"Yes."

"Who is currently managing the finance department?"

"I don't know."

"Wouldn't it be standard practice for you to head the finance ministry in its leaders' absence?"

"It's the senior pastor's decision."

"Don't you find it suspect the people being murdered are trustees and deacons in the finance ministry?"

"I do."

"What do you mean?"

"I do find it suspect."

Hawkins sat back in his seat. "Okay. Thank you. I need to question your colleagues."

They walked out of the room together.

With Nick present, Hawkins spoke to Paul first. He surveyed the pastor who was standing with his arms crossed in his customary posture when they entered the room. The gold silk shirt showcased a muted purple and gold tie. The purple three-piece, double-breasted suit set off by a purple and gold print pocket square. Hawkins remembered he was third generation clergy noting the pinkie ring with the engraved cross on his right hand. On his left hand was a wide two-toned wedding band.

"Pastor Mouton, thank you for coming down."

"You're welcome."

"Please have a seat. Pastor, besides pastoring the church, where else do you work?"

"I teach health science at the high school."

"I thought all your education was in theology."

"I also have a public health degree."

"Pastor, several tragedies have occurred within two weeks."

"Do you have a question for the Pastor?"

"Several months ago, the police commissioner's mother was murdered."

"Do you have a question for the Pastor?"

"Why didn't you tell the police the commissioner is a member in your church?"

"The police never asked about the commissioner's church life."

"Why was the commissioner's mother's murder kept out of the media?"

"You'll have to ask the commissioner."

"When was the last time you saw Pastor Sanchez?"

"Last Saturday."

"What happened?"

"We held our monthly clergy meeting. Afterward, David taped his Bible study series for social media."

"That was about a week ago. You haven't heard from him since?"

"No. He's an extremely busy man."

"Aren't we all?" murmured Hawkins. "What are you doing in the absence of Pastor Sanchez?"

"He has not been absent according to our calendar."

"Were you aware he was in a road accident?"

"No."

"Do you socialize with Pastor Sanchez outside church activities?"

"Yes, occasionally."

"How would you describe your relationship outside the church?"

"We live separate lives, Detective."

"Would you say you're friends?"

"Yes."

"What are you doing as a friend for Sanchez?"

"I don't understand the question..."

"Are you charging the Pastor?" asked Nick.

"One last question, Pastor. Who is overseeing the finances of the church?"

"The church administrator would have that information."

"Who is the church administrator?"

"Pastor Steven Barnes."

Nick interrupted. "Are you charging my client with a crime, Detective?"

"No."

"This session is over."

"One final question, Counselor. Pastor Mouton, don't you find it strange that the only people in the church who've been killed or hurt are trustees and anyone with accounting backgrounds?"

Nick tapped Paul on the shoulder. Hawkins watched Nick walk out with Paul. After a few minutes, Hawkins walked next door where Ernest sat.

Ernest wore dark shades covering his luminescent eyes. Hawkins looked at the suit with peaked lapels in a creamy white color. The black trousers were creased and cuffed. The open-collar shirt was in white with red stripes. A red monogrammed pocket square and red cuff links completed his look. Hawkins saw he was wearing red and white suede loafers.

"Pastor Carter, thank you for coming down."

Ernest smiled. Hawkins noticed the small diamond studs in Ernest's ear lobes. The door opened and Nick entered taking a seat beside Ernest.

"Pastor Carter or should I say, Dr. Carter?"

"Both are applicable."

"Why didn't you ever mention you have a medical license?"

"You never asked."

"What's your medical specialty?"

"Forensic pathology."

"I saw an article about you not long ago. Why didn't you mention you were a medical professional?"

"To who? Why?"

"What is your role as pastor in the church?"

"I cover the social ministries."

"And what are those, Pastor?"

"Weddings, funerals, graduations, and other events the church sponsors."

"When was the last time you saw Pastor Sanchez?"

"I believe Saturday last."

"Do you and the other pastors ever socialize as friends?"

"Yes."

"Where were you on the night of Sanchez' road accident?"

"I don't know."

Nick interrupted. "The pastor would have no idea when such an event occurred."

"What was your first reaction when you heard of the pastor's accident?"

"I haven't heard of Dave's having an accident."

"Now that you know he's been in an accident, how do you feel?"

"I'm alarmed."

"What will you do about your alarm?"

"Pray."

Hawkins, followed by Nick moved to the next room and sat across from Steven in his dark glasses. Hawkins observed how Steven sat with his feet planted on the floor and his arms loose in his lap. His footwear were expensive leather, soft-soled shoes that behaved like sneakers. Steven wore a black worsted wool suit with a white silk shirt, black and gold striped tie with matching pocket square. Hawkins noticed he was wearing the same style of black wristband.

"Pastor Barnes, thank you for coming down."

"Of course, Detective."

"You're a psychologist, Dr. Barnes?"

"Yes."

"Do you teach?"

"I have a mandatory grad course I teach every quarter. I'm a researcher primarily."

"What is your role in the church under pastoral care?"

"In my role as administrator, I oversee the clergy and deacon boards. I also lead the crisis and trauma ministry."

"A police officer was injured last week investigating an empty house. Did you know that?"

"No."

"Do you have any theories about why he would have gotten hurt investigating an intruder in an empty house?"

Nick stated. "Make the question relevant not speculative."

Hawkins glanced at Nick. "Do you know whose house it was?"

"No."

"It was Ms. Claudia Ginyard's."

Silence.

"Where were you on the night of Ms. Ginyard's disappearance?"

Nick stated. "The pastor would have no knowledge of said event."

"Dr. Barnes, my detective is in the ICU on life support because he was doing his job. Did you know two people from your congregation committed a murder/suicide?"

"No."

"What about Pastor David Sanchez?"

"What about him?"

"There's four of you here. Haven't you wondered where your colleague is?"

"No."

"You don't watch the news, Pastor?"

"No."

"Are you withholding information from this investigation, Pastor Barnes?"

"No."

"Have you and Sanchez ever socialized outside the church?"

"Sometimes."

"We can assume you have a friendship?"

"Define what you mean by your use of the word, friendship, Detective."

Hawkins held on to his temper. Silence ensued. He looked at his notes and looked up at Steven in his dark glasses.

"Who is currently managing the church finances?"

"We hired an independent third-party; an accounting firm."

"Don't you find it suspect the people who have died were trustees and deacons?"

"Only Sister Ginyard and Pastor Sanchez, are active trustees."

"What do you mean by active trustees?"

"They are the only two people legally able to oversee the financial records, sign checks, etc. The other trustees were retired."

"With both missing, who oversees the finances now?"

"The accounting firm."

"Pastor Barnes, is the church's financial records solvent?"

"I'm afraid I'm not at liberty to answer that question, Lieutenant."

"If there's nothing else, I'm taking my clients out of here."

Hawkins looked at Nick wearily. "I get the feeling you guys aren't being honest with me."

Nick looked at Hawkins. "Are you making an allegation, Lt. Hawkins?"

"Not at all" replied Hawkins testily. "But you'd have to agree the fact that none of you seem to be worried about the missing pastor or finance director is odd."

Hawkins stood in the hall and watched the pastor-lawyer collect the pastors. Their heights and body proportions dwarfed most of the police officers on the floor. Hawkins walked down the hall to the building's second set of elevators. He stopped on the second floor and stood by a window overlooking the parking lot. They each drove off the police lot in his own signature car. Hawkins stood at the second-floor hall window watching them split off. He sighed. They looked as if they were in shock. What did he expect from them?

Chapter 36

The pastors doubled around and sat across the street from the police building. They looked down on the police station as they sipped margaritas inside the Rooftop Café. Ernest looked at a menu.

He giggled. "I'm hungry after that interrogation."

"That *was* interesting," said Nick. "But what did you find out from David's car?"

Ernest gave them each a composite photo. The picture was in black and white with a smoky haze. The large, square shape was unmistakably an armored combat vehicle.

"This was the most powerful vehicle the military designed a few years ago. We're looking at a military veteran, combat arms."

"Active duty? A vigilante?"

"Since one of our hypothesis rested on the gender of this person, lets rule out women first. I can check the combat veterans database for this area," said Steven.

"How is David? What name is he under in the hospital?" asked Paul.

"Dave's conscious for a short period of time because of the pain medication, but he's improving daily. His injuries are healing. His memory is slowly returning as well."

Paul repeated his question. "His alias?"

"It's Dave Diaz only because he answered to Dave when he was brought in. I contacted the local police and explained he was working undercover and used the Florida credentials. They have an undercover posted at his door just in case our boy Hawkins is clairvoyant."

"What are his injuries?" asked Nick.

"Both legs and arms broken, crushed rib cage, broken collarbone, and concussion," said Ernest.

"Prognosis, so far?" asked Steven.

"He's healing faster than expected. We should be able to move him soon." said Ernest. "And he's ornery to see Raquel."

After a minute, Paul asked, "Ernest, what else did you find in Dave's camera?"

"Looks like Dave took a photo of a deed."

Nick looked at the picture and perked up. "Send me the picture. It looks like title to a land deed. I'm going to examine this more closely at home."

"It's time to move Dave to safer ground. I'm not thinking about Hawkins, but our vigilante. Dave is in a vulnerable position right now."

Ernest's turquoise eyes glowed. "I was thinking the same thing, Steve. Whenever you're ready."

"Paul, I'm going to need your spiritual presence when I talk to Raquel."

"What are you going to tell her, Steve? We can't let her know he's alive yet."

"They're in love with each other. She needs to know something," said Steven. "Besides, I don't want her caught off-guard."

Nick spoke up. "I'll be with you, Steve. Just so Claudia doesn't kill you being alone with Raquel."

"What's the matter, Paul? You left us for a moment."

"There's a pattern to these murders," said Paul. "They aren't random. It's the leadership he's targeting."

"Church leadership? Sure. We figured that out with all the people he's killed so far."

"There's no way we can possibly safeguard all the church leaders."

"Wait a minute, guys. All the people he's targeted so far have been the elderly."

"These are former trustees though," said Ernest.

"These people knew the financial history of the church. Their demise means dead men tell no tales. There's something he or she doesn't want us to know regarding this church and its finances," remarked Steven.

"Martin, Claudia and David were all working on the church audits. How far have they gotten?"

"Dave is going to take some time. He can't use either arm right now," said Ernest.

"Claudia is still having nightmares," said Steven, his voice quiet and still as the air about them.

"Nick, warn Raquel about the police and search warrants. I have a feeling Hawkins will pull something now that he knows where Dave lives."

"Excellent point, Steve. Let's get out of here."

The team quietly left the establishment.

Paul and Monaco were in their family room watching television when Ed called. Mary had collapsed at home, and he was now in Hot Springs Medical Center with her. Paul laid the phone down and walked upstairs. Monaco turned off the television and followed him.

"Oh, you don't have to come," said Paul, abstractedly.

"Nonsense. I want to pray with them, too."

Paul, having thrown on a sweatshirt and pants, sat in the chair and closed his eyes. He was learning not to argue. He was also learning it would take his wife at least twenty minutes to "throw on something and brush down her hair." She tapped him on the shoulder. She wore a light blue denim shirt tucked into white denim jeans. Her hair in a loose ponytail completed her look. He glanced at the clock on their nightstand. Fifteen minutes had passed. She grinned at him. He smiled, shaking his head.

When they stepped off the elevator they saw Ed at the end of the hall. The aged man was crumbled in a chair his gnarled hands folded together in his lap.

"Deacon Ed, thank you for calling me," Paul could see how tired the older man looked. The circles under his eyes were dark and deep. The deacon looked at him with vacant eyes. With a little cry, Monaco was in his arms. The deacon held her, tears forming in his eyes. Paul pulled Monaco away from Ed. They all sat down.

"What happened Deacon, if I may ask?"

"The excitement of these last few months has been too much for her, Pastor. All our friends dying such horrible deaths," his voice trembled.

Paul noticed Ed's once salt and pepper hair was now mostly white, and his head shook ever so slightly matching the occasional tremors in his hands.

"All we can do is pray, Deacon," said Paul.

The aged deacon gave him a wry smile. "Prayer does change things, Pastor. My prayer is that this villain is caught before anyone else is hurt. I have to be strong for my Mary, but..."

"Mine too, Deacon," Paul said, "look, let's pray with your wife. The doctor said we can stay for no less than a couple of minutes."

"Thank you, Pastor," said Ed.

Paul turned to Monaco. "Stay here, please. I won't be long."

He turned back to the deacon. He could see Ed's eyes were red and tear-filled. He could barely walk. He had a cane to steady himself. Paul gently held him up, and allowed him to lean on him as he was so frail. He admired the older man a great deal. Ed was helping to train the younger deacons in their roles, and on more than one occasional, was driven home when he collapsed. He always begged his fellow deacons not to tell Mary. As they made their way to Mary's room, Paul's heart went out to the old deacon and his wife. He prayed nothing happened to this couple. It would devastate Monaco.

Hawkins stopped at Hot Springs Medical Center to visit Stewart in Intensive Care. The hemorrhaging in his brain continued, and he was in danger of losing his eyesight. Emory had been spending more time at the hospital than on shift. The young man had black sockets under his eyes. Hawkins loved these men's dedication to their craft and each other, but he needed this healthy detective to refocus. He posted a police officer and took Emory home.

Chapter 37

The older man gingerly laid down mulch around his flower beds. The winter had been mild, and the spring was slightly rainier than usual, but as a gardener he had learned to use the changing weather patterns to his advantage. Lars Eliason was in excellent health as stated by his doctors at the Veteran's Clinic. He had little to no need for medication of any type and attributed his health to a lifetime of sensible eating, sustained exercise, and amenable companionship. The love of his life, Brad, had helped him reach a point of self-love to be able to acknowledge and stand up for himself. They had gotten married after a whirlwind courtship, and remained married for thirty-five years before cancer took Brad's life and heart from him. These past two years he had been living alone. Lars walked to the little garden in the back of his yard. He had dedicated a tomato plant to Brad as he loved tomatoes. Lars was not particularly fond of tomatoes and would often donate a basket of them to the church. He was busy pruning the tomato tree when the Sleeper attacked him.

Ed was driving his wife home from her weekly doctor's appointment. He was mentally thinking over his recipes of what to prepare them for lunch. Mary put her hand softly on his driving arm.

"Ed?"

He immediately pulled over to the curb and looked at her. "What's the matter? Are you alright? Should we return to the doctor's office?"

"Ed, I'm fine. I wanted to remind you that Lars asked Deaconess Hazleton to remind you about the tomatoes he's saving for us."

Ed smiled. "Thank you, darling. I had forgotten, and he told me himself a few days ago. Shall we do that now or later? I want you home. The new medication tires you easily."

"I'm good. I want those tomatoes so you can make that tomato aspic I love so much."

"Alright, my love. Anything for you. He doesn't live far from here. Are you comfortable? Warm enough?"

"Yes. Thank you, Ed. You take such loving care of me."

"I love you with all my heart and soul, Mary. This old, raggedy, worn-out man loves the ground you walk on. As long as I have breath in my body, I will take care of you."

Mary turned her head so he would not see the tears forming in her eyes. She felt blessed beyond measure. By the time Ed pulled into Lars Eliason's driveway his mind was already compiling the ingredients he would need for his tomato aspic. He saw Gordon Nillson, Lars' long-time neighbor, and waved as he knocked on the door a second time. Holding onto the railing, Ed painstakingly climbed down the porch steps, and was about to enter his car when Gordon called out to him.

"Ed, hold on a second." Gordon came scampering across the lawn. "Lars should be home. His car is still in the driveway."

"Good morning, Gordon. Does Lars drive everywhere he goes?"

"Just about Ed, just about," Gordon grinned. "If he's not answering the doorbell, he's most likely in his garden in the backyard."

"Oh?"

"Follow me," said Gordon. He had to wait as Ed adjusted his cane. The back gate was easy to push in and the two men entered the yard. Neither Ed nor Gordon saw Lars in the backyard. Ed turned around to exit the yard when he heard a gasp from Gordon. Both men stared in shock at the crumbled body of Lars Eliason lying just inside his open shed door.

Grant and Sanders were walking across the lawn when Hawkins cruiser pulled up. Hawkins noticed the calmness of the neighborhood as he surveyed the neatly cropped lawns and clear driveways. Eliason's home was in the middle of two tidy residences. Grant immediately pulled up his notes folder.

"Lieutenant, we have one deceased Lars Eliason, eighty-seven, killed in backyard and found in doorway of shed. He was stabbed with garden shears. The deceased has lived in this house for the past fifty-two years. Widower. No children. Retired accountant."

Hawkins' ears perked up. "Church affiliation?"

"Member of Hot Springs Cathedral Church."

"Sanders, get me a search warrant for Hot Springs Cathedral Church financial records," said Hawkins. "Who reported this in?"

"A man named Ed Joseph who had stopped by with his wife to see the deceased, and the next-door neighbor, Gordon Nillson" said Grant.

Hawkins walked over to Ed. "Hello, Deacon Joseph."

The older man was sitting beside his wife in his car. She was sleeping. Ed left the car and limped to the far side. His bad limp made Hawkins uncomfortable.

"I'm sorry, Deacon Joseph, to keep you out here. Is your wife going to be okay?"

"Yes, she's just sleeping," said Ed, smiling. He added, "I didn't know you were a police officer."

Hawkins smiled. "My official title is Lt. Hawkins."

"I don't know what to think, Lieutenant. I'm scared, my wife's scared. Who is doing this and why?"

"That's what we're trying to find out, sir. Do you live around here?"

"No. I was picking up some tomatoes. Deacon Lars grew them but didn't eat them. My Mary loves tomato aspic and spaghetti sauce. I make both the way she likes. Sometimes I make her fried tomatoes or just feed one to her in hunks. My Mary just loves tomatoes."

"When did you get here?"

"About thirty minutes ago. You all got here fast. Mary and I were coming from her weekly doctor's appointment. She has MS and..."

"Deacon, thank you for being so open and honest. Please, take your wife home. You get some rest, too."

"Lars was a good person. Quiet, industrious man. Wouldn't harm a fly. He was a good deacon."

Ed looked like he wanted to cry. Hawkins walked with him back to his car. He wanted to carry the older man so awkward was Ed's limp, and so slow his pace. Hawkins remembered something Ed said.

"Deacon Joseph, was Lars a member of the deacon board?"

"Yes, sir, he is. I mean, he was."

"Does your leg give you much trouble, sir?"

Ed smiled with a grimace. "The pain is nothing. Reminds me that I was lucky because many didn't make it."

"Deacon, would it be possible for me to get a listing of the men on your deacon board?"

"A listing, sir? We recruited a few new prospects from the military, and a few from the police department. Sound, active men." He paused to catch his breath. "I need to clear any requests with Pastor Barnes, sir."

Hawkins blood pressure elevated. He had to remain calm; at least, for appearance' sake.

"Thank you, Deacon. How soon can you give me that listing, sir?"

"Once I receive permission, I should have it for you by next Sunday's service. I need to find the box I put my catalogs in."

"How long have you been president of the deacon board?"

"I would guess about ten, fifteen or more years. No one ever wants to take on responsibility..."

The older man tired. He was breathing heavy, and losing his voice volume. Hawkins decided to stop talking. He watched the old deacon struggling to sit behind the wheel, wincing in pain, his wife still asleep. Ed waved back at Hawkins as the car ambled slowly up the street. A police officer approached.

"Lieutenant, a homicide occurred three blocks from here."

"Thanks, Smith." Hawkins ran to his cruiser sending for Emory along the way.

On his way to the address of the next discovered body Hawkins received the grim news that Detective Clay Stewart had died. Hawkins pulled over to the curb and rested his head on his hands. He closed his eyes. The answer was in front of him. Why couldn't he see it?

In the chapel of Hot Springs Cathedral Church Paul married Charles and Jayne. His mother, looking regal in a white satin gown with half gloves, stood beside Charles in a white tuxedo jacket with black tuxedo pants. Lisa and Nick stood as witnesses. Paul looked at Monaco, she was sitting with

Jasmine, and smiling. She had bought a light yellow wrap satin gown with full sleeves for the wedding. He smiled at his wife. She was feeling better.

Chapter 38

Raquel arrived at Steven's condominium promptly at four o'clock. He had asked her to pick up a book he was loaning to Jayne. Once she was inside, he sat her down in his kitchen, and plying her with food, asked her questions about her and David.

Once she stopped crying, she was ready to talk. "I didn't want to break up with him, Steven, but I had to. I don't want to force any man to marry me. That's not my style."

"Have you two discussed marriage?"

"No, I just assumed he understood fun and games couldn't last forever."

"That's not the way life always works, Raquel. Sometimes you must tell people what you want; give them instructions so you're both walking in the same direction."

"Well, I told him I was his girlfriend, not his wife. Hopefully, he read between the lines. That was easy enough."

Steven looked up. "Hi Nick, grab a seat."

Steven walked to the stove to prepare Nick a plate. Raquel frowned as she looked at Nick, seated at the counter..

"How has David been, Nick? Is he dating anyone?"

"Now you know I wouldn't tell you that even if I knew the answer," said Nick, with a grin.

Raquel stared at Nick as tears rolled down her cheeks. Giving Nick a hard look, Steven took Raquel by the hand, gave her his handkerchief, and guided her to a seat in the family room.

"Okay, some truth talking now. Do you love David?"

"Yes, I do."

"Well, he told me he loves you, too. Whatever else, you two must talk about it, okay?"

"Yes, I understand that. Steven, what's going on? Where's David?"

Nick stopped eating to listen to Steven and Raquel. He turned sideways at the counter and eyed Raquel.

"He's safe. I won't let anything happen to him. Trust me?"

"Yes, I do. David trusts you too. He always told me if anything happens to him, I am to find you." Tears flowed down her face. "He's not dead, is he?"

"No, and I'm going to make certain he stays alive so you two can make some babies together."

"Wait a minute... is that his car that they fished out of the lake? Is he okay?"

"I need you to listen to me carefully. No one can know he's alive. Only you, me, and Nick. Understand me? The police will want to question you. Call Nick right away, or me. But do not answer their questions without Nick being present. That's your basic right. Okay?"

"Okay." She laughed through her tears. "When can I see him?"

"Soon."

She hugged Steven. "Tell him I love him, and always will."

"Okay."

Steven stood up and looked at Nick. "Thanks, Nick."

Nick resumed eating. He smiled, waving his fork.

Nick carefully carried into the house the prepared meals Steven had sent from his kitchen. Lisa, already seated at the kitchen table, ate everything he sent over, including the hunk of pineapple cheesecake that was Nick's favorite dessert. Nick put the dishes in the dishwasher, and carried his wife upstairs to their bedroom. He sat her on the bed and brought her a laptop.

"Plenty of women become pregnant every day. I'm not an invalid, Nick."

"I don't want you to faint again."

"I promise, I won't be fainting anymore. Can't I at least sit at the desk? I am three months now."

Nick looked at her and walked with her from their bedroom to the spare room where the computers were.

"Okay, we can work together in here where I can keep an eye on you," he said.

He put Lisa to work identifying the contents of the deed. Ernest was developing the remaining roll of film. Nick sat down with the church ledger and looked at the numbers. Something was off. He needed the rest of the second page. He sighed. So far financial corruption had been going on under Pastor Clayton's nose. He decided to visit the public library via his computer terminal.

Hawkins arrived with a search warrant for David's home. Raquel called Nick who arrived as the forensics team was conducting a sweep of the premises. Nick had called David's estate attorney, Antonio Fernandez Garcia, who had arrived ahead of him. The search warrant stipulated David's bedroom, and the bedroom designated as his 'fiancée's,' which was next door to his own, were off limits. Hawkins, impressed that she had her own bedroom ahead of the marriage, watched the dark complected estate attorney on the phone. He walked near and heard rapid-fire Spanish which came to a dead halt as the lawyer glared at him. Hawkins looked at the card given him by the lawyer. Two more well-dressed men had entered the house. They ignored him and spoke to Raquel and Nick.

The Spanish-style mansion was expansive and elaborate, and Hawkins, wondered if he was wasting his time. He climbed the winding stairs to the second floor where a room caught Hawkins eye had been a study, but was now absent of a file cabinet, bookcase, desk, and technology of any kind. Another room was bare walls.

Taking another staircase to the floor below, Hawkins found himself in a Spanish-style courtyard. Rows of white rose bushes lined one side of the yard with a white wrought iron patio set on the other side. In the center of the yard a stone fountain decorated with cherubim playing a flute gushed water. The scent wafting from the roses was overpowering.

Retracing his steps Hawkins found a luxury guest house far enough from the main home to offer the ultimate in privacy. David was a man of discretion and painfully wealthy. To the detective, wealth trumped over justice. Hawkins vaguely mused what privilege had David's wealth brought him.

Hawkins made his way to the front of the house staring up at the arched windows when an officer approached him with a map of the property.

"Lieutenant, I believe this property extends beyond what this map shows."

"Why is that, Sergeant?"

The officer sighed. "I remember the news articles about this place when it was built. I think he has an air strip that's not shown on this map."

"Do we have an aerial view of this property?"

"Yes."

"And, is there an air strip, Sergeant?"

"Well, yes and no. It's not showing on this map, but there are markings indicating..."

"Sergeant, we have a search warrant to search his property, and we have done so. From the horse stables to the six-car garage to the outdoor swimming pool to the ten-acre garden. I'm not looking for anything else to search."

"But, Lieutenant, I believe..."

"Sergeant," interrupted Hawkins, "his lawyers are on the premises. In fact, we've been here all day. Let's not overstay our welcome."

Hawkins returned inside the main foyer of the mansion. He caught a glimpse of a framed photo on an ornate table. It was a couple on holiday.

Seated in his apartment, Hawkins studied the picture of David and Raquel he had borrowed.

Chapter 39

Hawkins was not in the best mood. This was a day dreaded by law enforcement. Having to pay final respects in a funeral service to fallen comrades who had given their lives in the line of duty. The fallen police officers would receive posthumous honors. Hawkins, in full dress uniform with a single gold bar, sat in the passenger seat with Sanders driving. After the ceremony, as Hawkins watched, Grant and Emory as pallbearers, carried the empty casket to the waiting hearse, he felt a chill. He scanned the crowds as casually as he could seeing only police officers in assorted ranks in attendance.

Hawkins was in the cruiser with Sanders driving when he passed a group of men in dark suits strolling away from the church. He glanced casually at them and his mouth fell open. All five pastors were in solid black suits with black eye shades heading toward the train station. Wait, what? Was that Pastor Sanchez with a long black cane?

"Turn this vehicle around," yelled Hawkins.

"Lieutenant, I can't do that!" Sanders yelled back. "We would be facing oncoming traffic."

Hawkins yelled again. "Damn it, woman! Pull over!"

He jumped out the vehicle and ran around to the driver's seat pushing her over to the passenger side. Sanders glared at him. Putting the police siren on top the car he cut across the traffic, barely being missed by an oncoming tractor trailer. He swung down a narrow street that expanded into a broader street. Stopping the car on the sidewalk, he jumped out the vehicle, looking up and down the street. Startled passers-by gave him dirty looks as they walked around the cruiser.

Where were they? He looked for the five men in black suits. Where had they disappeared to? As Hawkins looked for their cars, Ernest with Paul as his passenger, drove pass him in his black Corvette. Leisurely following in a black Lamborghini Countach was Steven with passenger David, and trailed by Nick in his new black four-door BMW truck.

Raquel, seated in the lobby of the Hot Springs Police Administration Building, powdered her nose. She was looking at her fingernails when she spotted black shiny shoes in front of her. She looked up at the Black officer in his uniform and smiled, ignoring his female partner.

"Yes?" said Raquel, staring at Grant only.

"Good afternoon, I'm Detective Grant, are you Raquel Mouton?"

"Yes. You asked me to come down here?"

"Yes. We need to ask you some questions. Please follow me."

Raquel stood up. Grant's eyes flickered briefly. She was taller than Sanders. Raquel tossed her long wavy hair over her shoulder sideswiping Sanders in the face. Sanders glared at the back of Raquel who walked beside Grant, not behind him. They entered an interview room, and Raquel walked to the chair opposite Grant. She took off the ice-blue trench coat revealing an ice blue form-fitting dress beneath hugged to a curvateous frame. She sat down and looked across the table at Grant.

Her light hazel eyes were slightly large and almond-shaped with arched eyebrows, long nose, and perfect Cupid's Bow lips. The dark, wavy hair created a voluptuous frame for the smooth butterscotch tan skin. She stared at him, and Grant forgot what he was going to say. He became aware Sanders was staring at him with a slight scowl to her mouth, and gazing at Raquel with veiled dislike.

"Ms. Mouton, my name is Detective Grant and this is my partner, Detective Sanders."

"My attorney should be here any moment, Detective."

"This is only a conversation, Ms. Mouton. We're just fact checking."

"You can fact check when my attorney arrives."

Nick stepped into the interrogation room. He and Grant shook hands. Nick sat beside Raquel, ignoring Sanders seated across from him.

"What are your questions, Detective? I've had a long day."

"I understand, Ms. Mouton. Thank you for being here. What is your profession?"

"I'm a high school principal at Holy Springs Academy."

"When was the last time you spoke with Pastor David Sanchez?"

"I believe it was the same day of his disappearance."

"Which day was that Ms. Mouton?"

"So much has happened, I don't remember the dates."

"Yet, you stated it was the same day of his disappearance. How do you know when he disappeared?"

"I don't. I hear the news. I watch the news. They all seem to know."

"You're in a relationship with Pastor Sanchez?"

"I was his girlfriend."

"Was?"

"Well, I haven't heard from or seen him in months. I'm ready to move on."

"Why have you waited so long to move on?"

"Because you all behave as if he's still alive. If that's so I want to be here. I don't know what to do anymore. I've been seeking therapy to help me during this crisis."

"Therapy? With whom?"

"Pastor Barnes, of course! Many people don't know he's a licensed psychologist. Did you, Detective?"

"Were you aware Pastor Sanchez was in a road accident?"

"What? Is he alright? Where is he?"

"We found a registration card with his name on it when we hauled his vehicle out of the water."

"Where was David?"

Raquel's nose had turned pink, and her eyes were holding tears. Grant had to stop looking at her.

"Miss Mouton, are you sure you have not heard from David Sanchez?"

Raquel frowned. "Don't you have any more questions for me than that, Detective?"

Nick, who had remained quiet during the exchange, stood up. "Unless you're charging my client with a crime, she is leaving."

Grant stared at Nick who guided Raquel out the room.

Hawkins, seated next door, was playing back the videotaped interview. He was listening to Raquel and Grant, but his eyes studied the man in the clerical collar seated beside her. Nick was wearing the identical black suit he had seen him in earlier in the day, and with the same dark eye shades.

Chapter 40

The Sleeper crouched low to the ground near the neighbor's rows of hydrangea shrubbery, and watched the home of Jose Lopez. There was a party occurring and the house and yard was full of people. The Sleeper looked at his watch. It was past midnight. He would wait one hour more. The weather was turning warmer now. Daylight savings would soon be on the horizon shortening the night hours. He looked across the expanse of yard again. Wait a minute! Jose was alone in the kitchen and the few remaining guests were on the front lawn between all the parked cars. He slipped across the yards keeping low to the ground and stood erect once inside the kitchen. Jose relied on his hearing device which worked if you made sufficient noise. The Sleeper was aware of this fact from previous contact with Jose. He slipped the knife out of its block. He was driving by the residence when he heard the blood-curdling scream of Jose's wife coming from inside the house.

Hawkins parked his cruiser and surveyed the scene before him. Police cars, undercover vehicles, medical trucks, and unmarked patrol cars were all vying for attention close to the property. Police were posted at both ends of the street to keep news crews out. He counted no less than three news trucks, although the alerts had been in code.

Hawkins walked up the driveway packed with parked cars and into the house. Bibles, rosary beads, statues of saints, and family photographs were everywhere in the house. Emory was in the kitchen with the assistant coroner. It was obvious there had been a party. The remains of food and a large sheet cake framed the cluttered kitchen table. Hawkins smiled at the empty cake pan. Either no one was on a diet or the cake was delicious.

Emory walked over to him. "Lieutenant, Jose Lopez was seventy-nine-years old. Stabbed once in the heart. Died on impact. Wife, Luz Maria, found him."

"How long ago was all this?"

"The coroner timed his death a little under fifty-five minutes. This is a fresh kill. The Lopez family had been celebrating his seventy-ninth birthday."

"No one saw or heard anything?"

"No."

"Was he a member of Hot Springs Cathedral Church?"

"Yes, him and his entire family."

"Deacon?"

"Yes, and trustee."

"Okay. I'm going over to the church. They're holding some sort of prayer vigil and I want to see who attends."

"That was last night," said Emory. "Next week is the town hall. Pastor Mouton will be addressing the church and community."

"Town hall? Big city sophistication in a small town. Cute."

"It's the second one."

Hawkins looked at him and proceeded to walk away. Emory called after him.

"Lieutenant? Forensics dropped off a manila envelope for you this afternoon. It's the completed diagnostics work on Pastor Sanchez' vehicle. I put it in your office."

"Thanks, Emory."

"Also, uh... Commissioner Novalski vetoed the search warrant for the church financial records. Judge Hall did as well."

"Why am I not surprised?"

"Deacon Joseph also left a couple of messages about a deacon's list?"

"Yes?"

Emory read from his notes. "The church lawyer stated it was a breach of confidentiality."

"That figures. Thanks, Emory."

Hawkins sat in his office going over the diagnostics report on Sanchez's vehicle. What stood out was the redesigned engine, reverse tint windows, and empty cavities underneath the vehicle that housed something that was no longer there. The only paperwork on the vehicle was the registration card to Sanchez and the owner's manual. A disturbing summary at the end of the report found when the forensics team attempted to examine the engine it self-destructed. Nothing was left of the engine but ashes on the lab floor. When they returned to the vehicle the entire console system had also self-destructed leaving a hole in the car. Hawkins sat back in his chair. He visualized each pastor's car. All designed for speed and durability on the road. Who were these guys?

Police Sergeant Edwards leaned across the open door jamb. "You just got here? There's been reports of a shooting in Oakland Heights. Guy shot is a pastor at that church you're investigating."

Hawkins ran past the policewoman so fast the papers in her hand shivered.

The Sleeper was irritated. The fact that David Sanchez whereabouts were unknown were bothersome and a constant source of irritation. He should have managed him when he was on foot instead of waiting until he was in his vehicle. Hindsight is the invention of regrets. Time to move on. Looking at the stilled picture of the photo gathering of pastors, clergy, and deacons all dressed in black for the last town hall meeting was a beauty. Huh? Wait a minute! A slower glance at each face. There was a missing pastor besides David Sanchez. Where was Pastor Ernest Carter that night?

Ernest admired the comely backside of Karen as she followed the hostess to their table. The off-white silk evening gown she wore embraced soft curves. Once seated, Ernest gave the wine order along with their dinner order before leading the doctor to the dance floor.

As they danced, Ernest looked down into mahogany brown eyes, and something in his chest fluttered. He stopped looking at her. What was happening here?

In the sultry voice he found pleasing to hear, she said, "I know you've heard Detective Stewart died from his injuries."

"Yes," he replied.

"Two other deaths came into the morgue recently. Lars Eliason, killed in his home garden, and Jose Lopez, fatally stabbed in his kitchen."

"The scenes of the murders have changed, but the victims are still senior citizens."

"Yes. The police are not releasing any information about the last two murders."

"They're busy looking for two of our people." He grinned.

She smiled up at him. "How is Claudia's arm?"

"It's healing nicely. I think almost getting killed has softened her attitude. She's a nicer, more improved Claudia."

Karen smiled despite herself. "Stop it."

He grinned and their eyes met. He looked down at her lips, and looked away again.

"Is there anything else? I see our food arriving."

"No, that was it. I have copies of the autopsy reports I can send you if you want them."

"Thanks, yes."

He escorted her to their table. She kept looking at him, but he remained silent for most of the meal. When he walked her to her door, he intended to shake her hand, and leave. Instead, she smiled, and he kissed her. When they parted their eyes locked. Uh-oh! He followed her inside her house. He inspected her house for safety precautions before joining her in her pink and green decorated bedroom. He was standing in the middle of the room. His heart was pumping hard. His breathing had become shallow. He sat in a chair with his bow tie in his hands. She stepped out of her closet in a pink silk peignoir set. Ernest stared at her and stood to his feet.

Sheepishly, he said, "for some reason I can't sleep with you tonight."

"Okay," she said. She was looking at him with a mixture of confusion and hurt. "Good night, Ernest."

"Good night, Karen."

He was across the door sill when he turned back. "I can't sleep with you because your worth more than a one-night stand to me."

"You hadn't called me in so long, I thought we were over before we had begun."

"Just busy. I thought of you every day and most nights."

"Same here."

"Karen, I want more from you than casual dates. For the first time in my life, I want a serious relationship, and I want it with you."

She smiled. "That's possible."

He smiled. "There's a spy thriller playing next week at the theater. I'll call you to see if you can make it."

"Oh, I'll make it. Your worth more than a casual affair as well."

They stared at each other. He walked over to her, and pulled her gently to him. She put her arms around his waist. This time when they kissed, it was deep and meaningful.

Chapter 41

The Sleeper was aware he dare not install any type of tracking devices on their vehicles. He noticed they paid attention to their vehicles now which meant no more automobile mishaps. The young postal worker, Rick, was dating Ernest's younger sister, Jasmine. He wished the young couple well. He watched the young man drive up in his black sport Audi, and they fairly floated to the car. He smiled to himself. Young love was a beauty to behold. The Sleeper was glad she had left the premises. He was waiting for Ernest to appear. He had no intentions of tackling him. Something told him the cat-eyed pastor was capable of handling himself. He had devised a unique plan for him. He watched Ernest with a broom sweeping his driveway. As Ernest turned to enter the open garage the Sleeper aimed his weapon. He had selected a SilencerCo Maxim nine-millimeter handgun. It came with a built-in silencer. A neighbor came out. He lowered his weapon. The woman walked over to Ernest and gave him what looked like a pie plate. Oh, for Pete's Sake! He used his binoculars to view her. A dark-haired brunette of a certain age; shapely, wearing a dress that emphasized her curves. He lowered the binoculars. She was following the pastor into his house. He leaned back and waited as Ernest walked in the house with the pie, and the neighbor followed him. The Sleeper smiled and sighed. The next instant he grew alert. The pastor had come out his front door and was walking the neighbor to her front door. Using the binoculars, he laughed aloud at the disappointed look on her face. Ernest walked to his garage and opened the door. The Sleeper aimed the handgun again and focused it on Ernest's head near his temple. As he pulled the trigger a blinding light caused him to blink, and the weapon jumped in his hands. The bullet hit the side of Ernest's shoulder and stuck in the garage wall. The Sleeper regained control, and fired again, hitting Ernest in the back. Ernest ducked and rolled to the other side of the garage disappearing inside. The Sleeper muttered curses and left the scene as he had arrived. Ernest sent out an alarm, activated the locked latch on the garage, and passed out.

Detective Grant jumped out of his vehicle and ran toward the open field. His partner Sanders ran in the opposite direction. Not finding tracks Grant doubled back to the other side with the same results. He looked out over the field. The sniper had come from beyond the trees.

"That's an open field," said Sanders. "If he had a high-powered weapon, which he must have had, he's long gone now."

"Agreed."

Sanders whistled as she looked up at the house. "This is some house. He's a pastor?"

"Pastor and doctor," said Grant. "He's also a millionaire. Some kind of family inheritance."

"Let me see if there's a way to get in this beauty."

Grant looked at the pastor's house and called for backup and medical personnel. There was blood on the sidewalk in front of the closed garage doors. He walked around the perimeter of the house and looked inside the windows. Blinds covered the view. He was concerned for the pastor. He could be dying. He kept one eye on Sanders as she ventured to the side of the house. He had lost one partner; he did not want to lose another.

Surveying the area on his car monitor Steven parked near the back of the house. He lightly scaled to the roof and slid down through an unobtrusive opening. He located Ernest on the garage floor and carried him to the kitchen. Surveying the body wounds, he located the bullet in Ernest's back, and retrieved it. Ernest flinched once. Steven bandaged his wounds and carried him out the back door to his car. He saw the detective outside on his phone and noticed the new blonde partner. He had to move faster.

Steven returned inside the house. Going to specific rooms he secured the locking mechanisms. Checking the photo room, he collected all the prints and the evidence from David's vehicle, and set the alarms. Going to Jasmine's room he located the extra weapons and ammunition.

Jumping over the stair railing Steven saw Grant and the new detective were now joined by Hawkins. He unlocked the garage door. Making his way to his vehicle as soundlessly as he entered, Steven backed up going a smooth one hundred fifty miles per hour before turning, and streaking pass the fire truck, medical units, police cars, and two news trucks.

The medical examiner appeared visibly upset at the absence of the body. She tried to cover it well, but Hawkins suspected she was intimate with this pastor. From his folder on the pastor he surmised this doctor would be the pastor's type. Hawkins looked at his phone. "What can you surmise about the condition of the missing pastor, Doctor?"

"From the amount of blood found on the garage floor, and in the kitchen, he's in dire need of medical assistance," replied Karen.

"My understanding is that he's a doctor himself. Couldn't he have removed the bullet?"

"There is no indication that occurred, Detective. From the amount of blood pooled in the garage, and on the kitchen floor, he would have passed out after a few minutes."

She walked to her car and drove away. Hawkins watched the police, forensics, and his detectives as they crawled over the home and grounds. The widowed neighbor next door was near hysteria at the news but had not seen or heard anything. The house occupants on the other side of the pastor were both white collar professionals who were at their respective employments. Hawkins surveyed the backyard. The entire area was fenced by twelve-foot deciduous trees forming a natural homage to the environment while also offering excellent privacy.

"That's crazy!" said Sanders. "This is the third body that's gone missing!"

Grant blew out his breath through his mouth. "The backdoor is locked. The patio door is locked. All the windows are locked. The front door is set with a sophisticated alarm system. Only the garage door was unlocked, but it was closed when we got here. How did the injured pastor and whoever else get out the house? They didn't come past us."

Hawkins spoke his thoughts. "That means someone else was in the house with him. Doesn't he have a sister? Where is she?"

"Look!" Sanders pointed to a chip high on the wall above the garage door.

Grant retrieved a six-foot ladder from the garage. Sanders climbed it and using her penknife pulled the bullet out of the wall. She dropped it in the evidence bag Grant held.

"Looks like a nine-millimeter," said Sanders.

Hawkins answered a call from his phone. "Okay, gotcha."

He looked at the detectives who were still surveying the house. "That was Emory. He has the pastor's sister."

"Was she here?" asked Sanders.

"No, they were at the movies," replied Hawkins. "The question remains, who was in there with him?"

Hawkins texted Emory. *Bring Jasmine Carter to police station.*

Monaco was in the kitchen breading pork chops and watching a best-selling novelist describe her new book on a talk show. A news flash came on preempting the program. The anchor lead in with the shooting at Ernest's house, followed by his photo, and live views of his house with yellow police tape surrounding it. The journalist described the police concern in lieu of his subsequent disappearance. The journalist put up his photo again, and asked the public's assistance in locating him.

Monaco doubled over. She felt the room spinning around her. She clutched at the sink for support. Her eyes stung with tears. She felt herself slipping into dizzying darkness. She opened her mouth and screamed. Paul ran into the house in time to catch her before she hit the floor. A few minutes later he watched helplessly as the emergency medical staff took his now comatose wife to the hospital. He faintly remembered the detective's advice, and later, when Steven gave him warning. For the first time in his life, he felt physically weak. He sent a text message to Steven and Nick. He walked inside the house and laid on the floor in tears and prayers.

They had enjoyed a nice evening at the movies. Emory knew he was falling in love with Jasmine and suspected she felt the same about him. She looked at him and smiled. He smiled and looked away. He looked at his phone. *Bring Jasmine Carter to police station.* He looked up and realized they were driving down her block. He spied the heavy traffic, and saw Hawkins standing in the driveway. He backed up, although he heard her speaking to him, he kept going in the opposite direction. Jasmine tried to unlock the doors, became hysterical, and grabbed at the steering wheel. He pulled her to him and kept driving. She collapsed on his chest, and began crying. He reached the church parking lot, turned off the engine, and wrapped both arms around her. All he could think to do to calm her was to kiss her. She kissed him back.

They sat there a long time. She was spent from crying and leaned on his chest. He had one arm around her and the other free on the steering wheel. He traded his dark shades for night goggles. Slowly he spoke to her about his childhood. He told her about his law enforcement father who spent most of his career undercover as a drug enforcement officer.

As the duskiness of the evening turned into darkness, he told her about his life in the Army and his forensic science background, and last, he told her how attracted he was to her. He asked her to seriously consider him as a suitor. She looked up at him, the large green eyes lightly rimmed with tears, and they kissed again.

"Rick?"

"You feeling better?"

"Can you find out about my brother, please? He's all I have."

"Yes, let's go inside the building. I feel vulnerable sitting here."

"Okay. I know the pass code."

Emory, keeping his hand near his holster, shadowed Jasmine as she unlocked the alarm system. She went to the ladies room to fix her makeup. He took a position by the door and called Hawkins.

"Where are you?"

"At the church with Jasmine Carter."

"I need you to bring her to the station. I'm heading there now."

"Okay."

"Get control of your emotions, Emory. You're her guardian for the moment."

"Yes sir."

"And, since you're in the church, look around her office. Different eyes, different finds."

The file cabinets were locked. He lightly tapped a drawer in frustration, and heard a sound. He stopped. He looked behind the file cabinet. Nothing. He looked down the side near the wall and found an old, faded ledger and inside, an old, faded property deed.

Emory told Jasmine he had to bring her to the police station. She called Nick. They held hands as Emory drove. Nick was parked out front when they drove up to the entrance. Jasmine rushed to Nick who held her and shook Emory's hand. The trio walked into the police station to meet with Hawkins. Nick walked in the interrogation room with Jasmine.

Hawkins walked in. "Hello, Sister Carter. My name's Lt. Hawkins. We've spoken on the phone briefly."

"I want to know what happened to my brother," said Jasmine.

Hawkins looked at Nick. "We don't know Sister Carter, and that's the truth."

"Why were the police and ambulance at our house earlier?"

"Your brother was hurt. That's all we know."

"He was hurt. What do you mean that's all you know?"

Nick laid a reassuring hand on her arm. "You asked Sister Carter to come here for what purpose?"

Hawkins addressed Nick. "Counselor, I received a report today that every person who has died recently has had some connection with Hot Springs Cathedral Church. Would you care to explain that to me?"

Nick coolly responded. "Isn't that your job, Lt. Hawkins?"

Hawkins turned from Nick to Jasmine. "Have you been aware of any disgruntled church members who might want to harm other members in the church?"

Jasmine looked at him with sad eyes. "No."

"When was the last time you saw Pastor Carter or heard from him?"

"His name is Ernest, and he's my brother," said Jasmine, looking indignant and angry through her tears.

"I understand that. That's why I asked."

"I saw him this evening around six o'clock. Rick picked me up for our movie date at six-thirty. That was the last time I saw my brother."

Hawkins scribbled on a card. "If you think of anything else, please do not hesitate to call me."

"Okay," said Jasmine, taking his business card.

Hawkins looked at Nick. "Please take her home. I need to speak to Detective Emory."

Chapter 42

Paul waited for the desk nurse to direct him to Monaco's room. He had brought her a bouquet of gardenias, her favorite flowers. He had been praying nonstop as she had been in the hospital for several days. He was inconsolable with silent grief. The nurse, a member of their congregation, decided to walk the pastor to his wife's room. She had another nurse stand in for her as she accompanied the sullen pastor down the hall. A large figure dressed entirely in black was standing over the bed with a pillow over Monaco's face. Paul's rage was insurmountable as he threw himself full force on the perpetrator. The man was his size, and they grappled about the room crashing into the walls and knocking over furniture. The man attempted to knock Paul out. He brought a chair crashing down across Paul's back. Using another chair, he caught Paul on the side of his head. Paul rolled over twice and kicked upward countering the next move as the perpetrator lost his balance. The nurse, knocked into the wall, managed to crawl into the hallway screaming and crying. Two male nurses appeared as the perpetrator tossed Paul head first into a wall. Paul swerved his upper body using his shoulder and arm to block the impact. The Sleeper gut punched the first male nurse, and used the second one as a battering ram against Paul, before fleeing the hospital on foot. Paul, bruised and battered, crawled to his wife's bedside. She was unconscious but breathing. The nurse gathered herself enough to tend to her. Paul sent an alarm out, hid his phone in his sock, and fighting nausea, crawled to a corner, and passed out.

Nick sped to the hospital which was in chaos. Hearing police sirens in the distance Nick walked confidently, but with haste, to Monaco's room. Two nurses bent over Monaco and barely looked in his direction as he bent over an unconscious Paul. Nick removed his credentials, the Glock in his ankle holster, and phone. A male nurse brought a cot and placed Paul on it. Nick hurried to the waiting area. Hospital security was swarming the floor. Hawkins stepped off the elevator on Monaco's floor, and spied Nick in the waiting room who waved at him. Hawkins turned his head and proceeded to the nurses station where his visitation was curtailed by Monaco's doctor who insisted she could have no further visitors that night. By the time Hawkins turned around and retraced his steps to the nurses station, the waiting room was empty.

Two hours later, the Sleeper walked the outside premises of the Mount Pleasant Nursing Home for Veterans where the man under alias as David Diaz was recuperating. He had to admire this team. They had nine lives. Paul surprised him with his skill level. The Sleeper changed into the outfit he had borrowed off the orderly lying unconscious from a sleep hold. He stashed the man's body in one of the broom closets.

As he walked leisurely down the hall, he pushed the cleaning bucket and mop along emptying trash cans and doing a custodian's job. He found the designated room and casually looked in. Ah, there he was. Laying there waiting for the nurse. His arms and legs bandaged the entire length. Steven had been guarding David for the past three months. But the Sleeper's attack on Paul and Monaco guaranteed they would pull over in that direction. He more than likely would send Nick and this time he would destroy the blue-eyed attorney.

The Sleeper slipped on his hood. As he redoubled his walk down the corridor he slipped into the room and closed the door.

The Sleeper was thrown into the wall and pummeled with fists that were like iron balls in his sides. He tried to grasp clothing, but his hand slipped on the rubberized top, as he was thrown head first into the wall. He managed to gain some traction and pushed against the wall into the giant who pummeled his head and body and flipped him onto the floor. He grabbed a leg encased in rubber that resembled an iron rod. Slammed bodily against

243

a door frame, he scrambled to his feet, grappling with the man. Brute strength for brute strength they railed against each other until the Sleeper staggered, his rib cage on fire from lightning-fast jabs.

He fell to the floor in pain, scattered and disoriented. He caught a glimpse of David leaning in a corner with a Glock in his hand and spied the giant coming at him. The Sleeper turned over to the wall and made it to his feet only to double-handed punch and sailed into the opposite wall where he nearly passed out. A male security officer entered the room. Grabbing the man's leg, the Sleeper threw him in the giant's direction, and rolled out the room. In the hall where general chaos reigned, the Sleeper rose to his feet swiftly, grabbed a nurse, and threw her in the general direction of the door. He fled down the fire escape stumbling on the second floor landing which sent him rolling down the concrete steps to the first floor.

In pain and gasping for breath, he removed the hood, and ran out the fire escape exit pushing startled people out of his way. He ran toward his vehicle parked beyond the bushes. The giant had left him. He sped wildly out the lot hearing police sirens; his vision blurry and fighting nausea. Bruised, battered, and bleeding; for the first-time, fear gripped his entire body like a vise. Through his scattered thoughts, and labored breathing, his perception was clear. The Sleeper had tangled with Steven.

Paul opened his eyes slowly and the moment he jumped up he saw the dark blue eyes of Nick standing across the room. He looked to his right. He was in a bed opposite Monaco. Nick walked over to him. Paul slowly raised himself from the bed and managed to stand. His head was hurting, and his hearing was coming in and out. Nick lightly pushed him back on the bed. Paul slid to the floor instead.

"I can't do this anymore, Nick. It was different when I was alone. I can't have her hurt. I can imagine how Steven must have felt when he found Claudia. He lost his first love and was about to lose the second woman in his life. I can barely process the thought of losing one."

Paul put his head in his chest and cried. Nick waited in silence.

After a few minutes, he said, "stay here with Monaco tonight. We'll strategize in the morning. I need to talk to Steven. Hawkins was by earlier."

Paul looked up. "What? How long was I out?"

Nick smiled. "Long enough. Don't worry I was here first. Here's your ID and your Glock."

"Thanks, man."

Nick turned on his watch. "Give me a description of your attacker."

Paul sighed. "Male, about my height and strength. He knows the martial arts, and some old Academy moves."

Nick whistled slightly. "Who are we dealing with? A renegade? Vigilante? Professional hit man? What does he want?"

"I think he was sent, but by whom, and for what purpose, that I don't know."

"Lisa and I are following some leads from the information Ernest supplied. How is he?"

"The latest input from Steven is a shoulder grazed by a bullet and one in his back barely missed his spine. His prognosis is good. Steven confiscated the bullet and having ballistics work done on it."

"Where is Jasmine? You know how Ernest is..."

Paul grunted a smile. "She's in the house with Claudia. Since Hawkins already interviewed her, and she wasn't home during the incident, they should be okay."

Paul was slowly stretching, assessing any physical damage to his body. He looked at Nick.

"I need you to fill in for me. I already talked to Steven about it. He's committed to guarding Dave. After my run-in with this guy, I'm reassessing our angle here."

Nick glanced at his watch. *Met the ninja. D with me. Stay safe.*

Looking at Paul he texted Steven. *See you soon.*

Chapter 43

Nick looked around Steven's new five-bedroom 40,000 square foot house, walking from room to room. Steven had spent time wiring the house and installing distinct types of alarms. He settled David into the guest bedroom with the attached guest bathroom. He laid out David's pain medications and showed him the stocked mini fridge that served as a nightstand which David loved. Steven set up his computer screens, showed him the surveillance monitors, gave him his guns, and left him alone. Downstairs Nick and Steven lounged in the living room.

"So how you feeling?" asked Nick.

"I'll survive. One thing the guy is physically strong but his fighting style is old. The moves he used were taught in the Academy about forty years ago. I believe that's the only reason I lived. He's strong, but that's it. His fighting style is way off, man."

"Only you would be studying old Academy fighting styles. So, we're looking for an old male operative?"

"Yeah, that's what I think. I put information in the data system."

Nick showed Steven the deeds he had lifted from Emory at the police station. They both grinned. A shadow fell across the stairs. Steven jumped and ducked as Nick rolled and both landed in kneeling positions with guns aimed at the figure on the stairs.

David waved his bandaged arm. "Calm down guys. It's only me."

Steven stood up shaking his head. "Please don't let the official reports read we saved you only to have to kill you."

David and Nick laughed. David walked over to the sofa using a cane.

Nick said, "I would've loved to have seen that guy's face when he saw you standing in that corner."

David laughed. "That makes two of us. His head mask blocks his identity, but his eyes were shocked to hell."

"Why are you down here?" asked Steven. "Do you want me to put you down here instead of upstairs?"

"No, I prefer upstairs. I just wanted to know if I could have Raquel come over?"

"A better deal. We need you to get well. Talk to her on the phone every day, but we don't need her here right now. I've talked to her, so she'll be glad to hear from you."

David nodded. "Good point. I'll call her instead."

Nick joined in. "Remember, no one knows where you are. She must keep the knowledge that you're alive to herself."

"Dave, on second thought, use social media. That way you can look at each other."

"Okay. Talk to you guys later." As David made his way upstairs, he turned back. "How did Ernest make out with the film?"

Nick and Steven exchanged glances. "He's cleared the image enough for us to make out it's an armored combat vehicle."

"Wow! That's interesting! I'm going to work on some of the other film Ernest sent me."

Nick followed Steven to the kitchen. They both listened to the sound of David climbing the stairs and the close of his bedroom door. Steven took salad ingredients out the refrigerator and four steaks. Nick watched him preparing the food. Steven made him a small salad. Nick grinned.

"Okay, where's Ernest now?"

"Hot Springs Medical Center," replied Steven. "He's doing well. No fever and no pain. The shoulder wound is healing."

"That should soothe Hawkins for a minute," said Nick, absently eating a piece of lettuce.

"Yes," said Steven. "After Hawkins visit, we'll bring him here."

"Where's Jasmine?"

" Jasmine's at Emory's apartment. They're inseparable."

"Don't say that to Ernest. Where's Claudia?"

"My old place. Everything is locked down. It's safe to say she listens more to what I say. How's Monaco and Paul doing?"

"Monaco's okay, now. They kept her a few days because she was dehydrated. Lisa's been at the hospital nearly every day."

"She's due soon, Nick. Keep an eye on her. When are you taking a leave of absence?"

"My leave began this morning."

Steven chuckled. "I wondered why you weren't wearing a tie."

"Yeah, it's difficult to dress down when you're in a suit every day." Nick licked his lips. "Delicious, my friend. I'm going to the hospital, collect my wife, and going home. Talk to you later."

"Here you are. A nice dinner salad for Mrs. Rodgers." Steven handed Nick a brown shopping bag. "And, this time I put two pieces of cake in there. Dad has to keep up his strength, too."

Nick smiled.

The doctor entered the room as Paul was zipping up the back of Monaco's dress. Looking at Lydia Khan in her white doctor's coat, Paul realized he had seen the woman during the parties Monaco attended prior to their wedding.

"Good afternoon, Monaco," said the doctor. "How are you feeling this morning?"

"Hi, Dr. Khan. Much better, thank you. This is my husband, Dr. Paul Mouton."

"Should I leave?" asked Paul.

Lydia smiled. "Not at all, Dr. Mouton. You need to hear this too. Monaco, you are going to have to find ways of dealing with stress. It's not good for you or the baby."

"What?" said Paul and Monaco together.

"Yes, you are expecting a little one in about five months. Monaco, my private office number is on that card. Your next appointment date is on there, as well." She smiled as she left them.

Paul took the scenic route home. Monaco was numb. She let the car window down to let the breeze blow on her face. Paul stopped in the park and turned off the engine.

"I've been mulling over something for a long time now. With you pregnant my priorities change."

She looked at him. "Whatever you want. That's what we'll do."

"I want to quit the church and teach full time in the university. I also received another offer to work for a research lab as a technical writer. It's work I can do online. I wanted to know how you'd feel as a full-time professor's wife."

"I would love whatever you love. But I don't believe you should quit the church you've worked so hard to pastor. You might need to take a rest. The church is closed now, isn't it?"

"Yes. I have a deacons meeting coming up. They will either sign me on permanently as their senior pastor or vote to have me terminated. Either way, we'll let God's people decide."

"Paul, whatever you decide I will back you. I will be there in your corner because you're my husband, and I love you."

"I love you too, more than anything in the world."

"Now can we please go home? I would like you to make me a peanut butter and bacon sandwich, and I need to call Lisa."

"Are you kidding me? Peanut butter and bacon?"

She laughed gaily. "That's my craving. Salty bacon strips between a smooth peanut butter sandwich. Lisa brought me one in the hospital."

"This is going to be one interesting pregnancy."

On the third floor of Hot Springs Medical Center, Ernest was sitting up in bed using a weight ball to strengthen his hand and arm. Karen walked in his hospital room in her white coat.

"Well, someone's busy," she said smiling. "How do you feel?"

"I'm feeling better than I look. How is your day?"

She was surveying him quietly. "I never expected to see you in the hospital. Who removed the bullet?"

"What bullet?"

"Very funny. Someone shot you and someone else removed the bullet. In fact, you were shot twice. The police want to know who removed the bullets."

"I have no idea. I'm sure I was unconscious when I was found."

"Do you remember how you came to be in the hospital?"

"No, could you please tell me?" He was looking directly at her. She tried not to smile, put her head down, and wrote on his clipboard.

"Are you experiencing any pain?" She looked up at him.

"Not at present, no." He smiled and she smiled and shook her head.

"Karen?"

"Yes, Ernest."

"Could you please give me a kiss? I'm sure that's what saved me. The thought of your lips on mine and vice versa."

She laughed, kissed him, and they both grinned.

"Behave yourself," she whispered.

"When can I leave?"

"It will be soon. Your health is excellent. Have a good night, Dr. Carter, and try not to get shot anymore. We have real patients to take care of here."

"Good night, Dr. Newbold. I guarantee nothing." He thought he heard her sigh as she left the room.

That evening Hawkins stepped into Hot Springs Medical Center and stopped at the nurse's station. No one had visited Pastor Carter except his sister, Jasmine. He walked in the room and noted the neatness. Ernest was reclining on several pillows.

Hawkins pulled over a chair. "How are you feeling?"

"Been better."

"Pastor, I have some questions that I'd like solid answers to."

"I'll do what I can," said Ernest, smiling. He closed his eyes.

"Do you recall where the shooting came from?"

"I don't recall much of anything."

"There was a bullet removed from your back."

"The doctors have told me someone shot me."

"Can you think of anyone with a vendetta against you?"

"Vendetta? No." Ernest smiled. He opened his eyes and looked at Hawkins. "Have you discovered anything on your end?"

"Not yet. Search teams scoured the area. We found large tire tracks belonging to a van or larger. Forensics is working on it now. The oddest thing is that our forensics people feel someone else was there before them collecting evidence."

Ernest stared at him. Hawkins looked beyond Ernest to the window and the drawn shades and curtains.

"Some good news for you about your colleague, Sanchez.. We believe he's lying low somewhere."

"Is that police jargon?"

"It means, Pastor, he's somewhere that he and others consider to be safe."

"Have the police found Pastor Sanchez?"

"No."

"So, he's still missing? You're confusing me, Lieutenant."

Hawkins glared at him. "I swear this is the damnedest, craziest case I've ever worked. You were missing until a day ago when you were found on the hospital lot, drugged, and bandaged."

"I just want to be able to thank the good Samaritan who found me"

"Do you think the hospital might receive the same delivery with Sanchez?"

"I hope so. There are good people in this world," intoned Ernest.

"I saw you and your friends at the memorial service. Sanchez was using a cane."

"What memorial service?"

Hawkins stared at Ernest whose turquoise eyes appeared unusually light. A slight shiver passed through Hawkins. Looking around he saw Steven leaning in the doorway. Behind him in the hall female and some male staff appeared transfixed by the handsome giant's presence.

"Am I intruding? Are you questioning him, Lt. Hawkins?" the deep voice reaching Hawkins was smooth and melodic.

"No, you're not intruding Pastor. Might I ask how did you know Pastor Carter was in the hospital?"

"He called me, sir."

Hawkins looked at Ernest who showed him his phone.

"So, your memory has returned? Tell me, Pastor Carter, do you remember what happened to you?"

"No, it's what Pastor Barnes is going to work with me on."

"True. He more than likely is suffering with short term memory lost, but I won't know that until he's released, and we can start working together on memory exercises."

Hawkins heard enough. He sighed, walked past Steven, and kept going up the hall to the elevator.

After his visit with Ernest, Steven taught his mandatory class at Hot Springs University. He would not be back in the university for another three weeks. He spied Hawkins entrance and watched him as he sat in the last row in the back. The large room was packed with students who quieted down when he stepped to the lectern. He always wore his dark glasses making it impossible for them to know who he was looking at or would call on.

Hawkins listened attentively. Steven spoke in such a soothing drone he nearly dozed off. There was a question-and-answer period, and the class was over. The lighting in the room became brighter. The students stood up, and so did Hawkins. He looked down at the lectern for Steven. Hawkins ran into the hall, but Steven had vanished.

An hour after visitation ended, Ernest waited for the night nurse to check on him. He smiled at her sweetly when she brought his pain medication. Once she turned out the light and left him, he took off the hospital gown, and put on a black pullover and slacks. He strapped his ankle holster in place, his wristband, and pulled the now empty knapsack onto his back. Slipping on his gloves and pulling his night goggles around his neck he looked down the hall. The semi-darkness proved to be expert camouflage as he deftly found the rigged fire escape and slipped through. He opened the outside door and looked right and left. He pulled up his night goggles and saw Nick's black Viper to his left. The car approached without head-lights, and he slipped in.

Chapter 44

Hawkins received the news the next morning that Ernest had left the hospital during the night. He checked with the undercover teams covering the hospital's entrances and exits. They had noted no changes. He paid a visit to hospital security. There was nothing on the surveillance monitors. Hawkins remembered not only was the church off limits to search, but they could not ask for membership lists or even the addresses of the pastors themselves.

If the pastors addresses were not on file in the church, how had the sniper found the pastors?

Hawkins mulled over the fact there were only two pastors not injured was Paul Mouton, and Steven Barnes. Hawkins mind replayed when he had spotted them after the memorial service leaving the area all of them dressed in black. There was something uncanny going on. His superiors were not questioning the apparent dangers these pastors were in. And, for their part, the pastors seem unbothered by the violence happening around them and to them.

As he pondered the last several months an idea formulated in his mind. This time instead of calling City Hall or Washington, D.C., and being side-tracked, he made a direct call to a friend who owed him a favor. He needed to know these men's real identities, and why they were in danger.

The incessant buzzing of the doorbell woke Monaco from an afternoon nap. She heard voices downstairs. She threw on a pair of blue striped pajamas and walked downstairs into the kitchen.

Jayne immediately came to her and hugged her. "Congratulations."

"Thank you, Jayne. I'll let you know when I feel like dancing again."

Jayne smiled. "Well, I was just telling Paul that we returned from our honeymoon and heard about your pregnancy. I also heard from Mary about your fainting spells, young lady."

"Oh, Jayne, I'm fine."

"I'm sure you are, and you will be better now that I'm here. If you think I'm going away, and you're carrying my firstborn grandchild. hush!"

Monaco smiled as she wrapped Jayne in a big hug. Paul and Charles looked on silently.

By five o'clock in the evening, Steven headed to his new house where he checked on David, showered, and changed clothes. David was already cooking, and put everything on warmers. He whistled when he saw Steven who merely smiled. David drove Steven's Land Rover with Steven sitting quietly beside him. David parked in the back, and they made their way to the side entrance where Paul's office was. Paul opened the door for them. He was in his black clerical robe. David, Ernest, and Nick were in solid black suits. Steven wore a white tailored suit with white alligator shoes.

"It was the request of my beautiful bride," he said smiling.

"What about the dark eye shades?" asked Nick, trying to keep a straight face.

"Ah! Fortunately, some things are negotiable." He took off the dark shades. "Where is my bride?"

"In the chapel with the ladies. They're waiting on my signal. Ready?"

"I am."

The men moved into the sanctuary and into position at the altar with Ernest standing next to Steven as his best man. Emory was doing duty as the group's photographer. Ernest reminded him more than once to focus on the wedding party, not just Jasmine, to everyone's amusement. Monaco's baby bump was noticeable. She wore a navy silk gown with an empire waist as the matron of honor. Raquel, Lisa, and Jasmine were in navy chiffon gowns in varying styles. Lisa's one-shoulder style complemented her pregnancy. Nick could not stop smiling.

Claudia walked down the aisle in a long white silk charmeuse gown that lightly grazed over her curves. The honey-blonde hair waved glamorously over her shoulders. She carried a dozen long stem white roses nestled in a bed of chiffon and tulle ribbon, courtesy of David's rose garden. Steven and Claudia held hands throughout their ceremony.

After the ceremony, the group headed to Steven and Claudia's new home to celebrate. Ernest locked the church doors and set the alarm system. A few hours later, Steven and Claudia left for their honeymoon. Paul and Nick took their sleepy wives home. Emory was allowed to take Jasmine home.

Chapter 45

Seated at the kitchen counter making a shopping list and cross-referencing recipes with her pantry items, Monaco glanced at the clock on the wall. She was planning a special dinner party. She picked up her phone.

"Hello? Ernest? This is Monaco, how are you?"

"Hello, sweetheart. I'm fine. How are you? Where's Paul?"

"Don't worry, he's on his way home now. I asked him, and he said it was okay for me to call you, and invite you to dinner here Friday night. Bring a guest if you wish."

"Who else has been invited?"

"Our usual group since Steven and Claudia are back from their honeymoon."

"What time, darling?"

"You don't have to bring a date. Is six o'clock too late for you?"

She could hear Ernest giggling. "You are so transparent. My date and I will see you tomorrow evening. Good night, dear."

"Good night, Ernest." Monaco smiled.

Ernest returned to the dining room. He adjusted the lighting, so it was not so bright and took his seat beside Karen.

"Okay, what did I miss Jasmine?" Ernest asked his sister.

"What do you mean, what did you miss? How do you know I was the one doing the talking?"

Ernest indicated a condiment which Emory passed to him. "I know your voice little sister. So, disclose the information."

Karen intervened. "We were talking about all the murders that's occurring in Hot Springs."

"It's not safe to walk the streets anymore," said Jasmine. She looked over to Emory. "I'm so glad Rick looks after me the way he does. I feel so safe with him."

Emory kept his eyes on his plate engrossed in cutting his steak. Ernest almost smiled. He decided to let him off the hook if he intended to get his sister married to the guy.

"It's good you have someone like Rick protecting you, baby girl. I don't have to worry so much now."

Emory looked at him. Surprise was written all over his face. "Thanks, Ernest. That means a lot, man."

Jasmine looked across at her brother with a happy grin he had not seen since she was twelve years old. Ernest looked at Karen she was smiling with her head cocked to one side. It was her happy look as well.

"That was my friend, Monaco. She invited us to dinner at her place tomorrow evening. Are you able to attend?" Ernest asked.

Karen looked at him. She nearly frowned but looked down at her plate instead. "I would love to meet your friend, Monaco."

"Oh, good!" said Jasmine, excitedly. "Sister Monaco is married to our new pastor. They are a great couple. She's invited Rick and me as well. After dinner, I want to show you some dresses I bought at the new boutique downtown, Karen."

Karen looked across the table, and a smile hit her face. "Sounds like it will be a great dinner party. I need to go shopping myself."

Ernest and Emory looked across the table at each other and Ernest grinned. "This is where we retire to my den or, if you prefer, the backyard where I can show you my golf swing."

"Either one is fine with me," said Emory. "I like the outdoors. Do you hunt or fish?"

Ernest grinned.

Ernest was leaning against the side of his black Corvette when Karen steered her white Lexus sedan up the driveway of the two-story town home where they had decided to meet. Karen had been nervous about meeting Ernest's friends, and it was an odd sensation. Ernest was just as nervous because this woman affected him in ways he had never dreamed possible. For the first time in his adult life, Ernest wanted to make a favorable impression on a woman. He had foregone his usual black suits for a dark blue gabardine that intensified his eye and skin color. For a moment Karen stood transfixed. The man's coloring was as red as fire, and those light eyes were mesmerizing.

"Hi, did you have trouble finding the house?"

"No. I live in this area."

He smiled. "It was dark when I brought you home."

"You look very handsome tonight, Ernest."

"And I don't at other times?" he asked, giggling.

She bit her lip to keep from laughing. They held hands and walked up the porch steps to the front door.

He whispered, "You look beautiful. Pink is your color."

They kissed just as the front door opened. Without skipping a beat, the couple walked through.

"Everyone, meet my lady, Karen Newbold," said Ernest.

Karen noticed a momentary quietness before everyone came forward to greet her. Dinner was a leisurely affair. Karen masked her surprise at seeing the 'ghost' of David in chef's hat and apron in the Mouton's kitchen. After dessert, the men retired to the patio outside, and the women retreated to the living room.

"Could I ask you all a question?" asked Karen.

"Sure, we're a friendly bunch of gals," responded Lisa to laughter.

"Why were you all surprised when Ernest introduced me? Hadn't you socialized with his lady friends before now?"

"Ernest has never introduced his current dates as his lady friend," said Monaco, matter-of-factly.

"Yeah," joined in Lisa. "We have known him practically all our lives and never, ever heard that title given to any of the women he dated."

Jasmine stared at her. "The way he looks at you is different, too."

"It's about time he settled down," said Monaco.

"We're rooting for you," said Claudia with a chuckle.

"Don't demonize Ernest too much," said Karen. "I've had my share of men friends overlapping sometimes. This is the first time I've not slept with a man I was dating on the regular. I think he's something special."

"Isn't it funny how you spend your free and not so free days looking for Mr. Right and when he comes along, you're unprepared for him?" asked Raquel.

"Only because you've spent so much time looking you haven't stopped to take stock of what to do when you find him!" responded Claudia.

"Wow! Now that's profound and so true," said Lisa.

"So, how are you and Rick doing with big brother standing by?"

"Ernest invited Karen over last night to our house for dinner. I think he's beginning to like Rick a little bit."

"Are you okay Lisa? Put that pillow under her feet."

"I'm fine, just feeling pregnant these days. Thanks, girls."

"Put your feet up, honey."

"How far along are you now, Lisa?"

Lisa smiled. "As of a week ago I am now a full nine months."

"You're glowing too," said Raquel.

"Do you think your baby will inherit your husband's blue eyes, Lisa?"

"I don't know. I hope so. I love the color of Nick's eyes."

"I don't know, girl. The baby can't go wrong either way. Yours are so dark they look black."

"They are black," said Lisa, laughing.

"Boy or girl?"

"We're keeping it a secret."

"The baby is going to be beautiful either way," said Monaco.

Karen looked at her. "How are you feeling?"

"How are you feeling, Monaco?" asked Jasmine. They all looked at Monaco in her blush-colored voile maternity dress with the gathered sleeves and handkerchief hem.

Monaco blushed. "I'm fine, ladies. We're due around Halloween."

"Oh, wow! That's not so far away."

"Congratulations, girl. I was about to ask where you bought that dress."

"I like your maternity wardrobe. Most of your dresses you'll be able to wear afterward."

Claudia and Raquel hit Monaco with a chorus of, "I want to borrow it when I get pregnant," to unabashed laughter for a few minutes.

"I know one thing. I must get married soon before I look like a whale in a pink dress," said Karen. "That dinner was fabulous, Monaco."

"Yes, it was! You outdid yourself with the dessert though."

Monaco giggled. "I didn't make the dessert. David brought it over."

"We didn't make the dinner either. David cooked and we helped," laughed Lisa.

Raquel giggled. "David loves to cook, and I love to eat. Thank God for his home gym, but I'm struggling to stay this size."

The ladies laughed. "That's the problem with love. You get too relaxed."

Karen turned to Claudia. "Ernest told me you're a newlywed?"

Claudia flashed her wedding rings with a grin. "Yes! It seems surreal at times. I never realized how lonely I was until I fell in love with Steven. I've known him all my life but never thought of him more than a long-term family friend, since he was engaged to my cousin."

Monaco looked at Claudia. She and Lisa exchanged glances before Lisa stood up.

"Speaking of long-term. I think it's time."

The ladies rushed to get the men on the patio. There was bedlam before Ernest and Karen took over. Lisa and Nick were driven by Paul to the hospital as the doctors tended to the worried parents in the backseat. Following Paul in their separate cars were David and Raquel and Emory driving Jasmine.

A few hours later, Richard Nicholas Rodgers, entered the world. Two hours later, David whisked away Nick, Lisa, and their newborn, along with Ernest and Karen, in his private helicopter.

Nick and Lisa's new home was a blue-gray Craftsman-style, four-bedroom home that sat on an incline with a wide front porch. Steven and Paul completed the wiring for the house alarms and surveillance footage in time for the baby's arrival. Monaco and Jayne decorated the new nursery in shades of baby blue. Lisa was surprised and delighted.

Chapter 46

Hawkins arrived a half hour early to find Hot Springs Cathedral Church's parking lot crammed with cars. Hawkins found a spot in the back of the sanctuary. He saw the pastor's mother and several women seated in the front pews. He saw Monaco when she stepped into view from a side door wearing a white maternity dress. He directed his attention to the lectern. He had a good view of the platform where the clergy stood. Hawkins watched as Paul, Steven, Ernest, and Nick walked onto the pulpit.

Paul stepped to the lectern. "I won't keep you long. As you all know, our church had to close its doors temporarily until we find out what's going on. As of this meeting the police still have not been able to discover the identity of the person or persons causing all this destruction. We, who are alive in Christ, know that the Church will have the final victory."

The congregation reacted with shouts of approval, and hand clapping. Paul waited until the applause died down.

"Church, I have come to a decision that I need your response to. I believe like Jonah I am the cause of the church problems. I don't know why or how, but I believe it is so. I am leaving this assignment as your pastor that you all may live in peace."

Deacon Ed, aided by two younger deacons, stood up. "My name is Deacon Ed Joseph, and I'm the chairman of the deacons. Pastor, you've worked hard to prove yourself a man worthy of the office of pastor/ teacher. Your leadership has been evaluated monthly, and you have not failed in all you've done. You have assembled a talented team of pastors who work as hard as you do. We approved your marriage, and we approved your closing the church temporarily. But we will not approve of you leaving us."

A trustee stood up, "Pastor Mouton, as acting president of the trustee board, I think I can speak for all the trustees when I say we will not approve of you leaving."

A deaconess was next. "My name is Deaconess Joy Candless. Pastor, we will not approve of your departure. We genuinely love you and your wife."

The president of the usher board was next. "My name is Brother Sam Craft, and unanimously the usher board will not approve of you leaving."

And so it continued. Each ministry leader stood and affirmed Paul's position as senior pastor of Hot Springs Cathedral Church.

Paul, visibly moved, looked down at the podium. "God's people have spoken."

The entire congregation of leaders stood and applauded the young pastor who was fighting back tears. Steven walked over and hugged him. The applause turned into a standing ovation. Hawkins, amazed by the scene, felt empathy for the congregation. It was some time before he was aware the second tier of clergy had taken over.

Hawkins felt a tap on his shoulder. He looked around and faced Ernest, who smiled. "Pastor Mouton asked me to bring you to his private office."

"Oh, I know the way there."

"Not to his private office you don't. Follow me."

As Ernest lead him down and around the halls Hawkins took notice of his physique. The built more powerful than he looked in business suits. The thin black pullover outlined taut muscles, and he walked on the balls of his feet. Hawkins had the eerie feeling he was following a huge dangerous feline. He shook himself. What! A side wall opened, and he entered a room. The wall closed automatically behind him. Hawkins surveyed the room. Nick was standing to his left, Paul was directly in front of him, Ernest had moved to his right, and turning his head slightly he glimpsed Steven behind him. He did not see the Puerto Rican pastor and that disturbed him. He walked forward into the room.

"Do you want me to do the transcription now?" asked Jasmine.

262

Hawkins snapped his head around. She was seated on the sofa and now moved to the door leading to her office. Hawkins felt slightly disoriented. Where he was standing would have brought him from the parking lot, and yet they had walked the halls.

"No, it's not that important," said Paul. "Go home."

Emory looked at Hawkins. "Stay with her."

Jasmine smiled, and the detective followed her into her office. Paul beckoned to the chair in front of his desk. Hawkins sat transfixed.

"That's a large number of church leaders you have out there. Do you mind telling me how many?"

Paul looked at his desktop terminal. "We have eighty-five deacons. Fifty ordained and thirty-five walking."

"I hate to sound like a non-believer but what's the difference, Pastor?" asked Hawkins.

"The ordained take the lead at communions, baptisms, and so on. The walking deacons are in training, you could say."

"Some of those deacons look, um..."

"That's why we pressured them to receive thirty-five younger men."

"How many ministers?"

"We have twelve married clergy couples."

"Why are they married? Your pastors were single."

"When I came on board, all the reverends were older and married. I happened to be single with the men I brought on. The fact that three of my team is now married, and the other two involved in long-term courtships with local women is looked upon favorably by the congregation and deacons."

Hawkins looked around. "Who's married?"

"Besides myself, Pastor Rodgers and Pastor Barnes."

Hawkins glanced sideways at both men. "How many trustees are there?"

"There were twelve active on the board."

"And five have been killed with eight former trustees murdered."

Paul eyed his monitor. His fingers moved across the keyboard. "If we're talking current deaths, we've lost four clergy, and eleven trustees, and I did not count the deacons or others injured. Most of these people were either former members or former volunteers."

"In other words," added Ernest, "they were former trustees and not actively involved on any of the financial teams."

"That doesn't mean they deserved to die because they were ex-members or volunteers," added Steven, his deep voice sounding deeper than usual. "What it means is that we are as dumbfounded as you why these older members are being targeted."

"You still haven't heard from Pastor Sanchez?"

"No," said Paul giving him the direct gaze Hawkins had come to appreciate was the pastor's way of communicating.

"It is encouraging that the church is standing behind you but, if you don't mind, could you please enlighten me how long you're going to play this game of charades with these people?" asked Hawkins.

Paul frowned. "What are you talking about?"

"Suppose it's an enemy from your past, Pastor? While you were out there playing the role of the biblical Jonah, I was wondering how long it's going to be before one of you gets killed; which might have already happened with Sanchez. I'm concerned about your lives and the lives of your families. Before I forget, congratulations Pastor Rodgers on the birth of your son."

"Thank you."

"Aren't you concerned for his safety now? Or your wife's?" prodded Hawkins.

Paul spoke before Nick could answer. "As the pastor of this church, I'm concerned about everyone's life, Lieutenant. We're taking care of our families the best we know how. And yes, Pastor Rodgers is not the only one worried about his family, I'm worried about mine as well, now that my wife is pregnant."

Hawkins stared at Paul. There was silence. Hawkins looked at Nick who was not looking at him. Instead, Nick's attention was focused on the open window. Both men ran for the window as Paul and Ernest went out the door. Removing the screen Hawkins and Nick scrambled out the window and stood back-to-back scanning the lot. Paul beckoned to them from the open door. Inside the office Steven pulled up the monitors to scan the outside perimeters of the building. The corner shadows shrouded the crouched figure. Steven zoomed in, but the shadow stayed crouched on the ground, and moved swiftly out of range of the camera.

"Where is your wife? No, don't tell me. Is she safe?" Hawkins asked Paul.

"She's not at the house if that's what you mean. She's with my sister and mother far from here."

"Hopefully, far enough."

Once again, Hawkins noticed how strategically placed the pastors were standing. No one was seated but him and Paul.

The Sleeper outright laughed with glee. Monaco pregnant! That's why she was in the hospital. Not much time left. The Sleeper retrieved the stray note he had found on the floor in the Trustees Office. Someone had scribbled the private address of Paul's home. That's where the wives were. He had a plan that would send that tight little group over the edge.

Chapter 47

Paul was awakened by the alarm on his wristband. It took less than a minute for him to understand the coordinates. He dressed as the team checked in. Ernest picked up Paul. Taking back roads hidden by an abundance of overgrown shrubbery and huge trees, Ernest entered the area where David housed his aircraft. He dropped off Paul near the air strip. David owned a redesigned warplane that could fly at three hundred fifty miles per hour. The original model was a one-seater, but David had a specially built backseat in which Paul now sat.

Steven and Nick met Ernest exiting the air strip, and each sped off toward Paul's boyhood home.

Over the river Paul parachuted down landing on the embankment. David circled a minute before moving on to the house. Viewing the home from overhead he sent the team a message.

Home on fire set around back entrance. Fire circling front and both sides of house. Fire moving steadily on left side of home due to heavy vegetation. No movement on ground.

Ernest arrived at the river bank. Both men softly treaded the water canal. Reaching the underside of the home, Paul climbed the embankment to the back of the house as he and Ernest looked for the water valves. Ernest reached the water pipes leading to the house, and worked releasing the pressure. Paul opened the locked valves and water gushed forth. They swam with the currents back to the embankment.

Nick skidded to a stop alongside the house, his taillights hitting the shrubbery. He jumped out the vehicle and headed into the home's entrance, kicking in the front door. Steven skidded alongside him facing the opposite direction and followed him inside. Steven smashed out the downstairs windows as Nick climbed the stairs to the upper floor.

They found the first floor bedroom where Lisa and Monaco had collapsed underneath a window with their faces covered with damp cloths. The women were unconscious with the baby between them with a towel over his face. Nick placed his sleeping son on his wife's chest, and picked up both, cradling them to his chest as he ran out the room. Steven picked up an unconscious Monaco and carried her gently down the stairs. Once outside, baby Richard let out a wail, and Lisa revived. Nick applied oxygen masks to both installing wife and baby in the backseat of Steven's Land Rover. Monaco was still unconscious. Ernest took a vial out of his ankle pocket and knelt before her. Paul watched wordlessly. Monaco regained consciousness, and Ernest nodded at Paul before placing a gas mask over her face. Paul picked up his wife and carried her to Steven's truck where he strapped her in. He headed back into the house through the front entrance while Ernest checked on Lisa and little Richard.

Nick, Paul, and Steven raced back into the house using a side entrance. Paul continued on down the winding hall to a set of stairs leading to a back suite of rooms. Nick and Steven found Jayne and Charles unconscious in a back bedroom. The couple were lying near a window with damp cloths covering their faces. Nick picked up Jayne in his arms, and Steven hoisted Charles over his shoulder. As they ran down the front hall the staircase collapsed under the weight of a flame-drenched roof. They turned and ran toward the back staircase. A whoosh sound alerted them that the front of the house had caved in. They descended the stairs aware the sides of the house was caving in with fiery flames and heavy gusts of smoke. They deposited the couple in Nick's BMW truck putting oxygen masks on both. Driving back highways and staying within the speed limits, Steven drove steadily keeping his eyes on the road and his police-dispatcher detector turned on. Ernest scanned for police as Nick's car sped along the roadway behind Steven's. Ernest would need to intercept if Nick got pulled over.

Back at the house, the smoke from the fire darkened and intensified as David hovered the aircraft above the rising flames. He turned on his sensors and watched his monitors. He saw the lone black figure carrying Raquel in his arms. He was staggering by the side of the house. The dark gray and black clouds of thick smoke made it difficult for Paul to see. The fire was creeping along the ground covering toward Paul. Using his bull-horn, David directed Paul to the embankment and the water. Paul had put his oxygen mask on his sister. He had ingested a great amount of smoke and could barely breathe. He staggered, and laid her down on the ground collapsing next to her. David hovered and landed. He gave Paul oxygen tank and worked on Raquel. She slowly revived, and they clung to each other. David, with Raquel's help, managed to drag Paul onto the plane. David sent a text.

All out. Stopping at medical center.

Everyone was wide awake by the time the three cars pulled into the garages of Steven and Claudia's new home. Nick carried his son as Lisa held onto his arm. Claudia alerted Ernest that Monaco was struggling with her breathing. Ernest carried Monaco to another bedroom and readjusted her oxygen intake. Claudia stayed with her.

"Where's David and Paul?" asked Nick.

"David took him to get checked out. He inhaled a lot of smoke. Raquel had gotten trapped in one of the rooms." replied Ernest, walking into the room and sitting down.

"What about Charles and Jayne?"

Ernest smiled. "Alive and well. They're both resting."

The men walked into Steven's new den. It was spacious and they each found comfortable seating. Steven was seated in front of a computer screen watching outside surveillance of his property.

Two hours later, Paul, David and Raquel, entered the house. The men gave David resounding applause. David, looking sheepish, kept shaking his head, and swallowing.

"Come on guys, we're a team. You did all the demanding work. All 1 did was get a chance to fly my baby."

"And, you were great, man," said Steven.

"Hey, Paul," said Ernest. "Are you okay?"

"Yeah, I'll live another day. How's my wife doing?"

"Claudia's with her," Ernest replied. He watched Paul take off his rub-berized pullover. "What about Jasmine? I know the detective is with her but, I'd feel better if she were here with us. I'll go get her."

"No, you won't, I'll go," said Steven. "Nick, help Dave get breakfast together, I'm starving. I think the ladies might want to join us."

Ernest looked at Steven. His eyes were shooting lightning streaks of green intermingled with blue, and his skin flushed cranberry red.

"I think we need to get Karen as well."

"Okay, Ernest. We'll get your women. Anyone else?"

Ernest grinned, closing his eyes to slits. "No, just them."

David grinned. "Come on Nick, help me."

"Help you do what? You're the chef around here!"

"Those mimosas Dave made for Monaco's party were great. Make those Nick," said Steven as he smoothly strapped his leg Glock back on.

Ernest was quietly standing by the door. They left the room soundlessly.

Steven headed for the young detective's apartment. He hoped they were in separate rooms, or more specifically, separate beds. He saw Ernest behind him. He had to smile but he understood. They entered the building with him in the front and Ernest coming in the back door. Emory was sound asleep on the living room couch. Steven stood over the detective, picked him up, and tossed him lightly to the wall. Emory scrambled to his side and pulled his weapon from his ankle before recognizing him. Steven smiled and helped him to his feet.

"Get dressed. We're moving you." he said.

Ernest appeared in the living room from Jasmine's bedroom and crouched to the floor. He looked over at the detective who was pulling on his shirt and shoes.

"What's going on?" asked Emory.

"You're coming with us. I want my sister safe."

"I was assigned to watch her."

Ernest stared at him. "Then how did we get in here?"

Emory gave Ernest a glaring look and turned his head. He reached for his phone and Ernest relieved him of it.

"What are you doing? I have to check in."

"I know you're a good detective, and you will get better as you go along...or get killed in the process," said Ernest in a matter-of-fact tone. "In the meantime, listen, look, and learn. We've been doing this a whole lot longer than you. You can be in our protective custody, or you can stay here and have Hawkins serve your behind on a platter to the mayor. The choice is yours, but I'm taking my sister."

Emory stared at Ernest whose light eyes were focused on him in a hard glare. The falsetto voice had deepened slightly, but the mouth had turned up in a slight smile. He was still crouched on the floor but had moved nearer to him. Emory saw Ernest was wearing black gloves, and he was not as low to the floor now. The hairs on the back of his neck raised. Ernest was poised to attack. He looked across the room at Steven languidly leaning against the wall. The dark glasses covered his eyes. Emory nodded, swallowed, and changed his light shirt to a black one and his shoes to black soft-soled ankle boots. He collected his night goggles, badge, and service revolver. Jasmine, in a white pullover and purple sweatpants appeared in the doorway with a pink overnight bag.

Ernest laughed. "It's not a sleepover, Jasmine."

She said, "I'm bringing it. I need my night creams."

"Whatever."

She walked over to Emory, and grasping his hand, followed Steven out the back door. Ernest watched them. Shook his head and sighed. Women!

Steven put Jasmine and Emory in his car and followed Ernest to Karen's home. He waited as Ernest disappeared around back. In his rearview mirror he observed the way the couple looked at each other. His thoughts traveled to Claudia, and he involuntarily smiled.

Ernest made his way to the back of Karen's home and lightly scaled the side of the house to the second floor back room. He entered soundlessly and walked to her bedroom. Karen was sitting up in bed reading a book. She looked up startled to see Ernest in her bedroom.

"Ernest, just what are you doing? How did you get in here?"

"Actually, I'd love to sit and chat, but there's not enough time."

"Why are you dressed like the grim reaper and in my bedroom? How did you get in my house?"

"I'm going to need you to get dressed and come with me. It's for your own protection, Karen."

She stared at him. "Are you serious?"

He sat down. "Look, Karen. I'm tired. I've had a long night. I love you, and I want you with me. The only way I will be able to rest is if I know you're safe with me."

"Where are you taking me?"

"I'm giving you two minutes to get out of that bed and get dressed. You will know all soon enough."

He leaned back in the chair. Watching him Karen walked into her closet. Ernest watched her shadow on the floor. When it moved out of range he walked to the hallway, and grabbed her by the back of her top. Without a word, he hoisted her over his shoulder, and jumped over the railing to the floor below. Karen was shocked into silence. He tossed her in the back seat of his car, gave Steven the thumbs-up, and shot off with Steven close behind him. Karen sat hunched in the corner watching the blur that passed for scenery outside her window.

Chapter 48

Steven and Ernest left Jasmine and Karen with the other women. Jasmine came downstairs and brought Emory upstairs with her. Ernest watched them but said nothing. David retrieved their stashed duffel bags, and they all changed clothing. The ladies came down each wrapped in a black top of Steven's as Claudia had helped them raid his wardrobe.

David and Nick prepared a buffet-style breakfast. Raquel and Claudia brought Charles and Jayne trays.

Monaco was in a different type of mood than Paul expected. She was quieter and more subdued. He remembered she was nine months pregnant with their first child. He looked at her in a black shirt of David's that was several sizes too large for her. She looked like a kid wearing her father's shirt. He smiled.

"Don't sit there smiling at me like that. You know I have trust issues, and you pull this."

"I was here to investigate your parents death not fall for you."

"Oh, so now all this is my fault?"

"That's not what I meant."

"When would you have told me?"

"Honestly? Never."

"That's what I'm talking about. And, look at what happened."

"What happened, Monaco?"

"We got into a relationship, and now we're married."

"And, that's the downside?"

"No, what I mean is you could not have predicted we would fall in love."

"Baby, if I had second thoughts about continuing in this world, when I fell in love with you those doubts flew out the window."

"Are you sure?"

"Trust me, baby. This is my last case. I'm getting too old for this stuff."

"You have to stay healthy to help me raise the twins, triplets, and quadruplets you want."

"Hey, wait. I know the Lord provides, but having one at a time is a better plan."

"Plan? With God in the middle? I could be carrying triplets right now."

"You love torturing me, don't you?"

"Are you quitting?"

"Already put in the paperwork. That life will soon be far behind."

"Keep your stories for our sons. I want them to know their dad is a hero."

Paul smiled, and shook his head.

Nick was looking at their son in his bassinet when Lisa handed him cutlery wrapped in a napkin. Nick studied his wife with her flaming red curls spilling over the black sweatshirt that swamped her. It reached just above her knees, and he could not help smiling.

"Stop smiling at me, Nicholas Rodgers. You're all working for the same agency?"

"The operative phrase is, 'was working.' I retired to practice law and pastor. This is my last assignment."

"Why didn't you tell me?"

"I couldn't risk someone asking you something. We don't know the identity of the person doing all this."

"No, I mean were you ever going to tell me?"

"It's not something I want to talk about. It's a job."

"A dangerous job."

"That's why I studied law."

"No more secrets, Nick."

Nick took her hand in his. "No more secrets ever."

Steven was feeding Claudia as she rested sitting in his lap. She had pulled the honey blonde hair into a high, loose bun on top her head. The black silk shirt never looked better.

"Are you sure you won't miss the excitement of that life?"

"With this last case, I'm done. I enjoy lecturing and teaching more than fighting crime."

"How can you be so sure?"

"When Cynda died, I didn't think I could breathe. You have given me new life, and I never want to be without you in it."

"But will I be enough?"

"Now that my dear is a resounding yes, because you are enough. I love you. I want to grow old with you by my side."

"Let's make that happen. We're expecting a baby next Spring."

"Slowly though. I'm in no rush to hit social security anytime soon." Steven stopped talking for a minute. "Did you just say you're pregnant?"

Claudia laughed. "I love you, Steven Barnes, and yes."

Steven wrapped her in his arms.

Ernest handed Karen a condiment. When she looked at him the intensity of her gaze floored his senses and grounded his vision. The black pullover was slouchy and silky.

"Are you retiring as an agent?"

"There's uncertainty in your voice when you ask that question."

"I've read and heard about your womanizing ways."

"Stop listening to others and reading old reviews. Since I met you, no other woman exists."

"Between the traveling, gun play, and women; are you sure a small-town doctor with minimal sex appeal is the one for you?"

"You don't know what you do to my heart. Please don't ever say you have minimal sex appeal because that is hardly the case."

"Are you sure you want to settle down with me, Ernest?"

"Hold out your left hand. Karen Newbold, would you please be my wife?"

"Yes!" She smiled happily as she held out her hand, and he slipped on the ring. It was an emerald-shaped turquoise solitaire. "Oh, my goodness! It's gorgeous!"

Ernest smiled. My! My! My!

David had said little upon his return. He insisted upon preparing a plate of food for Raquel. He handed her a mimosa and watched as she delicately sipped the frothy drink. The tan skin glowed beneath the black silk of the pullover and the glossy black hair flowed freely about her face. Her eyes lifted to his and lurking in their depths, he saw pain.

"So, everything was a game between us?"

"No, and you know it wasn't and isn't."

"Did you miss me at all while you were playing the role of a ghost?"

"My darling, I missed you morning, noon, and night. It is why I healed so fast. I can't wait to hold you in my arms again. My beautiful Raquel, will you marry me?"

"Why would I marry you knowing I could be killed any moment with the life you lead?"

"I'm asking you to marry me because this is my last job."

"When will it be over though, David?"

"When we catch this maniac. But I truly love you with all my heart and soul."

"I love you too. But who's to say this is really your last job?"

"No, baby, this is my last job. I'm only doing this one because of my relationship with Paul. I make way more money being a businessman, and it's safer."

"Hmm... then yes, my love. I will marry you."

David eased the diamond ring set in a cathedral-setting on her finger.

Emory and Jasmine cuddled together on the love seat. Jasmine's red curls and green eyes highlighted by the cowl neck black pullover. Emory gazed at her with rapt delight.

"Why have you been so quiet?"

"I will understand if you want to break it off with me," he said softly.

"Why would I break up with you?"

"The danger involved. Women don't like danger when they're trying to raise a family."

"Rick?"

"Yes."

"Please look at me. What were you going to ask me?"

"Will you marry me?"

"I want to, but I don't want to be a widow anytime soon."

"Would it help if I said I passed the crime analyst position which means I will be working behind a desk?"

"Are you sure you won't miss the action of detective work?"

"After this case? No, I'm ready to move to the white-collar division of law enforcement."

She smiled. "Yes, I'll marry you."

Emory smiled. He pulled the engagement ring out of his pocket, and placed it on her hand. The couple smiled looking at the emerald surrounded by diamonds on her finger.

It was late afternoon and the men were in Steven's den, when a timid knock at the door, and Raquel entered. She looked at David before looking at Paul. The entire group rose to their feet. Raquel swallowed and looked across the room to Ernest.

"What's the matter, Raquel?"

"Karen needs you right away, Ernest. Monaco's water just broke."

Ernest, followed by Paul close on his heels, took the stairs two at a time. Ernest stopped at the door where Jasmine was standing with towels across her arm. Emory and Charles were standing beside her.

"You all have to return downstairs," said Jasmine, as the rest of the men joined them in the hall. "Ernest is the only one allowed in."

"Okay," said Paul. "Come on, Ernest."

"No, Pastor Paul. Karen said only Ernest is allowed in the room."

"Jasmine, are you crazy?" Paul's voice rose. "That's my wife in there!"

"Calm down, Paul," said Emory, standing in front of Jasmine. "She was given doctor's orders. No need to shout at her."

Paul's right hand balled into a fist headed for Emory's head when Steven slapped it away, moving in front of Emory, and effectively blocking Paul's left fist. He pushed Paul into the wall away from Emory.

"Calm down, Paul. Ernest is a trained doctor and so is Karen," said Nick.

The door opened and Karen came out. She was in a white pullover with the sleeves pushed up to her elbows, and her hair in a messy bun. She stared at the people in the hall.

"Who is making all this noise out here? You're upsetting my patient. I need Dr. Carter's assistance."

"I want to see my wife," said Paul, slouched against the wall, with Steven and Nick standing in front of him.

Karen studied Paul for a minute. "Get scrubbed and change your clothing to something clean. Ernest, I need you, and you too, Jasmine. Everyone else can go downstairs."

The door opened again and Lisa, carrying baby Richard came out, followed by Claudia, who was looking ashen-faced. Raquel and Jayne were next. The group walked down the hall to the staircase. They remained downstairs in somber moods. After a quiet conversation with David and Raquel, Steven found Emory seated by a window in deep thought.

"Congratulations on your engagement to Jasmine. I know you love her, and I commend your heart, but don't ever do that again. You want to live to play with your children and grandchildren."

"I thought about it afterward," said Emory, sheepishly. "It was pure reflex."

Steven smiled. He took Emory to the poolroom where Charles and Jayne were setting up the game.

Five hours later, Jasmine came downstairs to find everyone had gathered in the dining room to eat a dinner prepared by David and Steven. Jasmine looked happily disheveled. The red hair was pushed together on top of her head, her face was shiny with perspiration, and she had the widest smile on her face.

"Monaco and Paul had twin boys. She and Paul named them Philip and Peter."

"Oh, wow! That's great!"

"How's Monaco?"

"She's fine. The doctors said you can visit her for a minute."

Steven prepared Jasmine a plate of food, and gave Emory seconds. They sat together eating and talking.

Monaco was sitting up in bed, her nose and eyes were red, and her hair was wild about her face and shoulders. She was wearing one of David's white dress shirts which made David smile. He handed her a frothy drink. Monaco drank it in huge slurping gulps.

Nick looked around. "Where's the babies and the doctors?"

"They took the boys to the hospital. They'll be back once they've finished examining them. Paul is with them."

Lisa walked to the bed and hugged her. Raquel came on the other side and laid beside her. Claudia brought over a hairbrush. Jayne took baby Richard from Nick and ushered the men out of the room.

A few weeks later, Steven was on his tablet in Paul's private office where David, still in hiding, was monitoring the church sanctuary and grounds on the video screens. Nick and Ernest walked into the office. Paul looked up from his desktop.

"Hawkins called me late this afternoon. He wants to see you Paul regarding the fire at your home last week," said Nick.

"We don't have time for Hawkins right now," said Paul, curtly.

"Agreed," said Steven. "Gentlemen and pastors, we've been productive with our online ministries, but as God's people, we are called to fellowship one with another. The Sunday-only services, while creative on my part, is giving too much power to our nemesis."

"I agree with you, Steve," said Paul. "But I'm concerned about this maniac that's still loose."

"So am I, Paul. We've got to do something, though."

"How so?" asked David, turning from the monitors which he left on.

"We are dealing with the fact this killer knows our identities. It's a fact we can't overlook with the assaults on us and the house fire."

"It just means we have to find out who he is."

"And how are we going to do that if we're fearful of moving forward?" asked Steven.

"If you're talking about opening the church to full operating mode, suppose he comes for the church next? We can't put the congregation in danger like that," protested Paul.

"I don't think he will come for the church because what he wants is connected to this church." replied Steven.

"I'm not concerned about this building. I'm concerned about our families. I have a feeling he's going to come after them next," said David.

"I'm with you on that, Dave," said Steven. He stood up and smiled. "Why not make it easier for him? He doesn't know Monaco has delivered because the women haven't been in the church."

Ernest looked at Steven. "Monaco? What are you getting at?"

It was Nick who responded. "Hawkins is preparing to arrest Paul for the murders, and while most of Hawkins suspicions are circumstantial, we know people have been found guilty for far less. We've got to lure the killer out."

Steven said, "I believe the attacks on Monaco have something to do with this church. The half deeds prove it. I found something searching through a file cabinet here a few years back. I sent it to you, Nick. If my suspicions are accurate, let's work out a strategy to draw this creep out of hiding."

The men gathered around the coffee table to view Steven's tablet.

Chapter 49

The reopening of Hot Springs Cathedral Church was met with great public applause. The weekend before the church's official reopening, the men of the church along with the deacons, staged a huge clean-up project on the church grounds. The first church meeting witnessed the congregation approving the hiring of armed security staff. A month later, the ordination service of thirty-five deacons-in-training, and installation of twenty new deacons-in-training saw a rise in church membership.

The unannounced wedding of Ernest and Karen was a subdued but elegant affair. Only church members, staff, and Karen's family and close friends received invitations for the wedding and reception held on Hot Springs Cathedral Church grounds. However, once news leaked out that the doctors were marrying, gifts and accolades poured in. The mayor sent armed police for the occasion. On the day of the wedding, most of the congregation attended. Ernest and Karen opened the reception hall for all to attend.At their estate, David and Raquel, hosted a private party for the newlyweds. Ernest took his bride to Belize for their honeymoon.

The Sleeper welcomed the suggestion to reopen Hot Springs Cathedral Church. He missed socializing with other church folks. After all, his only friends were church people. He was excited about the upcoming ordination ceremony with the new deacons-in-training. It was about time! He had heard that the pastor was considering ordaining new clergy, too. He assumed with the absence of Pastor Sanchez and with the low morale, these events would perk the church up again. Pastor Mouton was usually in a sullen mood. Pastor Rodgers walked with a cane now, and he mused if it was for his personal protection, or a physical disability. Pastor Sanchez's girlfriend was in deep mourning, and had taken a month's respite away from the church. Pastor Carter had recently returned from his honeymoon and wore dark glasses constantly. Pastor Barnes hardly spoke to anyone since the funeral of Claudia Ginyard. Sister Jasmine had changed her work hours to part-time and rarely seen since the disappearance of her boyfriend. The Sleeper was curious as to his whereabouts as well. He noticed that Lt. Hawkins stayed snooping around the church, but the pastors appeared to avoid him. Overall, the Sleeper did not concern himself with these people's problems. He had accomplished his mission. He had broken the tight pastors group. They were hardly together anymore. He watched and he waited. Pastor Mouton and his wife had settled fully in the townhouse. Deaconess Mary and Lisa had planned a baby shower for Monaco which was held on church grounds, and much of the female congregation attended. The Sleeper had trailed Monaco and Lisa visiting baby shops as the time drew near. He was going to wait a few weeks more. Once the pastors relaxed, he would kill Monaco, and the unborn child. He had wanted to avoid taking the baby's life, but she left him no choice. He lifted the weights high above his head and grinned at his reflection.

A month later at his summer estate in Puerto Rico, David married Raquel, in a weeklong celebration. Paul, Monaco, Lisa, Nick, Ernest, Karen, Emory, and Jasmine were flown out for the weekend finale.

David took Raquel to St. Croix for their honeymoon.

One Sunday after the morning service, Pastor Mouton announced his wife had put her childhood home up for sale. The Sleeper taken aback by the news was thunderstruck. What insanity was this? Why would she put the home up for sale when they were expecting a child? He had hoped she would hold on to it. His intentions were to thoroughly scour it from attic to

281

basement when she entered the hospital to give birth. But these new developments presented a problem. The best solution was to wait.

The home sold at last. The pastor announced from the pulpit that the church would hold a prayer vigil for the new couple.

The time had arrived.

In his apartment Hawkins sat on his couch looking at his evidence book. He was hoping he would not have to arrest the senior pastor but so much of the evidence his team had gathered so far, was pointing to Dr. Paul Mouton, senior pastor of Hot Springs Cathedral Church. He looked at the face of his detective, Rick Emory, who disappeared around the same time as a reported fire burned a home to the ground, thirty miles on the outskirts of town. City Hall records showed the owner of the property was the senior pastor. Hawkins summoned both the pastor and his secretary to police headquarters for questioning; twice. Hawkins received a cease-and-desist letter from Nick Rodgers, which had the endorsement of the police chief and the mayor.

There was only the senior pastor on the pulpit this morning with the auxiliary ministers. Where were the other pastors? None of the wives attended anymore. Sitting in the back row of the church he saw when the senior pastor left the pulpit and was waiting for him in the parking lot in an unmarked car. He followed the pastor, keeping a good distance behind, but two large trucks obscured his view. One was a Land Rover and the other was a BMW. For the life of him, Hawkins could not move around them and subsequently, lost the pastor in the heavy traffic flow.

Lost deep in thought, Hawkins fell asleep on the couch. He sensed rather than heard the presence of someone. He reached for his gun in his ankle holster.

Chapter 50

Sitting in the next-door neighbor's home the Sleeper watched Paul pull out of the driveway. He had placed the call that would send the pastor running across town. He smirked. He watched Monaco walk through the home slowly, each step seemingly labor-intensive, before sitting in her favorite spot in the window seat in the dining room. With her large stomach she tired easily now. He watched her lie back on the pillows. Time to act.

Monaco threw an arm over her face and closed her eyes. The Sleeper came in the house through the side window in the kitchen. The young mother-to-be was about to meet her fate. The shadow crept nearer. The long black hair draped like a veil around her shoulders. Her large stomach pronounced now, and her feet propped on pillows, she appeared to have fallen asleep. As the Shadow moved in on the sleeping woman, his instincts awakened, and he looked around. Too late.

Paul's headbutt careened him to the center of the room. The Sleeper turned in time to catch a black cannon to his eyes. He tried to swipe at Paul with the knife and missed. Paul kicked the knife out of his hand and the men grappled in a fierce wrestling hold. The Sleeper performed a series of sharp jabs in Paul's abdomen, and a quicker one to his head knocked him backwards.

The Sleeper turned into a twisted punch in the back of his neck from Nick. He swooped a leg out letting loose a backflip and caught Nick with a double punch in the midsection that sent him flying across the room. Ernest jumped in and caught the full brunt of a double fist in his side.

Returning his attention to the sleeping woman the Sleeper grabbed Monaco by the neck of the dress intending to twist her neck in a death grip. He felt a pain sharp in his eyes as she delved her fingers into his eye sockets. She jumped to the floor intending to crawl away when he recovered, and grabbed at her long hair. The wig came off in his hands. The blonde woman landed a fist to the center of his stomach, and flipped him over her shoulder sending him crashing to the floor. The Sleeper, enraged now, did a backflip landing near her and grabbed hold of one of her legs, sending her toppling downward. They both reached standing position with the Sleeper landing a solid uppercut to the woman's chin, airlifting her, and tossing her across the room into the brick fireplace as hard as he could. She grunted as her body hit the floor.

Nick hit him with the force of his body flipping him upside down. The Sleeper rolled himself toward the door but was airlifted and tossed head first back into the room and into a wall. Oops! It was Steven. A series of punches to his back and a knee to the groin further wounded the Sleeper. The Sleeper rolled over twice, climbed to his knees, and catapulted through the picture window landing on his feet on the lawn.

Paul grappled him from the back placing his arm around the Sleeper's neck. The Sleeper lifted backward and threw Paul head first into a large oak tree. Ernest with a double midair kick sent the Sleeper toward Steven who picked him up high above his head slamming him bodily to the pavement. The Sleeper rebounded but not fast enough to dodge the lightning punches from Ernest. The men locked into a fistfight with the Sleeper gaining enough leverage to toss Ernest over his shoulder.

Seeing Nick coming at him, the Sleeper grabbed him around the torso sending Nick flying toward a tree blocking Ernest's punch while slamming his fist into Ernest's kidneys. The Sleeper performed a butterfly-style uppercut punch under Nick's chin which sent him reeling backward. The Sleeper's jaw turned into Paul's fist, with Nick's balled-fist punches to his midriff. The Sleeper used his elbow to deliver a jab to Nick's kidneys knocking him into Paul.

The Sleeper flinched as his sides and back were pummeled by Steven, and he was picked up bodily and slammed to the pavement. He rolled over and backflipped to a standing position. He ran toward Steven and the two giants locked in a fist fight. Neither man gave way. Steven was quicker, stronger, and his punching jabs landed in crucial weakening spots on the Sleeper's body. The Sleeper attempted a deep knee kidney-groin maneuver which Steven sidestepped. The Sleeper staggered after Steven landed a solid right to his jaw. Steven bent his head and with a rapid two-punch to the Sleeper's torso, picked him up and threw him into the large oak tree on the front lawn. The Sleeper rolled into a sitting position. He reached into his waist belt, and put something in his mouth, slumping onto his side.

Breathing heavily, Steven helped Paul to his feet. Together, they walked toward the fallen figure with Nick and Ernest following. Steven calmly knelt beside the Sleeper. White foam had caked around the Sleeper's mouth and was seeping through the black face mask. Paul removed the mask. The pastors looked down upon the stilled deformed face of Deacon Ed Joseph.

Hawkins revived slowly. He was in Hot Springs Cathedral Church's parking lot, seated behind the wheel of a police cruiser. He solemnly surveyed the pastors standing around him. They were wearing black rubberized suits molded to their bodies from neck to feet. Their hands covered in the same black material. He looked at Steven whose wraparound eyewear was in place. Modern day ninjas. A black Rolls-Royce Phantom limousine was parked in front of the cruiser with David, dressed in black leaning against it. Hawkins noticed the stilled form of the man on the ground. He stepped out of the cruiser and walked over to the man. He looked into the face of the old deacon, Ed Joseph. He noticed he was wearing a similar outfit to the pastors. He inspected Joseph and saw he had taken cyanide tablets. Ernest handed him a thick yellow manila envelope. Hawkins offered his hand in a handshake to each man.

"Gentlemen, I know you don't have to, but could you please humor me?"

It was Paul who responded. "What is it, Detective?"

"What are you? Level with me. I know damn well you're not meek pastors, and you're not detectives. I had a friend in Chicago look you up, but he could find nothing."

Ernest smiled. "Come on, Hawkins. Don't play games now. You thought one or all of us were murderers at one time."

"What's your question, Hawkins?" asked Nick.

"Who are you guys?"

Steven grinned. "We're federal agents. Honestly thought you would have figured it out by now."

"We're here on assignment," said Paul.

"Why??"

"Same as you apparently, but on another wavelength."

Hawkins nodded his head. "It all makes sense now." He looked at Steven. "I suspected you were law enforcement with the hand skins and dark glasses. I began my career in the New York division. I remember when the skins first came out. But the rest of you..."

Nick laughed softly and showed Hawkins his hands. "We all wear them. Most people never notice. You were looking for the guilty party among us and focused on Steven."

Hawkins was looking at Steven again. "Have you gotten hurt? I haven't seen you much."

"I married Sister Claudia Ginyard."

Hawkins' mouth opened and shut rapidly. "What?"

"Before you get angry," said Steven, raising his hands in a gesture of surrender, "we had to protect her from this nameless, faceless killer. Since he assumed he killed her, we played along."

"No different than we had to do with David," said Ernest.

"So, what's next? Humor me."

"Retirement."

"All of you?"

When they all nodded their heads, Hawkins with a wry smile, shook his head. "You're a darn good team."

Hearing police sirens in the distance, Hawkins watched as they piled into the limousine, and headed toward the highway. He looked down at the manila envelope.

Several hours later Hawkins seated in his office received a phone call on the private line. After a brief, friendly conversation, Hawkins hung up. He walked over to his window seeing nothing but the image of five men posing as pastors. Five government agents situated in family residences in a small town. He questioned if they retired, or if it was another ruse. He stared at the photograph of his deceased parents. His father retired after a sixty-year career span. These men were his age and in the prime of their health. He smiled wistfully. Time would tell. He walked to the squad room to listen to the news broadcast.

Chapter 51

The evening had been a pleasant one as Paul and Monaco hosted a dinner party in their new home. Nestled on a broad expanse of land, their home included an annexed, two-story grandparent suite where Jayne and Charles resided. In the family room after helping themselves to dessert and coffee, the couples discussed the recent turn of events which lead to the capture of the Sleeper.

"Steven, what made you think the Valentine's deaths was anything but a strange twist of fate?"

"The money angle, Paul. Five federal agents killed within close time periods was suspicious in itself. The fact that they were retired was overlooked until Harris sounded the alarm shortly before his death."

"Was Joseph aware they were federal agents?"

"Joseph didn't know they were agents but Clayton did. He was enrolled in the FBI Academy with Victor Valentine and Cynthia Bartholomew."

"Clayton also knew Rev. Harris' background because they were teammates in the Bureau's training program."

Jayne said, "I don't understand any of this. Why bring them into the church's financial matters if you knew their business backgrounds?"

"The financial discrepancies didn't occur until the last four or five years," said David. "Before that time the books were clean, and the church was solvent."

"In fact, we had a surplus until just recently," added Claudia in a low voice.

"So, what happened?" asked Charles, intrigued. "Who was stealing and why?"

"I want to know why all the former trustees were murdered!" said Emory.

"The overview is that Joseph worked as a forensic accountant for the Bureau. He tracked the money," said Steven.

"We investigated the Wood Haven fire. We found old blueprints for church renovations that had been scrapped," said Ernest.

"There was a team of professionals involved in the renovation effort from the Wood Haven trustee office. The names included Wright, Lewis, Bennett, Hines, Novalski, and Clara and Raoul Whitfield," said Nick.

"The two men who headed the finance team were Martin and Joseph," said Steven, producing a photo of the group on his tablet which he passed around the room.

"I believe Bergson was killed because he stumbled upon something," said David. "He conducted his own internal audit, and might have been tracking Joseph that night."

"Eliason was killed because he held intimate knowledge of the background story to the founding of Hot Springs Cathedral Church," said Steven. "Joseph needed to kill him off before Eliason realized who Monaco was."

"Which was the same story with Martin. He had been a long-standing member of the community and Hot Springs Cathedral Church. It was only a matter of time before Martin would discover the identity of the check forger," said Nick.

"I believe he did discover the identity of the person forging those checks," said Claudia. "He called me that night, remember?".

"What about Jose Lopez? What was the reason for his death?" asked Emory.

"Lopez was one of the last people to work with Glenn, Claudia, and David on the audits. Joseph knew if Lopez saw the ledgers he would recognize his handwriting as Joseph had worked alongside Lopez for years."

"Unbelievable," said Charles, rubbing his hand across his face.

Paul said, "I guess we need to begin at the start of all this. As Steven has mentioned Clayton knew the Valentine's history because it mirrored his own. All three worked in the Bank Fraud Division in the Bureau. Clayton moved on to become the director of the International Fraud Division."

Steven picked up the story. "Clayton was home-grown. Once he retired from the Bureau, he became involved in church. Fast-forward and Clayton is now senior pastor. He coerced his old friends Joseph, Martin, and the Valentine's to join the finance ministry."

"At that time, Martin was serving as the trustee president. A Wall Street stockbroker he enjoyed configuring numbers," said David. "About five years ago, Clayton cooked up a scheme with Joseph to pilfer the surplus account as no one was keeping watch over it."

"Around that time, Valentine had grown bored with the finance ministry, and wanted something different. Clayton pushed him toward the trustee board. The trustee soon brought his wife on board," said Steven.

"They began their new role with an audit and soon found the ledgers they had weren't balancing with other accounts, and they brought the matter to Clayton," said Paul. "Clayton, in turn, told Joseph who ultimately decided to kill them."

"After her parents deaths, Cynda discovered the discrepancies in the church's accounts. Her mistake was in going to Clayton about it. No one, not even me, considered her death a murder for hire."

"Wait, I'm trying to wrap my head around all this," said Charles. "You mean to tell me Monaco's parents were murdered because they discovered the bank thefts?"

"That's right. Joseph killed Johnson and Wallace when they confronted him about the thefts. Johnson had been a handwriting expert with the Bureau, and Wallace, a forensic accountant," said Paul.

"The clergy had always approved purchase orders," said Steven.

"The absentminded Reverend Harris was a close friend of your late father's, Monaco. He was not only a federal agent, but a mathematician. He had extensive experience working bank fraud cases," said David. "The reverend might have been absentminded, but he was smart."

"When he discovered Joseph was behind the thefts he was on his way to the church to retrieve the ledgers. Unfortunately, he made the mistake of calling Clayton and informing him of his discovery. Clayton called Joseph," said Steven.

Paul straightened his back. "With the deaths of the Valentines, and the other agents, the Bureau began an investigation."

David smiled. "As I stated earlier, Harris was a smart man. He sent two copies of the ledger out. One to Eliason who hid it in his garden, and the other to Raoul Whitfield. Joseph found Whitfield's copy, but not the copy Eliason had."

"Joseph might have assumed Harris made only one copy," said Claudia.

"Hmm, that's a possibility."

"So, all this chaos and people dying was because of money? Did Deacon Joseph need money that bad he had to kill innocent people?" asked Monaco.

"Didn't the Josephs have medical coverage?" Raquel asked.

"Of course, they did," said Lisa. "They were very well-off. I guess Ed felt it wasn't enough."

"Greed overcompensates for common sense," murmured Emory.

Holding his new wife's hand, Ernest sighed. "It's a sad situation. Mary Joseph suffers from multiple sclerosis. It's a disease in which the immune system eats away at the protective covering of nerves. Mary's health has worsened drastically over the last few years. Meantime, Joseph was losing his mental balance."

"That's putting it mildly," said Claudia. "He certainly did not give a darn about anybody else' life or their loved ones."

"But he loved his wife," said Ernest. "The money he was stealing from the church was to fund long-term MS treatment for Mary. I read her medical records upon her admittance to the hospital after his death. Once, the courts unsealed Joseph's medical records, we found he had stage four cancer. He would have died before he reached prison or while in there. Knowing his own mortality he was preparing for Mary's long-term medical care."

"It didn't help that his medication was too strong for him," replied Jasmine.

Ernest looked at her. "His medication was fine. It was the illegal and unapproved drugs that sent him over the edge. He was on untested steroids, and a few other miscellaneous items to keep him physically active and alert."

"And to deaden pain, Ernest," said Karen. "He was popping pain pills like they were candy. It was only a matter of time before his vital organs gave out."

"The money stolen was only one facet to all this. Joseph was on a personal mission to find the lost property deeds once reading Mary's paperwork and realizing her family connections to Monaco," said Nick.

Jasmine looked startled. "What family connections?"

"Claudia is related to Monaco on her late mother's side, but Mary is related through Monaco's late father. Mary is a distant cousin to Monaco. Her maiden name was Valentine."

Tears came into Monaco's eyes. "I never knew that. I wonder why she never told me. I wish I could talk to her now."

Everyone in the room became silent. Jayne, seated next to Monaco, hugged her. Mary Joseph collapsed into a catatonic shock when she learned of her husband's death, and never fully recovered.

"The interesting plot twist to all this is that Monaco is the sole owner of the land the church sits on and the church itself," said Lisa.

Emory looked at Monaco in awe. "You owned the church?"

"I'm trying to understand how Monaco could be the owner when the church traded hands several times over," said Raquel.

"There was no trading hands," Nick explained. "The deeds found described the ownership of the plot of land the church sits on. That land belongs to the Valentine family and their heirs. When Victor and Cynthia Valentine died, they passed on this property to their daughters, Cynda, and Monaco. Cynda was aware of the deeds to both the church property and the family home."

"We pieced together the first deed which shows Marcus Edgar Bartholomew as the owner of the land the church sits on. Marcus is the great great-grandfather of Monaco," said Lisa.

Nick joined in. "The second deed outlined the property lines and clearly shows the signatures of Agnes Wright and Glenn Martin, the two murdered trustees."

"Out of the murdered trustees, Raoul Whitfield, sent the faded copy of the last will and testament of Cynthia Bartholomew Valentine to Lars before he died," said David.

"Lars Eliason knew about the original signatures. He had the original copy which the killer did not know about," said Claudia. "Steven and David returned to the property and found the copy in a plastic bag among his tomato plants."

"Very ingenious," Ernest said, with a smirk.

"Something only a gardener or chef would think about," said Paul.

Jayne leaned forward. "Money was the main purpose behind all these killings?"

David sighed. "Clayton and Joseph got in over their heads fast. They were after a substantial windfall to fund retirement dreams. But once Ed discovered he had stage four cancer, he planned and plotted to find the original deeds."

"It was a highly strategic plan if they had stopped once the Valentine's were murdered. But unknown to Clayton, Joseph had discovered the property deeds existence. He thought he could get his wife to sign over the deeds, and he would sell the property. Monaco had been gone long enough to either be forgotten about or expected to want to sell."

"Monaco's appearance back in town was not expected. I remember how he looked when he saw her for the first time. I just thought he was surprised like the rest of us," said Lisa.

"What is truly ironic about all this is that the original deeds were never in Monaco's house. His wife, Mary, had given the original deeds to Eliason a long time ago," murmured David.

"Once Joseph killed Wallace, Johnson, and Harris, Clayton feared for his own life. He developed health problems because he wanted to get out of town and away from his partnership obligations.," said Steven, "and he also feared being murdered by his deranged partner."

Paul said, "Steve, why didn't you seem surprised when you removed the hood?"

Steven sighed. "It was something Hawkins said when we had the private meeting with him. He distinctly said that Joseph knew who he was."

"And Joseph never said anything to us about knowing Hawkins was an undercover cop," Nick said.

"Exactly!" said Steven. "I have monthly meetings with them. He never mentioned he'd been questioned by Hawkins after Eliason's death."

"That's when you began to suspect him?" asked David.

"I didn't think it was him at first because of his age and the fact he was so physically disabled. I did think, however, he was orchestrating with someone else," said Steven. "That's why I was watching a few of the newer deacons and younger men in the church."

"I could see that," said Ernest.

A soft whimper could be heard coming from the baby monitor placed on the fireplace mantle. It was followed by a gurgle and a soft laugh. The group in the family room smiled.

Chapter 52

A year later, in Hot Springs Cathedral Church, Jasmine and Emory were married by Paul in a lavish wedding ceremony hosted by her older brother. The equally lavish reception gifted to them by David and Claudia, and their honeymoon trip to Dubai was arranged by Jasmine's uncles-in-residence: Steven and Nick.

Monaco sat in the front row holding twin sons, Philip and Peter, on her lap. Nick and Lisa sat on the same row. Lisa cuddled their newborn daughter, Ava Maria, and their son, Richard, playing with his toy train sat beside his father. Sitting in the next row were Steven and Claudia. Their daughter Lily, seated on her father's lap, was busy enjoying a tasty treat in her baby bottle courtesy of her father. Claudia, pregnant with their second child, was busy enjoying her own treat courtesy of her husband. Seated behind them was Ernest and Karen, who held their son Kyle, in her arms. Occasionally his pale green eyes looked toward the altar where his aunt was marrying. Next to them were Raquel and David. Their son, Robert, was not happy. Jayne and Charles took the colicky infant and carried him out of the sanctuary. When Charles and Jayne were not traveling, they were happy to be doting grandparents. They were constantly, and lovingly, being scolded for spoiling all the grandchildren.

Hawkins flew in from Chicago for the wedding. He stood as Emory's best man. Grant and Sanders, attending the wedding as guests of the groom, were now actively dating.

THE PASTORS